The Thin Line

Camilla Draymarch

Copyright:

ISBN: 978-0-359-67476-3

For John Moser Jr. – Who taught me to think for myself.

And for Jeffrey Moser – Who I will always miss.

Book One:

Memory

Prologue

The Sun Rises

Take a sunrise. Hold it in your mind. Try to make it as real as possible. Imagine the clearing of the colors as they reach for the horizon line. Are the clouds the bright, fluorescent pink of a neon sign or the soft pink of a cloud of cotton candy? What about the horizon line itself? Are there trees, houses, buildings, the ocean? Is the moon still high in the sky behind you? What about you yourself? Are you tall, skinny, fat, short? It's likely that by now, you've diverged from memory. When I asked you to take a sunrise and hold it, you started with a memory, but memories can be cloudy and faded, so your subconscious stepped in. When I asked you what shade of pink the clouds were, your mind tried to compare the colors, but it's most likely that what you remember isn't quite the truth. By the time I asked about the moon, your imagination will have fully stepped in, creating an image of the world and yourself in it that's been fabricated by the mind.

Does the fact that this particular sunrise has never been seen make it any less real?

Maybe it does, but not for you. By now it's another memory and since your mind had its way for those critical moments, it's twisted around the original memory. One leads into another. In three years, you might look back on this moment and think about your sunrise. You probably won't remember that it's not real. That there are impossible details in your mind. But you'll remember the sunrise.

Now try to think about something you've forgotten. Forgetting is… like a missing book in a library shelf, isn't it? It's obviously missing. There's a giant hole where neat little volumes usually are. Run a hand down a shelf of books and across the missing piece. It's obvious where it was, where it should be. Take a moment to think of the other books around it. Stroke their spines, read their titles. With some deduction, you might figure out what the missing book was titled, what it was about. The longer you think of it, the more it comes back to you. All of a sudden, you might run your hand down that bookshelf and find that there's no hole anymore.

If it came back, did you ever really forget it? Was it really gone or was it just misplaced?

Look up at whatever's in front of you. Now look back down. Think of three things you just saw. Hold them in your mind. Identify some details. Now, leave the room. Go and putter about for an hour or two working on something. Bake a loaf of bread. Then, think about the three things. By now, they're probably a bit blurry. The edges aren't so crisp. If you do a lot of staring at those objects, you might know them like the back of your hand, but what if you didn't? What if your eyes passed over them once or twice a day and you never really thought of them? Then, your memories might as well be of different objects.

There's a thin line between reality and what we perceive. The mind plays tricks on us and even on itself. Psyco-somatic illnesses can kill the body. Problems that exist only in the realm of fantasy can destroy relationships. Men see pools of water where they find only sand.

With all of that in mind, how do you know what you remember happened?

How do you sort it out? Do you? Or do you just trust yourself to remember with clarity?

Maybe you never thought of this before. Maybe you don't want to think about it. It can be scary, I know, but its important to realize the boundaries of your own abilities. It's important to know that you can't be certain what is and isn't real. It's to help you understand what I was thinking, what I was doing. What I was trying to show.

Chapter One

Ludwig didn't wake up when the van turned a tad too sharply, pressing his body against the side and jostling his head. Medical school made heavy sleepers of the best of them. As a young doctor, fresh from his Residency, Ludwig still retained his student habits. Had he been able to see himself, Ludwig would likely be surprised that he could manage to sleep at all. Excited didn't suffice to describe the doctor's state of mind when they set out on their journey to Albuquerque. Though he was a very young doctor, Ludwig had been invited to work with one of the foremost neurosurgeons and researchers in America. For Ludwig, who had never dreamed that he would manage to go farther than Houston from his beloved Fredericksburg, it had been a chance too good to pass up. So, along with Thomas – his roommate and best friend – he set out across the plains and into the high desert.

Blinking, Ludwig looked up into what seemed to be too-bright lights. "Vhere-?" And his world exploded into pain and noise. It was everywhere. He felt as if his body had been tossed against a wall and held there for a long moment before bouncing off and back. It felt slow, as if the gravity had been turned off, and at the same time, it was nearly instantaneous. He didn't know how long he lay there, but there was something digging into his side. It was uncomfortable and hard to breathe, harder to move.

"…We have two vics in the van!" Someone was shouting, but not screaming. There was a professional sound to the voice.

"One more in the car!" Blackness closed in again.

Bright lights. Too bright. "He's waking up! Someone get him back under so we can operate!"

"Stubborn son of a-!" Ludwig was trying to blink himself awake, trying to understand what had happened. There was a tube in his throat, forcing him to breathe. Something in him didn't want to breathe, wanted to stop breathing, because breathing hurt. Everything hurt. His body had become a sea of hurt.

"Just do it!" Blackness, a surprising lifting sensation. Some kind of relief. He became less and less aware of the ocean of pain sensors in his flesh. It felt like falling asleep, but more like being dragged into its embrace.

Ludwig reawoke to voices and to the sound of machines, monitoring heart rate and oxygen. "…He's waking up, Doctor." A soft, feminine voice.

Ludwig couldn't feel anything in his body. He had to be up on Morphine.

"Ludwig? Ludwig, can you hear me?" The Doctor leaned over him. Doctor… What was his name? He was the man who had called Ludwig here, called him to help him with his wonderful machine… Berlioz? No, not right… Berwick.

"...Doctor... Bervick?" Ludwig forced his lips to work.

"Ludwig, you've been slipping in and out of consciousness. You were in a terrible accident."

The bright lights, the jolts, the pain... All came back like a tidal wave. The feel of his broken body and the shouts of paramedics. How could this have happened? "Thomas...?"

"That doesn't matter right now. I'll be honest, Ludwig, you're dying. You're going to fall into a coma and there's not going to be a way to wake you up."

Ludwig forced himself not to fall down that particular well. "...Nozhing to do?"

"There is one thing. If you consent, we can connect you to the CORD machine, and you can help further our research." Doctor Berwick was becoming fuzzier. There wasn't much time. "You have to sign this form. It's the only way I can help you."

Ludwig's hands twitched. They felt weak, like kittens. "...Gife me..." He tremblingly lifted his fingers, barely managing to grasp the pen in a fist. With his arm being steadied by the nurse, he scrawled his name in the crudest of child-like letters. "...Save ozhers..." He managed to mutter as his head fell back to the pillow and the darkness closed in again.

Of all of the scenarios that might have greeted him in Albuquerque, Ludwig had never imagined that he would never reach the city. As drives went, it hadn't been a long one. Thomas had once taken a wild hair to go down to the Florida Keys for a Christmas Holiday and they had driven together. They had crossed four states from Texas and ended up on the road in Thomas's camper van for over two days before they reached the small cabin Thomas had rented. It wasn't especially dangerous either, unless they were unlucky enough to run out of gas, but Ludwig had been confident in their usual caution, certain that they could manage the road trip as they had before.

The young doctor had been afraid that it was a mistake. That the letter and the subsequent e-mails inviting him to join Berwick in Albuquerque – working on a device that would connect directly to the mind of comatose patients – would have been meant for someone else. A different Doctor Bonhoeffer.

The opportunity had been too good to miss out on. Ever since Ludwig had first learned of Berwick's work, he had idolized the man. He obsessively collected medical journals with his studies published on their precious pages and memorized each one. CORD – Doctor Berwick's miracle machine – claimed to be able to touch and observe the processes of the human mind in such detail that it could even read thoughts. Or at least, that was the idea. Results were sketchy and few and far between, but Ludwig's imagination was on fire. With this kind of technology, they could cure the insane, train the autistic, and reach the unreachable unfortunates trapped inside their own minds by accidents or disaster.

Was it any surprise that he had torn through the house to blurt everything out to Thomas the instant he received the invitation? Was it any surprise that Thomas – responding to his best friend's enthusiasm – had agreed not only to drive with Ludwig, but to apply for a nurse's position at the same hospital?

They had both been so young...

Ludwig woke up on his mental train. The same train that he always visited in his dreams. Sitting on the plush seats in the comfortable cabin, watching the world go by. They were driving through the same landscape they always did, and the rich colors of the trees in autumn stretched towards the horizon line. His head was buzzing like the static on a radio and it was cold. It was so, so cold.

Shivering, he pulled himself up, achingly slowly. His face had been pressed into the velvet of the seat and his glasses were askew. Neatening himself with one hand, he called out. "...Hallo? Hallo?" He wrapped his arms around himself and looked out the window. The bright colors were becoming colder as he watched. Winter. It was winter outside his train now. Winter, and it was so cold.

He wouldn't have imagined being inside the CORD machine like this. Was it cold here because he was inside it now? Was CORD itself cold?

"If I ever vake up, I must mention zhat to Dr. Berwick." Ludwig grumbled to himself.

The landscape outside continued to change as the train began slowing down. "Zhis is new."

Pausing, he considered himself. "It seems zhat zhoughts are translated as vords here, und it is impossible to keep silent vhile zhinking. Strange. I vonder vhy I can still hear mein accent. In my subconscious, I zhought I vould pronounce perfectly." The accent that he had cultured as a child in a German-Speaking home had haunted him for all his life. It irritated him to think that he couldn't escape it, even in his subconscious.

Ludwig looked back out the window and saw that his mental train was coming to a stop on a snowy platform in the middle of the countryside. "Vhy is zhe train stopping? It has never stopped before." He didn't want to leave the train. Cold as it was inside, he knew that outside it would be even worse. The dreary air and the blowing wind stirred a bank of icicles hanging threateningly above the train. With timid hands and feet, Ludwig finally gathered his courage and pushed open the door, dashing beneath the safety of the sheltered porch and into the station to get away from the cold platform and the ominous icicles. As he ran, the gathered ice came down in a sheet, shattering into sparkling bits of shrapnel that spiraled out in all directions.

Ludwig cowered inside the station, barely aware that it was significantly warmer here. It seemed a shelter, however brief, against the elements. This was his mind in CORD? It was a far different experience than he had expected. Still, if this was CORD, eventually someone had to show up and explain to him what was going on. "Bitte, anyone? Am I alone in here?"

There was a chime like music from somewhere outside, in the bitter cold. Ludwig mentally refused to go back out there. "Hallo?" He cursed his thick accent as he went to the door and called out. In his mind, he should have perfect diction, verdammt!

The chimes continued, outside, trying to draw him out. "I vill not come out!" He called out to it. "Nein, I cannot! Come to me, Bitte!"

The chimes grew louder, but they didn't seem to come closer. It was a musical, tinkling sound. A teasing sound. Ludwig began to have the horrible, sinking feeling that he would have to follow those chimes if he wanted to find anyone else in this frozen wasteland. If only he was better dressed for this cold!

Warming himself as much as he could beside the fire, he looked around for anything that could carry the warmth of the room with him. There was nothing much: A couch with a simple throw over the back of it. He gathered this around his head and torso, wrapping it up into something resembling a shawl. It was not much against the chill of the weather, but it would have to be enough. He needed to find someone else, perhaps someone who could explain all this to him. That was the point of CORD, ja? To connect minds for the transfer of ideas and information as well as to wake up those who were comatose.

How many people had Dr. Berwick's letter said he had gained access to? Five? Six now that he was here? There was a man about twenty-seven, a woman of seventy-six, a man of thirty, and a girl of sixteen, yes... Then there was himself, and that made five. Who was the sixth?

The cold bit into him as he stepped out onto the platform, almost stealing his breath and his thoughts away. The train was still there, covered in a thick layer of ice and snow already. It would not be moving for a very long time.

The chimes in the distance drew him on. If there was music, someone had to be playing it. The wind was like ice on his face and he had to force himself to walk into it, towards the chiming. The closer he got, the better the music sounded. They were like wind chimes and cathedral bells all at once. The music was light, airy, like a dance. It promised warmth and fun, if only he could reach it.

Ludwig's hands trembled in his armpits as he pressed them there. He couldn't afford to be frost bit. He relied on his skill with his hands too much to let his fingers turn black. Why was it so bloody cold? He was not a man out of shape and falling down after climbing the stairs, but this cold... It seemed to sap his strength from him and make him tired. He wanted nothing more than to lie down in the snow and go to sleep, out of the wind.

The chimes were growing louder again now, beckoning him onwards. His feet felt like they were frozen, both stiff in their thin, silken socks and the clogs he always wore.

Suddenly, the chimes vanished. The music faded and he was alone in a white hinterland with no sense of direction, no way to guide himself through. "Hallo? Hallo?" He called into the wilderness. "Vhere are you? Bitte, don't go!"

He stumbled on, a few steps more, and fell, face-down into the white. His body was numbly aware that it was warmer here. If only he could rest a moment. He was so tired.

There was a sudden stir above him, like great wings had decided to beat over him, pushing frigid air down onto his shaking form. He turned over to deliver some scathing reply and saw a dark figure in the sky. It was barely visible, but he could see that it was too large to be a bird, too organic to be a plane. In the next moment, he blinked and the thing was gone.

"What are you doing out here?" A strong, American voice questioned, and a looming figure wrapped up in black ski wear stood over him. It was a woman, but far, far too tall and broad to be a woman. Nevertheless, her blonde braid draped out of the back of her black cap and over one shoulder, and her lips were a painted red against her pale face – what little was exposed.

"Bitte… Bitte…" Ludwig could barely force his lips to move. This was an American, she did not speak his language. "Please… Please… I cannot mofe. Mein legs…"

"You've walked too far in the snow already." The giantess reached down and pulled him into her arms. She was warm and dwarfed him with her bulk. His hands slipped suddenly – almost without his bidding – into the front of her coat where it was warmest.

"Es tur-!" He cut himself off as he tried to force his hands away from her chest. Had he lost all sense of decency? "I'm sorry! Many apologies!" Slowly, his fingers began to slip away from the silky, warm lining of her coat, but one of her hands went from his knees to cover them.

"Don't. They need to be warmed more than I need modesty." She told him. "Though your apologies are gentlemanly and your manners much appreciated. Stay still and try to stay awake. My lodge is not far from here. Hold on, little one."

"Ja... Danke..." Ludwig pressed closer to her warmth as she carried him away from the indentation his body had left in the snow. "So cold... Ich bin ice..."

"You feel it. Hang on. Almost there." A warm light was pouring over the snow now, coming from something obscured in the heavy snow. It was a window. A window that glowed gold with the light coming from within. It was a warm, flickering, merry little light: A fire. A fire meant heat. Ludwig's frosted glasses fixated on the light. He almost gave a scream as he was drawn into the warmth of a cozy room, protected from the cold by doubled doors. The giantess laid him on a couch in this foyer and stomped the snow from fur-lined boots. In spite of her size, she easily moved through this home of hers. It was as if she was the normal size, and he was merely tiny.

"Perhaps," some insane rambling in the back corner of his mind spoke, "Perhaps ve are shrunken! Vouldn't zhat be somezhing? Zhis is you. Zhis is you on CORD. Questions?" Accompanying diagrams of himself at normal size and himself as small as a fairy popped into his head, drawing almost hysterical laughter from his frigid throat.

"I see you haven't learned how to keep your thoughts to yourself yet." The giantess pulled off Ludwig's snow-covered shawl and began divesting him of his other garments. She must have heard his supposedly internal monologue. "Don't worry, you will catch the trick in time."

"Vhere are ve?" Ludwig questioned, his head buzzing with pain. He still wanted to sleep. He wanted to sleep so badly, but he felt he couldn't. Not like this. He didn't know where he was or who the giantess was or why she was so giant.

"How can such a little man hold so many questions?" The giantess pressed a warm palm to his forehead. "Sleep now. Tomorrow, we will have time to talk. So much time."

Ludwig found his eyes fluttering shut. Unresisting, he went with the giantess's urgings and found himself in a dark, warm sleep that felt like floating in a sea of liquid caramel. Vaguely, he was aware that someone was lifting his nude body and carrying him from the bench to somewhere else, cradling him like a baby or a newly-wed bride.

Chapter Two

Ludwig woke up and everything was blurry. His eyes roamed the blur of color in front of them. Someone had taken off his glasses. Lifting his head, he found himself lying in a soft bed, between silken sheets and under a bearskin throw. The deep, thick fur was soft under one of his hands and the other was tangled up in something equally soft and smooth. "Bitte…? Hallo?" He called out.

"You're awake." The giantess was at his side in a moment, her figure a dark shape against his eyes. "Here. I couldn't let you sleep in your glasses." She set them on his nose and the world came into focus. "How do you feel?"

"Varm und sore." Ludwig sat up. Something soft clung to him as he moved and he looked down. He was draped in a red shirt, far too large for him. One of the sleeves was rolled up to his elbow and the other had fallen down over his hand, tangling his fingers. "Wot is los?"

"One of my undershirts." The giantess replied with a shrug. "Your clothes were soaked, and you needed to wear something. All of my pants are too big: Sorry. I can get you something later."

"It's fine." He gingerly rolled back the sleeve and examined his hands. They were pale, pink at the tips, and seemed to be intact. He could move each finger and wiggle them all at once. "No permanent damage, Danke Gott."

"I made you some breakfast. If you like, I can bring you a tray." Now that he could see her, standing beside the bed, Ludwig realized that he had been mistaken about her relative size. She was much, much larger than he had thought. Each of her arms was as wide around as one of his calves and she stood near the high ceiling, looking down on him with large, gentle eyes. She had to be eight feet tall and she was built like a horse – a large, strong back and legs leading down to surprisingly dainty feet.

"Danke." Ludwig looked up at her, intimidated and slightly afraid. "Fraulein, vhy are you so large? Or is it zhat I am so small?" Once again, his mental monologue popped out of his mouth without a filter.

"I am this size because I choose to be." The giantess replied, shrugging. "It is not so bad. I can see farther this way, and run faster." She left the door open as she stepped out and her voice carried down from wherever she had gone. "And I like people being smaller than I am. It makes everyone so cute and non-threatening."

"That does not seem odd at all." And, the more Ludwig thought about it, the more it made sense. Being here, in CORD, had disoriented him badly. It had thrown him into a frozen wasteland and turned all that he knew inside out. Perhaps being so over-sized was this woman's defense mechanism more than anything else.

"I should hope it wouldn't." She replied, walking back in with a tray of porridge and coffee with milk and sugar on it. The porridge was mixed with some kind of berry jam and with cream. "This is not a friendly place, Ludwig." She sat beside him on the bed to watch him eat. "You are lucky I caught that Father of Lies in my domain before you stumbled into his trap. If you had reached those chimes, you would have been no more." There was an earnest sadness in her voice, as if she had tried to save others before and had failed.

"Who vas calling vith zhe chimes zhen?" Ludwig questioned.

"He calls himself Lucifer, but the man is no more a demon than I am a giantess. He likes to think of himself as a great and dark power, but the truth is, he just has a stronger will than most and the sadism to put it to use, entrapping the others in here." A bitter note entered her tone. "I can keep him out, but it's more difficult to protect others from him."

"How many of us are zhere?" Ludwig questioned.

"In truth? I do not know. It seems there are a great many, though I suspect that most of them are the imagined products of one of the others." The giantess tapped his bowl with one finger. "Eat before it gets cold. You need to keep your strength up."

"Ja, danke…" Ludwig took another few bites of the porridge. "Is gut, but I am afraid I haf little appetite."

"You're in shock." She nodded agreeably. "You need rest and to recover. As long as you stay inside this house, you should be safe from all intruders."

"Ja?"

"I promise."

The next time Ludwig woke, the giantess had a clarinet at her lips and was playing something soft and sweet, almost Celtic in its cant and turn. One of her feet was tapping in its shoe and making the wooden floor ring slightly. The soft smell of burning herbs came from an incense burner nearby. It was a clean, pinewood smell. There was a bowl of soup made with meat and vegetables, egg noodles floating in the dark broth, beside the bed and he reached out to take it gratefully. His appetite was returning, it seemed, and it had brought reinforcements.

The giantess's eyes flashed to his as he moved and she blinked at him over the clarinet, still playing. When she had finished the tune, she set the instrument aside. "You're awake again. How do you feel?"

"Much better." Ludwig smiled back at her, scooping up a bite of the noodles. "Danke."

"You're welcome." She sat down on the edge of the bed. At some point, the bearskin throw had been changed for velvet. He stroked a hand over it, enjoying the softness of the more refined blanket. "I thought you would prefer that. You seem a man of refined tastes."

"Ja, I am. I am a doctor. My name is Ludwig Wolfgang Bonhoeffer, but please, call me Ludwig." He hadn't meant to spill his whole name like that. As a doctor, he usually only went by his last name, but with his thoughts translating into words, there was little he could keep secret.

"That is a name that will get you teased as a child." The giantess observed with a wry smile. "Still, it is better than a name so common that everyone has it."

"Perhaps. I vould not know." Ludwig shrugged, polishing off the last of the soup. "How long haf I been here?"

"Not long enough. You should rest more." The giantess fiddled with the fasteners on her gloves and pulled them off. Her lambskin slippers followed. "I never get used to this cold." She stated conversationally. "But Winter has always been my happiest season, so my own mindscape is often icy."

"I take it you're fond of Christmas ten?"

"Yes, I am." She pulled off her sweater and laid down on top of the sheets beside him, putting her hands beneath her head to support herself. "Just leave the bowl on the nightstand. I'll take care of it later."

"Vhat are you doing?" Ludwig questioned, watching her stretch out on the bed beside him.

"If you don't mind, I'm going to take a nap. This is the warmest room in the lodge and I can't sleep anywhere else." The giantess replied. "I can keep my hands to myself, if that's your worry."

"Nein, nein… You are fine." Ludwig waved off the offer. "I vas merely confused. Ve haf not known each ozher fery long und I don't efen know your name."

"Call me Mara." She pulled a black sleep mask down over her eyes and made herself comfortable beside him.

"Zhat's Biblical." Ludwig looked down at her, wondering if you could truly sleep inside CORD.

"Of course, you can sleep in CORD. It's still your mind. It still needs time to relax. The experience is a little different, though. You won't feel the same drowsiness before hand. It's more of a pain – an ache. And when you wake up, you'll wake up faster." She peeked out of one side of her mask. "And yes, Mara is Biblical. It's the name Naomi took after coming home to Israel with nothing."

"Is zhat your real name?"

"Ludwig, is anything here real?" She let the mask snap back down onto her face and Ludwig felt it would be unwise to continue speaking to her at the moment.

His legs and hips still ached and the bed was deliciously warm. Ludwig laid back down among the pillows, occasionally glancing at his bedmate. It was impossible to tell her age with her eyes covered up. Even when they weren't, she had a sort of ageless quality that made it difficult to think of her as especially young or old. Perhaps she was simply middle-aged. But middle-aged women didn't tend to think so much of size as strength.

It didn't really matter, he supposed. Inside CORD, they were mind-to-mind. Their thoughts were patterning onto each other, spinning out in crystal-clear communication. There was no room for miscommunication or misunderstanding. With a clear conscience, he laid down and let his mind drift.

This was starting to become a habit. It seemed that every time Ludwig woke up, there was food waiting for him. This time it was a simple mug of broth. Mara was sipping a similar one, staring down at him with an intense, almost hungry expression.

"Vhy do you look at me like zhat?" Ludwig questioned. "It's like you're starfing und I am a drei course dinner."

"You are the first man I have seen in far, far too long who isn't completely insane. I'd like to remember this, when you leave." There was a mournful note in her voice.

"Leafe?"

"Yes, leave. Everyone does, eventually. They get tired of my company or they want to see what else there is out there and they leave. Lucy gets most of them, and the few who can stand up against him go insane looking for something they can't find." Mara replied, looking away. "He would have gotten you too, if I hadn't been there. He's slippery, and good at luring people in. It's safe here: This is my home. Lucy can't touch it. But the moment you leave my company, he'll be back after you. He's always hungry. Always searching." Her eyes had gone dark and dead, the pupils expanding until they seemed to fill her eye. It was not a happy look and it frightened Ludwig with its intensity. "You can't leave."

"I von't leafe." Ludwig assured her. "Zhis is temporary, Ja? Doctor Bervick vill get all of us out und ten ve vill not need to vorry anymore, und I do not vant to die before ten."

The sardonic tilt of Mara's head told him more than anything else that she didn't put as much faith in Doctor Berwick as he did. "Mmm. Perhaps. I have given up on ever waking from this place, myself, but perhaps you are right." She gave a slight toss of her head. "Well, how did you end up here, if it's not too personal a question?"

"I vas…" The memory of bright lights and being flung across the confined space of the van flooded him. Operating room lights and the sound of a heart monitor sputtering filled his senses. He smelled sterile alcohol and iodine, steel and soap.

"We're going to lose him if this keeps up!"

"I'm working as fast as I can. Panic won't help anyone." His head in a brace, his body strapped and bolted, papered down to a table. Video monitors blipping, his heartbeats beeping away. All that he was and had been, ticking down the drain. "He needs more blood. Someone get a transfusion going, I've got to stop this bleed."

"Wait, what's that? Beside his lung? Where did that come from?!" Panic, noise, and confusion all around him…

A green face-mask hovered close and the giantess inside it pulled it down. "Breathe, Ludwig."

Ludwig came back to himself, seizing on the messed bed. He had tossed off sheets, blankets, and pillows in his fit.

"Don't worry. It gets easier." Mara told him from where she had bent over him. "The memory stops being so sharp, you begin to lose the details, and it doesn't affect you as much. It's just this part, where it's fresh, that it hurts so badly."

"Vhy…? Vhy did tat happen?" Ludwig panted, raising himself on his elbows. "All I did vas remember…"

"You're in your mind. Memories have power here." Mara tried to explain, gesturing outwards at the pine walls. "Your perception – your assumptions – shape the world. To a lesser degree, the assumptions and imaginations of others shape your world as well. However, if you decided that I was a 5' 0" Chinese man, then – to a certain degree – I would become that. Depending on how strongly you believed in that perception, how much you demand that the world conform to your imagination, I might even find myself looking up at you. But when you try something like that, you open yourself to attacks of the same kind and you might quickly find yourself the one being influenced." She picked up the blankets and sheets and pulled them up around him. "When you remembered what happened before you were put in CORD, the world became that memory – however briefly."

"Is tere any vay to stop it?" Ludwig faintly questioned. If every memory he recalled changed the world, how was he ever going to separate what was his memory from what was happening in CORD?

"Practice. Time. You'll get the hang of it eventually." Mara tucked him back down into bed. "I slept a lot when I was trying to catch the rhythms of this place. It seems to help straighten out your processes and adjust them to CORD's. Then again, I've been told I'm a strong-willed person, so it might just be that I have a brain that's made to control this world. If that's the case… I would suggest living, and not thinking too hard about it."

"Vhy are you here?" Ludwig questioned as one of Mara's hands reached for his glasses and pulled them off of his face, laying them on the night stand.

"I was in an accident. I fell off of a lifeguard stand onto a pool deck and smacked myself a good one in the noggin." She replied flippantly. "No big deal. I would have walked it off if I could have woken up."

"You're lucky to be alive!" Ludwig shot up from the bed and stared into the blurred surroundings towards where he knew she was. "How could you fall from a lifeguard stand?! How did you survive a fall onto concrete?!"

"Dickens if I know!" Mara protested, her blurred figure moving towards something on the wall. It had to be some sort of light control because the room was soon plunged into darkness. His eyes stopped straining as he used his ears to track her progress through the room and back to the bed. "I woke up here, in CORD. Everything was confusing and difficult. I was lucky: I made myself invisible automatically. Lucy didn't notice me until I was strong enough to fend him off."

"Did no one try to communicate vit you? How functional is CORD's interface? How much can Dr. Berwick see and understand?" Ludwig had so many questions.

"Ludwig, I'm tired." There was a bite to her tone now. "I don't want to talk about this. Especially not now."

"…All right." Ludwig sighed, crossing his arms. "I just want to understand." His tone was plaintive.

"Don't we all." Mara sighed. "Tomorrow, I'll try and explain more. Tell you about some of the people, but right now… I'm just so tired, Ludwig. So tired."

So, he let her sleep. When he felt around beside himself, he couldn't find his glasses. They had to be somewhere, but it was dark and there was little he could do. He folded his hands in his lap and waited to fall asleep as well. The gears in his head were turning once again, as he tried to keep his thoughts to himself. Mara had given him some interesting clues since they had met. He was fairly certain he knew which of the subjects in CORD she was.

The mug of broth was still gently steaming when he picked it up and put it to his lips. It was acidic and spicy with a tang of something distinctly Asian as well: Warm and soothing.

In the morning, Mara was gone. There were odd noises coming from outside: The roar of a great beast and the responding cries of something that chattered and screeched. Then, a different roar split the peaceful morning: The roar of fire. Ludwig grabbed hastily at the side table and found his glasses. Throwing them on, he tossed himself up out of bed and rushed up the stairs. The forest surrounding the peaceful lodge was on fire!

"Mara?!" Ludwig cried out, looking for his giantess protector. "Mara, vhere are you?!"

There was a harsh cracking sound and one of the nearby trees snapped off. Ludwig scurried for one of the sliding doors as it landed with a crash on the roof. Tripping on a step separating the foyer from the rest of the lodge, he landed on his face and his glasses cracked. As he picked himself up again, he blushed, realizing that he still wasn't wearing pants, just Mara's silken undershirt.

There was a white, double breasted coat hanging on the rack next to Mara's Ski wear and a fur lined Ushanka beside it. Ludwig grabbed those and hastily stuffed his feet into a pair of over-sized boots before dashing out into the snow. "Mara?!" He yelped. A flaming pinecone almost hit him as he pulled on the woolen coat. One of the massive boots almost fell off of his feet as he tried to run. "Come on!" He pulled the boot out of the snow and lunged away.

The lodge behind him was on fire. The tree had caught the roof in a blaze that spread down the walls. "Nein!" He hissed. Mara hadn't been in there, he reminded himself.

There was another, reverberating roar and Ludwig snapped his head around to see what could possibly make such a horrific sound. The answer stole his breath away. There was a dragon rising above the tallest trees, its head a mass of crested, golden spines and deep, multi-colored scales. She – he somehow knew instinctively it was Mara – looked like she had been carved out of charcoal and set on fire. Blue pulsed over the onyx of her scales and red and gold layered themselves on over it. But the fire wasn't hers. From her mouth, a beam of pure, white light radiated: The purest form of plasma. The fire was coming from something else, something Ludwig couldn't see.

"Vhat is going on?" Ludwig questioned aloud as he stood, stunned in the relative safety of a clearing in the snow. The snow was melting back from the burning forest, putting out the smaller fires and dampening the wood and forest floor, preventing the blaze from spreading. Nearby, there was the harsh crack of ice breaking as the whole of the mountainside went into an early thaw. The Ushanka cushioned his ears from the noise and he felt as if he could breathe easier.

Then, Ludwig felt a tickle like something was looking over his shoulder. He turned, wary, and found himself face-to-face with a man. But not just a man. He was ethereal. There was a lethal grace about him that lent him the trappings of power and the grace of an angel. Even his shoulders had wings sprouting from them. "Who are you?"

"Call me the light-bringer." The angel smiled easily. Something about him put Ludwig at ease. He felt as if someone was soothing their fingers through his dark hair. "You should get out of this fire-fight. It's not safe here."

Ludwig looked around. Most of the nearby fires had died down, though the lodge was still burning and the dragon – Mara – still roared occasionally. Her calls sounded distant and faint. "It seems safe enough here for now. Anyvay, vhere is there to go? It's all hinterland for miles."

"Take my hand, and I'll fly with you." The angel offered one, pale hand and an easy, inviting smile. "You don't need to be afraid."

Who was this? Had Mara chosen a different form? Were there other friendlies around? "...I'm not entirely sure I should trust you. Ve're strangers, after all."

The angel gave a not-quite angelic snort. "Whereas you should trust the person who changes into a dragon and burns down half the forest... and dresses you in her underwear. That doesn't seem the slightest bit creepy to you?"

Ludwig looked down at his bare legs peeking out from beneath the long coat. "You might be right." He admitted. "But Mara hasn't hurt me yet, and if I'm right, you're more dangerous than you look." His reasoning was kicking in. Lucifer meant "Light Bringer," didn't it? And Lucifer was the most beautiful of the angels before his fall.

"Everyone is more dangerous than they look. It's not so much a question of appearances as of intentions here." The angel gave Ludwig a cat-faced look and walked about him in a slow circle, bumping their shoulders together and trailing one hand over the coat. "Mara seems perfectly nice on the surface, but she wants to control you. Has she told you that you can't leave yet? I wonder… What is she willing to do to keep you here?"

"I know vhat you're trying to do." Ludwig made an effort to keep calm. If this was Lucy, he hadn't yet made any effort to take him prisoner. It seemed that – for the moment anyway – he couldn't "take" Ludwig. That Ludwig would have to go willingly with him.

There was rustling and the crash of footsteps through the trees and Mara was on them in a moment. "Get out of here, Lucy. I think I've thrashed about with you enough for today." She had a Butterfly Knife open in one hand and cleared the distance between them in two, massive strides. There was a cut on her cheek and the cloth on her side was damp with something that looked suspiciously like blood.

Lucifer hissed at her, his angelic form merging with something much darker and more menacing.

"You cannot keep up this constant vigilance forever. Someday, your guard will drop and I will have what is mine."

"Whatever." Mara twirled closed her knife and hid it away. "Get behind me, Lucy." She pushed out at him and Lucifer hissed as he was forced back and away from them by a sudden gust of gale-force winds. "Are you all right, Ludwig?"

"I am fine. You're hurt!" Ludwig rushed to brace her up as one of her legs trembled.

"Fighting Lucy can take a lot out of a body." Mara shrugged slightly as she limped back towards the lodge. "Don't worry. I just need some time to recover."

"Vhat happened? I tought you said it vas safe!"

"It is safe." Mara assured him, raising a hand towards the lodge, which had burned down to cinders by now. "I was careless, I'm sorry. I was trying to repel him quickly and I forgot to keep the lodge from burning down this time." Pointing at the foundation, Mara carefully raised her hand, restoring the lodge and – it seemed – upgrading it. "Don't worry about the forest. There's a snowstorm coming. By the time it's over, the trees will be fine again."

"Zhe lodge burning is a commonplace zhing zhen?" Ludwig felt one of the boots drop off of his foot. "Ach! Vait a moment..." He felt around in the snow for where it had fallen off and found it filled with snow by the time he got his foot back in it. "Verdammt..."

"Hold still." Mara gripped his thigh suddenly and the boots shrank to fit his feet. "Better? I've been a lacking hostess, I'm afraid. I forgot to get you a wardrobe, or at least teach you how to get your own."

"If zhat is vhat you are dealing vith, I can forgife some forgetfulness." Ludwig looked back over the trees. "Does he attack often?"

"Often enough that I've learned to fight him off at all times." Mara replied. "Sometimes, it's every morning. Sometimes, it's only once in a while. He seems to think that he can wear down my defenses if he just works at me long enough. But don't worry: You handled him well."

"Danke." Ludwig considered the event and looked up at her again. "It is odd: I felt so... relaxed, vhen I vas speaking to him."

"That's him influencing your mind. You resisted pretty well, for being so new. Probably because you knew who he was and what he wanted. It's important to know where you stand with people." Mara stepped up into the foyer of her home. "There's a first aid kit on the breakfast counter. It should have everything we need to treat this."

"Ja." Ludwig set her down on the bench and kicked off the snow-laden boots before scurrying into the lodge proper. The first aid kit was a white, plastic surgery kit with a red cross on the front. It was well stocked and supplied, more than he would have expected from a civilian's kit. Hurrying back to her side, he found she had pulled off her jacket and shirt and was applying pressure with one hand, waiting.

"You haf a very good first aid kit." Ludwig opened the box and tapped the back of her hand. "I vill take zhis."

Mara moved her hand away so he could press a handful of gauze over the gash and cast her eye over the kit, nodding. "Thought so. Ludwig: There was no first aid kit."

"Wat is los?" Ludwig questioned, looking up from the bottle of iodine.

"There was no first aid kit on the counter. I didn't put it there. All I did was tell you it was there and it would have everything you need." Mara explained. "Congratulations: You just imagined your first object into reality."

"Really? It vas zhat simple?" Ludwig's eyes widened as he threaded a curved needle.

"Yep. Well, it might be harder if you don't have anyone suggesting the object to you beforehand. It's all about believing in the object, making it real that way. You believed me when I told you there was a first aid kit on the counter because you trusted me. It's a little more complicated to make yourself believe something because you say it, because there's no boundary of trust. You know that the object doesn't technically exist." Mara obediently sat through the sutures that Ludwig used to pull her side back together.

"So... To affect zhe vorld, I must confince meinself zhat vhat is not true... is true." Ludwig shook his head. "I'm sorry, but zhat seems quite beyond me."

"I was afraid you would say that." Mara lowered her arm as he wrapped up the injury in gauze and surgical tape. "You're a man of science: You need to see to believe. That's not going to help you out here... Or maybe it will. Just because your mind works differently than mine doesn't make it particularly better or particularly worse. Maybe knowing what isn't real will help you in the future. But if you accept everything you perceive, you're going to end up badly hurt."

"How?" Ludwig questioned. "I mean, how can I keep myself from being hurt? Vhat can hurt me here? And what are the consequences?"

"So many questions with you. Always questions. Questions I'm not sure how to answer. Let me think." As she was thinking, she reached up to the peg beside her and began pulling on a change of clothes. Ludwig noticed that a suit of clothing in his own size was hanging beside it.

"Mara?" Ludwig took down the hanger. "Is zhere anyvhere I can change?"

Mara swept the room with a slightly sardonic eye. "Well, if it's modesty that's holding you back, there's the bedroom, of course. I added on a few rooms this time, so you could step into the sauna or into the bath."

"A bazh?" Ludwig perked up slightly.

"Yes, a bath, and no, you don't need my permission to use it." There was a slight, lop-sided smile on her face. "Go on. Relax some, and I'll think of a way to explain your questions."

Ludwig headed for the two new doors with the clothes slung over one shoulder.

"Ludwig… You're very young, aren't you?" Mara's voice was distinctly sad. "Not on the outside: I can see you're a silver fox. But on the inside… You're terribly young."

Ludwig drew himself up, half in offense. "I am forty-zhree years old."

"Maybe physically." The giantess waved it off. "I mean no offense: It was simply an observation. You seem so naïve, still."

"I haf had… a sheltered life." Ludwig admitted. "But I am not a child. I know how zhe world vorks and how to lif in it. I simply choose to put a little more faizh in people zhan ozhers."

"…I wish I could say the same. Enjoy your bath." Mara stood up and stepped outside into the snow storm that had blown over the lodge.

Chapter Three

Mara didn't return as quickly as Ludwig would have liked. He was done with his bath, dressed, and sipping a china cup of tea before she emerged back from the snow-strewn forest. The clothes he had found were tasteful and warm: A long pair of slightly loose khaki slacks, a dress shirt, green tie, and a cable-knit, cashmere sweater.

"You look good in neutrals." Mara observed as she pulled apart her much more dramatic attire, stepping through from the foyer to the warmth of the living room. There was an armload of freshly-cut wood in her hands and the pine scent mixed with the smoke from the already-blazing hearth.

"Vhere haf you been?" Ludwig questioned at once. "It has been hours."

"Did I worry you? I'm sorry. I needed time to think." Mara huffed out a breath as she stepped close to the fire and pitched two more logs onto it. "I was just outside."

"Cutting vood in a snowstorm?"

"The world is what you make it, Ludwig, remember?" Mara retrieved a second cup and poured tea into it. "I see you found the tea."

"Vas it meant to be hidden?" Ludwig raised an eyebrow as she made for the sofa he was stretched across.

"If you don't move your legs, I'll just sit on them." The giantess threatened mildly.

Ludwig lifted his legs, then dropped his feet into her lap as soon as she had sat down. "Zhere. Now I haf you trapped."

"So it seems." She amiably watched him. "And now that I am trapped, what are you going to do with me?"

"I'm going to make you answer my questions." Ludwig set down his tea cup on the table in front of the sofa. It was a strange piece of furniture: It seemed the perfect height to pull over the sofa itself, but it was far too large a piece to be that kind of table. On the other hand, it was too high to be a coffee table and too low to be a dining table. There was a jigsaw puzzle laid out on it. "How much danger am I in? Vhat can Lucifer do to me if he efer catches me?"

"…Lucy is… Boundlessly creative, infinitely curious, and endlessly cruel. If he ever gets ahold of you, he's going to try to kill you. But it's not going to be quick. I've seen what he does to the unfortunates he catches, and it makes me sick to my stomach. He tortures people for fun… and uses them in barbaric "rituals." They suffer for a very long time before they die." Mara coldly sipped at her tea, eyes shifting towards the fire.

"Vhy? Vhy vould he do zhat?"

"Aside from the fact that he's a sick freak?" Mara bitterly questioned. "He thinks that if he kills enough people, makes them suffer enough, that he'll become a demon. He wants the devil himself to take notice of him." She gave a crooked smile. "It seems that CORD has finally given him the ability to carry out his plans."

"Vhy isn't he stopped? Does Dr. Bervick not know vhat he does?"

"If Dr. Berwick knows what goes on in here, he doesn't care and he doesn't say. To be perfectly honest: I didn't even know his name before you came in." Mara hissed slightly. "As for why I haven't put a stop to him: I don't know if I can. There are... Well, I can't seem to decide how many exactly. The numbers change. The people leave or die, but there are at least four others in here with us, along with the Shadows Lucy keeps around: Those being people who died in CORD and their mental presences left an imprint. There's an old lady, a guy who thinks the world has gone mad, Lucy, me, and then there's... Well, I'm not sure. The fifth one can be hard to pin down." Mara shook her head. "The point is, the four of them are locked in some kind of combat for control over CORD. They're pretty evenly matched and they don't seem to get along well enough to team up against other people."

"Vhy aren't you fighting vith zhem?"

"Look, Ludwig, I have a strong enough mind that I can pretty much keep everyone out. I let them get a foothold occasionally because I like to tussle. Breaks up the monotony. But I don't know if I can defeat any of them on their territory, and I don't think

it's my place to do so. I'm not a killer, or a policeman.
I'm just... me."

"But if you allow zhem free rein... Isn't zhat zhe
same as being... Permissive? Allowing zhem zheir
vays?"

"I think you mean enabling, and that's a subject
I've grappled with myself. I didn't decide to take a
sidelines role easily, Ludwig. I'm not the kind of
person who lets themselves be benched easily. But I
genuinely don't know what to do. I am not a judge,
jury, or executioner and I don't want to be responsible
for anyone's death. That's not who I am." She
reached up to her blonde head and plucked a hair out
of her braid, running it between her lips until it stood
straight in her fingers. "There's a thin line between
justice and murder. I don't trust myself to walk it."

"...If you vere in danger und to safe your life,
you had to kill... Vould you?" Ludwig gave her a
piercing look.

"...That's different, Luddy. I have a right to
protect my time of Grace, after all."

"Vhat if it vas mein life?"

"...That's not a fair question." She stared
through the far wall, deep in thought. "Yes. I would kill
to save your life."

The jaws of the trap snapped shut around her.
"Vhy me und not zhe ozhers?"

"Do you want me not to save your life?
Because that's how you make me not save your life."

Mara poked one of his be-slippered feet. "And the reason is, I took you in. You're my responsibility now. I can't save everyone. I have to pick my battles, or I'll over-extend and I won't be able to save anyone."

Ludwig nodded. It was logical. Cold and analytical, but logical. "…Can you actually die here, Mara?"

"Yes." Mara's eyes darkened again. "Your perceptions shape reality here. If you perceive yourself as dead – if you believe it – then you will be dead. Your body will die and all that will be left is a Shadow – the memory of you that the rest of us have."

"…How many hafe you seen die?" He was a doctor. Death was a reality that he had faced before. One slip with his tools, after all, and his patient would never wake up. That was the reality of being a surgeon. But murder… Death because someone had wanted you dead. That was not an easy truth to face. Not even for a surgeon. Especially when the reason was so… insane. So petty.

"…Too many." Mara whispered. "Just plain too many."

"How many left… after you tried to protect zhem?"

"Five. Five and now you. You'll leave, in time, and you'll die like the rest. There won't be a thing I can do then. Not a damn thing." And she shut her mouth and refused to open it, or to let go of his foot, for a very long time.

"How necessary is food?" Ludwig questioned Mara as he cut into a broiled lamb chop. They were sitting at a dining table, across from each other and Mara was still brooding into a glass of zinfandel wine.

"Not at all." Mara replied, setting down the elegant crystal glass. "It's a pure indulgence. Something to do, something to keep yourself sane. In its limited way, it makes me feel better about life."

"So, if I didn't eat, I vouldn't starfe?" The lamb was perfect: Salty with just a hint of a slightly caramelized crust.

"I didn't say that. You'd likely think that you're a bit weaker, more tired. It's all in your head, Ludwig. If you think you need to eat, you'll need to eat." She stabbed a Brussels Sprout with her fork and held it up. "I realized that everything I used to need was a luxury long ago."

"Is it possible to ofer-eat?"

"If you think you've over-eaten, you'll feel full and maybe even pain, depending. But it won't result in weight gain. Well, not unless you believe it will."

"Ah… So, it really is all in mein head…"

"That is generally the answer to every question you'll have, yes." Mara snickered suddenly. "When did you realize you didn't need to go to the bathroom?"

Ludwig's eyes popped wide. He hadn't even thought of that. "Oh!"

"Yep. You won't need to use any sort of facilities either, unless you think you have to or just want to for some weird reason." Mara shrugged. "It's your life: I'm not gonna tell you how to live it."

"Shut up!" Ludwig tossed his napkin at her, blushing. "You are being crude!"

"Perhaps I am." She caught the napkin one-handed, folded it up, and tossed it back. It unfolded as it flew and burst into a dove on the wing, made of sparkling, silver snow. It sprinkled flakes over the table and the diners and then burst into nothingness. "But anything to stop brooding."

Ludwig had to clap appreciatively. "Zhat vas amazing."

"It's nothing. The world is limited only by your imagination." Mara waved the applause off. "But thank you. I live to please."

"Vell, zhis has been fery nice, but I am tired." Ludwig looked down at the table. "I suppose it is silly to ask if you need help vith zhe dishes?"

"A little bit silly." Mara stood up and pulled the tablecloth towards her swiftly. Leftovers, plates, candles, and roses, all went down onto the floor and vanished into thin air. When she was done showing off, she smoothed the tablecloth back down. "To bed then."

"…You didn't make a second bedroom." Ludwig observed as they stepped out of the dining room and through the lodge.

"I didn't. Would you rather I did?"

"Nein, nein… Not if you don't vant to." Ludwig gently pushed the lambskin slippers off of his feet. There were two dressers in the bedroom now. One of them was ornate and dark, the other streamlined and light. Ludwig pulled open the drawers of the lighter one and found neatly folded cardigans and pants. Nothing else. "Zhere is no undervear, Mara."

"I can fix that. Here." Mara handed him a familiar red, silk shirt. "Forgot nightclothes too, I suppose."

"Zhis is a razher clumsy attempt at seduction." Ludwig turned his back to her. "Don't look at me und I von't look at you."

"Who said I was doing that?" Mara retorted. "If I was trying to seduce you, it would be blindingly obvious." When Ludwig turned back, she was already wearing her sleep mask. "Besides: I'm ninety percent certain that I'm asexual."

"Vhere does zhe ten percent uncertainty factor in?"

"Look, I don't lust after people casually. Sex isn't a big thing for me. Relationships are, you get my drift? I've had two people exactly in my life that I've wanted to sleep with. Both of them I knew for a while, and I was close to them before I wanted… You know. Even then, it didn't happen. They didn't see me the same way." Mara gestured with one hand in the air.

"Ah. You are Demisexual." Ludwig found the word after a few moments' thought. "It means you are only sexually attracted to zhose you are in a deep, committed relationship vith."

"Yeah well… Apparently it works if it's one-sided too." Mara picked up her sleep mask. "Do you sleep with the lights on or off?"

"It does not matter." Ludwig settled between the sheets while she laid down on top of them, crossing her ankles. She was always wearing fuzzy socks, he noticed. The ones she had on currently were purple with blue polka dots. "I cannot see much vizh or vizhout zhem."

"If you need it, there's a sleep mask beside you."

"Is zhis anozher trick? Vill mein own mind fill in zhe blank vhen I turn ofer und zhere is not a mask already zhere?" Ludwig turned to the bedside table beside him and found the offered sleep mask – a duplicate of Mara's – waiting.

"Maybe it was, maybe it wasn't." Mara smirked. "Try it on: They're very comfortable."

"Nein, I do not like zhe vay sleeping masks press against mein eyelids." Ludwig folded his glasses and lay back on the pillows.

"Good thing this is less a sleep-mask and more of a face-bra then." Mara mused, snapping her own down.

"…Vhat?" Ludwig leaned up, squinting at her.

"You heard me: It's a face-bra. The mask has cups that go over your eyes so it doesn't press against your eyelids the way normal masks do."

"Zhat seems... Vell, I suppose it is a logical name." Ludwig gently patted the night stand and found the "face-bra." It was made of semi-stiff foam and lined with something soft. "I vill try anyzhing vonce." The inside of the sleep-mask was dark and soothing, true to Mara's word, it didn't press against his eyelids and it was more comfortable than he would have expected. "Hmm... Zhat is fery nice..."

"Told you." Mara rolled onto her side so that her back was to him. "Now, shh... Wanna sleep."

"Guten nacht, Mara." Ludwig laid back down.

"Good night, Ludwig."

A thought suddenly occurred to Ludwig. "...Vhat stops Lucy from attacking vhile you sleep?"

Mara sighed through her nose. "We still need to work on keeping our thoughts to ourselves, I see. As for your question, I don't know. It might just be a function of CORD. People don't seem to "appear" the same way they do when they're awake. Not that I've had much experience with that. As a general rule, I don't go prodding around the others."

"Oh." Ludwig laid his head back on the pillow. "...Zhat seems razher fortunate."

"I tend to count my blessings and not push my luck."

Silence fell for a few minutes more before another thought occurred. "You vere a dragon earlier."

"…If I promise to take you for a flight tomorrow, will you shut up and let me sleep tonight?" There was a slight growl to her voice.

"Verzeihen mir." Ludwig meekly settled in.

"…Ugh, don't do that."

"Do vhat?"

"That! That thing you do when you're acting all cute and harmless! It makes me feel like a jerk for snapping at you." Mara grumbled and turned over. "I'll answer all of your questions tomorrow. I promise. But right now, I'm going to ignore you, okay? Don't wake me unless the lodge is on fire."

"Not funny." Ludwig pouted, remembering that morning's close call.

"Shhh…" Mara pushed one hand down on his side, forcing him back into a sleeping position. "Quiet."

The doctor swallowed another few thoughts and struggled to go to sleep without speaking again.

Chapter Four

"Mornin'." Mara muttered as she pushed herself up from the bed. She had a lumbering grace, even when half-asleep, though the effect was ruined when she walked into her dresser while fumbling for the drawers. In the end, she gave up and – with a snap of her fingers – she dressed herself. "That's better. Ludwig?"

Ludwig had already been up for a while and he was upstairs. "Up here!"

"…I smell bacon. How crispy did you make it?" Mara climbed up the polished steps to find Ludwig standing in front of the stove with a massive, draping apron wrapped around himself and a spatula in the other hand. He looked like a doll or a child, wrapped up in borrowed clothes and working at a stove not meant for his size.

"It vas just started." Ludwig replied, looking up at the giantess. "How crispy do you like?"

"I like it with a bit of a lop to it." Mara took the spatula gently from him and turned the bacon. "I'll make you a step-stool if you're going to insist on cooking. I don't want you burning yourself." The bandages on her side had vanished during the night, along with the sutures.

"I am not a child." Ludwig crossed his arms. His temples were dabbed with grey and seemed to become more prominent, as if he had something to prove.

"No, but you're very short and everything in here is at my scale." Mara reminded him, one hand fluffing his pomaded hair. "And you're absolutely adorable."

"Ach. You vill insist on zhat." Ludwig adjusted his glasses with one hand. "I do not need a stool."

"What if you want to get up in the cabinets?" Mara thumbed at the large, over-counter pieces.

"…I can get a chair from zhe table." Ludwig looked up at her. "Are you… Taller zhis morning?"

Mara quickly compared their heights. "…Hmm… I seem to be nine feet tall this morning. Sorry, sometimes I think of myself as taller or shorter depending on the mood I'm in. Let's scale all this back down." Spinning one finger in the air like she was turning a dial, Ludwig seemed to grow up a little beside her as the lodge shrunk. "That should give you less trouble."

"Danke." Ludwig took his spatula back and began scooping bacon onto a rack to drain. "So… Yesterday, you vere a dragon."

"Still on that, I see." Mara reached up into the cabinets to pull down a tea pot and a box of jasmine dragon pearls. "After everything that you've seen, it's the dragon you're hung up on. Oh, and while we're on the topic, I prefer 'Wyvern.'"

"A dragon is a bit more fantastic zhan everyzhing else!" Ludwig protested, digging through the refrigerator for eggs. "A giantess is a simple matter of scale, but a dragon…"

"A WYVERN is a simple matter of imagination." Mara countered. "If you can envision it, you can be it here."

"But how-?!" Ludwig smashed one of the eggs in his frustration and it ran down onto the stovetop. "How do you force yourself to beliefe in somezhing so impossible?!" Another egg, smashed.

"Once you accept that this world is impossible, it gets easier." Mara shrugged. "Imagine all the things in this cabin: The lamps, the stove, the radio… but there isn't a generator. Everything needs electricity to run, but there's no power-source. That is impossible, and yet here we are." She gestured up at the bright lights and around at the sizzling stove.

"But just because I cannot see zhe generator does not mean zhere isn't vone!" Ludwig protested, smashing another egg, and then another. He didn't seem to be aware of what he was doing. "…Vell, in zhis case, it does, but zhat is not zhe point!"

"Ludwig. You're going to get trapped in a mental loop at this rate." Mara took him by the shoulders and shook him, forcing him to drop the next would-have-been-smashed egg from one limp hand. "Look: You're making a mess."

Ludwig shook himself and blinked at the eggs dripping down through the metal grating and onto the burner below it. "Ah! Vhy did zhat happen?!"

"Because your mind is designed to give people triggers and warnings when you're getting too upset and need to calm down. Usually, this manifests in expressions, but it also happens when you're doing certain tasks-"

"Ja! I know zhe jargon! But if zhis is truly inside mein head, und I can do vhatefer I vant, zhen vhy did zhat happen? Vhy didn't zhe eggs just go into zhe pan?" Ludwig protested.

Mara tapped a foot and put her hand over her mouth to think. "...Hmm... Something in your mind must have realized that you were getting upset and wanted to give me a warning. A subconscious urge to communicate that something isn't right? That seems... logical, but it doesn't seem like I explained it well."

"...Ja, you did not." Ludwig sighed. "It seems zhat efen here, zhe vorkings of zhe mind are a mystery."

"Did you really expect anything different?" Mara poured boiling water over the tea pearls in the pot. "Just because your perspective has changed, it doesn't guarantee immediate understanding. You're staring into an ocean, Ludwig, you can't expect to see the bottom."

"Ja, but... I had such high hopes for zhis machine." Ludwig sighed, cleaning his glasses with a soft cloth. "Vhen Doctor Berwick invited me to vork vith him... It vas a dream come true! I hafe alvays vanted to help ozhers... Und I am a sucker for zhe underdog. I vanted to find a vay to reach people zhat ozhers had gifen up on."

"...You're a good man." Mara was flipping over two perfectly fried eggs when he put his glasses back on and there was no sign of the mess he had made. "But you're fighting a force of nature. It might take decades of observation – even with machines like CORD – to understand the most basic part of the human psyche."

"Ja, I know." Ludwig sat down in the breakfast nook and laid his head in his hands. "Und now... Zhis has happened und-"

Bright lights. The retinas in his eyes were burning. Where were his glasses? He couldn't see without them. "He's back – we need to finish this!"

"He's losing oxygen in the blood. Those lungs need to be cleared and sealed!"

Ludwig tried to be still, but – he needed his glasses! He tried to tell them, "I am a doctor!" But no sound came out of his mouth. Then, he was rolling to the side and tumbling off the cold, steel table.

One of the assistants broke protocol, reaching out and catching him in one arm. The other hand came in front of his eyes, a blur of tightly curled fingers.

Mara snapped her fingers in front of his face. "You were doing it again."

"I fell! I fell off zhe table... Zhey let me fall!" Ludwig babbled at her, eyes rolling, terrified.

"Compose yourself!" Mara slapped him across the face, bringing him out of his shock. "You had good doctors, Ludwig. You didn't fall off the table: You fell off the chair." She pointed up at the seat he had been in before tumbling.

Ludwig took stock of his position and where he was. His operations had to have been completed days ago. "Vhen does it get better?" He clung to her shoulders.

"I don't know." Mara admitted, picking him up off of the floor. "I just don't know. I had hoped it would only take one episode before you learned to keep your memories and your reality separate, but… The memories must be just too raw for that. I guess we have to assume… That it's going to be a while. Maybe it never will."

"I can't do zhat… I can't go back zhere again… Zhe operation vas days ago… I should be able to remember zhat." Ludwig was barely aware that he was squeezing her shoulders in his hands with a grip that was too strong to be comfortable, but Mara wasn't complaining.

"First off, Ludwig, if there's anything I've learned about the mind from being in here, it's that scars can run deep. I had flashbacks to my tumble for a very long time before I learned how to sort myself. This is going to take time." She hadn't put him down yet. Of course, he hadn't asked her to. It felt safer here. "I blame myself. I should have been actively training you from the start. Maybe we can't avoid episodes in the future, but we can at least try."

"I'll do anyzhing."

"I hope so, 'cause this won't be easy. Now, I'm not in the mood for breakfast anymore, and if you aren't, then how about that flight I promised you?"

Mara's dragon form was even more magnificent up close than it had been over the trees. Her scales were a cool, glassy black that looked almost liquid as Ludwig ran his hand over their smooth surface. As she moved, spreading out her great wings and stretching herself like a cat, the light caught and shattered, reflecting itself into blues, reds, and golds. Her spines were covered in leathery skin, though her claws were burnished and razor sharp. "Do you think you can sit comfortably right below my neck?" There was a saddle carefully wedged there. "I can add safety straps, if you want."

"Nein, I can hold on. Just don't go too fast." Ludwig securely pushed his feet into the stirrups. The fur boots had a non-slip tread that locked easily with the steel imprint on the stirrup.

"Don't kick my sides, and I'll see what I can do." Mara stood up and beat her wings a few times, testing them, letting Ludwig find his balance. "Ready?"

"Do it!" Ludwig gripped onto the spine in front of him as tightly as he could. "Do it now!"

"All right!" With a sudden push and toss, Mara threw herself into the air, wings forcing them up.

Ludwig gave a delighted shriek and pressed his eyes closed as they ascended, the large wings pounding on either side of him. They leveled out only once they had breached the cloud layer and crystals of ice were forming on the surface of his glasses. If his hands weren't so busy with their death grip on Mara's spine, he would have checked the tie on his fur-lined Ushanka, fastened carefully beneath his chin. The scarf wrapped around his neck flapped behind them in the wind.

"Mara! How high are ve?" Ludwig called forwards towards her.

"High enough that we would require oxygen tanks... If this were the real world." Mara twisted her body in loops, twirling the clouds tickling her belly into swirls and peaks.

"Zhis is impossible! Zhis is amazing!" Ludwig loosened his death-grip slightly to extend his arms on either side of him in a bright, joyful gesture. "Faster!"

"Andale!" Mara bugled and dove forwards, whipping through the reaching fingers of cloud and forcing him to grab onto the spine once more, her sinuous frame moving beneath him like a river. He could feel every turn and heave of her wings.

"Mara, look!" Ludwig pointed to their left. "The sun! Fly towards the sun!"

"If you insist!" She threw herself into the turn and spun herself.

At this altitude, the sun was blinding. It reflected off of her scales and shattered over and over into a million fractals of light. Ludwig squinted against the radiance, his eyes beginning to stream and he lifted his voice to howl, "Diese frau brennt!"

Mara only held on her course for a few moments more. With a tilt of her body, she dove back beneath the clouds and into the snow-white wonderland. Spinning into her dive, she tumbled down towards the frosted river, trailing her claws along the ice to make it sing. Ludwig held on, helpless and grinning like an idiot.

"Having fun?" Mara turned her massive head to look back at him and nuzzled his head.

"It's brilliant!" Eyes widening suddenly, Ludwig pointed forwards. "Look out!"

With a press upwards, Mara was scraping over the tree Ludwig had pointed out and soaring back up into the sky. She did an easy loop-the-loop and landed in front of the lodge.

"Vhy are ve stopping?" Ludwig questioned. "Let's go again!"

"We'll go again tomorrow, Ludwig. And we'll start training then as well. But for now… Let's just have fun, and a nice, calm day. I don't want to over-stress myself." The dragon was shrinking and the saddle under him became a pair of arms. Ludwig found himself gripping hard onto Mara's shoulders while she held him up in a seat made of her arms. "There will be time. I promise. There will be time."

"All right." Ludwig sighed and looked down at the snow. "Vell, are you going to put me down?"

"I don't want to." Mara grumbled, setting him on his feet. "…Well, I didn't mean to say that out loud."

"Now, who's having trouble keeping zheir zhoughts to zhemselves?" Ludwig chuckled humorously.

"Oh, shush…" Mara gently pushed him backwards into the snow.

Contentedly, Ludwig waved his arms and legs, making a snow angel. "Help me up so I don't spoil it!" He reached up with his arms, sitting up carefully.

"Pick me up, put me down, pick me up… Make up your mind." Mara reached down and helped him out of the impression in the snow. Then, she let out a surprisingly high-pitched laugh. "…Your snow angel is wearing an Ushanka."

Ludwig looked down at the oddly-boxy impression his head had made. "It is, isn't it?" He laughed as well, gripping her arm. "Vhat else are ve going to do today?"

"Have you ever been sledding?"

"Only once. Is zhere a good hill nearby?" Ludwig looked up at her.

"Yes. And the best part is that the lodge is halfway up it." Mara gave him a crooked smile. "Come on, it's a nice hike."

"All right. Should ve pack some lunch or a thermos? How long a hike?"

"Ach! Always logic with you! Very well, let's get some lunch." And the giantess headed up into the lodge. "I have to find where I put the sled anyway."

"Did you lose it? How can you lose somezhing here?" Ludwig questioned.

"I didn't "lose" it. I just haven't been sledding in a while and I need to think of what it should look and feel like." Mara explained as she unwrapped her black ski mask. "Sometimes, it helps to think of things as being "lost" instead of forgotten, savvy?"

"I get it." Ludwig nodded. As they were stepping through the front door, he closed his eyes. "Prosciutto, basil, and Havarti." He muttered beneath his breath, focusing, and trying to visualize what he wanted.

"What?" Mara questioned, looking over her shoulder. "Are you trying to order an antipa-?"

A bit harshly, Ludwig shushed her. "Prosciutto, basil, and Havarti."

"Tiramisu while you're at it." The blonde giantess muttered, hanging up her coat and setting her boots in their stand.

"Shh! I'm trying to focus!" Ludwig thrust his Ushanka onto a hook and ran into the kitchen. There, on the counter, was a platter of Italian Antipasti – slices of cured meats and cheeses with dishes of olives and garnishes all arranged on a wooden block. There was even a plate with a Tiramisu on it – the layers of ladyfingers, creamy mascarpone, and cocoa powder all picture perfect. "I did it!" He called to Mara as she came in behind him, more sedate and slightly confused. "I did it!"

"What is it that you did?" Mara stepped into the kitchen and her eyes landed on the block of antipasti. "Wow. Yeah, you sure did. Was that what you were trying to do?"

"Yes!" Ludwig happily picked up the square loaves of Ciabatta bread and split them in half with a serrated bread knife. "It seems I vent overboard, but at least zhere is a gut selection! Vhat do you vant on your sandvich?"

"I'll… I'll let you decide." Mara sat down at the counter and picked up a tasting spoon, dipping it into one of the garnishes. "I… Wouldn't know where to start. I've never even seen an Antipasti before. Italian isn't my favorite, so I don't know half as much about these things as you."

"Wot is los? But you knew about zhe Tiramisu… You vere the one who suggested zhat." Ludwig looked suspiciously over at her, drizzling a light layer of olive oil onto the bread.

"Well, everyone knows what Tiramisu is. I mean, it's like Zuccoto, it's everyone's favorite." She pointed at a bowl of Nicoise olives. "I wouldn't know these olives from the Castelvetranos…" Immediately, she seemed to recognize her mistake.

Castelvetrano Olives were a ubiquitous snack in Italy. A mild, green, buttery olive with a smooth finish and no hard edges, they made for an excellent palate cleanser and their firm flesh made them easy to eat out of hand. But in America, the Spanish olive was much more common and it was difficult to find Castelvetranos outside of specialty Italian stores. Further, Tiramisu was certainly popular enough in America, but Zuccoto – a similar cake made with ice cream instead of mascarpone – was not. In fact, it was virtually unknown outside of Italian restaurants and homes.

"Vhy vould you…?" Ludwig's blue eyes cleared as he looked down at the Antipasti board. While there were several varieties of Italian cheeses, none of them were the Havarti he had been envisioning. "…Oh."

"…You okay?" Mara looked worriedly at him.

"Ja, ja… I am fine." Ludwig sighed through his nose. "I really thought I had it for a moment there."

"You'll get it." Mara assured him. "I bet you would have gotten it, but when you spoke out loud… Well, I guess my mind was filling the blanks before I could stop it."

"Maybe next time." The doctor squared his shoulders and picked up the bread again. "Vell, now zhat ve've established zhat you are a terrible liar, what do you vant on your sandviches?"

"Prosciutto with mozzarella and basil leaves." Mara crisply answered. "And then the white wine garlic garnish with chicken and salami."

"Someone doesn't vant to be kissed." Ludwig teased as he spread the garlic garnish on one of the loaves of ciabatta.

"…I can suck on a peppermint." Mara replied – a bit nonsensically. She shifted uncomfortably, then stood up. "What kind of tea do you want with this? I'll put together some chicken soup to carry along."

"Tea and Italian food?" Ludwig rolled his eyes to heaven. "I'll warm some wine to carry." He reached up into a cabinet above his head where he had seen her draw wine from before. "How does a Chianti sound?" He went up on tiptoes, trying to read the labels and spotted one that was vaguely familiar.

"Well, it's not my favorite, but it's good enough, I suppose." Mara looked over her shoulder, watching as he pulled out a green bottle with a silver label, nearly tugging it out and onto his head. In one, smooth motion, she reached out and caught it by the neck. "Careful."

"Danke." Ludwig took the bottle and opened it up, pouring it out into a small double boiler from the rack of pots over the stove.

"…Ludwig, what does the label on that bottle say?" Mara questioned, her voice carefully modulated and casual. She was stirring a pot that smelled better by the moment.

"It's a Chianti from Italy. Zhe maker is Sicilian. It's called – razher nonsensically – Zhe Road to Rome. Do you vant to smell zhe cork?" Ludwig offered the light brown plug to her, their shoulders brushing as both shared the stove. "I must say: You hafe excellent taste. Zhis is mein favorite."

"Ludwig…" Mara smirked down at him. "I hate Chianti. It's the last thing I would stock my wine closet with."

"Vhat? But zhe bottle…" Ludwig looked back down at it. No, it was still a Chianti and his glasses were clean.

"Ludwig… You got it." Mara fluffed up his hair with her off hand.

"I… I did, didn't I?" Ludwig didn't even bother to push her away from his usually crisp hair. "Of course, it wasn't really somezhing I did alone, vas it? Zhere vas zhe suggestion. It vas from zhe vine cupboard. But I did do it…"

"You did good, Luddy." Mara stirred the soup a few more times and put it off the heat to cool down some. "Unconsciously making things appear is the first step. Consciously doing it is harder. But you'll get it. I know you can."

"Don't call me zhat…" Ludwig grumbled, his cheeks heating.

"What? Luddy? Why not?"

"It's too much like Wolfie. I was called that all the time when I was a child. I hate it."

"What should I call you then? Princess?"

"Nein!" Ludwig turned horrified eyes on her. "You vouldn't!"

"Too late, princess. I'm going to call you that forever now." Mara smirked as Ludwig smacked the back of her head with the spoon.

"Dummkopf." Ludwig muttered. "Vatch zhe vine. I vill make zhe sandviches." He stomped over to the other counter.

"Whatever you say, Princess." She ducked the olive he threw at her.

Chapter Five

Perhaps as a direct response to the new nickname, Ludwig insisted on pulling the sled with their picnic basket tied onto the back.

"It's a long hike. Are you sure you wouldn't rather ride?" Mara was walking behind the sled, far too amused for Ludwig's comfort.

"Nein. Valking is good for zhe blood und zhe body." Ludwig replied, nose stuck firmly in the air. The hiking path Mara had chosen wasn't steep, but it was drifted with snow that tickled the top of Ludwig's boots.

"All right... If you change your mind, all you have to do is say." Mara reminded him, walking easily with her long stride. Ludwig had to take two steps for every one of hers.

"I vill not change mein mind!" Ludwig replied, pulling the handle of the sled a little harder to guide it over a bump.

"Careful of the basket." Mara was carrying the thermos of wine and soup in one hand to keep it from spilling as the sled jostled over the snow.

"I am being careful!" Ludwig insisted.

"Be more careful then."

"Who is pulling zhe sled?"

"If you don't like me criticizing your sled-pulling, just let me pull the sled."

"I can pull zhe sled!" Ludwig looked back over his shoulder. "I am un grown man und I do not need assistance vith efery single task."

Mara's eyes went to a spot above and behind his shoulder. "Hi, Lucy."

"Verdammt!" Ludwig twirled at once and found himself face to face with a pine tree he was about to walk into. "…Liar."

"It got you to watch where you're going." Mara easily brushed off the accusation.

"You could hafe just said: Vatch out, tree!"

"I could have, but which option would have been more fun?"

"You are impossible!" Ludwig huffed and smoothed himself down. The white double-breasted coat he was wearing marked too easily to let himself walk into trees. Schooling his eyes ahead, he kept pulling the sled.

"Are you really that mad over a silly nickname?" Mara questioned, following behind him.

"It's not zhe nickname! You are alvays doing zhese zhings!" He dropped the sled rope and poked a finger accusingly into her black-clad front. "I am a grown man und not a child! I do not alvays need coddling und caring! I am off balance, ja, but I am not cute! In fact, I am probably older zhan you!"

Mara stared down at him. Then, she took a step back and bowed, gesturing to the sled. "Of course. I suppose I must have overestimated you,

Doctor. Do carry on. I won't offer to help again."
Straightening, she looked down at him. "Oh, wait,
does my height threaten your masculinity? Many
apologies. Allow me to fix that. While I'm at it, shall I
put on a skirt?" She shrank down to a normal height
and looked at him with a raised eyebrow.

"...I vas not insulting your independence, Mara,
I do not vant you to change."

"Yes, you do. Now, it's an insult to my
independence as a woman that you are pulling a sled
for me." And, with that, she pushed him backwards so
that he landed on the sled and picked up the rope.
"After all, oh-so-very-grown-and-not-cute-at-all old
man, the young should take care of the aging. Catch."
She tossed the thermoses to him.

Ludwig folded his arms grouchily over the
vessels of warm liquid. "If you still vant to, zhat is fine.
Tell me vhen you get tired."

Mara set off at a pace that was more a run
than a walk and Ludwig simply held on for dear life.
"Is zhis not a bit too fast?" He called as they went
over a bump. "You should be careful... Of zhe basket,
of course, not of me."

"I tied that basket down with three different
belts. It will be fine. Oh, look! A shortcut!" She tossed
herself up a much steeper slope, pulling the hapless
Ludwig behind her.

Ludwig gave an exclamation as he was hit in
the face with a tree branch.

"Whoops! Sorry!" Mara cheerfully pulled them back onto the path. "Clumsy of me, wasn't it? Maybe I should be more careful!"

"Nein, it is fine." Ludwig had the distinct feeling that they were fighting over something a bit more than a nickname and surrender was not an option.

"Oh, of course, I forgot. You don't need to be taken care of. Well then!" And she set off at a full-out run.

Ludwig's Ushanka flapped slightly as they sped along. Every turn and bump threatened to dislodge him. It was not a sensation that he enjoyed. "Perhaps I could valk for meinself?"

"No, of course not! I wouldn't dream of letting you do that! It would be downright irresponsible of me!" Mara raced up around the next curve and Ludwig gave a sickening lurch in the seat.

"Und zhis is not?!" Ludwig's statement rose in pitch and panic as the sled tipped over entirely, sending him into a snowdrift, scattering the thermoses.

"Oh, carp!" Mara swore as she dropped the sled and ran to his side, picking him out. "Are you all right?"

"...I zhink so... Nozhing is broken." Ludwig sat up. "Do not pick me up, please."

"I'm going to pick you up." Mara stubbornly replied, and Ludwig saw that she was back at her giantess height as she pulled him out of the drift.

"Criminey, Ludwig, what are we doing? It's just a dumb nickname. I won't use it if it really bothers you so much, but I don't see why it does."

"Because I am not a voman!" Ludwig burst out, pushing her away. "I refuse to be one for you!"

Mara reared back. Something dark flooded into her eyes and she raised a hand, which changed into a scaled claw. "How dare you..."

Ludwig threw a hand up over his face to protect himself and flinched back, but after a frozen moment of waiting, nothing came. When he pulled his hand away and looked, Mara was gone like a puff of snowflakes. "...Zhis is ridiculous." Ludwig muttered. "Lucy is right. I hafe to get avay from her."

The doctor climbed to his feet and took up the sled's rope. He would need the supplies – meager as they were – if he was going to survive the journey. He needed to make it back to his train station, his train, and figure out a new strategy from there. With Lucy loose, he would have a hard time trying to defend himself. If he could get the train moving again, he would be able to make himself into a moving target, prevent Lucy from catching up to him.

Now, which way was out? In a white wonderland like this, nothing stood out. Of course, with the way this world was set, shouldn't he just need to start walking? Eventually, he would be out of Mara's mind. Picking a random direction – that just happened to coincide with downhill – the much better-prepared doctor set off to leave his guardian's home.

The snow sapped his strength and the cold bit at his nose. Every step was weighted by a hundred pounds of lead. "Mein gott... Does it hafe to be so cold?" He opened the thermos of warmed wine and took a sip. It was hot, which was all that needed to be said, though any other time, he would have mused over how the warmth changed the flavors of the Chianti and made the pallet brighter over all.

It was a very long time before he felt like he was making progress. The trees were becoming thinner, though the snow was no less thick. By the time he had sipped his way through half of the thermos of heated wine and started in on the soup – the last thing he needed was to be impaired in any way – he was up to his knees in snow. It was going to be impassible if he wasn't careful.

"Snowshoes." He seethed silently. "I vish I had snowshoes!"

"Wishing never got anyone anywhere." Lucy was walking beside him. Ludwig gave a slight shudder.

"How long hafe you been zhere?"

"Leaving the dragon's side, I see." Lucy ignored his question, turning his eyes on him. "Decided to take my advice?"

"Go avay, Lucy. I might be less experienced zhan Mara, but zhat doesn't mean I von't defend myself." Ludwig quietly told the demon. That was how you dealt with demons, wasn't it? Tell them to go away and refuse their gifts. Unfortunately, this was not a demon.

"You might try, but you see… Well, here's the thing." Lucy snapped his fingers and the ground fell out from beneath Ludwig. He tumbled for what seemed a long time and landed in a chair that came alive the moment he touched it, binding him into place. "You've wandered into my territory. And I don't take kindly to that." It was a dark room, lit only by some unseen source that illuminated a very small area around the chair he was bound to. The chair felt slippery and slimy beneath him and one glance confirmed that it was, in fact, made out of human flesh and bone, arranged into sickening patterns.

"It vas an accident." Ludwig stiffly replied. "Just like you said: I vas leafing Mara."

"And now you've come all this way to me. Look around, Ludwig, because you're going to be here, for a very long time." Lucy leaned over him, his angelic features twisted up into a cruel smile. "Did she manage to get you into bed this time?"

"Vhat? Nein!" Ludwig pulled back his lips. "You may torture me, Lucy, but I vill not play your sick games. I am an accomplished brain surgeon und I know vhat you are doing. You vill use mein death to zhrow in Mara's face. Vell, it von't vork. Zhe reason I left vas zhat ve had a fight und doubtless she is not zhinking fond zhings of me." He forced himself to stare right into the eyes of evil.

"Oh, my dear doctor… Haven't you figured it out yet? Poor, stupid, child." Lucy patted his cheek, tutting.

"I am not a child." Ludwig bit out, glaring at Lucy.

"Perhaps not. But you are very stupid." The demon produced a knife from thin air and sank it into his shoulder suddenly.

Ludwig howled, flinging curses at Lucifer as he dug the blade in deeper until it met bone. "Look how little it takes to make you scream." He marveled, pressing lightly around the wound – exploring. "I can't wait to rip you open and see your soul. It's probably a very large one: After all, you're a doctor! Then again, I have met another doctor in here, and let me tell you… His soul is not very large at all."

"You are completely insane."

"Perhaps." Lucy shrugged. "She's listening, you know. I always let her listen in. Poor thing can't do anything now, but she can't help herself either. She'll be here until the end, you poor, little imbecile." He pulled the knife out with a jerk that caused a spasm of pain through Ludwig's body. The surgeon forced himself still after an initial jerk and bit down on the outcry, glaring out his pain and hatred.

"I see we've decided to be tough. Let's see how long that lasts. It's usually only a few hours. Oh, but don't worry. I have myriad ways to make you suffer until you finally break. Why don't I cut out one of those blue eyes and see how you feel then?" Lucy took off his glasses and crushed them in one hand. "I should give you better eyes. Needing to wear glasses just takes something away from this experience. There's something wonderful about being able to see what's coming slowly towards you..."

The world was reduced to smears of color and Ludwig was briefly glad that he couldn't see Lucy's sick smile, but when the point of something hard and steel touched his eyelid, he flinched backwards. Ludwig struggled as Lucy gripped his skull with a steel hand. "No!"

"Of course, I'm not going to take your eyes." Lucy scoffed, scoring the knife down his cheek. "The eyes are the window to the soul, don't you know? They're so important for what I'm doing. I'm going to watch your soul, Ludwig. I'm going to watch it squirm and twist until it turns black and dies. And then I'm going to kill you. Don't worry: By then, you'll wish you were dead."

"...You're insane." Ludwig didn't dare shout while the knife was working away, making shallow cuts on his face. One false move and he would touch a facial nerve.

"You know what they say: The wisdom of God is foolish to men." The knife briefly moved away from him and Lucy forced a kiss on the doctor, his foul breath and slimy tongue making themselves known as Ludwig ground his teeth together, resisting him. "Hmm... I see what she wanted from you... You are sweet. Not like the last one. Oh, Ludwig, this is going to be so much fun... For me, that is. Not for you."

Ludwig's head sagged when Lucy released his death grip. There was blood trickling down the back of his neck from where Lucy's fingers had pierced his scalp. "…Mara." He whispered.

"Speak up, Ludwig. I'm not sure she can hear you." There was a horrid sound, like a thousand shards of glass, grinding on each other. He had to be doing it on purpose, making it so loud. "I must say, I'm surprised by how fast you broke. Most take a little more punishment before begging her to come."

Ludwig ignored him. If Mara could hear everything, he would make her hear him. "Mara, shut your ears. Don't dvell on this. You can't help me now." He forced his voice to be steady, forced his head up. His glare could freeze Lucy. It would have to, because he had no other way to stop the demon from simply cutting his tongue out. Lucy thought this was him breaking? He had no idea. The surgeon planted his feet and lifted his head. "It's not healthy to obsess. Zhis vas mein choice. Turn avay."

A massive hand smothered his mouth. Lucy stabbed him in the throat, cutting through his voice box. "Oh, you stupid little –"

"Let go of him."

Lucy hissed and whirled, the knife dropped from his hand. Ludwig struggled for breath around this thing that was blocking his windpipe. He could barely hear it as Mara and Lucy grappled with each other. What little breath he could get came in horrible wheezes and tasted like blood.

Then, the blade was being removed with careful fingers and there were pricks of agony as a needle and thread sewed him back together. "You moron." Mara berated him. Her voice was trembling. "You won't die from a scratch like this."

Ludwig let his head loll and the needle prick and believed her.

Chapter Six

When he woke up, he was whole and pain-free. He stretched out on the cotton sheets, smiling, and breathed in the smell of the sea.

The sea?

Ludwig sat up and reached for his glasses on the nightstand. This wasn't the lodge high up in the mountains. This was a charming little beach house with large, bay windows where curtains fluttered in the breezes. There were seashells hanging in ribbons from the ceiling. They clattered and clinked in the breeze and made their own strange music. "Mara?" His voice sounded fine. When his hand went to his throat, the only remains of the hasty, unskilled sutures were a thin, bumpy line.

"I know you're here." Ludwig stepped out of bed. He had been dressed in pajamas and there was an outfit hanging on the closet door nearby. "You safed me. I zhought it vas impossible."

Mara didn't respond. Ludwig glanced out the window and spotted a black figure flying away over the ocean. ...Where was she going?

Ludwig squared his shoulders and got dressed. The beach house was the pink of a child's cough medicine on the outside and trimmed in something sickeningly blue-green. It was the sort of charming ugly that he would expect from the neighborhoods of South Padre Island. With his pants rolled up over his knees, he went down to the water to see what he could see.

The island – as it turned out – was no more than a few miles around and set into a lagoon created by a ring of coral. The beach house was the sole inhabitation. It had the same lonely, peaceful quality that the lodge had, but none of its warmth. The inside was cool and soothing. The outside was bright like a warning. It was not a place where one retreated when they wanted visitors and, hard as he looked, he could find no egress. The ocean spread to the horizon, the only visible land the spits of sand that had formed on top of the reef.

"Vell... Zhis is certainly a retreat." Unless he could grow wings, he wouldn't be leaving any time soon. Maybe that was the point. Sitting down on the sand, one hand dropped to the beach and stroked it gently. The sand was soft, but not clinging, like normal sand was. He doubted that this sand would irritate him with its grittiness or get into every crack and cover the floors. With an abandon he hadn't felt since he was a child, Ludwig stretched himself out on the beach and looked up. In spite of the bright light and the warmth, the sun was filtered through fluffy, white cloud cover.

He could spend some time here, easily. If Mara wasn't going to speak to him, he could keep himself occupied. First on the agenda: A quiet nap on the beach. He might have just woken up, but there was still an ache in his head and back that needed attending to.

Ludwig woke up feeling oddly unsatisfied and lacking. In spite of that, he was still comfortable. The sand had made a good bed and he pulled himself up with ease. A brisk walk across the porcelain beach would be just what the good doctor ordered.

Ludwig rubbed his toes through the white sand and enjoyed the breeze teasing at his hair. Reaching up a hand idly, he ran it backwards through his pomaded locks. The resulting spiky mess would have mortified him in front of his peers, but here… here he was alone. With only the song of the gulls to keep him company.

An hour's walk brought him in a full circle to the indentation where his body had lain. On his journey, he had passed several exotic fruit trees, some of them tantalizingly sweet-smelling, and various bits of beach detritus such as shells, crab casts, and even the occasional piece of seaweed. It was, in all, a pleasant little island. Entirely suited to rest and relaxation. It was the sort of place that would have been considered a cure-all during the Industrial Revolution. There was even a deep, cold, freshwater spring on the other side of the small patch of jungle that the house backed up to. Exotic birds gave the occasional call, but the soundscape was otherwise a rhythmic, white noise. He would have no trouble sleeping here.

Inside, Ludwig found that the kitchen was all at his size. In fact, everything was exactly the right height for a normal, six-foot stature. There would be no teasing about stepstools. The refrigerator was full of various trimmings and the doctor put together a simple lunch – a salad with orange segments and delicately steamed crab – fit for a king.

After lunch was eaten and the dishes washed, Ludwig went searching for entertainment. There was a bookshelf full of volumes. Ludwig adjusted his glasses as they read their titles. Classics for the most part and what weren't classics were medical journals and textbooks. Ignoring these, he reached for a copy of the works of Shakespeare and settled on the beige couch to read it. It was lovely to sit down on a couch that he didn't have to compete for and read without someone resting a hand on his shin. Absolutely lovely.

Chapter Seven

Safe and alone had a charm that wore off too quickly for Ludwig's taste. It was with a reluctance that he attributed to apprehension that he admitted he was lonely. There were only so many times one could read through Grey's Anatomy without finding themselves bored. Life on his island was rhythmic, peaceful. Too much so.

He had long learned to keep his thoughts to himself. At first, that had been a game of his. It had been weeks since he last burst out with a sentence that had begun as a mental observation. In the end, when he got the hang of it, it was a deceptively simple matter.

"I seem to be getting zhe hang of zhis." He told a mirror that he suspected was a two-way one hanging up on the wall across from the sofa where he did a majority of his reading. "Maybe I vill start trying to change zhis vorld again soon." He glanced up into the mirror and saw a glint of a golden braid before it was gone. "I know you're zhere. Zhis is your beach house. You can't help but hear me."

If Mara heard, she wasn't talking. He laid down his book and huffed, folding his arms. "Now who is being childish?"

"Vell, am I going to be alone forefer or are you going to come out?" Ludwig addressed this question to the ocean one morning as he sat up in bed. The ocean didn't answer and the shells above his head were equally unhelpful.

"Join me for mein efening valk. I found somezhing I vant to show you." He told the guava tree where a songbird was singing out.

"Doesn't zhat smell delicious?" Ludwig questioned the empty kitchen the next day as he stirred a pot of sauce made with shellfish and white wine. "You could join me, if you vanted. I made more zhan enough of zhe sauce for two. You could even pick out zhe pasta."

Ludwig peeked over his shoulder. No one was there. But, when he put his hand out for the pasta he had intended to use – a simple mid-sized shell that would cup the sauce and incorporate with the mussels and shrimp easily – he found that it had been replaced by a bag of ruffled, over-sized monstrosities. "Fery funny." Ludwig scolded the empty room, shaking the bag. But he still opened it and poured them into the boiling water.

"...Vhat day is it?" Ludwig questioned, lying back on the beach. "How long hafe I been here? I've lost track." He had built up quite a tan as well, walking and napping on the beach and wading or swimming in the lagoon.

There was a simple, counting calendar/white board hanging up on the wall when he returned to the house. A date had been marked with a red circle and black X's led up to a different day. Ludwig counted them carefully. From the beginning of what Mara had decided had to be a year, there were five unmarked months. Then, the red circle. That must have been his arrival on the island. Almost four months later, the X's stopped. "One hundred and seventeen days is surely a long enough time for anyvone to stop sulking." He told the living room. "I'm sorry your feelings vere hurt, but I hafe had enough of zhis. Am I a guest or a prisoner?"

Ludwig suspected – as he nibbled a truffle with his after-dinner coffee – that he was some strange combination of both.

"You really should come out. It's quite rude to just slink around and ignore your friends." Ludwig blew the steam off of a morning cup of strong, green tea. "I made your favorite: Jasmine Dragon Pearls. Vhy not sit und hafe a cup?" He had laid a second cup and saucer out on the table and brewed too much tea for this very purpose. "It's all going to go to vaste if you don't hurry. Green tea can't be allowed to steep fery long."

When Ludwig turned his back to pull his poaching eggs off of the stove, he turned around to find that the extra tea cup had been set upright on its saucer and there was a small pool of dregs at the bottom. "Und taking it zhis vay is cheating!" He huffed.

Ludwig had been collecting the small, black turban shells that the snails left on the beaches for a few weeks before he began drilling holes into them and making a necklace. There was, as usual, a bouquet of hibiscus and bird of paradise on the table in front of him. The bright, flaring colors of the bird of paradise blended surprisingly well with the pinks and reds of the hibiscus flowers. "…No offense to your hibiscus, but I miss roses." He told the bouquet. "Plain old, hot house roses."

When he next glanced up from the turban shells and his auger, there was a dozen, round, flourishing sunset roses in the vase. "Dankeschon, mein friend."

A strong breeze toyed with his spit-curl and faded.

Ludwig didn't immediately reach for his glasses when he woke up one morning. He folded his hands in the blanket in front of him and sat up, just listening, not getting up yet. "…I von't say I'm sorry. I am not a voman, nor a child. I hafe no desire to be eizher. But I do miss you. In your own, odd vay, I zhink you are vone of zhe few people I can truly call my friend. I vish you vould come and fisit, at least, if you von't stay."

When he eventually put on his glasses, there was a flash of bright red in the cream-colored room. A familiar, too-large undershirt was hanging over the back of the nearby chair. It smelled like pine and smoke when he picked it up and tucked it carefully into a drawer.

Ludwig woke in the middle of the night to the sound of heavy footsteps in the water. Without bothering to dress, he threw himself forward in the draping, baggy undershirt and jumped out the window, running down to the beach. When he reached the place where the tightly woven grass met the white sand, he stopped. The moon was very bright – it was a rare, clear night with the stars above and the sea a reflecting pool below. Mara was up to her hips in the soft, open waves. When he came out, she looked back over her shoulder at him. "…Hey."

"Hallo." Ludwig stood at the saltstrand, the waves barely licking his toes. "I've missed you."

"I know." She looked back out at the ocean and Ludwig began carefully wading closer.

"I'm not a fery strong svimmer." He warned. "If zhere's an undertow, it vill carry me off like zhat!"

"There's no undertow here." Mara pointed out at the encircling reef. "The lagoon is almost completely still."

The water was up to Ludwig's chest when he reached Mara, but she didn't offer an arm to anchor him. Her hands were in the water, fingers spread, and hundreds of tiny fry and fishes had gathered to nibble at her skin. A few of them grouped around Ludwig as well and he could feel them on his bare legs. "Ja. Und

I am grateful for zhat. I do not like to svim in open vater alone. It's fery dangerous."

"…I love the solitude of the ocean." Mara replied. "I've never met a fish that judged me as anything but a potential meal or a threat. None of them have ever told me I can't be anything but what I am. Or called me out for not being normal. They just want to nibble at your skin, bask in your shadow, then leave."

Ludwig fell silent. There was clearly something deeper here. Something he had missed. "…Who vould tell you to be ozher?"

"…You tried." She stared ahead. "I don't think you're a woman. I'm very aware that you're not a child. But when you accused me of making you one…" She trailed off, one hand coming up to her utilitarian braid and playing idly with it. "I don't believe God makes mistakes."

Ludwig decided to remain silent and let her order her thoughts.

"But he does make it hard sometimes… for people to fit in." She traced a finger through the water, interrupting the gentle pattern of the waves. "Some people are different. And that's not a bad thing. But there's a stigma associated with being different. It's the price you pay." She looked miserably down at her reflection. "…Why can't people accept that sometimes… Sometimes, people are going to fall outside the norm?" She looked down at him. "All women want to protect, care for, and save the ones they love. Especially the ones they see as being strong or fearless. We want to be needed. That's why there are so many crummy romance novels about a good woman reforming a criminal or saving a scoundrel. They seem so strong on the surface, but we've convinced ourselves that they have to be broken deep inside." A blink of sad, strong, soft eyes and she was looking up again. "In the end, we all want to be someone's Guardian Angel. I'm just more forthright about that than others. I'm honest about what I want. Is that so bad? Does that make me a man?"

"...Nein, it does not." Ludwig looked up into the stars as well, seeking answers there. "...Do you zhink...? Do you zhink you should hafe been a man?"

"No." Mara's answer was simple. "God doesn't make mistakes. I am what I am. But... it would be easier, I think, if I was."

"...I can see you in armor." Ludwig gently plucked at the red sleeve of the now-soaked shirt he was wearing. "You hafe such a strong mind. I take it... zhis isn't vhat you look like in real life?"

"No. It might be simpler if it was. This is a shell. A shell for someone who can't seem to relate to the world, or to fit in." And she was moving, walking slowly forwards, towards the reef. "I didn't mean to threaten your masculinity. I thought... I always think... that I might find someone who would understand."

Ludwig pressed after her, past the point where his feet could touch. "Let me try." He got his fingers around her elbow. "You're right: I vas threatened by your size and the vay you acted. I didn't try to understand vhat you were doing: I zhought you vere molly-coddling me because you zhought I vas veak."

"Well, it's not like you can go head-to-head with Lucy." Mara let him hang on with one hand as she moved forwards. "But I've seen other men and women try the same, and fail. I don't think you're weak. I think you need protecting. But that's not... that doesn't make you weak. Everyone needs someone to lean on."

They reached an exposed section of the reef and Mara lifted him up over the corals before heaving herself up onto the small strip of dry land. "You're more... upfront, about who you are, than anyone I ever met before." She admitted to the man sitting beside her large form, slowly bleeding water down into the white sand. "I thought – when you were comfortable with me – that I had found someone who was like me. Maybe I pushed too hard. I do that a lot. The point is... I thought you liked it. Being taken care of. Being carried and protected. You seem... tired. I just wanted you to be able to rest. I just wanted to keep you safe and well cared-for."

"...I do like zhat." Ludwig quietly replied. "I did like it vhen you carried me around. And zhe flight... zhat vas amazing. But vhen you called me 'princess...' I guess I read too deeply into it. I don't like nicknames. Zhey're almost nefer meant kindly."

"...I call everything I love 'princess.'" Mara admitted suddenly, then blushed so deeply he could see it in the moonlight. But she didn't take back the words or try to cover them up. She stood by them.

"…Me?" Ludwig pointed at himself. "A broken down old brain surgeon? Me, of all people?"

"Don't talk about yourself like that." Mara grumbled. "You're a beautiful, analytical mind, trapped in a body that will age, die, and fall apart before your eyes." That was a bit unnecessarily graphic.

"…How romantically morbid."

"Oh, shush." Mara stood up and prepared to dive back into the lagoon.

"…Calypso." Ludwig looked up at her, still sitting. "You should hafe called yourself Calypso."

"And why would I call myself after a titan trapped on an island by the angry gods?"

"Living alone. Doomed to fall in love vizh zhe stranded travelers to come to your island. Knowing zhey can nefer stay."

"…Titans are monsters. The children of the most primeval of the gods." She raised her arms and made her hands into claws. "Wouldn't you be sensible enough to be afraid of such a person?"

"Nein. Apparently, I am not." Ludwig smiled softly up at her. "After all, you followed me into Hell, und wrested me back from zhe defil."

"Lucy's idea of Hell is a cheap horror attraction." Mara muttered and jumped into the water. "And he's no devil."

"It doesn't matter. If you hadn't come, I vould be dead." Ludwig held out his arms and Mara helped him back over the spiky coral.

"…Yeah. I guess I got tired of seeing everyone who left dying."

"You didn't tell me you vatched zhe ozhers. Or listened, vhatever."

"It didn't matter." The tide was coming in. The water was reaching far up the beach by the time they stepped out onto the sand. "What does it change? I listened as they screamed and cried and pleaded. They had left me. They didn't want my help when it was offered, even after all my warnings. I couldn't reach them. Perhaps I didn't want to reach them. I can be a very cruel person. But I was always there, at the end." She heaved in a deep, shuddering breath. "And let me tell you… you idiot!" She turned and shook him by the shoulders. "No one ever pulled a stunt like you tried to."

"Vhat did I do?" Ludwig let himself shake and be embraced like something precious directly afterwards.

"You asked me to leave you. So I wouldn't hurt. So Lucy couldn't hurt me. You moron, how could I leave you after that? I had to risk getting into his head… if only to get you back safe and never see you again. Criminy… I almost died pulling that stunt. I could feel him trying to push me back."

"But you weren't in real danger were you?" Ludwig looked worried. "If you don't believe it's real, he can't hurt you here... that's what you said."

"Yes. But it still felt... He has a very strong will. When he tries to force his vision of reality on me, it's hard to repel. Especially in his realm. Harder than anything else I've ever had to do." She shuddered and shrugged. "But it's not impossible."

"I don't understand entirely how the realms work." Ludwig pressed a hand to his chin, thinking. "They seem simultaneously to be physical locations and subconscious visions."

"It's confusing. I doubt anyone in here understands fully." Mara lifted him up when they reached the sand and carried him up to the scrupulously clean porch. "You're soaked to the skin."

Ludwig looked down and nodded. The silk undershirt was clinging to his thin form. "So are you."

"Yes, but I'm wearing a wet suit." Mara smirked back at him. "Go on inside and get dried off. You can't catch cold here, but it can't be comfortable to walk around soaked either."

"Aren't you coming vith me?"

"...No. But I'll be back in the morning. I promise. I just have to make some changes to the world." Mara assured him. "I'm a dragon, so I can go wherever I want, but you need to be able to get around too."

"You could alvays fly me."

"I could." She smiled. "But I want you to be free too. You're a guest, and a… a friend. Not a prisoner."

"…Dankeschon, Mein Liebling." Ludwig quietly told her and turned to go inside.

"…You don't mind then?" She questioned suddenly from behind him. "…That I… That I love you?"

"…I zhink, in a vay, I alvays knew. Ve vill hafe to talk. Zhere are complications – practicalities. But no, I do not mind. In fact, I'm fery flattered." He adjusted his salt-spotted glasses. "I had zhought I vas too old to be zhought of like zhat, und my profession is a lonely one."

"…Well. I don't care about that. I love people who listen. Always have. Good night, Ludwig."

"Guten nacht, Mara."

Chapter Eight

Ludwig woke to the smell of tea. His face was pressed into someone's side and he was pleasantly warm. There was a hand tangled up in his hair. He almost didn't want to move. But, of course, he had to eventually.

"I brewed tea." Mara told him and that was the final nail in the coffin. Ludwig sat up with a slight grunt and stretched from his head to his toes.

"A late night swim is supposed to leafe you calm and refreshed." He told Mara as he pulled off his mask. "All I feel is sore."

"That's probably because you were using my shoulder as a pillow for most of the night." Mara pointed out, her large hands coming up in front of his blurred eyes and setting his glasses on his face. "You remember what happened, right? It wasn't a dream."

"Ja, I remember. Ve still need to talk. I vant to be clear about my boundaries. To prefent future misunderstandings."

"I can talk for hours, love." Mara sighed and slid her legs out of bed, standing up. She was already dressed in casual, linen slacks and a long-sleeved beaching shirt, buttoned all the way up.

"I've never seen you in short sleefes or shorts." Ludwig observed. "Hiding somezhing?"

"Nothing you need to worry about." Mara blushed. "Just a tattoo."

"Zhat must be a substantial tattoo."

"Well, it changes. It is a very large tattoo in general, but when I'm shorter than my "full height" it only shows up in pieces. How much is showing depends on my height, what day it is, and how I feel." Mara shrugged. "I can get the whole thing on me if I stand at twelve feet."

"Someday, perhaps you could show me?"

"…I'll think about it. It's a personal thing, you know." Mara reached up and ran her hand along the ribbons of shells hanging from the ceiling. "Come on. Let me show you what I've made for you." She held out a hand and pulled Ludwig out of the bedroom.

"I'm not dressed yet!" Ludwig protested.

"Hurry then!" With a sigh, she let go of his hand and did a backflip, seemingly letting off a great deal of nervous energy.

"I vill do my best." Ludwig did try to hurry through his routine, but Mara was still anxiously tapping her foot by the time he came out. "Now vhat is zhis you hafe to show me?"

"I built you a land bridge." Mara took his hand again and pulled him outside. The island had become the tip of a peninsula, covered in the same, tropical fruits and flowers. "Basically, what I did was fill in the blanks between my domains." She gestured out towards the north, where the mountains rose into snowy peaks. "There won't really be seasons. I can conjure storms, though, if you like, and I can raise or lower the temperature, if you need it."

Ludwig looked up at the thin layer of clouds, filtering the light and making it soft and dim. The clouds spread across the whole of the sky. He couldn't even see the blue of clear sky in the far distance. "Vhy are zhere alvays clouds?"

"I hate the sun." Mara replied, looking up. "My eyes are sensitive and my skin burns easily. Sun isn't my friend." They were walking along the vague line between the shaded forest land and the sand, up the beach and towards the mainland. There was a black line in the distance with a shining speck sitting right at the end of it.

"So, in your perfect world, the veather is always cloudy und shields you from zhe vorst of zhe sun's light." A mischievous idea struck and Ludwig looked up and held out one hand. "It does look like rain, zhough. Perhaps ve should hafe brought an umbrella."

As the first drops touched his palm, a yellow silk dome with a red Zia sun painted onto it went up over his head and the rain began tumbling down. Mara stepped close to him. "You spoke of the devil?"

"Und here it is." Ludwig smiled, watching the rain hitting the sand all around them. The shining fleck and the black ribbon were growing larger: A road and a car. "Mara… Is it possible to make a city? People?"

"It's possible, but I'm not particularly good at it. Sometimes I do, but I never really interact with any of my facsimiles except to purchase a sweet or a cup of coffee. I've never been social." She was walking him out to a car. He could see it in the distance. It seemed such a commonplace object in her usually fantastic world that he was briefly surprised. Then, he noticed that it was a champagne rose painted Stingray and the world made sense again.

"Vhere are ve going?" Ludwig questioned.

"I'm taking you out to the aquarium and lunch." Mara replied. "I thought we could talk somewhere nicer than the beach house or the lodge. I have a more urban mansion that we could retire to as well."

"A mansion sounds too large for my taste." Ludwig replied. "But I vouldn't mind going back to zhe lodge... For zhat sled ride ve never took... I'm sorry. I lost your sled."

"I got it back. Don't worry." Mara walked him around to the passenger side of the car. It was raining lightly, like kisses, but the drops were big and soaked through clothing as they fell. "...Here. I made you a hat." She pulled a light brown Gatsby hat out of the glove box and set it on his head. "You're cute in hats."

"Danke." Ludwig closed the door and waited for her to come around to the other side and join him inside. The Gatsby was light and unobtrusive. It wouldn't do much in the way of protecting him from the rain, but that was what the bright, yellow umbrella was for, after all.

"I don't drive stick." Mara commented as she settled into the driver's seat and turned the key. Her keychain had a brass abacus attached to it and several different keys that didn't seem to be related to any of her houses. Ludwig hadn't seen a lock on any doors in the lodge or the beach house. Being in a world of solitude made such things unnecessary. "Never have."

"I hafe nefer eizher." Ludwig admitted as Mara threw the modified transmission into drive. "Do not go too fast, for mein Herz's sake."

"No promises." Mara's eyes flashed mischievously and she slammed a foot down on the gas pedal. The resulting squeal of tires and skidding forwards of the whole car tossed Ludwig back against the seat, none too gently.

"Mara!" Ludwig cried out, grabbing onto the armrests as she slowed them to a more reasonable acceleration.

"Sorry." The woman was laughing, tears in her eyes. "I couldn't resist. You're okay, right?"

Ludwig fixed his Gatsby and glared at her. "I'm fine. Do not do zhat again."

"Sorry, sorry…" Mara slowed down dramatically and looked out the windshield. "We should be in pseudo-Atlanta soon. The rain should clear up by then."

"Pseudo-Atlanta?" Ludwig questioned, looking over at her in confusion. "Vhy not just call it Atlanta?"

"Because I only went to Atlanta once." Mara explained, turning into a graceful curve. "So I only remember vaguely what it looked like. The city I built here is little more than a dim imitation and combination. It's false: Pseudo. Therefore, Pseudo-Atlanta."

"You like vord games?"

"Of course. For a while, they were my only way to pass time. Here, try this one on: If the square root of all evil is money, and money equals time, then time must equal the square root of all evil. Therefore, you have just mathematically proven that idle hands are the devil's playground."

Ludwig put a hand over his mouth in thought. "Vait... So, money being zhe root of all evil –"

"The square root." Mara corrected. "There's a difference."

Ludwig shot her a look of annoyance. "Yes, danke, I'm avare. Money is zhe root of all evil. Und time is money. Zherefore time is zhe root of all evil. Vhich implies zhat idle hands are zhe devil's playground. Ah. I see now."

"Good one, wasn't that?" Mara shot him a cocky smile.

"Yes, yes, it vas quite good." Ludwig tipped his cap back. "Vord games aren't my strong suit. I prefer solitaire und riddles."

"Riddles?" Mara's eyebrow quirked and she recited. "Thirty white horses on a red hill. First they champ, then they stamp, then they stand still."

"Child's play." Ludwig scoffed, folding his arms and recalling long nights reading fantasy novels to pass the time. "Teeth. I feel, but do not zhink. I beat, but do not hafe fists. I am zhe strongest of your parts, but you vill nefer see me. Vhat am I?"

"Your heart." The woman took a moment to think. "Rushing into various egresses – Rainstorm."

"…Is zhat efen a riddle?" Ludwig was confounded.

"It is. But not in the way you're thinking. It's all about the words themselves. The letters they make. I suppose it's more of word play than actual riddling, but you can figure it out if you think about the words and not the meaning."

"…Rushing into farious egresses – Rainstorm… Zhat's not fair, Mara, a riddle is supposed to hafe clues in it zhat point to zhe meaning."

"The words I chose do have clues in them, but the answer is plain as the nose on your face. It's River."

"River? Zhat doesn't make sense at all. Is Rainstorm supposed to point to vater?"

"R-I-V-E-R. Rushing into various egresses – Rainstorm."

Ludwig's eyes widened behind his glasses. "It vas an acronym!"

"Exactly." Mara chuckled. "I like writing down puzzles and riddles, so they end up having more to do with reading than reciting."

"Zhat isn't fair." Ludwig crossed his arms over his chest again. "Pick a different riddle."

"I devour everything. Mountains, trees, horses, men... I will not wait for you. What am I?"

Ludwig twisted his lips into a grimace as he thought. "...Time? You're time. Time vaits for no man."

"Go on. What's your next, fair and proper, riddle? And don't pull out the Riddle of the Sphinx. Everyone knows the answer to that."

"...Zhe man who builds me doesn't vant me. Zhe man who buys me doesn't need me. Zhe one who needs me doesn't know it."

This one bought him several minutes of silence as he took in the beautiful, piney countryside. Mara hadn't built interstates. Instead, she had chosen to create long, looping country roads and – as he was only now noticing – go at a truly alarming pace.

"We're not going to crash." Mara told him when he turned to look at her, his mouth opening to ask. "I'm far too careful for that. Further, it's my world, my rules, and I choose which laws of physics we actually obey."

"...Of course. How could I forget?" Ludwig looked up at her face. "Vell?"

"Shush. Don't rush me. I'm thinking." Mara took another turn and a city suddenly opened up before them.

Ludwig had never seen Atlanta, but he had seen Houston and Dallas many times. The arrangement of the skyline, of the buildings that soared up to meet the sky, triggered his old memories of driving up to visit more city-minded cousins. "Hafe you spent much time in Texas, Mara?"

"I have an Aunt in Dallas and a divorced grandfather in Houston."

"Ah." Ludwig looked up at the top of one of the buildings nearby and noticed the slowly rotating, disk-shaped restaurant on top of it. "Zhat explains a lot."

"Yeah. I suspected my mind was filling in the gaps with familiar skylines." Mara pulled into a parking garage and drove them up to the highest level to sit there. The aquarium was right beside them and the garage overlooked a tiered park filled with azaleas and magnolia trees. It was so beautiful, so peaceful. Johann found himself slipping his hand into Mara's as they both stepped out of the car. "Do you want to tool around the garden first and then go in?"

"...Zhat depends. Vill ve talk in zhe garden?" Ludwig gave her a sharp look. He strongly suspected that she was stalling.

"...I suppose it can't hurt to see the garden later, when it isn't so hot." Mara ran a finger beneath her collar. "Come on then. Straight to the main attraction." They headed out into the staircase.

"Excellent." There was a strange pulling sensation in his arm and hand and Ludwig looked up at Mara. She was growing taller. "Mara, are you nerfous?"

"…Yes. Is it obvious?"

Ludwig hand to raise his arm above his head to reach her hand at this point. "You are growing razher tall." Actually, he noticed, the world around Mara wasn't changing in proportion to the giantess. It wasn't her growing – he was shrinking.

Mara jumped. "Whoops! Sorry, Ludwig." The doctor shot back up to his normal place just below her shoulder. "I- I must have been thinking too hard. I'm sorry."

"No harm, no foul." Ludwig dismissed it. "But if you do it again, I vill insist on you carrying me. I do not vant to hafe to run along beside you."

"…You're still going to let me carry you?" Mara's eyes widened.

"As long as ve are clear zhat I can valk on mein own, und I am not a voman." Ludwig elbowed her gently.

"You're not weak, you know. You just need to get used to this place." Mara skipped down four steps faster than Ludwig and used the height difference to grab him around the knees and lift him up. "And until you do, you can lean on me. I won't think less of you for needing a leg up."

"Yes, but do you hafe to take such joy in it?" Ludwig didn't need to hold onto her as she set him up on her shoulder, but he did anyway.

"Why wouldn't I? I love this. I love being large and strong enough to carry the people I love." Mara gave a fierce smile. "I've never –" She broke off and her expression changed, becoming dimmer. "Come on. I need to be sitting down for this."

There was a bustle of background people in Mara's Pseudo-Atlanta. They were little more than dim shadows. Whenever Ludwig tried to look at one properly, they would fade away until there was nothing. It was enough to distract him from further questioning – and from the way that doorways seemed to stretch high enough to easily allow them to pass under – until he found himself being set down on a soft couch, sitting in the middle of a large, open observation room. And in front of him was one of the largest viewing windows into an aquarium that he had ever seen. Passing in front of it was a massive, spotted fish with a mouth wide enough to swallow him whole and a lazy, smooth swimming pattern: A whale shark.

"…Woah…" Ludwig quietly exclaimed. "Is this…"

"Real? Yeah. I have a bad memory. Details all run together. But some things are crystal clear. This window is one of them. I remember all of the fish, the wobbegongs, the manta rays… Especially the whale sharks." Mara reached out as if she was going to touch the glass. "…But we didn't come here to talk about the aquarium."

"No, ve didn't." Ludwig sighed, watching as a Manta Ray waltzed by, its fins flapping in gentle motions. "…We're moving razher fast, aren't ve? How long hafe ve known each ozher?"

Mara hummed. "…We've been connected on a mental level. Assuming that we're right, and we are here in this machine – connected somehow – then there are wires and computer chips, circuits… Either that or all of our minds have been linked more directly. Constant communication, familiarity… That's a great environment for relationships – and for us, all we've had is each other. Besides Lucy."

"Lucy vould not be a relationship candidate." Ludwig shuddered.

"I never said he was." Mara ribbed him gently. "But that leaves us two alone – some sort of messed up Adam and Eve. Maybe that's all this is. Maybe we're just lonely. But that's all human relationship drive is, right? People being lonely and reaching out."

"Mmm… From a fery basic point of fiew, perhaps. But it is more complex zhan zhat. Humans seek different kinds of relationships. Ours began as nurturing und has been evolving into somezhing stronger. If ve vere simply lonely, I do not zhink ve vould valk zhis pazh."

"Maybe we've both been unlucky in love and we found someone who could understand that." Mara shrugged. "It doesn't matter. You're here and I'm here and we're together. That's all that matters."

"Vell, it is not all zhat matters. How long hafe you been in here, Mara?"

"…Total? I don't know. Years. At least five. It's not easy to keep track of time here. I think 'days' are about the same, but I can't be certain." Mara cut her eyes to him. "What you're really getting at is 'am I legal?' Am I right?"

"Ja, zhat is part of it." Ludwig steadily met her gaze. "Zhe ozher part is, how can I be certain zhat you vill be stable und not change your mind? Adolescence is a trying time for bozh males und females."

"You can be certain because I went through puberty early and because I've always been stable. At least, stable enough that people often think I'm older than I am. That's not bragging: Simple facts. I have a wild imagination, but I'm not a child. Not anymore."

The strangest part of this situation was that Ludwig believed her. Here, in this mindscape, even if she had come in as a budding adolescent teenager, she had grown out into a woman and made her peace with herself and her desires. Some adults didn't manage to do that until well into their thirties. "…I believe you. But that doesn't answer the first question."

"…I'm legal. Even if I've only been in here for two years, I'm legal." She shrugged, looking up at the light filtering through the water. "I fell off that lifeguard stand on December fifth. I was sixteen and a half when I fell. I've been here ever since."

"…What happened?"

Mara's eyes darkened and she stared blankly at the glass of the aquarium's tank. "I had been up late studying for an exam. The pool was quiet and peaceful, warm. I couldn't keep my eyes open. Then, I must have slipped out of the seat and tumbled down to the ground. I remember fumbling, trying to save myself by hooking an ankle around the steps leading up to the seat itself. All that did was flip me upside down so that I hit head-first instead of feet-first. When I woke up again, I was here. I don't know why I was put in here, but I can't figure out a way to get out."

"...Zhe damage must hafe been substantial." Ludwig mused, thinking. "Doctor Berwick designed zhis machine to contact zhe minds of zhose in comatose and fegetative states. It's supposed to help zhem find a vay to vake you up, but somezhing must not be vorking." He looked up at Mara. "Maybe, if ve try, ve can find a vay to vake up and rejoin the vorld of the lifing."

"Maybe." Mara neutrally replied. "I've made peace with never waking up. It's not so bad here. I never get bored: That's certain. And there are other benefits." She shrugged her broad shoulders. "I was weak, sick, and afraid out there. In here, I'm different and I can be different. I like that. I like myself better here."

"But it is not real." Ludwig looked up at the aquarium. "Zhe vorld is a faried und interesting place. Vouldn't you like to see more of it zhan you hafe already? It vould make for efen more interesting imaginations, vouldn't it?"

"I have seen many places already. I've been to Florida and California and Texas… And, of course, I've lived here in Albuquerque for all of my life. It's enough. Maybe it's not perfect." Standing, she gestured down at herself. "Besides, there's no tolerance for someone like me out there."

"Does vhat ozhers zhink of you matter so much? Vhat about vhat I zhink?" Ludwig questioned, not getting up. It seemed like the light was being sucked out of the room, the only source centering in the aquarium's tank, throwing Mara into a sharp contrast. "I zhink you are beautiful. Und I hafe seen you here, vhere you truly are. Zhere is nozhing wrong vith you, und if ozhers cannot see zhat, zhey are zhe ones who are blind."

"You say that now, here, in the privacy of our minds, Ludwig. But what would happen out there? Where the others can cast an eye over us and wonder why you married a woman who never wears a skirt. I would be an embarrassment to you among the other surgeons and their trophy wives."

"Zhose empty-headed bimbos can paint zheir lips und eyes all zhey vant. Zhey know nozhing of beauty." Ludwig stood up and stepped up beside her. "Und who is to say vhat I vould be embarrassed by?"

"Ludwig… I don't want to talk about this." Mara reached out and pressed a hand to the glass. "It's impossible anyway. I've been here for years and I've never even felt like I'm close to waking up. Nothing can change that. Put it out of your mind." And, with a press, she bent the glass of the tank inward like a bubble. "Care to walk with me?"

"On a fantastical journey zhat vould not be possible anyvhere else? Alvays." Ludwig took her hand, though his mind was still whirling. He wanted to convince Mara that life outside of CORD could be as good as it was inside, but she clearly had experiences that had convinced her otherwise and her mind couldn't be budged. Still, this subject was – by no means – closed, and he would try again later.

Ludwig was not surprised when the glass bubbled and bent around them. Mara pushed a bubble of the glass out from the tank and they stepped directly into the water. "Have you ever wished you could do this?" Mara grinned over her shoulder at him as she continued to push the bubble out into the middle of the tank.

"Nein, not really. But now zhat ve are doing it, I vonder vhy I nefer did." A curious pufferfish flirted around their bubble and Ludwig pressed his hand to the glass. "Has zhis been a fantasy of-?" He turned and found himself alone in the glass bubble. "Hallo? Mara? Vhere did you go?"

A dark shadow passed over the sand beneath him and he whirled to look up. There was a squeak of something scraping over the glass. There were several long moments where he was unsure what was going on. Then, a musically soft laugh rang through the glass and Ludwig whirled about to see the third impossible thing that had happened to him that morning. There was a mermaid outside of the glass bubble.

It was not a mermaid in the sense that Ariel was a mermaid. There was no definite divide between fish and human. As Ludwig studied Mara – who else could it be? – he found that he could trace out webbed arms from her scaled torso. There were gill slits on the front of her ribcage, similar to a stingray's. The only really human thing about her was her face. Golden spines, laid neatly against her neck and skull, simulated her hair. Her ears were replaced with fan-like fins.

The tail that extended down from the sloping curve of her waist was long and serpentine, like a sea crate's, with fins that fluttered slightly as she moved, curling her tail around and over the bubble. Frankly, it was incredible. "Come out and join me. You can do it. Just push out of the bubble and believe you can breathe and you'll be able to. Don't let a doubt enter your mind."

Ludwig put a hand on the glass and found it solid and cool beneath his palm. "I don't know –"

"Come on. You saw me do it. You can do it." Mara pressed one of her webbed palms to the outside of the bubble. "Grab my hand."

"There's at least eighteen inches of glass between us. I'm not ready for this." Ludwig shook his head. "Eighteen inches of glass… I would have to melt my way through. My hands would burn. I would die. I can't do the impossible, Mara. I can't bend the world."

"…It's not impossible. You've seen me do it. You can do this." Mara encouraged, circling the bubble. "Just reach out. Just believe. It's not a cage unless you think it is."

"It's not that easy. It's impossible for it to be that easy." Ludwig quietly replied.

"It's possible. It's realistic. You can do it." Mara's whispers reached him. "Think about it. This is already an impossible situation, but it's happening. All around you, millions of gallons of water are pressing down on this bubble of glass. The glass itself is resting on a sand and gravel bed."

Suddenly, Ludwig's mind kicked into over-drive. Yes, this was impossible. Mara had pressed outwards from the glass of the tank to make this bubble. That implied that either the viewing window was compromised or that the bubble itself was too thin to adequately repel that much water from this isolated pocket of air.

"…Oh, don't do that." Mara breathed and lunged forwards as cracks laced the bubble. "No, stop! Ludwig!"

The force of sixty feet of water rushing down onto Ludwig all at once was crushing. He pulled in a desperate gasp of air before the bubble failed entirely and glass and water rained down on him. He was nearly skewered by a shard of glass as long as his arm and was only saved by the scaled, slick shield that forced itself between Ludwig and the encroaching water and glass. There was a strangely pitched and modulated scream as the combined pressure of three atmospheres crashed down on Ludwig. His head blazed in pain as water rushed into his ears and up his nose.

The doctor scrabbled and scrambled as sea-slick arms gripped him and began towing him upwards. A webbed fist came out of nowhere and punched him in the abdomen, forcing him to exhale – hard. When his mouth opened in a plea for breath, salt water rushed in instead. He choked, thought he would drown, and there was a moment of pure terror as he couldn't see anything but white lights. Then, he was lying on a surprisingly dry, hard and solid, deck, and air rushed into his lungs as his headache receded.

Mara threw herself up onto the deck next to him.

"Was zum Teufel?!" Ludwig screamed at her. "You hit me!"

"Think!" Mara demanded at once as she caught her breath. "I hit you because if you hadn't exhaled, then your lungs would have popped as we ascended!"

"I vouldn't hafe needed to ascend so rapidly if you hadn't been so careless!" Ludwig was scraped and scratched from the shards of glass that had rushed down around him. His clothes were shredded, but he had been protected from the worst of it. "Vhere are mein glasses?"

"I wasn't the one who decided to think about exactly how impossible the situation was! I didn't say to make that the reality!" Mara bounded to her feet, recovered and whole. "And your glasses are probably on the bottom of the tank, where they fell."

"I need mein glasses!" Ludwig demanded, angry and frightened. "I almost drowned und I need mein glasses!"

Mara gestured at the tank behind her and called the glasses up from the bottom. They were intact, miraculously, and she fiddled with them as she thought for a long moment. "I know you're scared." She finally stated. "I would be too. But I was there. And I saved you. Next time… Next time, I'll make sure you're all right. I'll make sure you're ready." She placed the glasses on his face and the world cleared. "…On the other hand, I have a theory for how you can control the world. But it's a very, very bad idea."

Ludwig was slowly calming down. "Tell me your bad idea."

"This is only for the direst situations." Mara explained to him. "So, when you have Lucy bearing down on you in his Lord of Hell garb, what would you do?"

"I would probably run away, fast." Ludwig replied, giving her a look. "Can this conversation wait until I have dry clothes on?"

"…Sure. Lucy's not here and there's nothing else that can really hurt you here anyway." Mara stood up and offered a hand. "Let's get to the showers and the washing machines."

Chapter Nine

"Vhy does zhe aquarium in Pseudo-Atlanta hafe a shower room und vashing machines?" Ludwig questioned as Mara loaded their clothes into one.

"Well, first off, the real Georgia Aquarium has a diving program that allows patrons to Scuba with whales. So, I assume they have to have some kind of shower. You can't just dive into one of the most expensive aquariums in the world with the risk of having bacteria on your body. Marine tanks are delicate places." Mara explained. "The washing machines are my addition, as is the restaurant that I replaced the gift shop with."

"Good replacement." Ludwig stepped into the shower stall and turned on the water. "Vhat kind of restaurant?"

"Churrascaria and Sushi. I know, I know… Odd combination. But they were my two favorite types of restaurant and I can do what I want, so, bleh." Mara pulled a face at Ludwig's back as she stepped into the shower stall next to his. Ludwig couldn't help but glance down at her feet. They were bare as usual, but the height of the stall also allowed him to see the space above her feet – her ankles. There was black ink on them, lines and lines of miniscule words. And, right above the joint, the stem of something that extended up from the ankle. The words seemed to twine around it and it was almost like the rose was part of the text.

"...Vhat is your tattoo?" Ludwig questioned. "It looks like... vords."

"Peeking? Naughty." Mara playfully stepped to the side so he couldn't see more than her feet anymore. "Do I need to bring out the riding crop?"

"No, Danke, not now." Ludwig blushed, turning up the water slightly.

"Good, because I do not see you that way right now." Mara's feet turned. "Hey, heads up." A bottle of shampoo and one of conditioner flew up over the stall's wall. He barely caught both of them. "Those are great. My favorites."

"...Rose oil?" Ludwig read the label.

"Yes, you will smell like a rose for a while, but don't worry. It fades after awhile." Mara explained. She stepped out of her stall. "I'm going to get us some clothes and make sure the restaurant is ready. Come on down when you're done."

"You're just leaving me alone? Just like zhat?" Ludwig questioned, rubbing heavily scented shampoo into his hair. "I did not expect zhat."

"Yeah, well, someone informed me that you are a strong, independent man with a mind of his own and sometimes I need to back up and give you space." Mara's steps walked out towards the door. "Don't worry: I'll have an eye on you."

"By zhe vay, zhe whole "all-knowing" zhing? It's more creepy zhan reassuring." Ludwig called after her. "Und ve still need to talk!"

Mara sighed heavily on her way out.

Ludwig finished his shower and stood under the warm stream, just enjoying the feeling of the water on his skin. The minor scrapes he had collected were faded and healed. Mara and her pastes again. The towels were pleasant and fluffed as he wrapped up in one and mused gently. After the fright of the bubble, he had never thought he would be calm again. It seemed a warm shower did work wonders. Either that, or perhaps... If Doctor Berwick had seen a change in his vitals that correlated to panic, he might have added a calming drug to Ludwig's system. It all depended on how much Doctor Berwick had achieved with CORD.

Ludwig thought back to what Doctor Berwick had told him about the CORD system. According to Doctor Berwick, it was still in a highly experimental phase and the system itself was not entirely stable. Apparently, there had been deaths, but that was expected with the technology he was working with. It couldn't be helped. There would always be a few problems. That was the nature of experimentation. The fact that he was here and alive seemed to suggest that Doctor Berwick had finally stabilized the interface.

Doctor Berwick was one of the top neurosurgeons in the world, but he dedicated his life to research. His journals and experimentation with the nervous system and computers made him famous. Of course, that kind of fame could only go so far. People were not lining up to be put in CORD and the inherent risk of an experimental kind of treatment frightened families for whom the reality of a permanent comatose or vegetative state had not settled in yet.

In their communications, Doctor Berwick had mentioned that he had five surviving patients connected to the CORD machine. But he had been unwilling to share just how much he had accomplished with them yet. He hadn't mentioned if he could see into their minds yet. There certainly hadn't been a mention of any kind of interaction between the people inside of CORD. As far as Ludwig had been aware, the CORD system was the only interface to each individual.

Of course, this suggested that the CORD system had become, somehow, a communications link between those who had entered. Perhaps CORD acted like some kind of translator between the individuals – sending thoughts and feelings to the others. The denizens of CORD lived in some kind of lucid dream. Like any lucid dreamer, they could control their own world to an extent that was limited only by the imagination of the individual.

It seemed he had a very poor imagination. Either that or his sense of reality was too well grounded. Mara's ideas were insane and her control over her mindscape was absolute. Ludwig envied her. Not least of all because she was bullet proof here in her mind and he was weak. Lucy had already proved that he would make short work of him if ever Ludwig dared to go alone.

But Mara was also clearly depressed at the very least. Her nature appeared to be solitary and the lack of photographs of family or friends in her home seemed to support that idea, but even the most reclusive person requires a little human contact for the sake of mental stability. She stood alone, out of the apparent chaos that was the rest of CORD, but she had apparently spent a great deal of time collecting and protecting other men who had come into CORD, only to see them leave and be caught by Lucy.

And yet, she had decided to leave her armored home to save only one of them. Him. For no real reason except for a moment of pretended bravado and selflessness. Perhaps she had taken that as a sign that he really could love her, and it seemed… she had been right. Or at least, she had been right that there was some attraction, some affection. Whether it was love or loneliness, he couldn't say.

"You look a million miles away." Mara's voice interrupted him. She had changed into a pair of black jeans and a soft-looking turtleneck. There was a sleepy kind of affection in her face as she offered him a clean set of clothes. "I don't think you'll need your sweater here."

"In Atlanta Georgia? Probably not." Ludwig took the shirt from the top of the pile and began pulling his clothes on, buttoning up each button and tying the red tie around his neck. "Danke."

"You're welcome. Food's ready downstairs." Mara hovered, trying not to look at him as he put himself in order.

"Gut. I am starfing." Ludwig neatly knotted the red silk and smoothed himself down. "Lead zhe vay."

Mara offered an arm in escort and led him down a set of stairs to the main floor. True to her words, where a gift shop should have stood, there was an upscale restaurant with the distinct look of an imagined place. Nowhere on earth could there have been such crisp, white tablecloths with black napkins folded upon them. Neither had he ever seen a restaurant use antique, upholstered chairs with the deep, soft cushions he could see beneath each table. Nor would there have been such an attentively bland wait staff. At first glance, they were nothing more than the ghosts that teemed throughout the aquarium. However, unlike the ghosts, when the waitress at the greeting station saw them, she smiled broadly. "Welcome! Come in. Do we have a reservation?"

"The Marisol table. It should be reserved, as always." Mara replied easily as their server picked up two menus and led them off to a table surrounded on two sides by a display of Brazilian orchids and bromeliads.

"The wait staff seem much more real than everyone else." Ludwig pointed out, looking around at the other diners. Like the ghosts outside, they eventually vanished if he stared too long at them. "Is that on purpose?"

"Of course. I need the staff to be solid at the very least, or it quite ruins the illusion here." Mara sat down on one side of the table and Ludwig took the other. The scale of the restaurant seemed to be a carefully enforced "happy medium" where both of their needs were easily encompassed by the height of the chairs and the tables. Ludwig had to reach up slightly and Mara had to lean, but neither was particularly favored.

"How do you maintain them?" Ludwig questioned, looking around.

"Well, each person is slightly different, but if you look carefully, they're all practical copies of each other." Mara pointed out, gesturing across to a man carrying about a long skewer of curled sausages. "He, for example, has ebony skin and slicked back hair with brown eyes. But his nose, mouth, and forehead are all the same as his Caucasian Aryan compatriot over there. The same rule applies to that lovely young Korean lady mixing cocktails and the Irish red-head who just showed us to our table. Further, they're lacking in personality. All they really need is a smile and a few, carefully chosen phrases."

"Ah. So more like computers than actual people."

"Exactly." Mara opened her menu. "The Churrascaria is all-you-can-eat, of course, but I'm going to order a few Sashimi roses to go along with it. Is there anything you'd like?"

Blushing, Ludwig had to admit that he had little experience with Sushi except for the ubiquitous California Rolls.

"There's nothing wrong with that." Mara looked down at the menu. "If you like, we can start you off with something easy: Like the Philadelphia Rolls."

"Wat ist los?" Ludwig opened his own menu, which contained an assortment of different kinds of sushi and sashimi, with tempura mixed in.

"Philadelphia Rolls are the Japanese version of the Lox Nova. They contain salmon, cream cheese, and cucumbers all wrapped up in Nori and rice." Mara explained, pointing them out on the menu which – now that Ludwig was looking – lacked any mention of price or payment. Imaginary world, naturally.

"I suppose yes, ve can try zhat." Ludwig looked around. "I almost vish you hadn't made zhis a combination restaurant. I vant to try everyzhing."

"You can try everything. It's an imaginary world. You could gorge yourself for hours and never be over-full." Mara reminded him, tapping her plate and turning over a green and red tumbler to summon the Churrascaro. "For that matter, why not make a small alteration? I can't believe I hadn't thought of this before." Turning towards the salad bar in the middle of the restaurant, she waved a hand at it and the trays of salads and extras became a buffet of various kinds of sushi, laid out and elegantly arrayed with bowls of wasabi and pickled ginger.

"Now zhat looks very tempting." Ludwig stood up. "Vell, shall ve begin eating?"

"You go ahead. I'm going to pull some Churrascario first." Mara smiled at her paramour and

Ludwig went to the bar to fill his plate with little bits. When he came back, she was carving at a pair of lamb chops and looked up easily as he settled down across from her.

"…Have you been to many Brazillian restaurants?" Ludwig questioned her, probing.

"Only two, unfortunately. One of them was our favorite for special occasions."

"Our?"

"My brothers and I. Every time we went up to a Spelling Bee, we went to Tucanos afterwards. I got second place in my class twice in those times. I've always been clever with words. Never a champion, unfortunately, but always a competitor." Mara explained. "One year, they nailed me with the world 'Nuzzle.' I thought it was spelled N-U-Z-L-E. Of course, I was quite embarrassed. One of the rules of spelling had turned against me." She held her fork in her left hand and her knife in her right as she peeled the meat back from the t-shaped bone in the center of each chop.

"Ah, you expected two consonants before zhe e instead of zhree." Ludwig nodded. "On a basic anatomy test, I got zhe muscles around zhe eye mixed up and identified zhe muscle zhat closes zhe top eyelid as zhe one zhat closes zhe bottom eyelid and vice versa. I passed zhe test, but if I had just remembered zhat one little detail, I would hafe been top of zhat class." The doctor smiled slightly. "In zhe end, it doesn't matter. Zhe person who beat me dropped out – became a nurse instead. Pressure got to zhem."

"Medical school isn't easy. I was thinking of being a doctor or a lawyer before I fell off the lifeguard stand. Now… I don't know what I am."

"Did you efer decide? Doctor or lawyer?" Ludwig questioned out of pure curiosity.

"Neither. Engineering was going to be the life for me. Electrical Engineering, like my parents before me. I guess it was fate. My whole family is engineers."

"Do you have a large family?" Ludwig popped one of the Philadelphia Rolls into his mouth. It had a pleasant mouthfeel, the cucumbers crisp and the cream cheese rich.

"Only in the sense that anyone does. I have two brothers and my parents, grandparents, uncles. Five sets of grandparents. Cousins by the bushel… I would trade you a few relatives for some peace and quiet and the chance to skip out on family gatherings." A waiter appeared at their table and slid a piece of filet mignon wrapped in bacon off onto Mara's plate without being asked. "Would you like a piece of steak?"

"Ja, please. Rare." Ludwig held his plate carefully for the waiter and carved into the piece of meat as soon as he had a chance. It was perfect – red in the center and juicy. "Vould you und your family go to zhis Churrascaria togezher?"

"At first, yes. When I got a job, and a car, I went alone a couple times. It was a nice place. I wanted to go." She had a far-away look all of a sudden and her knife and fork paused. "They would have long skewers of chicken hearts… roasted over the fire. I never thought of chicken hearts as delicious before that restaurant. I never would have thought of them as food at all."

"Do you miss zhem? Your family, I mean."

"What kind of dumb question is that? Of course, I miss them. Everyday. They are my family."

"You don't keep any pictures." Ludwig took a sip from a glass of a dark, fruity red wine.

Mara looked up at him, suddenly probing. "Why are you asking?"

Ludwig shrugged, looking back down at his plate to pick apart a sashimi rose. "I vas zhinking, zhat's all. It's just a matter of curiosity."

"…I don't mind questions. I have curiosity in my list of character traits as well. But if there's a reason you want to know something, I'd like to know." Mara bit into another piece of steak.

Ludwig sighed and sipped at his glass of wine. "I spent time in psychology before I became a neurosurgeon. It vas a tipping point betveen zhe two disciplines. I've alvays vanted to help people vith mental illnesses. So, vhen I cannot fix somezhing by cutting someone up, I talk to zhem and try to find an answer vith zhem."

"And you think I need fixing?" Mara raised an eyebrow into an arch. "I don't think I like the insinuation."

"I do not zhink you are broken, Mara. I zhink you are a puzzle. A psychological puzzle. Und I cannot resist zhat." Ludwig chewed another bite of rare and tender meat. "So tell me: Vhy don't you keep any pictures of your family?"

"Because I never thought of this place as permanent. It's just a stop-gap for the real world. Except that that was ages ago and I've been here for longer than I care to think about. I don't remember my family's faces anymore except as blurred images. I would rather not fill in the blanks with other faces."

"…Ah." Ludwig sighed. "You hafe lost zhe dearest zhings to you. I am so sorry."

"Don't be." Mara waved a hand and pulled a photo from the air – a photo of a little girl with practically white blonde hair. "Everything here is based on memory and imagination. And memory gets faded and old." The photo began wearing away in her hands and becoming stained and dog eared. The details of the little girl became unrecognizable. "When it reaches a certain point, imagination steps in." The photo began to come back into full color, but the color was too sharp, too detailed, and as Ludwig studied the picture, he realized it was a different girl entirely. "And the memory changes."

"So, you did not put out pictures…"

"At first because I thought I would wake up any day. Then, later on, because I realized that any pictures I did make wouldn't be of my family. They would be of the people who I had imagined to replace my family. I couldn't do that. Not to them. So, I go without pictures on my walls, and if I'm here forever... So be it." With an air of finality, she ate the last of her filet.

"And by zhe time you do get out..." Ludwig whispered. "Your family vill hafe changed."

"My parents will be grey in the hair. My brothers will be in high school. I will never be the same. Nothing will be the same. Better to go in with a blind side and a clean slate. Leave my imagination out of it." Mara looked up as another server brought barbequed chicken thighs. "Yes, please." She addressed him for the first time since she had spoken to the waitress that seated them. It seemed the subject was now closed.

"I'll have one too." Ludwig told the waiter. It was the African-American waiter and, as Mara had pointed out, he had a generally pleasant and handsome face, but a generic outlook and the black and white uniform just added to that impression. The saucy piece of poultry was slid onto his plate with a vacant smile and the waiter stepped away. "...Zhey're creepy."

"I don't think anyone inside of CORD can make convincing facsimilies of people. Well... Except the Other One."

"Zhe Ozher One?"

"I don't know what to call it. There are five people in here. Old Lady, Engineer, Lucy, Me, and the Other One. The Other One – no one knows anything about them except that they create hundreds of different people and they look like real people. The only reason I know they can't be real is that there are too many of them. They wander everywhere. Lucy gets a lot of them. I think the Other One is fascinated by him."

"So, zhis Ozher One... Is zhe only one who can create realistic people?"

"I like to call them Facsimiles."

"A fitting term." Ludwig sighed. "Fakes."

"Yeah. Between them and the Shadows, sometimes I have no idea what's going on in here."

"You mentioned zhe Shadows once before. Zhey're people who hafe died in here. Or at least, zhe memories of zhem." Ludwig cut into the chicken thigh.

"Yes. I'm not entirely sure if it's our memory, though. I think this machine... You called it CORD, didn't you?" Mara looked to Ludwig for confirmation and as soon as she had a nod, she continued. "I think CORD has memories. Memories of the people who have been in here. They're less alive, but they're... fuller. Better than the waiters. You won't mistake them for anything else. I keep them out, but they tend to wander. The only good thing is that, unless they specifically died while Lucy was having his way with them, he can't touch them. I'm sure that would only add fuel to his fire if he could collect wandering souls."

"He is razher obsessed vizh souls. It vas zhe only zhing he talked about, besides showing off for you." Ludwig nodded to his table mate.

"He hates me so much." Mara smirked at her three chicken thighs and picked one up by the bones, eating away at it. "But souls, yes, I can believe that. He's such a freak. He's a sick freak."

"He said he vasn't going to touch mein eyes because he vanted to see my soul."

"That sounds a hell of a lot like him and a hell of a lot like horrifying." Mara reached across and took his hand, rubbing her fingers down his wrist and up to the knuckles. "And then he stabbed you in the throat to keep you from talking. That was… not one of his signature moves. Usually, if he wants to shut someone up, he gags them, but he tends not to want to shut them up. He likes hearing people scream and cry and plead."

"But he doesn't like it vhen zhey show some backbone."

"You know, the ultimate enemy of a bully is someone who shows no fear." Mara pointed out. "Someone who, no matter what you do to them, doesn't back down, but stands up on what they know is right. Lucy's the bully – and you stood up." She lifted her goblet for him and toasted. "And to that, I will drink happily."

Ludwig blushed and clinked his glass against hers.

Chapter Ten

"Vhy did you put zhe road so far from zhe house?" Ludwig picked his way back through the flotsam down the beach at Mara's side.

"I like the walk. It's pleasant and cool and the sand feels good between my toes. Plus, I don't usually bother with a car. I just teleport or fly."

"If you had offered, I vouldn't have said no to a flight."

"Well, after how my mermaid went earlier, I didn't think you'd want to do something supernatural so soon." Mara explained, lifting his hand to her lips and pressing a kiss to the back. "I'm still sorry for that, by the way."

"It vas mein own insecurities zhat ruined it." Ludwig pressed her hand to his own lips. "I just… I cannot seem to understand zhe zhing zhat makes it vork for you. I cannot let go of reality so easily."

"Do you think it was always easy for me? I could let go of reality because my mind was shattered. I was traumatized and my sense of reality was gone. When I realized that I could use that lack of reality to control my reality, I kept the talent and learned to harness it." Mara explained, helping him up and over a log.

"But zhen vhy did I not have zhe same ability? I vas in a car accident und my friend is dead, most likely."

Mara reflexively picked him up and pinned his arms and legs against her chest. "Are you all right? Still with me? Not having another flashback."

"I'm fine, Mara." Ludwig's eyes widened. "I'm fine!"

"Ha." Mara grinned. "I think my crazy ideas are coming true."

"Ah, ja, your crazy zheory. Mind telling me vhat zhat vas?"

Mara gently set him back on his feet. "I think that you're so grounded in reality that you can use it to affect the world the same way that I use my sense of unreality. Of course, given that it's not as predictable, I don't think you'll be able to use it as fluidly. But I think you can use your sense of reality to defend yourself against Lucy. When it comes down to it, he's a twerp, isn't he? Just a skinny little brat playing at being a demon. You can beat up someone like that, right?"

"Ja." Ludwig nodded. He wasn't a scrapper, but he was no weakling.

"Then when Lucy's bearing down on you in his Lord of Hell garb, think of exactly what he is: That little twerp in a costume. And you'll be able to beat him up." Mara grinned. "The same way you thought of the bubble of glass being impossible – physically – and made it shatter. It's funny how powerful you are. You managed – in my mind, on my turf, against my home-field advantage – to fight off my control of the world against all the force I could bring to bear – with a single, out of line thought. That's how powerful your sense of reality is."

Ludwig thought about it. "Zhat... Makes sense. Too much sense. It's so simple, could it be possible?"

"Of course it can, Mr. Genius Neurosurgeon. When it comes down to it, all of the fancy-dancy little solutions that people come up with have no chance against the simple, plain truth." Mara pushed open the door to the beach house.

"And zhe plain truzh in zhis is zhat I can affect zhis vorld by zhinking about how impossible it is." Ludwig stepped into the house behind her and they left their sandy shoes beside the front door. "I vill not be helpless vhen Lucy next shows up..." A grin cracked across his face, crooked and slightly off-kilter. "I cannot vait for round two."

"You want a crack at Lucy?" Mara returned the grin, six shades of crazy all rolled up into one. "I can let him in for a scrap, let you have your twelve rounds."

"...Please do." Ludwig smirked as he stepped back into the bedroom.

In the morning, Mara was out in the water, catching shrimps in her mermaid form. She raised her golden spines in greeting as Ludwig stepped out onto the beach and came down to the water. "Good morning, Ludwig. Do you feel like shrimp for breakfast?"

"Shrimp sounds wunderbar. I'll make some corn pancakes to go vith it. Or maybe ve could cook zhem in grits." Ludwig sat down on the beach in his light, linen pants.

"Polenta. Not grits." Mara pulled herself out and let her scales slowly retreat over his body, revealing a wetsuit. "We're not back woods hicks here."

"I can't beliefe you efer zhought I vould buy zhat you don't know anyzhing about Italian food." Ludwig looked over at her. "Polenta, Antipasti platters… Tiramisu. Are you sure you don't hafe relatifes in New York?"

"Shut up. You can enjoy Italian without a drop of Italian blood." Mara pushed him gently on the shoulder with still slightly webbed fingers. For once, she had shrunk down her size. She must have been feeling secure that morning.

"You're short." Ludwig smiled at her. "Six feet. Only as tall as I am."

"Is that a problem?" Mara questioned, looking over at him, at his clear, blue eyes. "I can always put the extra feet back on."

"Nein, it's not a problem." Ludwig's lips curled up as he took her in. "I feel like I am seeing you for zhe fery first time." She looked different this morning. There was a slight change about her mouth and eyes – like some tension had released. She looked so much better than normal.

"…Thank you. I think." Mara pulled up her net of shrimps. "I got two dozen good-sized ones. Let's go clean them."

"I'll put on zhe grits – Ach, I am sorry: Polenta."

"Oh, hush." Mara stood up, putting her feet on the ground. "Come on."

"So, vhen's zhe showdown with Lucy?" Ludwig questioned, stirring milk and cornmeal together.

"I don't have an assistant that manages appointments. This is going to be off the cuff. I've set some cracks up in my defenses. He'll be able to get in and once he's here, I'll know, but I have to wait for him."

"All right. So, ve just vait for him to abush us?"

"It's not a trap if you know it's coming." Mara pointed out, peeling out the shrimps and arranging them on a plate beside a skillet. "Butter? Garlic?"

"Parmesan as vell, if you hafe it." Ludwig pointed towards the fridge. "Or vhatever you do to magic it up."

"Oh, hush. Want some avocados?" Mara opened the fridge.

"Not to mix into mein polenta. But if you hafe zhem sliced into a flower on a plate, I von't say no to a few." Ludwig poured the shrimps into a skillet and began frying them in butter.

"Your wish is my command." Mara handed him a head of garlic and a box of shredded parmesan and sat down at her table. "Anyway, I think we can continue training today. Nothing dangerous, of course, but I still think you can try and change this world to fit your whims. Just a matter of learning how."

Ludwig took the pan he had been stirring the polenta into and added the shrimp and parmesan. "Mara, ve must hafe tried a million times."

"Then today we're going to try a million and one times. What else are we gonna do? Besides, I want to show you Atlantis and if we're gonna do that, we need to get you breathing underwater." Mara pointed out, laying out a set of silverware.

"Atlantis? Ach, nozhing should surprise me at zhis point, but... Atlantis?"

"Yep. And not the ancient Atlantis that's dead at the bottom of the sea in the shadow of a volcano, the kind of Atlantis that's filled with artwork that looks brand-new and soaring towers that look like they grew straight out of the seabed. You'll love it."

Ludwig scooped out two portions of polenta into shallow bowls and brought them to the table. "All right, all right. Ve try again."

"Don't think of it as a transformation. Try and think of the water as air. You're lying back on a soft pillow of water and breathing in and out slowly. Then, nothing changes." Mara had Ludwig lying against her shoulder, floating perfectly in the waves. She began slowly bending her legs, lowering him further into the water. "Stay perfectly still. Don't think of the water. It's just a thicker form of air."

Liquid touched Ludwig's nose and he sat up straight, coughing. Mara raised him back up at once. "Zhis is not vorking!"

"You can do this! You're just thinking too hard." Mara encouraged. "Look, let's try again. Lie back down."

"Nein!" Ludwig struggled free of her grip and treaded water. "I hafe had enough of zhe vater up mein nose!"

"Your accent gets thicker when you're upset." Mara sighed, paddling about beside him. "All right. We're done with this exercise and I'm sorry it's not working. I don't understand why we can't get this together. Maybe it's my fault..."

"Nein, if anyzhing, it is mein fault." Ludwig began swimming for the shore. "I vill not be able to do zhis. I am sorry."

"You don't have to be sorry. It's not a matter of can and can't. It's a matter of – it's a matter of finding the way to do it."

"Und you hafe anozher idea?" Ludwig asked wearily.

"Actually." Mara ducked under the water and came up with golden spines instead of hair. "I do have another idea."

"...Just one more try." The Doctor sighed. "After that: I'm tired."

"Come here. I'll hold you this time." Mara reached out for him.

"All right, all right, but no more vater in mein nose."

"No water in your nose." Mara promised, wrapping scaled arms around his bared chest and pressing him back against her gills. "Close your eyes, just listen. I'm gonna help you."

"All right… But I zhought ve vere doing zhis vizhout your suggestions."

"We are. But I think maybe you'll be able to do this again if you know how it feels." Mara explained. Her long, serpentine tail supported his legs. "All right… Can you feel my scales? They're all soft and slick, smooth. Imagine your own skin is covered with those scales. Breathe in, breathe out. Do you feel your scales slowly sliding up your arms and down your chest, covering your legs?"

Ludwig felt like a thousand tiny splinters were bursting out of his skin. "Mara? Mara, it hurts. I feel like my skin…" He opened his eyes and looked down and his entire body had been coated in a layer of translucent, light blue scales. The same color as his eyes. "Oh…"

"See? Scales. Now lay back, we're going to keep working on this." Mara pressed him back against her. "Come on. Now, the tail. Your legs are pressing together and your scales are merging. Your toes are pointing, flattening. Everything is merging and changing. You feel your skin moving, becoming fins on either side of your legs. Your legs have lengthened and flattened. They're not legs anymore. They're a tail with a paddle. All right. Open your eyes, check."

Ludwig opened his eyes and looked down. "Mein Gott!" There were two, twining, paddle tails below him. One was bright, clear blue with a set of white fins and the other was black with velvety, dark fins.

"Good. That's great. Now, all we need is to get you some gills. All right. Close your eyes again."

Ludwig closed his eyes again, his tail twitching beneath him. "Zhis is going to be hard to explain in mein memoirs."

"You know what? Let's just focus on getting you to the point where you can write up a set of memoirs and then we can talk about how to explain it." Mara sighed. "Okay, gills are complex. Sections of your chest are lifting up and the scales over them are expanding, growing to cover them. Seamlessly merging together. They're like doors. Open and shut. Okay. I think that's good. You still have a human head, but my spines are more like decorations than anything else."

Ludwig opened his eyes and looked down at the set of six gills growing out of his chest. "Oh. Oh, zhat feels funny..." They were pumping water in and out like he was breathing, but he couldn't feel it in his chest. "Mein Gott, zhat feels..."

"Come on. Let's get you back under." Mara pulled him down into the water. "Still good?"

"Of course, I'm good. I hafe gills!" Ludwig wiggled away from her arms and swam a circle around her. "Look at zhis!"

"I see! You look great! Come on, let's go explore the reef." Mara lifted herself up, a flash of black and gold and Ludwig pitched himself into following her – only to end up with his head buried in the sand, literally.

"Whoops…" Mara came back over. "It took me awhile to learn how to swim too… Are you okay?"

Ludwig pulled himself out of the bottom of the lagoon. "…Zhat vas humiliating."

"Try waving your tail from side to side instead of up and down. Go slowly." Mara instructed, maneuvering herself beneath and to his side, trying to support him from beneath.

"This feels wrong…" Ludwig muttered, focusing on moving himself side to side.

"I'm sorry. Our tails are designed like a sea snake's tail, and they move the same way other sea snake tails do." Mara assured him. "You'll get it soon. It's all about the rhythm."

"Zhe rhyzhm…" Ludwig sighed, moving back and forth clumsily. "Oh, zhis vill nefer be fast…"

"When you catch on, it gets faster and faster. That's the nature of the beast." Mara assured him. "For now, let's get you learning how to swim."

Chapter Eleven

Mara shook his shoulder. "Ludwig, get up." She pulled him out of bed. "How do you feel like going toe-to-toe with Lucy?"

Ludwig muttered and blinked himself awake, then leapt to his feet. "He's here?" Now that it came down to this, he began to feel nervous.

"You know I'll be right there – tossing his dumb butt out – the moment you give a shout." Mara promised him, throwing his clothes at him. "But for now, I have to go blaze a trail towards where he's doing his thing. Get dressed and do a walk-about. He'll find you."

Ludwig pulled on his full outfit. Mara had moved them back up to the lodge – according to her – this was Lucy's favorite staging ground for the conflicts he and Mara regularly had. As a result, all the layers in the world couldn't keep Ludwig entirely from the chill of the wind outside. It touched his nose and cheeks beneath the Ushanka, chapping them almost from the start of his stroll.

The lodge didn't burn this time, and the roar of the dragon was less frightening than it had been the first time he heard it. The crack and roar of plasma and flames were farther off. Ludwig stepped out on the snow, heard the crunch of it under his boots and his eyes closed. A deep breath and he summoned strength from the middle of his chest. Out into the fray.

Ludwig chose a random direction, away from the sound of the pitched battle, and began walking calmly. Looking about, he spotted a tree that had been covered in glowing fairy lights. Mara had begun getting anxious for Christmas, it seemed. Either that or this was a trap Lucy had set up and Ludwig was about to walk right into it. Oddly enough, he felt fine with it going either way at this point. He stepped boldly up to the tree and looked into the branches, noticing that the tiny lights were filled with bubbles.

The tree being a trap turned out to be the more likely almost at once. Ludwig felt a breath of wind on the back of his neck and dove aside. Lucy was descending on him with a scythe – thematically appropriate, since he was also masquerading as a skeleton. Apparently, this was an attempt at disguising himself as the Grim Reaper.

Oddly enough, it was the skeleton garb that Ludwig focused on. When he was twelve, he had insisted on going as a skeleton for Halloween. Not just any skeleton either: An anatomically correct skeleton. He and his mother had spent a great deal of time working with glow in the dark paint and a copy of *Grey's Anatomy*.

Lucy became a blonde twerp running around in a skeleton costume in a moment's thought. His scythe was reduced to a plastic toy. Ludwig snatched the handle and cracked it in half. Lucy's face was priceless. At once, he went from the frightening Grim Reaper to a frightened child. "What?! You can't – you can't do that!"

Ludwig fixed Lucy with an unhinged grin as he remembered the pain of a knife driving through his voice box. "Vhy not?" He pulled the toy away from Lucy and turned the pieces on him, slashing through the cheap robe he was wearing. "I vould run." He took to his feet, chasing after the fleeing wannabe-Demon. Lucy put his head down and ran away from Ludwig as fast as he could until Ludwig stopped, catching his breath. "Und do not come back! I may hafe done schtupid zhings before, but ve are ready for you! You vill nefer zhreaten us again!" Feeling alive, Ludwig almost didn't notice when Mara landed beside him.

A dragon's tongue caressed his cheek. "I saw everything. You did well, Ludwig." Mara nuzzled him and Ludwig turned around to hug her broad leg.

"Ve did it!" He said fiercely. "But, ja, I vas amazing! Zhe moment I saw zhat schtupid costume he vas in, I knew vhat to do!"

"I get the feeling he'll never be bothering us again." Mara settled beside him in the snow and shrank down to an unusually tall – but not gigantic – woman. In fact, she wasn't an inch over five foot six and Ludwig stared down at her, suddenly realizing that this was her natural height. Nevertheless, she looked invincible. "We're too much for him."

Ludwig put his arms around her and pulled her close, relishing the level of trust Mara showed him. "Ja, ve are. Shall ve go home? Or vhat about zhat sled ride ve hafe alvays been meaning to take?"

"How about a sled ride that ends back at our beach house?" Mara gave him a broad smirk as she began growing again, returning to the height he was used to seeing her at. "The world's longest sled ride ever."

"I vould like zhat." Ludwig agreed and as they turned, a bright, red sled appeared beneath one of the trees nearby.

Chapter Twelve

"All right. Same thing as with the scales, but think of feathers this time. The same feeling, but longer and broader." Mara was instructing. "You're a bird. Think of it that way. Legs shrinking back into a feathery body. Face changing. Dark, beady eyes."

Ludwig opened his eyes and stared up at the dragon in front of him. "Did it vork?"

Mara stared at him with her huge, draconic eyes and pitched her head back and laughed into the clouds. "Good job, Ludwig, it worked."

"Vhat?" Ludwig questioned. "Vhat is so funny?" He hopped forwards and looked down at his feet. They were delicate and sank only a tiny bit into the snow.

"You're a sparrow, Ludwig." Mara dipped her nose down to where he was and stared at him with her golden eyes. "A cute, little sparrow."

Ludwig pecked her nose. "Shut up! Are ve flying or not?"

"We're flying." Mara lifted her massive wings. "Ready or not, here we go!"

The two lovers launched into the air in tandem. It had been almost a year since Ludwig had had his twelve rounds with Lucy – as Mara put it. In reality, as with all fights against a bully, it had been a surprisingly quick match. Lucy had never been resisted so mightily by someone like Ludwig before.

Since then, Ludwig had learned more control over the world, though his control was not half as strong as Mara's and he often needed her help – her suggestions – to help him work through it. Still, he could now transform into his aquatic form at will and had decided that he wanted to have the freedom of wings as well. This was his first time transforming into a bird.

Mara's massive wings created an excellent breeze to surf on just above them. Below them was a tumbling gale, and Ludwig quickly learned to stay out of that. His tiny sparrow form was smaller than one of Mara's scales and he had to be careful. But he was so much more maneuverable than her massive dragon. He flirted around her nostrils and ears, settling himself directly on the bridge of her nose between her eyes and fluffing himself in the strong wind that blew before them.

The world was peaceful below them. There were no lights to interrupt their star-gazing at night and no bustling of cars to keep them up when they both wanted to sleep. Ludwig was even used – by now – to the lack of conversation and to amusing himself with activities. He had taught himself how to play the violin – at least mentally. As it turned out, Mara had a strip of musical talent and shared it with him when he asked. Her clarinet had a pure, amateurish sound. She was careful with each note and played every song at a slow, easy pace.

It was up in the air – as far as Ludwig could tell – how much of a skill that he had learned here was really real. Mara knew how to play the violin and the clarinet, so she had offered him lessons. But where his mind might be certain of how to hold the bow and touch the strings, he had never touched the instrument in life. When he woke, he intended to find a violin first thing – after making sure that Mara saw her family again – and test out exactly how much he had learned.

"You feel fluffy against my face, Bon." Mara had finally found a nickname that he had approved as well – though not without her wearing him down over it a bit. "That's not a complaint. It just feels really adorable."

Ludwig pecked at one of her eyelids, making her blink. "I am not adorable. I am zhe sparrow! One of zhe most agile und adaptife of all zhe songbirds."

"Adorable to me, Bon." Mara went into a spin that dislodged Ludwig from his comfy perch. "Look at those widdle wings!"

Ludwig flew around her head, harassing her and calling at her with his angry sparrow-like screech.

"Oh, shush. You know I love you." Mara caught him in her mouth and blew him out into a cloud before she let him settle back between her eyes again.

"Ja, Ich liebe dich." Ludwig began preening himself free of the dragon's spit. "Und vhat hafe I said about keeping zhat tongue to yourself?"

"Oh, shush. You know perfectly well that you don't want me keeping my tongue to myself at all." Mara made for the ground and landed in an explosion of loose snow that rained down over her iridescent scales.

"Hmph. Zhe tongue I do not vant you to keep to yourself is not forked." Ludwig pointed out as his perch began a black-gloved finger and the eyes he was staring at went from being slit by a lizard's pupil to the rounded, soft eyes of a human woman. Mara gently pulled the little sparrow close to her and tucked him into the collar of her black coat. It seemed he was staying in this form for a bit.

"It could be." Mara stuck out her tongue and showed that it was forked like a snake before it became her normal tongue and retreated into her mouth.

"Bitte, nein." Ludwig admonished her with a few flutters of his tiny wings.

"All right, all right." Gentle fingers went to the back of his neck, giving him scritches there. "I have a surprise for you."

"I hate surprises. Vat is it?" Ludwig looked up at her, unable to see her expression because of his vantage point.

"Nothing bad. In fact, I think it might change your mind about surprises." Mara confidently strode forwards through the trees. Ludwig's sense of direction told him that they had been flying and were now walking away from the lodge. It had to be three miles away at this point.

"Zhat vould hafe to be quite zhe surprise." Ludwig studied the forest in front of them. They seemed to be heading towards a clearing where a soft light was glowing.

"You can turn back into a human now." Mara told him as they stepped through and Ludwig saw what was waiting for them.

The clearing had been decorated with a thousand floating lights in all of the trees. A warm fire blazed in the center, made with logs piled up into a cone right there in the snow. A table was laid only a little bit away, covered in dishes that Ludwig didn't doubt would be piping hot and ready when they sat down. Red flowers were scattered all around. Somehow, Winter and Summer had collided in the frozen clearing.

"Mara, zhis is... Beautiful." Ludwig stared around at it all, taking in the beauty and the care Mara had used. It was warm here too, warm enough that he was not sure he would need his coat. "But vhat is it for?"

"Do I really need a reason?" Mara questioned, shrugging as she sat down in one of the wooden chairs beside the table. "And if you do need one: It's our anniversary."

"Ah, is it so?" Ludwig smiled. Of course, he should have known. "I vish you had reminded me. I vould hafe made or bought you somezhing."

"No, no... It was nice to surprise you." Mara smiled down at him. "Besides, what can you get for the girl who can snap her fingers and have anything?"

Ludwig chuckled. "Fery vell. Vhat is dinner?"

"Lamb chops with mashed potatoes and asparagus for the main course. Creamy chicken soup for the first. For dessert, a decadent chocolate cake right off the pages of the last word on that all-consuming passion: Raspberry Fudge Torte. And, all the way through, a bright, bubbling champagne." Mara gestured to the grand spread.

Pulling off his gloves, Ludwig settled down in the second chair and lifted the cover over his bowl of soup. "What are ve vaiting for, zhen?"

Mara didn't actually like to make conversation during dinner. Ludwig had learned that while she would speak if engaged directly, she would much rather tuck in and eat before devoting herself to conversation.

With that in mind, Ludwig raised his eyebrows when Mara looked up from her bowl of soup. "A year is a long time."

"In zhe grand scheme of zhings, it is a very little time." Curious, Ludwig replied. "But I vould say zhat zhis year has been a much longer one zhan most. Much has happened."

"Yeah... I mean, it's been more than a year since you came, and then there was the thing with Lucy..." Mara took a bite of her soup. "Anyway, it's been a long time."

"It has, but... I hafe enjoyed every minute of it." Ludwig tipped his head to the side, studying her. "Are you nerfous, Mara?"

"What? No, no… I mean, well, a little, but it's not important."

"Vhy is it not important? Vhat is vorrying you?" Ludwig studied her. "Do you feel sick? Is zhere somezhing wrong?"

"No, there's nothing wrong… and there's no danger. I don't feel sick." Mara assured him, pushing her bowl of soup aside. "The only thing I'm worried about… Is what you're going to say."

"Say? Say about vhat?" Ludwig sat back from the table, staring at the taller woman.

"About this." Mara reached into her coat and pulled out a small box. It was too small to be a watch case and covered in burgundy velvet with a clasp on the front. "Go on. It's for you."

Ludwig took the box in steady hands and gently fiddled open the clasp. The little box was heavy for its size, though that could be his apprehension making it feel heavy. Somehow, he knew exactly what was in this box.

Mara held her breath as he finally flipped the lid open and revealed the contents.

Of course, it was a ring. A masculine piece made of platinum. It looked like someone had taken a pair of Mara's talons from her dragon form, patterned them with the scales from her aquatic form, and then topped it with a five-petaled rose. And in the center of that rose, a bright, red ruby winked up at him like a faceted drop of blood. He didn't need to try it on to know that it was exactly his size. Running around the inside of the ring was an inscription: "The ropes that have bound you to me, have bound me to you as well." It had the ring of a quote in his head.

The silence lingered as the ruby winked and he stared at the simple question, promise, and symbol he had been offered.

"...Please, say something." Mara whispered when she couldn't take the silence any longer.

Ludwig glanced up at her through his black lashes. She was a good woman: Loyal, exciting, and honest. He could really do no better. In this world, though, they were equals. And outside it, what would they be? She was young there. Half his age.

Still, here they were equals. And it was not Ludwig who had created this ring. If she ever wanted to take it back... Especially in the real world, where it had never technically existed... He would let her. Without a fuss.

With this in mind, he slid the ring onto his finger and looked up at her with an amused smile. "Vhat? Zhe cake und zhe champagne flute vere too cliched vays of asking?" Ludwig questioned.

Immediately, Mara relaxed and her easy manner returned. "You know, I thought of slipping it into the cake, but I was worried you'd choke on it, and you'd definitely see it in a champagne flute: You're not blind."

"I vill need to find one for you." Ludwig gave her his hand to hold. "Und zhere are practicalities to consider, but... Perhaps at a later time, Ja?"

"That's fine with me." Mara sighed deeply and settled in more comfortably. "I was so worried you would be offended."

"So long as ve are clear zhat ve are equals, I hafe no problem. One of us had to ask." The doctor smirked slightly. "Und I vould not hafe been bold enough to try."

"You're certainly bold enough." Mara scoffed. "But I will concede that I have a little bit more flair." She pulled the second covered dish in front of her place. "Now that I'm not shaking in my boots anymore, why not move onto the second course and enjoy the rest of the dinner?"

"Vhy not?" Ludwig raised his flute of golden champagne to his fiancée and gently rang it against Mara's own. "After all, efery union needs a celebratory banquet."

"Oh, hush... I can't wait until you meet my parents. You'll find out what a celebratory banquet really is then." Mara assured him and picked up her fork to carve into her chops. "Now, let's eat, and then we can talk all night for all I care."

Chapter Thirteen

Ludwig rested against Mara on their over-sized chaise lounge. It had been Mara's idea to share a sweater and cuddle after their long flight through the cold. Ludwig's arms were trapped by the red wool, but he was warm and cozy. Mara's hand was stroking the small of his back.

One topic of conversation was guaranteed to make the evening a bad one: Leaving. There was no two ways about it. Mara was paranoid and she had good reason to be. Thinking about how Lucy had stabbed him in the throat always made Ludwig's spine tingle as well. But they couldn't stay here in CORD forever.

"Mara?" Ludwig questioned, almost hoping she was too far into sleep to answer. "Are you avake?"

Mara hummed, turning over onto her back and pulling him with her. "Yes. For now."

"Hafe you ever zhought about… trying to vake up?" Ludwig looked down at her expression and found it hooded and guarded.

"Many times. But it's not as easy as you make it sound." Mara reminded him. "If there was a way to wake up from here, I would have found it. I've tried everything."

"Vell, zhen, maybe zhe answer's not in here. Maybe ve hafe to leafe to find zhe vay home." Ludwig gently suggested.

"You want to leave?! After what happened last time? Don't you remember what happened when Lucy got ahold of you? He could have killed you, Ludwig!" Mara sat up abruptly, forcing Ludwig to straddle her lap.

"Ja, I remember, but he only caught me because I did not hafe you vith me!" Ludwig reminded her. "You profed zhat you can fight him efen on his own turf. I zhink ve should go und try to vake zhe ozhers, so zhat ve can learn how to vake ourselfes!"

"This isn't a bad place to wait. I think we should stay here, where we're safe. We can have a good life here." Mara reminded him.

"Ja, a good life, but not a real life! I vant to be vith you in zhe real vorld!"

"I'm not –" Mara looked away from his blue eyes and towards the dying coals. "I'm not like this in the real world, Ludwig. I'm small and weak. I have health problems and I don't like them. Here, I can be strong and we can be together in a world we control. Out there, something as simple as a car accident could take you away from me."

"Ja! It is life! Not zhis. Ve may hafe forefer here, but it is a forefer vizhout risk, vizhout safor. Zhis is not a future. It is stagnation." Ludwig argued with her, pressing his hands to her cheeks. "Bitte, Mara, I do not vant our lofe to grow stale. Ve need room to grow."

"I can create room for us here!" Mara pleaded, a note of desperation in her voice. "Anything you want: I'll give it to you. Just say the word."

"I do not vant zhe zhings you can create, Mara. I vant you. Zhe truzh of you, und all zhat comes vith it. Do you not trust me, mein liebling? Do you not zhink I know I can lofe you in any form?" Ludwig pressed close to her, their foreheads touching. "If you do not zhink zhat, zhen ve hafe no hope, eizher vay."

After a moment, Mara put her hands on his face. "It's not a matter of you loving me. I know you will. It's a matter of... everything else. Everyone who looks at us will know you're older. They won't understand everything we've been through. They won't understand how I feel and what I've seen. I may be young, but I feel so old."

"You've had to grow up before your time." Ludwig cooed to her, pressing his lips to hers. "Und zhat means you've seen too much. If I could undo vhat vas done to you –"

"Don't say that." Mara pressed a kiss to his lips to silence him. "If I had never been here, I would never have met you. I wouldn't trade the world for that. Not even the world."

Mara's hands kneaded helplessly at his neck as she worked through what Ludwig was asking of her. Her expression was far away and alternating between helpless and despairing. She truly didn't want to do this. But Ludwig had seen others conquer their fears and knew Mara could too. "Bitte, Mara. Ve must try."

"…All right." Mara murmured. "I don't like this at all, but all right. I can't refuse you anything. But what are we going to do with the others?"

"Ve're going to help zhem Vake up." Ludwig let his lips curl up into a smile. "So, ve must find out vhat keeps zhem asleep in zhe first place."

"…You have a plan, don't you?" Mara gave him a side-glance. "You think you can figure this out."

"As I said before, I vas almost a psychologist. I zhink I can find out what zhe ozhers need." Ludwig kissed her forehead. "Und ve vill alvays be able to come back home for rest."

"Ah, yes, 'rest.'" Mara nodded saucily. "We must get plenty of that. …When you're ready, of course."

"Are you?" Ludwig challenged, his eyes dancing.

"I believe I am."

In the morning, Ludwig found Mara in the lodge's breakfast nook, eating a muffin and reading a newspaper whose headline read TERRORISM IN NEW YORK. There was a picture of the New York skyline with a pair of newly demolished towers missing. "I hafe nefer seen you read a newspaper before, Mara." Ludwig sat down across from her.

"I only ever read for the comics. You can have the rest if you want." Mara pulled out the colorful comic section and handed the rest of it to Ludwig.

"This was the last newspaper I remember reading." She casually told him. "Terrible thing that happened. I was at school when the news came in – the whole place shut down. Crazy day."

Ludwig's eyes flashed to the date on the newspaper: September 16, 2001. "…Mara, I know how old you are." He told her suddenly. How had he been so stupid? "Ve hafe nefer discussed dates."

"…We're stupid." Mara replied, putting down the paper a little more emphatically than necessary. "We're so unbearably stupid. It was 2010 when I fell off the lifeguard stand."

"It vas 2018 vhen I vas in mein accident!" Ludwig threw his hands up. "You are twenty-four at zhe least!"

Mara made a fist and pumped it. "Yes! I can drink! Well… Not that it ever stopped me from drinking before." She shrugged. "And we can get married as soon as we wake up!"

"It's better zhan ve could hafe hoped." Ludwig smiled, settling down. "Vell, how should ve prepare for our journey?"

"…I had hoped you would forget that." Mara groaned and sat up. "I don't want to rain on your parade, but I need time to prepare. If we leave my estate, we might have to fight, and constantly."

"A few days more cannot hurt." Ludwig agreed. "So long as zhey are a terminable number."

"Will a month satisfy?" Mara offered, looking up at him in her long-sleeved red shirt.

"A veek at most." Ludwig kissed her forehead. "Und ve can come back to rest as often as you need, don't forget zhat."

"Hmph. All right then. A week." Mara wrapped her arms around him and pulled him close until her face was pressed into his sternum. "You smell funny."

"Ve could bozh use a bazh." Ludwig stroked her loose hair. It had come undone from it's usual, tightly-laced braid and she had left it loose. He wasn't entirely sure what it meant, but he stroked the silky waves and let them gather in his fingers as he drew them through the golden streams.

"What are we waiting for then?" Mara questioned finally, standing up and gripping his arms with an attitude that seemed intent on never letting go.

Chapter Fourteen

"So, vhat should ve take?" Ludwig questioned from his half of the bath tub. One of Mara's gangly legs was dangling out of the side and the other was a bit awkwardly positioned near Ludwig's hip.

"Well, I would guess that the other worlds we touch work the same way that this one does. So, there isn't really anything we strictly need to bring. On the other hand, it might be a good idea to show up with things so we don't have to build them on the fly." Mara laid her head back. "Personally, I'm fond of the idea of showing up with a submachine gun."

"Nein, do you vant to scare eferyone?" Ludwig scoffed and kicked at her knee gently.

"No, but I do want to be scary enough that dangerous folks don't mess with us." Mara thought for a moment, then pulled an NYPD cap out of nowhere. "Think this might work?"

"No, Danke. I vould razher not impersonate a police officer." Ludwig declined and Mara flipped the cap into a green beret.

"This one's almost true." Mara hummed when she held up the beret.

"You vere too young to be in zhe Army." Ludwig reminded her.

"Yes, but I have a cousin who gave me his uniform."

"Zhat vould only vork from a distance. You vould not be able to vear any sort of rank badge." Ludwig leaned back and pressed his foot against the outside of her thigh. "Relax, Mara, ve vill be fine. I can't imagine zhat zhe voman who pushed back Lucy on his own turf is considered an easy target."

"If I know Lucy, he didn't exactly brag about that." Mara replied, her eyes becoming dark and distant. "I still don't like this. It's not safe out there and I don't want to leave."

"I know you don't, but ve must." Ludwig moved to his knees and then laid himself out across her so he could nuzzle at her face and nose.

With a sigh, Mara returned the affection. "We may be strong, but I'm afraid that there may be stronger forces than you and I at work here. We don't understand how this world works or what the consequences to waking up the others will be."

"Ve vill nefer know if ve nefer try." Ludwig pointed out. "It is not such a bad zhing not to know somezhing. It only means zhat ve vill find zhe answer."

"Ugh. You're such a sap." Mara brought her long-fingered hands up to his head, baring the lines of black writing on her forearms. There was a line of flames running up the outside of her left arm and the words caressed it like a frame for the elegant picture. Ludwig took one of the hands in his own and began reading.

"The tongue also is a fire, a world of evil among the parts of the body. It corrupts the whole body, sets the whole course of one's life on fire, and is itself set on fire by hell..." Ludwig read aloud, his lips forming the words with care. "Zhis is a Bible verse... You hafe a copy of zhe Holy Bible tattooed onto your skin?" He looked up at Mara.

"With accompanying illustrations, in some places." Mara raised herself out of the water slightly and covered up her left breast. A heart with a crown had been inked in there and it was surrounded by "For God so loved the world, that he gave his one and only son..."

"Zhis is amazing... Mara, I do not know if zhis is efen possible in zhe real vorld, but it is amazing." Ludwig continued to read through the Gospel of John as it spilled down her ribcage. "Did you choose zhe illustrations or vere zhey automativ vizh zhe text?"

"I chose them, for the most part. I tried to choose things that were symbolic. For example, I have all of the pieces of the Jesse tree my parents and I used to put together. This angel is right here in the book of Daniel." Mara lifted one hip out of the water to show off the stylized angel surrounded by the prophecy of the messiah. "And this rose is Isaiah." The rose was directly above her ankle, and Ludwig traced through it with gentle fingers. "Careful, my feet are ticklish."

"I vill be extremely cautious." Ludwig kissed the rose's bloom and lowered the foot back into the water. "Vhere is Genesis?"

"Across my back." Mara turned over with difficulty. Each of the days of the Creation was illustrated with a stylized illustration. Light from dark was set with white text against a black background. The firmament was a circle within a circle and so on. Ludwig ran his fingers down the text. "...Are you a Christian, Ludwig? I always meant to ask, but never had the words." Mara murmured.

"...I beliefe in Jesus Christ, in zhe resurrection, und in zhe history of zhe bible." Ludwig sighed. "But zhe seven-day Creation... Zhat I find harder."

"Yeah, well... I think you got enough there. It only takes faith in salvation to get to Heaven. Good." Mara stretched, the text moving with her. "Come on. My skin is going to wrinkle up if we stay in here any longer."

"Ja, but it is so comfy, isn't it?" Johann raised his eyebrows at her.

Mara laughed and gently pushed him off. "Maybe later, Don Juan. For now, I think we need to discuss strategy."

Chapter Fifteen

They sat down at the kitchen table and Mara pulled a notebook towards herself. "Now, we're here – the two of us." She made a series of five circles. "And these are the other four people we have in here with us."

"Lucy, zhe Grandmozher, zhe Engineer, und zhe Ozher." Ludwig rattled them off by the nicknames Mara had given each.

"Yep." Mara sighed. "I only know Lucy well, but he should be our last target, I think, not our first."

"Why? He's surely zhe most dangerous." Ludwig apprehensively looked down at Lucy's circle.

"Yes, but he's also the most predictable. I'd like to save him for last." Mara sighed through her nose. "Besides, I have the rather horrid feeling that we'll have to kill him when we go after him and I don't want to have to do that."

"Ve von't hafe to kill him. Ve can vake him up and ve'll tell zhe police about zhe zhings he's done. Zhey'll stop him from hurting anyone else." Ludwig assured her.

"I'd love to believe that, Ludwig, but I get the feeling that the crimes people commit here aren't prosecutable in any sort of court. This is new territory." Mara shook her head. "Anyway. I think we should go to the grandmother's circle first."

"Zhe easy target?"

"I hope she's the easy target." Mara drew an arrow from their circle to the grandmother's. "We should visit each circle on the sly at first, try to gain as much information as possible before we have to approach the controllers directly."

"Can't ve try to speak to zhem?" Ludwig questioned Mara. "Zhey must vant to vake up as much as ve do."

Mara raised an eyebrow at him and Ludwig remembered that she didn't really want to leave at all.

"As much as I do anyvay." Ludwig amended. "Vouldn't zhey vant to help us find zhe vay out?"

"You would think so. I don't know if it's true or not, though, and I'd like to know for sure before we do anything." Mara explained, drawing arrows between the other circles. "We should avoid Lucy like the plague until we have to. He'll figure out what we're trying to do and use his wiles to turn the others against us."

"Mara, vill Lucy be able to get into zhis vorld vhile ve are in ozhers?" Ludwig questioned, anxious at the idea.

"I don't know. I don't even know if this world exists while I'm not in it. I don't understand how this world works entirely and there's no way for me to know if there is a change when I leave. Well, there's no way that I would risk. The last thing I want to come back to is an empty lodge and Lucy's calling card." Mara decided, crushing the idea of the experiment. "Regardless, I don't think that Lucy could take up residence here. It's not a shell like a hermit crab might toss aside. If I re-enter, anyone in it should be pushed out."

"Zhen zhere should be no risk to our lofely home here." Ludwig was soothed. "Und no surprises should be vaiting vhen we do return."

"Of course not. I wouldn't allow that." Mara assured him. "And, with that in mind, I think it's time we do have somewhat of an expedition. Let's take a picnic and get outside of my world."

"Vhere should ve go?" Ludwig questioned in curiosity. Mara had been adamant that before she would not leave for this pilgrimage for a week at the least.

"Your world. Let's try and find that train you told me about. If we can find that train, we'll be in your head instead of mine and it should give me a chance to feel how this is going to go." Mara explained to Ludwig. "It's been a long time since Lucy and I had the square over you, and I need to prepare myself somehow."

"You'll be sparring with Lucy this week then?" Ludwig questioned. Ever since he had turned Lucy into a child in a costume, the would-be demon had left them alone except for the times that Mara "invited" him over for a fight to break up the time.

"If he takes the bait." Mara decided. "It's been too long since we had a good match. Perhaps we should spar at some point. See if my belief in unreality can match your solid belief in reality." She nuzzled at his face gently. "But for now, we should go and find that train."

"I'll get the saddle-basket." Ludwig at once set for the kitchen. "Italian today?"

"The dish with the lamb chops, please. I'll bring down the spare blanket." The "spare blanket" was – in the fashion of the world – less of an actual spare blanket and more of an idea of a worn and stained old blanket that Mara always dragged out when they were going to have a picnic.

Ludwig seared and baked the lamb chops while Mara brought around the outside to be more conducive to travel. It seemed that they wouldn't be flying with Ludwig aboard her dragon-form, but driving in a car. Mara considered this precaution to be logical. "The last thing we need is for us to cross the border between our minds – so to speak – and for your belief in the real world to strike us both from the air."

"I don't zhink zhat vould happen." Ludwig frowned. "Vhenefer my belief in zhe real vorld strikes, it doesn't affect you."

"That's here, in my world, where I rule what is real." Mara explained. "In your world, it might be more of a struggle, as it is in Lucy's world. I don't know if that's the rule for every world or just for the ones where I'm fighting with the controller."

"So, I might be able to control vhat you und ozhers can do in my vorld?" Ludwig thought on the subject.

"Well, to a point. It's all about perception and belief here, I've told you before. From my experience, it can be complicated to decide who will be the victor in a battle of minds." Mara shrugged. "Lucy and I have given each other "wounds" that would certainly be fatal in the real world, but here they're little more than scratches. Our fights are play fights at the best. It's only when I took you that we really did battle, and it was hard to breach his defenses. I think that each Controller sets the rules of the world based on their preconceived notions, and it's only when another Controller engages them that those notions are challenged. From there, it seems to be a battle of stubborn will. Of course, I've only ever really engaged Lucy. I don't know the other Controllers well."

"Do you zhink you can defeat zhem should it come to zhat?" Ludwig questioned.

"Ludwig, this world isn't real. I know that. No one here can hurt me with that in mind. I'll always be able to walk away from an engagement." Mara assured him gently, packing up some mashed potatoes and brussels sprouts. "Now, if the lamb chops are ready, we can get on our way."

The car was a more sensible one than Mara's ostentatious sports cars. "My dad's pick-up." Mara explained when Ludwig questioned her choice. "The most real car I could think of. Four wheel drive, so if we do get stuck, it'll be even farther from help, and plenty of leg room." She shot him a teasing grin. "But don't worry. I can't count the places we've been to in this old thing and never got stuck."

"I'm more concerned vith skidding." Ludwig looked out apprehensively at the snow-covered road. "Did you put snow chains on?"

"Of course I did. And don't worry, the tires have a no-slip grip. The snow will clear up as we get down the mountain." Mara put the truck into gear and they headed out. "I'd worry more about finding our way into your head. I want you to concentrate on your train. Give me a heading. Think hard about it."

Ludwig closed his eyes and imagined the train. He had spent so much time on it in his dreams that it came to his mind with ease. He imagined the way he had last seen it – frozen over by a sheet of ice and driven from the warmth of the station into a blizzard – chasing fairy lights. It had been a long walk, but by truck, it shouldn't be far at all. The pick-up would cut through the snow and Mara would find the station. After all, she had found him in that snow-filled wasteland.

"Is that the station up ahead? That was fast." Mara pointed ahead at a building coming out of the snow. "I thought your mind would be a little more temperate." She looked around at the drifted snow all across the land. "At least, the road seems clear for now."

"It's not actively snowing." Ludwig looked up. "And zhere aren't any clouds. Vhat's causing zhis snow?"

"Well, do you feel cold? Are you thinking of ice and snow?" Mara questioned as they pulled up to the station. The little train was hidden behind it entirely, but with the condition the station itself was in, Ludwig didn't doubt that the train itself was still completely iced over – unable to go anywhere.

"Nein. I hafe been nozhing but varm und cozy efer since you rescued me from Lucy's domain." Ludwig glanced up at the threatening icicles hanging in sheets from the station's roof. "Und zhose look dangerous."

"Well, thankfully, they're only dangerous while they're up there." Mara climbed out and kicked the snow away from a pile of rocks next to the steps up to the station. "Stand back." She warned him unnecessarily as she pulled back her arm and threw one of the rocks up at the icicles. With the tinkle and clatter of a thousand glass panes, they came tumbling down and shattered on the porch.

The path cleared, Ludwig pulled the basket out of the back and they went inside the station. Inside, it was warm and cozy – fires still burning in grates and the furniture soft and ready for them to settle in and rest. Mara pushed a pair of chairs and a table close.

"…Vhy is zhe outside so inhospitable und zhe inside so nice?" Ludwig questioned, looking out the back windows. As he had expected, the train was iced over and rows of icicles had re-grown from the station's roofs and become a maze of jagged daggers pointing down towards the wooden platform.

"Hmm." Mara looked out at the train as well. "I'm not sure. It could be that your mind subconsciously recognizes that you're in danger and wants to protect you by making the world outside your shelter as inhospitable as possible."

"In the hopes of scaring avay intruders, of course." Ludwig connected the dots. "Zhen it makes sense zhat it seems so dangerous, but ve should be perfectly safe."

"The only thing I can't make fit in with that supposition is why the train is iced over." Mara gestured out at it. "You would think that a moving target would make a better shelter. Force him to look for you."

"Ja, but perhaps my mind has already constructed itself like a maze, so zhat Lucy cannot get in. Perhaps zhat is vhy he had to lure me out." Ludwig settled down into one of the chairs. "If ve do not eat quickly, ve vill hafe cold lamb chops."

"We can warm them up next to the fire if we need to." Mara unpacked the picnic blanket and tucked it down around Ludwig, sitting in the other chair.

"Ja, but zhat vould add smoke to mein sear." Ludwig pushed two chops onto her plate.

"Oh, of course, how could I forget?" Mara teased him as she picked one up by the bone and began nibbling on it. "Did we remember silverware?"

"Of course, I did! Do you zhink I am a barbarian?" Ludwig smacked the back of her hand with the handle of her knife. "So do not eat like one!"

"Owie, all right, all right." Mara accepted the knife and fork. "You don't have to be snappish, geez!" But the look she shot him was all puckish mischief.

"Ja, vizh zhat look, I do." Ludwig waved a speared brussels sprout threateningly at her. "How do you feel? Is it different being here?"

"No, not that I can feel. Possibly because you're not fighting me. Well, let's try something out. I think I forgot to pack any wine – let's see if I can make some." Reaching into mid-air, she concentrated and found herself holding a bottle of Zinfandel. "Okay. So, that works."

Ludwig looked at the bottle of wine and began thinking of exactly how impossible it was that the bottle existed. It had been pulled from the air. Either it had been teleported into her hand or Mara had rearranged the atoms of air itself into different patterns to create the bottle. Impossible without the introduction of silicon of some sort.

The bottle became less and less real. Mara frowned and looked down at her hand. She focused on the bottle, trying to keep it in the world with them. "Are you fighting me?"

"I'm trying to see if I'm more powerful here." Ludwig explained, releasing the wine bottle and letting it remain real.

"Are you?" Mara questioned, pouring out two glasses of wine and passing one to him.

"I'm not sure. I just zhought of zhe bottle being unreal and felt you fighting me." Ludwig looked down and the wine glass in his hand vanished in a moment as he thought of its own unreality. "It seems I am. Zhat vas much faster zhan normal."

"Interesting. Perhaps we could use that somehow." Mara thought quietly to herself. "But only if we had to lure someone into our own worlds."

"Ja, und zhat vill not happen. Ve can take zhem, Mara." Ludwig's confident smile bolstered her own.

"Yes, we can." Mara nodded. "But it won't be easy. I'd like to stay here for a bit before we set out. Let's do some training off of my own ground."

"I don't know if zhere are beds here, but I suppose ve could alvays improfise." Ludwig looked around. He hadn't explored all of the station before he left and there were doors leading away from this cozy main room.

"Well, if I am right and your mind constructed this place to keep you safe and comfortable, then it makes sense that there would be a place to sleep." Mara stood up. "Come on, let's do some exploring."

Ludwing followed after her, abandoning their plates. The station had a second room, which contained a stove, cupboard full of canned food, and a closet with hinges along the floor instead of the walls like normal. It didn't take long for Ludwig to realize it was a pull-down bed.

"Zhat makes more sense." The Doctor sat down on the end of the slightly-bouncing piece of furniture.

"Indeed." Mara settled down beside him. "…I'm very tired. I'm not sure why."

"Do you feel sick?" Ludwig looked over at her worriedly.

"I told you: That wouldn't matter unless it was my body that was sick." Mara thought for a long moment. "And I don't think it's that. I've been bodily sick in here before and it was miserable – not just tired."

"It might hafe been exertion. It can be so hard for you to remember zhings. Like your fazher's truck."

"Maybe that's it." Mara settled back on the bed. "Or it could be that it's cold and I always want to curl up in warm places when it's cold – What's warmer than a bed?" She patted the spot beside her. "Join me?"

"Of course, mein Engel." Ludwig laid down beside her and pillowed his head on her shoulder. "Let me keep you warm."

Chapter Sixteen

Mara's training consisted of performing the activities she did normally with minor difficulty in her own world in Johann's. It turned out that it exhausted her quite easily. Though, as they were fighting, Mara pointed out time and again that Johann's sense of reality was almost impossible to defeat. She had to mine cracks in his attention, sweep for infinitely small holes – even duck and dodge out of his direct field of view – in order to change forms or to summon up objects whose appearance couldn't be explained by sleight of hand. Even when she managed, it was a struggle to hold them as Johann turned her dragons into animatronics and her houses into mirages that cleared from his eyes with a few blinks.

"You… Are… Immensely powerful here." Mara panted, sitting beneath a tree after Ludwig had turned her dragon in flight into an impossible aircraft and caused it to plummet.

"You're getting stronger too." Ludwig told her, reached down with a hand to pull her up. The recent reversal in their usual dynamic hadn't affected their relationship. If anything, it strengthened it. "I felt you fighting back zhat time."

"I should hope so!" Mara exclaimed as she allowed the doctor to pull her up, out of the remains of the dragoncraft which had been grounded by high winds. "I put everything into that one." They limped home through the snow.

"Vell, I zhink you are doing vonderfully, but I cannot beliefe myself." Ludwig kissed her cheek. "I am so much more – able here."

"It's your world. In this place, you rule." Mara replied. "And it seems I drool."

"…Vas zhat a mofie reference?" Ludwig questioned.

"Yep. One of those classic children's films. Why?"

"It is zhe first one I hafe heard you make zhat vas not from a vork of classical literature originally." Ludwig replied as they walked up the steps into the station with care. The icicles, whose presence had become constant, did not rattle or shake as they walked under them. It seemed they were – as Mara had once supposed – a defensive measure, designed to come down upon the heads of intruders alone.

"I don't watch a lot of TV. Even before CORD became my home, I didn't. I'm not a passive entertainment person." Mara replied.

"Nein, I suppose zhat is logical. You are alvays up und about, making somezhing. Zhough, I hafe seen you read quite a bit." Ludwig helped her to sit down in a chair and brought the first aid kit.

"Reading is different. It's a mental challenge to read a book and imagine myself in that story. It's not to watch a movie and see everything in front of my face played out for me." Mara explained as she rolled up her pants leg to reveal an afflicted ankle – quite sprained.

"Oh, my. I'm going to have to pack zhis vizh some snow."

"Do you have to? We just came out of the cold." Mara winced as Ludwig prodded the joint gently and manipulated her foot in his hands.

"It vill keep zhe joint from swelling und make zhe healing go a little faster." Ludwig stood up and pressed a kiss to her nose. "Und it vill not be so bad. You are beside zhe fire und zhe rest of you vill be toasty."

"All right, all right. Heaven knows, I can never argue with you. Bring on the snow pack then."

As Ludwig happily tended to her bruises, they fell into a contented silence.

"Are you really, really sure you want to do this?" Mara questioned as they sat inside her Aston Martin – preparing for their trip across imaginary lines.

"Of course, I'm sure." Ludwig nodded, his expression firm. He was dressed in a green cardigan this morning and a pair of light, khaki pants. There were coats in the back and both wore light clothes as well – prepared for all sorts of weather. "We have to find a way to save these people and get out."

"…Of course, you're sure. Well, then, to Grandmother's house, we go." Mara stepped on the gas and they began driving through seemingly aimless miles of greenery gradually giving over to gold and rusty red.

Ludwig kept his eyes glazed an on the landscape, letting Mara take the lead. He spotted a few, tiny antelope as they drove and watched as the sandbank plum gave way to cacti and back again. They seemed to be entering a high desert, not unlike that which surrounded Albuquerque. Glancing behind, he was not surprised to see mountains.

Mara's teeth were grinding and Ludwig could hear them in spite of the music she was playing. "You really hate this place, don't you? Where are we?" He looked more closely at the landscape.

"Between Albuquerque and Clovis, New Mexico." Mara roughly replied. "It seems we've passed Fort Worth as well." The speed dial on the car was dangerously high. In a real world, Ludwig might be worried.

"You live in Albuquerque, isn't zhat right?" Ludwig questioned as they picked up speed and he began to feel just a tad apprehensive. It had been a car accident that brought him here and killed Thomas, after all. His hands began to clutch the armrests.

"Yes. I have for all of my life and my relatives aren't far from it. It's a convenient place to life, close to family." Mara was babbling, something was truly bothering her.

"Mara, is something wrong?" Ludwig almost timidly asked as they blazed through another small town. "You seem so tense... Zhis woman is just a Grandmother, as you say – vhy is she so fearsome?"

"Just a Grandmother..." Mara mockingly repeated – to date, Ludwig had never heard her belittle him in such a tone. It was quite clear that she was not joking this time. In her mind, he had said something unforgivably stupid. "Nothing is as it seems here and this woman is an abscess of evil almost as great as Lucy. Perhaps more so for how maliciously she pursues it. I refuse to believe that she can simply be so stupid as to not know what she is doing. No one is that stupid."

"Mara, I do not understand." The doctor humbly told her. "Please, explain to me."

"..." Mara's head seemed to clear briefly of all the hatred that had to be tumbling through her. "Ludwig... I'm sorry. I shouldn't... shouldn't be angry at you. It's her I'm angry at. Her and everything she's doing here. I hate her so much, Ludwig. I despise, loathe, revile her. There aren't enough words in the Thesaurus to say how much I hate her." And Mara's eyes teared up as she thought of it. "I hate her so much... that nothing compares."

"So you say, Mara, but you hafe yet to explain vhy..." Ludwig looked up into her eyes. "Is zhis somezhing I must do alone? I can go in und keep in contact vizh you surely. Zhere must be some vay to make a cell phone vork." The doctor reasoned with his fiancée, who had never looked more dragon-like as she snorted in immediate dismissal.

"No. I refuse to leave you unprotected in that woman's clutches." Mara replied. "She will just have to weather my hatred – or perhaps give up her thrice-accursed disguise."

Ludwig quickly realized that he would get no more sense out of Mara until they had gathered their information and were well away. She was locked in her own mind at the moment – all of her emotions gathering up into a maelstrom and Ludwig didn't want to be the unfortunate it was directed at when they reached the end of all this. He doubted that Mara, even in this clearly compromised state, would turn her full powers on his destruction – and if she did, would he be able to defend himself? Best not to think about it.

The city that they came to was a small one – barely a city, really. But it had hotels, a gym, grocery stores... Even a Chinese Buffet that Mara glanced at on their way in. Ludwig began to notice a pattern. This was Clovis – a city a mere three hours away from Mara's own home. It was statistically unlikely that both a grandmother and a granddaughter would be trapped in the same circumstances inside a machine such as CORD. This "Grandmother" had to be raising Mara's ire for the same reason that she never put out any pictures of her own family in any of her homes. By taking the form of Mara's remembered grandmother, this Grandmother must be corrupting those memories – destroying them passively.

No wonder Mara hated the woman with every fiber of her being. Ludwig resolved to keep both an eye on her and his own reality-bending powers at the ready. They had to suffice – if he dared – to prevent Mara from doing something rash.

The neighborhood they drove into was full of brick houses set against a golf course. Ludwig stared out the window as families – seemingly as real as anything could be – were moving about around them. "Mara, I zhought you told me zhat no one could create Facsimilies zhat stand up to observation except zhe Unknown."

"I did. And I didn't lie. It's just that it's not just the Grandmother creating these. She's filling in all of the gaps with her own memories, but, Ludwig… If you haven't figured it out by now you will soon. These are my memories. This is my grandmother's neighborhood – in Clovis. It's how I remember it almost exactly. Maybe it even is how it really is. But I can't know for sure. Do you see?" There was a wild desperation in her eyes – the black of her pupils had consumed her changing, oceanic iris. "Do you see why I hate her so much?"

"I see, Mara, I see." Ludwig assured her in murmurs. He turned his head back to their destination. "Which house are we going to?"

"The dark brown brick with the oak tree in the front yard." Mara grimly parked the car across the street from it and stepped out. "She's going to try to appeal to you as well. I don't know if she'll use your own memories or just try to manipulate you using mine, but be prepared."

Ludwig set his black shoes down on the plus, green grass and straightened to his full height – an almost useless gesture against Mara's bulk. His glasses flashed with the New Mexico sun. "I alvays am, Mara."

"That's my Ludwig." Mara grinned viciously. "Let's meet the witch."

The brown house was a single-floor home with pink and fuschia roses planted in front of the door. A pile of droppings drew Ludwig's eyes upwards to a mud and grass nest for a family of small, black, blue and orange birds. The babies made high-pitched chirps and shrieks down at them as the Westminster chimes played inside the house. Mara had rung the doorbell and then turned to look at the birds. She was tall enough – here – to peep into the nest directly. "…Just like I remember." The woman agitatedly whispered to Ludwig. "Almost perfect. There's no difference between what we're seeing and what I remember, but I know how this world works: There are differences. The details are wrong."

"Human memory is rarely so perfect. Zhere are associations zhat allow for zhe mind to remember a great deal more zhan ve could if ve remembered all details." Ludwig agreed, running his hand over the smooth bricks. "But zhe voman is likely just so lonely zhat she reaches out to anyone she sees und tries to create forms zhat vill allow her to draw zhem close. She is most likely not malicious und unavare zhat vhat she is doing has such deep effects on you, Mara."

Mara couldn't argue because at that moment, the screen door opened and an elderly woman with sandy-silver hair was stepping out, arms cast wide. "Come in this house! My precious grandchild!" And she hugged Mara around the middle as Ludwig stared. There was no denying the similarities between this woman and Mara, but there was no denying the difference either. Where Mara was tall and built of straight lines and angles, the Grandmother was all soft curves and a short, plump frame. Mara could have thrown her about like a sack of apples, but the blonde woman was frozen. There were tears in her eyes, streaming down her face and her form was shuddering – it looked like she might change if Ludwig didn't step in and break her free from the spell.

Mara had been understating the effects that this person had on her. Ludwig put a hand on her arm. "Aren't you going to introduce me, Mara?"

And just like that, Mara snapped back to herself. She put out an arm and pulled Ludwig close to her body, pushing away the grandmother gently. "…Dora, this is Ludwig. My fiancée."

"You've finally found someone!" Dora – was that Mara's grandmother or this person's true name – put her arms around Ludwig in another warm, comforting hug. "And what a handsome man too!"

"Danke, madam." Ludwig put all of his best effort into the smile he let creep across his face. It took less than he thought it would. She was so disarming, so pleasant, and warm. It was a safe, gentle feeling. "Is Mara's grandfazher here as vell?"

"Oh, dear…" Dora's eyes turned sad and her face fell. "It's been so long since I thought of poor

Sam… No, dear, my husband is long dead." She patted the doctor's elbow. "The cancer took him long ago. Now come in, come in. Don't sit out here on the porch."

The inside of the house was neat and cozy, decorated with glass pieces of art that shimmered in the sunlight that suffused the house from a bank of windows that filled up the front wall of the dining room. They were directly in front of a living room filled with three, large, plush couches and a reclining arm chair across from a home entertainment set – a flat-screen television surrounded by cabinets of movies.

"You must be so tired." Dora ushered them into the kitchen where a table – carved and painted out of some kind of white wood and stained artfully in blue – was set with bowls and spoons and a large, stainless steel soup pot was filling the air with a creamy, spicy scent. "Come in and eat something, then you can rest." She pressed her hands to Mara's shoulders and gently shook her. "Your fiancée is skinny as a stick, Mara. Do you not cook anymore?"

"I do, Dora, but Ludwig and I run and exercise. It tends to keep the weight off." Mara laid her coat across the back of a chair.

"I can see that. You look amazing, my dear granddaughter." The Grandmother ladled bowls of the spicy cream of chicken soup out for them and Ludwig found himself picking up a spoon.

Before Ludwig took his first bite, he flashed his eyes at Mara, checking to make sure it was safe. The blonde woman gave him a quick little nod and began eating for herself. Her form was… odd. It seemed as if something was still trying to change her. She certainly didn't fit as well in this world of the Grandmother's as she had in her own. Perhaps the Grandmother's dimension was trying to force its vision of her on Mara. If they stayed here long enough… Ludwig might have a peek at the real Mara – free of any imagined changes.

The Doctor couldn't decide if the prospect pleased or terrified him.

Mara pushed back from the table when their bowls were emptied. Dora tried to ply them with cheesecake. "You have to have at least a little piece before you go." She cajoled. "I know this was only a day-visit, but surely you can stay a little longer! You just got here."

"I know, Dora." Mara replied, standing up and nearly hitting her head on the angled skylight set into the roof. The stained glass piece of art hanging from it brushed the side of her hair and the change in angle sent a beam of lavender light across the kitchen. The iris seemed to wink at Ludwig as the yellow center of the flower disappeared and reappeared in the petals. "But we'll be back. We're not going far."

Ludwig didn't mention that they had learned almost nothing from their expedition as Mara forged a path to the door that left no room for Dora to persuade them into staying.

Mara drove them to a hotel not far from the golf course where the Grandmother lived. "We're back in my world. I can't explain how, but we are." She told Ludwig as they stepped into the lobby and went straight through to a suite on the top floor. The woman was morose and withdrawn. As Ludwig watched, her form became completely solid once again and that hatred that seemed to have vanished before Dora came back to her eyes.

"Then ve are safe?" Ludwig questioned, watching Mara from beside the veiled window with sharp, surgical eyes.

"I think so." Mara turned weary eyes up to him. "Still think she's a sweet, lonely old lady?"

"It vill take more efidence before I beliefe zhat she is so malicious." Ludwig slowly approached her, like a tiger or a lion, and settled at her side on the blue couch. "But I can see zhat she is hurting you, und zhat vorries me. Perhaps I should do zhis alone. I might hafe a better chance. It is not mein grandmozher, whose face she has stolen. Zhat gives me a slightly clearer head." He argued gently, rubbing his fingers tenderly into her shoulder and unbinding the knots of muscle.

"But that might also leave you open to her attacks – it might make you vulnerable. I can't allow that, Ludwig. I can't. I can't see her take you apart and put you back together some other way and I won't see you wandering around like a ghost. Some of the people here are Shadows – I've told you that – people she's killed, somehow. Maybe that's the secret. Maybe we have to find out how they die, but I can't risk losing you. Don't ask me to risk that." Mara was babbling now and Ludwig looked around for something to calm her. The only thing that presented itself was the remote control for the television.

A few hours of General Hospital seemed to calm Mara down enough to rest and Ludwig left her on the couch while he took a pad of complimentary paper and began scribbling down notes and ideas, laying them out in a web across the desk. He needed to put all of his thoughts together. This was a mystery he couldn't rely on Mara to understand or explain. It was up to him to rescue the Grandmother.

Chapter Seventeen

When Mara woke, Ludwig was collapsed over the desk with notes laid out in a star shape on the desk. His head was pillowed on his arms and she gently fixed his glasses for when he woke up before looking down at the pieces of paper. Picking up one, she read off. "Mara – Imaginative, young. Doubts self. Creates illusions to convince herself of the strength she possesses. Was put into CORD as a result of accident – Fell from lifeguard stand." The notes seemed to be on the people inside of CORD. Mara picked up Lucy's notes next. "Lucy – Believes or wants to believe – that he is a demon. Psychopathy, sadism, and sociopathy. Uses his imagination and strength of mind to attack and torment others. Disturbed."

Mara frowned slightly. Disturbed was one way to put it. She would probably have used a few words that would offend Ludwig's scientific tendencies.

Ludwig leaned back against her as she read. He had woken the moment she came close to his uncomfortable position. "…Vhy did you let me sleep like zhat?" He groaned as he stretched his shoulders and back.

"Good morning to you too." Mara was still reading his notes. "And I didn't – I was asleep myself. On the couch." Her eyes sparked a little mischief. "Am I in trouble?"

"Of course not." The doctor scoffed and pushed himself up with effort. "Zhough some tea vould not be amiss."

"Raspberry or Anise?" Mara offered, gesturing to the pot and pair of cups that had appeared on Ludwig's desk. There were bags of tea beside the porcelain pot and Ludwig picked Raspberry. He preferred Anise, but Mara couldn't stand the flavor – it reminded her too much of black licorice – and they both liked Raspberry.

The scent of bright berries and earthy green tea filled the small room soon after. Mara had moved to the window, was staring out over the small city. Ludwig poured her a cup of tea and offered it up with one hand, sipping with the other, as he came to join her.

"Thank you." Mara's eyes were foggy. "…My grandmother is dead. My real Grandma Dora. It was cancer that took her, but not Grandpa."

"Zhis Grandmozher… She has created an alternate. Somezhing zhat allows her to maintain control und is close enough to the old story zhat you might grow to accept it." Ludwig dissected the admission and the relation to their current target easily. "…On a more human lefel, Mara…" The doctor turned up to her and laid a hand on her arm. "I am sorry, zhat you had to go zhrough zhat."

"…It was a long time ago." Mara's voice sounded dead and her eyes were blacking again. "I hate her… for making me see this. For trying to fool me. It's not making it better, Ludwig. Having her…

alive in front of me again... hurts worse than knowing she's dead."

"I understand, Mara." Ludwig pulled her closer. She was taller today – ten feet at least. She was in no danger of knocking her head here, where the world was made for her, but she would never manage the Grandmother's tiny house, with the hanging decorations made of stained glass and the delicate furniture unless she managed to shrink herself back down. With how insecure and pained she had to be feeling, Ludwig didn't imagine she would manage it.

"...Maybe you should go alone. But take something... something that will let me keep track of you." Mara was digging in her pockets and pulled out an old-style flip-top cell-phone. "That'll do."

"Danke, mein Engel." Ludwig smiled softly. Mara trusted him – that was the only reason she would let him go alone. "I vill fisit your grandmozher und try to get more information from her."

"If there's any trouble, call me." When Ludwig opened the phone, it had a single, large, red button that was labeled "Mara."

"I zhink I can manage zhis. After all..." Ludwig's blue eyes twinkled behind the panes of glass. "She is just a grandmozher. Surely I can imagine zhat I can defeat her, if necessary."

"Call me if there's trouble anyway." Mara kissed his nose and then his lips. Hers were papery and had been nibbled and bitten in anxiety. She had to bend almost in half to reach him. "...And it seems

I've grown too tall in the night." There was a moment's pause. "But if you're going to be out, I'm going to indulge in a larger height."

"Do that, Mara, if it helps you." Ludwig ordered. "And I'll go face zhe vitch."

"Don't let her manipulate you into cleaning her house for three days in exchange for a flaming skull." Mara told him.

"...Vhat?" The doctor blinked owlish eyes up at her, uncomprehending.

"I take it you've never heard of Baba Yaga?"

"Un monster from Russian folklore..." Ludwig shook his head. "Nefermind. I understood zhe sentiment, Mara, but zhe oddities of your education could drife me to distraction."

"We're all mad here." Mara's eyes sparkled briefly and Ludwig noticed that she had dropped a foot. "Now go before I kidnap you back to our mountain lodge and abandon this insane plan entirely."

Ludwig didn't need any further warning. Stopping only to put himself in order, he kissed Mara on the cheek and walked out the anonymous hotel door. He felt rather like a child in Mara's world as he walked along the hallways and into the elevator. The world didn't become normal again until he stepped outside and spotted a small car with a giant, red bow on top and the keys dangling from the ignition. Mara's idea of a joke, doubtless.

Ludwig waved up at the fourth-floor window where he knew Mara was still standing and staring and settled in the car's driver seat, turning the key.

The way back to the Grandmother's house was printed out in Ludwig's mind, but even if it hadn't been, the doctor was certain that this world would not allow him to be lost on his way to Grandmother's house.

Sure enough, Ludwig pulled up the long, concrete driveway to the pine trees that shielded the cars from any stray golf balls. As he turned, looking over at the house beside them, he saw a dog... a rather pitiful looking creature, all locked up in a wire enclosure too small to play in. It was covered in dirt and holes, the only shade coming from a single juniper bush. There was a long worn-out rope toy and the dog didn't seem to have even the spirit to bark. Ludwig's soft heart went out to it.

"Hello, zhere, boy." He softly spoke to the dog as he approached the enclosure and held out a hand to be sniffed. "Hello, zhere. I'm a friend."

The spotted brown-and-white dog was so starving for affection that it came up to him and sniffed his finger tentatively before coming close to the fence and pushing against his hand as Ludwig rubbed his ears and head. This poor dog... In a real world, he never would have been able to do anything about it except call animal control. It occurred to him suddenly that the Grandmother wasn't going anywhere and that there were no police to stand in between him and his urgings.

"…Hang on, Sveet." Ludwig cooed to him, disregarding the dirty collar except to loosen it around the dog's neck. "Ve vill get you out of zhere, don't you vorry. Just hang on."

The dog let him pet it and loosen its collar and Ludwig wished he had food to offer it. He seemed such a sweet animal, if a little timid. Somehow, he knew Mara would love to see this wonderful dog free of this depressive pen.

But first, he had come here on a mission. With a look of regret over his shoulder, he walked around to the front of the Grandmother's house and knocked on the front door.

The baby birds were making good progress, if the row of heads too big to hide in the nest were any indication. Ludwig smiled up at them as the Grandmother opened up the door. "Oh, Ludwig, I didn't expect you back so soon!" She looked almost exactly the same as she had yesterday. "Please, please, come in."

"Danke." Ludwig stepped over the threshold and took off his shoes out of habit. "How are you today, Grandmozher?"

"Oh, I do like being called that by my only granddaughter's fiancée." The old woman smiled up at him. "Come and sit, we can talk over some coffee – or would you prefer tea?"

"Tea please." It was served iced with lemon and Ludwig didn't object when Dora offered him sugar. "Dankeschon."

"Well, Ludwig, it's been quite a long time since I could pick a young man's brain before he whisked away one of my children." Dora told him as she sat on her couch. "I only had one daughter, you know, and of course, only one granddaughter. I'm so glad that she's finally found someone. Perhaps we could break this pattern finally." The old woman gave him a charming smile that looked absolutely radiant in her doughy face. She was the image of a perfect grandmother.

"I vould like zhat." Ludwig smiled charmingly back. "Mara und I hafe not spoken in detail about children yet, but ve vould like to hafe zhem someday." He couldn't just accuse her outright of deception. That would put her off in a millisecond. He had to do this right – earn her trust and subtly find a way to work the oddities of their world of CORD in.

"Good. Children are a responsibility, but they're such a joy as well." Dora smiled up at a group of five photographs on the wall. The one in the center was a photograph of a younger Dora with a man that had to be the surviving Grandfather, the four around them were photographs of their children with their own brides and husband. There was a thump in Ludwig's chest as he realized that he was looking at Mara's parents. They were unmistakable – flanked by three photographs of blonde children. The only blonde children on the wall. Mara had a school-girl smile with a string of blue beads around her neck in her photograph. Her parents were standing with their hands entwined before an altar – her father in a dress uniform, her mother in a flowing, white dress.

Mara had her mother's face and her father's smirk. They were at once so similar and so different – these two people and the vivacious woman he knew. And then, it occurred to him. He had no idea what Mara's parents looked like. His imagination had to be filling in the gap and that meant that these were not her parents – never had been. His mind settled as he calmed himself. For a moment, he had been excited to see what they looked like.

Re-focused, Ludwig returned his gaze to the Grandmother as he raised his blue glass to his lips. The glass had little nobs of glass over the surface that made gripping it easy. "Has it been fery long since you last saw your children?" He began to probe gently.

"To a mother, it's always too long since she's seen her children." The Grandmother easily deflected. "But that's the problem when they scatter to the four winds. Christmas and Thanksgiving are the best we can hope for and anything extra is a blessing."

"Vhere did Mara's parents go?" Ludwig questioned, curious. "I met Mara in Albuquerque, of course…" This was a trap of a question and he knew it. He was hoping to find out how much Dora knew and whether it was all accurate. Mara's parents had set out and had their start together in Florida, but had moved to New Mexico when she was born.

"Oh, they went somewhere near Tallahassee I think. At least at first. I was very glad when they came back to New Mexico." Dora revealed, sipping at her own iced tea. "Imagine poor Mara, Ross-Boss, and

Atticus growing up in Florida, my word. The weather down there is quite abominable."

"Ross-Boss?" Ludwig was briefly thrown off of his questioning line by the absurd nickname.

"Ross-Boss is Mara's younger brother, dear. All of his siblings had more than one syllable in their name, so it felt quite silly that he only had one." Dora explained easily. "So, he became Ross-Boss. Because it rhymes."

"Of course." Ludwig should have guessed at that. He would have to ask Mara how much of this was accurate when he returned to the hotel. Any discrepancy might allow him to understand this woman and her psyche as well as how to get her to reveal the truth. "Do all of your children hafe nicknames?"

"I was never able to figure out good ones for them. Ross is a grandchild and his parents nicknamed him. You should have heard them calling their children back from the duck pond. They always tripped over Ross or said his name twice because it only had one syllable. Then, Mara called Ross "Ross-Boss" while they were having an argument and it stuck."

"Zhat seems... Fery like her." And it did, in a strange way. This Grandmother knew Mara better than Ludwig would have expected an imposter to. Perhaps he would get no further taking this subtle route. Perhaps it was time to probe directly. "Madam, I am avare zhat you are not really Mara's grandmozher. You are vone of zhe fictims inside of

CORD. Do you understand vhat I am saying? You hafe been in a coma by some means und you are here to heal und to vake up. I am here to help, but you must help me."

"Dear, what are you saying?" Dora scolded him. "I'm not in a coma and I am Mara's Grandmother. I'm the only one she has – her mother's mother is long dead and I've always looked out for her when she needed it. It's not kind or right to lie to an old lady like that."

"Madam, I am not lying. Mara is here in CORD because she slipped into a coma after falling from a lifeguard stand. I am here – " the flash of operating lights in his eyes, the sounds of his own heartbeat monitor in his ears. " – Because I vas in a horrible accident und I too slipped into a coma. Ve are all inside of a machine called CORD zhat allows zhe human brain to interact vizh a computer interface."

"That sounds like something out of my husband's science fiction novels, Mr. Ludwig. What you're saying resembles real life about as much as Star Trek does." Dora waved the notion away. "I don't know why you're teasing me like this. I don't want to hear this nonsense. I thought you were here to speak to me and to get to know me before you marry my granddaughter, but I see that isn't the case. You're here to tease me and drive me mad." She stood up and loomed over him with her arms akimbo. "Well, if you're going to say such wild things, then you can just leave and not come back until you're willing to be polite. It isn't nice and it isn't fair of you." Dora pointed at the door. "Come back when you're ready to be reasonable and not a moment before."

Ludwig stood up with painstaking dignity. "Madam, I am not a liar und I am not teasing you. I take no pleasure in our situation, but it is vhat it is. Ve cannot change it by lifing in denial. I vill return tomorrow und I vill talk to you more, but my position cannot change: Hafe you never noticed anything different? Anything vhatsoever? Mara and I have. Many times. Und if you ask Mara, she vill say the same to you: Ve are not in the real world."

"I said come back when you're ready to be reasonable!" And she chased him from the house. For a long few minutes, Ludwig sat under an oak tree and thought about the situation. How could he reach someone who was determined not to be reached in a world where the mind ruled?

Perhaps by some will of Ludwig's own, perhaps by the manipulation of the Grandmother, Ludwig heard a dog begin to bark and was reminded of the neglected pup in the enclosed pen next door. Standing, he went at once to free it. As soon as he walked into sight, the dog stopped barking and wagged its tail. He seemed much more lively than he had before and Ludwig reached in to rub his ears affectionately. "I'm back, boy. I promised I vould come back und I did, didn't I? I am your friend." With a sneaking look around himself – the golf course and the neighborhood was deserted – he opened the gate and let the dog out. "Come, come mein freund. Ve vill go und you vill hafe a good home at last. No more pens und lonely days."

The dog easily bounded into Ludwig's car and licked his cheek as Ludwig started the ignition. The doctor kept a hand on his neck, stroking him, as they moved out. The soft fur beneath his hand was dirty and dust covered the seat where the dog was lying, but Ludwig couldn't bring himself to care. In this world, if he wanted the car to be clean, it would be clean, after all, or he could always drive up to a car wash and ride through it a few times – take out the vacuum from outside of the wet wash and clean the inside. This wasn't a real world – no need to worry about having enough change.

His eyes fell on a "House For Sale" sign and he briefly tried to imagine what it would be like to return to the real world. For Mara to introduce him to her real grandfather, and to take him to a house that was – by all accounts – remarkably similar to this one. Would they be impressed that she had found a doctor or simply horrified that he was so much older than she was? Even if Mara was twenty-two – her high end estimate – that left him twenty years older than she was.

Maybe Mara was right. Perhaps this imaginary world was a good enough place to live – insulated from the harsh realities that would plague them in the real world. Family and money and age.

The dog licked his hand and looked up at him with adoring eyes. It seemed that even here, in this imaginary world, there could be variation. They had never had a pet before.

Ludwig closed his eyes and shook his head. No. This was not him. These were simply his anxieties and fears. Even if Mara's parents worried because she had chosen an older man, they would learn to accept that he adored her for the woman he saw inside her. Even if they worried that she would regret her decision, they would come to understand that there was nothing that could weaken the bond they had formed. In going home, they did not have to fear. They had only to rejoice.

Gathering that resolve around him, Ludwig took a deep breath and nodded to himself. He would go back to the Grandmother tomorrow and he would try again. And he would go again and again until she revealed what they needed to know. They would save the Grandmother. If it was a solution that required imagination – Mara would provide it. If the sheer strength of reality was what was needed, then Ludwig would put himself to work. Nothing could stand in their way – not if they worked together.

Book Two: Intuition
Prologue

The Rattlesnake

Memories slip through our fingers just when we need them the most. Still, they linger – not in details, but in fuzzy kinds of feelings. Sometimes, something just doesn't smell right, and our brains can fill in the gaps. Sometimes, these leaps of logic – that nebulous thing that we call intuition – don't make sense, even to those who see them in their mind. Consider the rattlesnake.

The rattlesnake is a creature with a most unique system of defense. Equipped with venomous fangs and with the ability to leap several times its body length, it does not immediately recourse to its offensive capabilities. Instead, it uses a rattle made of dry scales coming from the end of its tail to warn intruders. It is a very American creature – in my estimation.

Now, think of your childhood. Unless you live in the countryside, you've likely never heard a rattlesnake before. Maybe you could find an audio file online. It's not a discomfiting sound. In the peace of the country, it's one that stands out, certainly, but if you had never heard of a rattlesnake before and had no knowledge of the toxin in its venom or its bite, then you might not want to run away at first. Perhaps you'd simply be curious and wander towards the sound. The exact opposite of what the snake wants you to do to avoid having to break its neutrality and bite you.

Curiosity – it seems – is not a failing limited to humans. Merely, it is most prevalent in us.

But I digress. The point is not curiosity. The point is intuition.

If you grew up knowing what a rattlesnake was and what it sounded like or – heaven forbid – have ever been bitten by a snake, then you most likely associate the sound with danger or disaster and an ominous pit opens in your stomach whenever you think of it. But a rattling noise is not in itself a bad thing. It's simply a warning. A warning that might trigger a subconscious reaction in the most innocent circumstance. To me, a cellphone on vibrate against a metal table sounds like a rattlesnake giving its warning.

When you hear that sound then, the sound of the cell phone on the table, your subconscious might hear the rattlesnake. Instinctively, your fuzzy memories – made so by age and the likelihood that you do not re-visit your encounters with poisonous snakes with fond eagerness – think they have heard a rattlesnake. Your conscious mind begins to prepare you for danger – igniting your adrenal gland and sending warning tingles through your fingers and toes. Immediately, you begin to feel dread as you look down at the source of the noise and find your phone rattling on the table. It is clearly not a snake, but the feeling remains. That feeling of paranoia.

What has happened? You wonder. Reaching for your phone, you think of all the horrible things that might have happened to those you hold dear. Perhaps your mother has been in a car accident and is badly injured. Perhaps your boss finds your performance lacking and has decided to fire you. Maybe your significant other has found someone else. Expecting the worst, you pick up the phone.

If it's bad news, your subconscious is vindicated: You were expecting it! A leap of intuition and your mind has prepared itself to receive bad news before the news itself was confirmed. With a feeling of relief – that you were right, that the problem, whatever it was, is revealed to you – you can breathe again. The rattlesnake has given its warning and you heeded it.

If it's good news, then relief floods through your whole body. The tingles and prickles stop and you have a good laugh at yourself. What a silly mistake! Appeased, your subconscious soothes itself back into a sleepy state of lethargy and you can rest easy. All is well in your world. Your intuition was wrong: It happens! You've already forgotten the sharpest of the sensations, the edge of that dread.

What if you were sitting on a subway platform? Trains rattle, sometimes. That sound might remind you of the proverbial snake. Suddenly, your senses sharpen. You're certain that something terrible is going to happen and your eyes survey the crowd in front of you. Some instinct – the same instinct – is preparing you for disaster.

There! A little girl has been playing with her ball and suddenly the toy is rolling away – towards the tracks! You rush forwards and grab her shoulder, pulling her back from danger, as the rattlesnake pulls into the platform and its scales glimmer in the yellow lights. The snake gave its warning and the warning was heeded – the child will live to see another day.

The fuzziness of the memories of the rattlesnake is what enabled intuition to step in. Intuition is nine-tenths association with one tenth vindication. When your intuition is right, when you save the child, you feel invincible. Your mind – that glorious neural machine – has predicted successfully that disaster was imminent and you stepped in and stopped it. When your intuition is wrong, then no harm is done. There was no child. The ball was not dropped and no one was running towards the train. The snake rattled in vain and your mind forgot the rattle as soon as it realized it was safe.

Intuition can save humans from unknown dangers. Sick gut feelings allow us to identify that poisonous stranger for what he is. Dread, fear, association… Intuition. It was so important – so important – to see intuition in action. To examine that and to understand it. To reveal what intuition could tell us about the human mind and how we could manipulate it.

It was so important to see them react and interact. To see if they would learn to trust each other. If they would allow their instincts free reign. It was about possibility and defense.

Chapter One

Mara was shocked when she saw the dog walking along beside Ludwig. "Patches!"

"Patches? You know zhis dog?" Ludwig questioned as Mara called the animal to her and rubbed its ears, feeding it salami from a sandwich in her hand.

"Only by the name I always called him." Mara hugged the dog close and rubbed its back. "I used to see him in that enclosure his negligent owners had put him in and I wanted nothing more than to break him out and take him home with us." She scratched his neck and took the ugly collar that had been wrapped around his neck off. "Look at you! Look at you, baby." She cooed to him.

"Patches isn't a fery creatife name." Smirking, Ludwig knelt beside the woman – who seemed to have shrunk down to seven feet as she petted and played with Patches' ears.

"Shut up – I was a child when I named him." Mara's eyes teared up and watered. "If this was the real Patches, he would be thirteen years old."

"It's a good zhing zhat he is not!" Ludwig declared over Mara's emotion. "Zherefore, he could be a puppy for all ve know."

"You're right." Mara hugged him. "Thank you, Ludwig. I never like to see animals suffering, but Patches was always haunting me and I never had the courage to do anything about it."

"In zhis vorld, zhere is no reason to leafe zhe dog unhappy." Ludwig kissed her cheek and Patches licked his own. "Ach! You silly dog." He stood up, getting out of the range of Patches' tongue.

"Did you have any luck with her?" Mara questioned Ludwig as she played with Patches on their hotel room floor.

Ludwig had retired to the desk and taken a second pad of paper out, making notes. "Mara, is one of your little brozhers called Ross-Boss?"

"Yes." Mara dourly replied. Ludwig didn't need to look at her to know that her pupils threatened to invade her iris again. "I regret telling her so much – she used my grandmother's face against me. I was vulnerable, new. I just wanted that familiarity, but instead of making herself into my friend, she tried to abscond with my family ties."

"She used you. She's using you. I'm just not sure vhy. If the intention vas to make you feel at home und to ease your transition, zhen surely she vould allow zhe disguise to fall vhen she realized zhat it is only hurting you." Ludwig was making notes again, his hands scribbling across the paper, thinking over all he had learned. "Her disguise suggests zhat she is a cold-reader, vhich is a technique often used by Mediums to confince ozhers zhat zhey are really psychic. It is a simple illusion – not uncommon vizh zhose who practice sleight of hand und other illusions."

"So, what? You think she was a magician in the real world and that she's using her gifts to impersonate my grandmother? But why?"

"Zhat I am less sure of. If she is fery old or has grandchildren of her own, she may simply be missing zhem und seeking replacements." Ludwig leaned back in the straight-backed office chair and thought. "I still zhink zhat malice is a step too far. I beliefe zhat loneliness und desire for company are far more likely."

"They are." Mara grudgingly agreed. "But it would be so much easier if it was just someone's sick idea of fun."

"I agree, zhat vould be simpler." Ludwig arranged his notes on the desktop again in the star pattern. "But life is rarely so simple. She seems to be keeping to zhis fantasy quite vell, und her narrative leafes little to be doubted. Ve vill hafe to go ofer vhat I discussed vizh her to see if zhere are any discrepancies. Zhere must be a crack zhat ve can exploit somehow."

"There isn't one. I told her everything, when I trusted her, and then, when I came to visit her again, I found myself in grandma's house with Grandma Dora waiting for me." Mara cut her eyes to Ludwig and away as she thought. "Well... You saw me yesterday. She looks and sounds exactly like her."

"You lofed your grandmozher dearly." Ludwig didn't need to be a psychologist to see that Mara needed his ears more than his mind at the moment. He abandoned his deductions and notations and sat on the couch beside her, resting against her and encouraging her to lean against him as well. "Zhere is no shame in vishing zhat she vas here vizh you. If you had created a Facsimile of her, I vould not hafe judged you und I vill not judge you now."

"…Thanks." Mara tucked him into her arms like a plush toy and Ludwig realized that she had expanded – in her anxiety and grief – to nearly four times his size. He hugged an arm – now large enough to squeeze the life from him with a careless press and stroked the skin at the wrist. Patches hopped up as well and sat in the crook of her elbow, resting his muzzle against her breast and looking up at her eyes with his own, soulful ones. They sat like that for a long time before she began to shrink back into her normal size again.

Ludwig and Mara parted again in the morning – Ludwig back to Dora's house to try and get more information, Mara to play with Patches. This time, the doctor decided to walk and try to think over how exactly he was going to play this. If he went straight for the heart of the matter, Dora would become hostile again. There was no way for him to pry away at the knowledge that Dora had of Mara's family since – according to Mara – she had told the woman everything. In the context of CORD, that probably meant that she had opened her memories up for inspection and Dora had read them off, memorizing them to use for herself.

If that was true, though, it meant that Mara's mind had been completely open – both to reading and to manipulation. Why hadn't the Grandmother simply taken or forced Mara to do or give her whatever she wanted then? The only logical supposition was that the Grandmother wanted Mara's affection, but she wanted it given willingly. It was highly likely that she created similar illusions for all other visitors to her world, but she had never had to face two people at once.

Bringing Ludwig into the Grandmother's world with her might have saved Mara from further manipulations. If Ludwig was correct and the Grandmother had woven some sort of emotional spell around each of her victims, then the web was determined and exactly created to entrap one particular individual. By adding a second person, they had defeated the most basic portion of the trap: Isolation. The Grandmother couldn't target Mara's weaknesses if Ludwig's own strengths were covering her. And, since Ludwig had come with Mara and the Grandmother had been forced to reveal herself in this form – Dora – she wouldn't have a chance to create a similar web to entrap Ludwig.

In short, by sheer luck, Ludwig mused, they might have blundered into the only way to keep themselves safe and alive against this opponent. Now, Ludwig had to apply his medical training to convince the Grandmother that they were not a threat and that it would be wise to drop her illusions and let them help her to wake up. It was likely that the Grandmother had created this world and entrapped others as a means of simulating the family that the coma she was in had separated her from. Convince her that they could help her get back to them, and her need to entrap Mara would vanish.

"Good morning, Dora." Ludwig addressed the old woman. She had dressed in a lilac sweater this morning and he noticed that the air felt a touch chillier. It seemed that this world was rapidly approaching either fall or winter. "I've returned. Mara is still debating on vhat dress to vear to our vedding."

"I do hope she chooses something in Velvet. I know she always loved that material." Dora stepped back from the door. "Come in, then, Ludwig. I'm baking pumpkins and you can help me."

"Ja, of course." Ludwig noticed that a shrug of fall leaves had been laid out on top of the mantle and that there was an arranged cornucopia on the table. Thanksgiving then, as only a family Thanksgiving could be. "Pumpkins for pies?" He laid his coat on the back of a chair.

"No, don't leave that there." Dora scolded him. "Go hang it up in the office where it belongs." The Grandmother retreated into the kitchen and Ludwig was forced to explore the house in the direction that Dora had pointed. Opening a door, he found himself in an office that was dominated by bookshelves and a bed, neatly made up and prepared for guests. The cover over it was green and gold with a rusty red woven into it. Ludwig found the closet full of various coats – most very thick and waterproofed.

There was a sled – one with red runners and familiar braided candy-cane striped rope – leaning up against the back of the closet. It was Mara's sled. Ludwig hung his coat up among the heavy winter wear and smiled at the sled.

Dora had three pie pumpkins on the counter when Ludwig joined her. She was splitting them with a meat cleaver. "There you are. Take this over, please. Your hands are stronger than mine."

"Of course, of course." Ludwig took the heavy knife and wedged it into the pumpkins, pressing down against the back of the blade until the pumpkin split in two. "Do you hafe a rubber mallet zhat I could use?"

"No, unfortunately. That would make the job so much easier." Dora was mixing together pie crusts made with plenty of butter and what smelled like bourbon. "I always mean to get one every year, but then Thanksgiving sneaks up on me and I can't seem to remember to get it."

"Mara has zhe same problem sometimes." Ludwig smiled fondly. "Eferyone seems to at some point or anozher."

"It's one of the foibles of being human." Dora agreed, patting her curled hair as the stand mixer churned together the butter and flour. "Have you ever rolled a perfect pie crust, Ludwig?"

"Nein, I cannot say zhat I hafe. It alvays tears holes in zhe middle und I have to patch zhem in zhe pan." In his defense, the doctor almost never made pies anyway. Usually, he and Mara would put together a strudel if they were going to make a dessert. Mara preferred the braided look and he found them, on the whole, less fussy.

"Then stick close and let me teach you." Dora told him. "But first, pumpkins into the oven. They need to roast before we can fill the pies."

Chapter Two

Ludwig found himself eating a slice of creamy pumpkin pie filled with spices and the soft, fruity flavor of the squash itself. "Danke, Dora." He accepted a cup of hot chocolate with nutmeg and cinnamon sprinkled over the top. Now that they had had such a companionable afternoon, it was time to bring up the explosive topic once again. "Dora, now zhat ve're here und ve are calm, I vould like to bring up somezhing zhat you vill not like."

"Oh?" Dora sipped her own cup of tea. "And what's that?" Her blue eyes were tired and knowing. It was clear that she realized exactly what he was getting at.

"You must hafe realized zhat zhis vorld is not zhe real one." Ludwig gestured around them. "Mara, she is too tall, after all, is she not? She barely fits in zhis house."

"I haven't noticed anything of the kind." Dora told him with the weary tolerance of someone who was convinced that their conversation partner was quite insane. "Mara looks exactly like she always has to me. And so what if she is a little tall? You surely don't mind that – you're marrying her."

Ludwig rolled his eyes and stood up, raising a hand up towards the roof to illustrate how tall Mara was. "Ja, und I do not mind her height, but it is a physical impossibility zhat a voman could grow naturally to tvelfe feet. Efen Goliazh vas only nine feet tall."

"Ludwig, really. There's no need to make fun of an old woman. I can see that you're clearly disturbed, but this is a little too far. You're a doctor, you should realize that what you speak of is insane. Mara has never been twelve feet tall." Dora set down her cup and stood, patting his shoulders. "I'm going to call Mara to take you home."

Ludwig sighed and leaned his head on his fist as Dora picked up a phone and dialed. This would be interesting – he had never seen Mara use a phone before. Perhaps it worked like everything else in this crazy world. Think hard enough about the person you're trying to reach and they would know and hear you.

"Mara? Ludwig needs to go home. Can you come and take him?" Dora was speaking into the phone and Ludwig folded his arms, listening in shamelessly. "If you want my opinion, I wouldn't take up with someone so obviously mentally disturbed. How can you expect him to be a good husband?"

Ludwig stood up – not wanting to listen anymore – and went back to the office to take his coat. His eyes scanned over the shelves of books, looking for anything that could help him. The titles, he noticed, were oddly regular – two copies of Stephen King's "The Shining" and three sets of the whole Harry Potter series. Ludwig reached out and touched them, studying the shelves. This had to be it – the puzzle, the weak point. Something was hiding here and he would find it.

He pulled aside the Harry Potter books and revealed a photograph in a stained glass frame. It was of a family of smiling, dark-skinned people. Ludwig studied it and realized that the Grandmother was in the picture – in the center left, surrounded by three grandchildren, a granddaughter the most prominent of all of them. As Ludwig studied the photograph, he heard the front door open and close and dropped it. As the glass broke, Ludwig swore and he had the guilty feeling that he was about to be caught out doing something bad.

"Ludwig?" Mara's voice, oddly strained and stressed. She had come to pick him up after all. The doctor grabbed his coat and stepped out, hurrying. "There you are. Dora called me saying that you were overwrought."

"She seems to zhink zhat I am crazy for pointing out zhat zhis vorld is not real." Ludwig calmly agreed, pulling on the tan-colored wool coat. "Shall ve?"

"I suppose we should." Mara put an arm around his shoulders. "Ready to give up yet?"

"Nefer!" The doctor fiercely replied.

Dora came out from the kitchen, holding a container with a quarter of the pumpkin pie they had made that afternoon. "Mara, be sure to be back later this week for Thanksgiving." Dora instructed her "granddaughter." "We would miss you terribly."

"Of course… Dora." Mara seemed about to say something else before she stopped the words. Her

visage was shifting, fuzzy, again. "Come on, Ludwig."
She opened the door and practically fled. "…It's
always either Christmas or Thanksgiving here." She
told Ludwig as they collapsed into her car, Mara going
briefly boneless against the seat. "Sometimes it's
summer, but only rarely."

"Zhat aligns vizh my obserfations." Ludwig told
her. "I beliefe more zhan efer zhat zhis voman is
using you to replace her own family. Und I may hafe
found somezhing zhat vould allow us to confront her
vizh zhe truzh. In zhe office, zhere are false books on
zhe shelfes. Zhey vere hiding a photograph: It vas of
a different family vizh zhe Grandmozher right in zhe
center. Zhere must be ozher piece of efidence zhat
she is not vhat she seems."

"False books? Now that sounds like something
out of a novel." Mara chuckled. "Well, we always
come to spend the weekend for Thanksgiving – that
should give us plenty of time to explore and make a
case against her. Now, come on. Patches is waiting
for us at the hotel."

"A whole veekend? Do you zhink you can
stand zhat?" Ludwig questioned, turning to look up at
her as he pulled the seatbelt across himself. "Ve still
don't know how zhis Grandmozher ends up killing her
fictims."

"I do." Mara replied. "It happens when they fully
accept her as their grandmother and surrender. Their
minds open and she floods in, buries them under her
own madness and they suffocate. Her force of
personality cracks the mind open and she just takes

whatever it is she wants and then you're a Shadow, wandering around here… Part of this place for forever."

"Mara… Ve're avare. Ve're ready." Ludwig placed one of his small hands over hers. "If ve must spend a few nights sleepless, zhen vhat of it? If vorst comes to vorst, ve could pretend to go shopping und retreat for a few hours of sleep. But ve must find zhe vay out, und to do zhat, ve must make sure zhat ve can find zhe vay, or else ve might just get stuck in anozher layer of zhis vorld."

"…You're right." Mara sighed. "I hate that you're right, but you are. If we're going to do this, best let it be done properly and quickly. But I'm not going to sleep in that witch's house and I don't want you to either."

"I vould nefer let you or I let down our guards so badly." Ludwig agreed. "Ve vill stay at zhe hotel und be at zhe house during zhe day for zhis Zhanksgiving. Ve find zhe ozher photographs und ve confront her!"

"You make it sound so simple, so possible. Why do I feel as if everything is about to go horridly wrong?" Mara bitterly threw the car into gear and Ludwig could feel that her hand was cold with fright.

Thanksgiving had always been something of a lavish affair for Ludwig. Christmas was a more private holiday for the doctor, but he would have moved worlds to be home with his family for Thanksgiving.

The idea that they would spend this one together with the facsimiles of Mara's family wasn't appealing. For the past two days, they had been resting almost constantly – trying to make sure that they wouldn't have to sleep during the holiday. Now, Mara was dressed up in one of her suits and Ludwig was wearing a cardigan and tie.

"You look adorable." Mara told him. She was carefully controlling her height at a good-sized eight feet and her tattoos were swirling. The text was leaking out of her sleeves and collar. Ludwig had never known her to have that happen before. It had to be a terrible strain on her systems.

Ludwig wrapped his arms around her neck and pulled himself up to her level, feeling the muscles tense as she supported his weight with ease. "Danke, you look fery cute too." He pressed a kiss to her lips. "Ve vill be fine." They had packed a suitcase for camouflage.

"I hope so." Mara gently set him down. "If she's anything like me, though, she'll know as soon as we try to start searching for these false books you found."

"Ja, and you'll hafe to hold her off until I can find zhe proof, but I know ve can do it." Ludwig assured her.

"It's going to be more complicated than that, I can feel it." Mara pushed the button for the lobby on the elevator. "And you know it, I bet."

"I do." Ludwig nodded slightly. "But zhat does not mean zhat ve should look on zhe bad side. It means zhat ve must be vary und look on zhe bright side as much as possible. Ve vill keep our spirits up und our vork vill be good."

"There isn't a think on earth that can break you down, is there, Ludwig?" Mara questioned. "You always bounce back to your feet and keep on rolling."

"Ja. Zhat is vhy you lofe me."

"I know. That doesn't mean I understand it."

The house's driveway was filled with cars and Mara and Ludwig were forced to park on the street. Mara suddenly became very weak in the knees as she looked up at the house, with its lit windows. Ludwig could see why. In the windows, there were people setting the long, dining table and laying out plates and glasses – stemmed, for wine. And Ludwig recognized them from the photographs on the wall.

"My God... Don't do this to me." Mara's mouth was dry and her lips were chapped. "Please, don't make me do this."

"Mara..." Ludwig took her hand. "Ve can do zhis. Ve can."

"I can't! I just can't!" Mara backed up, trying to pull herself away from him and get back into the car. "I want to go home! I want to go home!" She was getting taller again and Ludwig was finding it harder to keep ahold of her fingers with one hand. He grabbed her with the other as well, pulling back.

"Mara! It is not real! You know zhey are not real!" Ludwig held on and dug his heels in. "You must do zhis, because I cannot do it on mein own!"

"Let go of me!" Mara jerked back and Ludwig closed his eyes. He had never done this to Mara before, but he pressed out – trying to let her see through his eyes. Mara's family couldn't be here – therefore they weren't here. Grandma Dora wasn't alive, therefore she wasn't here either. It was all so impossible that there was only one other option.

Mara stopped struggling suddenly as Ludwig reached for her. Blinking, she came back to herself and her hand shrank in his. "Ludwig, what are you doing?"

"…It's different now?" Ludwig opened his eyes and turned his eyes back on the house. "Vhat's happening?"

"It's- it's still Thanksgiving, but look – The people inside the house. They aren't my family anymore. Ludwig, they're… Well, there's no nice way to say this, they're my family, but imagine my family being African." Mara pointed through the window glass.

Ludwig looked back up through the windows. There was Ross-Boss, but his skin had darkened and the crew-cut he was sporting was made of tightly curled, black hair.

"…Oh, my god… that… witch!" And there was something dark and deeply dangerous in her voice. Her skin was puckering with scales and her eyes had turned almost completely black with an ember of burning blue and gold at the center. "That witch used my memories! She pushed her own family into my mind!"

"Mara! Vhat are you doing?!" Ludwig ran after her as she continued to transform. "Mara, hafe you gone mad?! Ve cannot hurt her! Mara! Stop!" But his objections were lost. There was no stopping a force of nature – not of Mara's kind.

Mara threw the door from its hinges and her cries of rage filled the otherwise peaceful night. The family assembling dinner in the dining room scattered and the whole house began to shake as Mara expanded into her dragon form. The roof ripped off and fell in front of the house, blocking Ludwig from reaching it.

"Mara!" Ludwig shouted helplessly. He ran around the house to the back door and forced it open. "Mara, stop, Bitte!" The house was aflame. Mara had set the dining room on fire and the Grandmother was scrambling. She headed for Ludwig.

"Help! Help me!" The old woman had grey cornrows – just like she did in the photograph. "Monster!"

Mara roared. "Evil witch! Take my family from me, will you? Twist their images, will you?! I'll burn you alive!" The flames leapt from her mouth and the pieces of art glass on the mantle and hanging from the ceiling melted. Ludwig dodged a dollop of the falling glass as he rushed to put himself between them.

"Nein! Mara, zhere must be anozher vay! Ve must find a vay out for her! Some vay for her to vake up! So ve can vake up! Ve must get her out of here! Mara, are you listening to me?" But Mara was beyond reason and Ludwig would have to have been blind not to see it. His glasses cracked in the heat and he cried out, running outside, dragging the Grandmother with him.

"The pond!" The grandmother's voice was cracked and dragged out of choked vocal cords. "We have to get to the duck pond!"

"Vhich vay?" Ludwig pulled her out of the backyard as Mara rampaged out through the house. "Vhich vay!"

"There!" The Grandmother pointed. "If we get there, we'll be safe!"

Ludwig doubted – privately – that anywhere would be safe from Mara's rage and pain, but for now she was determined to ensure that nothing remained of the copycat house. "Hurry! Ve cannot afford to dawdle!" With the old woman on his arm, they staggered down the green as the world was reduced to ashes behind them. The winds blew smoke and flames after them as Ludwig pulled the Grandmother along.

Finally, they reached the pond and waded in. It was shallow – only up to Ludwig's waist. "Zhis vill not safe us vhen she comes zhis vay!" Ludwig told the Grandmother. "You must tell me eferyzhing, now!"

"Yes, yes, all right! Just let me catch my breath. That's a hell of a power you have, boy, if you can reveal the truth of a matter just by willing it." She shook her head and brushed down her sweater, now stained with slime and pond water. "No, I'm not Dora. I'm just an old woman. I was very, very lonely and I created a world. I wanted Mara to stay and keep me company, but she ran away. I couldn't explain to her that all I wanted was to be at home! I gave her her family! Everything she wanted!"

"…You changed her family." Ludwig breathed. "How long vould it hafe been before you made her beliefe she really vas your granddaughter? Zhe little girl from zhe pictures? Before you erased eferyzhing zhat vas her?"

"I wouldn't have done that! I don't do that!" The Grandmother protested. "When I take a person in, I give them their family! I never would have erased her identity! Swear on my life!"

"Zhat fow means little vhen ve may as vell be already dead!" Ludwig pushed her away. "Hafe you been avare zhat zhe ozhers you took under your ving are Shadows now?"

"No! All I knew was that after they had had a few months or weeks coming to visit me and the rest of their family, that they stopped coming back! I didn't know they were dead!" The Grandmother reached for him again. "I just wanted visitors! And not to be so alone! I swear! I didn't know what I was doing!" Then, the cloud of ashes and smoke blew over them and

Ludwig could feel the steam as the pond evaporated from underneath them.

"It is too late!" Ludwig cried, covering his mouth and nose. "Mara, Bitte! Do not do zhis!"

"I must." Mara's voice was angry, hurt, and above all – determined. "It is the only way." Her head emerged from the smoke, her scales covered and dulled by ash. Ludwig couldn't think of how many times he had been on her back, right there behind her neck. He could only see her fangs as she opened her mouth again and fire flung itself down from her throat, straight at the Grandmother.

"Bitte!" Ludwig threw himself away from the pillar of flames. "Mara, you cannot! You cannot!"

"I can." Mara's voice rumbled and roared. "I must!"

Ludwig shielded his eyes as Mara reduced the old woman to dust as fine as the air itself, scattering her into the winds. A dying scream rocked the world.

Chapter Three

Ludwig opened his eyes to find Mara – twelve feet tall, surrounded by shadows, all visible skin covered in ink – standing in the midst of the ashes. Her head was downcast and her hair had come loose from its braid and was flopping over her face. She was sitting directly in the fine, white and grey powder and clearly felt terrible. Her shoulders were shaking and the shadows surrounding her were reaching out for Ludwig. Was this some form of hers that Ludwig had yet to see?

The doctor reached out and touched one of the lingering shadows. It curled around his arm and pulled him in close. He let it.

"Mara... Vhat hafe you done?" Ludwig whispered, putting his arms around her and pulling her close.

"She took my memories and changed them. She made them into her own family." Mara's voice trembled as hard as her body did against his shoulder. "She took them, Ludwig..."

"...I know." Ludwig patted her back, eyes running with his own tears. "Ve vere supposed to safe her, Mara. Ve vere supposed to help her find her vay out..."

"I'm sorry. I'm sorry..." Mara whispered. Her shadows and arms bound themselves around him. "Forgive me... Please, don't be afraid of me..."

"…Shh…" Ludwig kissed her forehead and smoothed the golden hair back from a face that had never looked so young and vulnerable, even as verses of Scripture – some in an angry red – passed over it. "I am not afraid. I promise."

"You should be." The shadows tightened their hold on him. It was rather like being in a tentacled embrace. "I'm a monster."

"Nein, you are not." Ludwig dismissed the self-accusation with another kiss. He could taste ash on his lips – a burned and fragile innocence. "You are human, und humans must sometimes be dragons. To protect zhemselfes… Und ozhers."

"I killed her. I burned this whole world. And I'm not sorry, except that it upset you." Mara reared up, expanding and seeming to fill the world around him. Her eyes were dark – her pupils had filled her whole eye, covering the white. "What does that make me?"

"Human." Ludwig argued. "Human, pure and simple. I vould hafe razhered zhat zhis go a different vay, but I should hafe known. You do not like ozhers taking zhe zhings zhat you lofe or hurting zhose you do." That seemed such a trite statement in hindsight – such an obvious generality. Who, after all, did like that?

"Humans are not good things, Ludwig. We are comprised of urges – all for evil and few for good – and we are untamable. We are monsters." Mara's tears cleared trails in the ashes that covered her skin. "I try so hard to be different, but nothing ever changes…"

"Shh... You are human. You hafe made a mistake. But you vere attacked on a lefel zhat ozhers cannot comprehend. You hafe been fiolated, Mara. Your memories hafe been twisted against you. You defended yourself in the only vay you knew." Ludwig cupped her cheeks and rubbed away the ashes. "Written here, on your skin, zhere is zhe tail of King Dafid, Ja? Und Dafid murdered a man for simply hafing a beautiful vife." Ludwig took her hair and pushed it back over her shoulders, putting her in order. "Und he is zhe man after God's own Heart. Vill God not forgife you for a far less malicious und far more profoked act?"

"...I never know how to answer questions like that." Mara sighed. "If I say 'No' does that mean I believe he will forgive me?"

"I zhink so." Ludwig smiled softly and tried to gather all of her up into his arms. "If you do not mind, Mara, I vould like to care for you for now. Shrink so zhat I can carry you, Bitte?"

Mara's shadows wrapped themselves around him and he felt rather like he was carrying a very young woman wrapped up in a robe with a life of its own. He could feel her frame in his arms and the shadows wrapped around his shoulders like a sling. "...Thank you, Ludwig... For not being afraid."

"I vill nefer be afraid of you." Ludwig promised her. "No matter vhat you do."

Chapter Four

When Ludwig tried to go back to the Grandmother's house, he couldn't find the way.

"It's like her world has been removed." Mara commented when she eventually joined him in the search. "Either because she died or because she disconnected from CORD. It's not unexpected, is it? I killed her. Her body wouldn't be kept on CORD just because she used to be here."

"She vas going to die of old age soon, Mara. You cannot afford to go to pieces." Ludwig told her as they walked in aimless circles in a patch of arid desert remarkably like that which surrounded the Grandmother's parody of Clovis. "Ve must find out as much as ve can about zhis."

"Why? Why is it so important? She's dead. She's gone." Mara kicked a rock beneath her feet and scared a Pronghorn Antelope. The small deer bounded away across the yellowed plain.

"Because I am a scientist, Mara, und zhis interests me." Ludwig explained, watching the deer go as well. "Here, ve hafe a chance to obserfe zhe triumph of mind ofer matter. Zhis is unprecedented und I vant to hafe as much data as possible." The scientist was writing notes into his graph in their hotel – they had yet to return to the lodge – and seemed to exist in a constant state of cautious excitement.

"Well, if you think it's important, I suppose the least I can do is help out a little." Mara grumbled under her breath. "But we're not going to find anything by walking in circles out here. All of the data you want is out there." She thumbed up towards the sky, which had become their signal for "Outside CORD," and shrugged. "We don't have access to heart rhythms, O2 capacity or anything from in here."

"Ja, but ve hafe zhe first hand vitness! You und I vatched as zhe Grandmozher vas remofed, und I zhink zhat ve hafe some insight, but I vish to see if ve can find anyzhing else." Ludwig told Mara once again.

"Ludwig, I hate to break this to you, but we've been in my world ever since we left." Mara explained. "I can feel that this is my domain, that I'm its source. We're not going to find anything of her here."

"Are you sure, Mara? If zhere is anyzhing zhat zhis experience has taught me, it is zhat ve all leafe our marks on zhe ones we meet in life. Zhere may be an echo – a pattern – of zhe Grandmozher's domain in your own head, und if ve can find it, zhen perhaps ve can use some basic forensics to find out vhat happened exactly, Ja?" Ludwig had been searching for the Grandmother's Shadow, but it had disappeared. The Shadows that were left behind when her realm was destroyed had scattered, fading in and out of existence within CORD.

"…I'll try." Mara folded her arms and bowed her head, closing her eyes as she focused. Then, she began to walk forwards, through the prickly pear and the saltbush. "Follow me. I think I have something. I don't know how useful – " They came out of the desert and into a pit of ashes. "…Well, that worked."

Ludwig reached out and took a handful of the ashes in his hand, letting them sift through his hands. "You vere fery zhorough. I doubt zhat ve vill find much of anyzhing in zhis."

"But you still want to rake through the ashes for what little is left." Mara reached out and plucked a partially burned photograph – miraculously intact among the fine, white dust. "…She took them from me. I couldn't be certain of my memory before, but now I doubt everything I thought I knew. Do I even have two brothers, Ludwig? Or three uncles and an aunt?"

Ludwig took the photograph from her hand and looked down at it. It had burned the faces from each member of the family and it crumbled to a fine powder almost as soon as he touched it. Putting an arm around her, he pulled himself in and pressed a kiss to her cheek. "Mara, you are growing again."

"I know." Mara sighed, looking down at him from twelve feet. "I hate this place. Do what you want, Ludwig, but I can't stay here."

"I know. I vould not ask you to stay vizh me. I vill come home vhen I am done." Ludwig gently pushed against her hip. "Go on. I vill be fine."

"Come back to the hotel as soon as you're done, it should be just back over that rise." Ludwig had learned to recognize when Mara was manipulating his own sense of space to allow him to travel through her own world without her.

Nodding gratefully, he bent back to the ashes, looking for the pieces left behind when a house inevitably burned to the ground. Of course, given the nature of the fire that had taken place – a dragon's pure, plasmic fire – and the nature of CORD itself, there was nothing "usual" left. Ludwig found no bones and no walls, nor bricks. There was only melted slag where there should have been stone.

But, at the same time, he dug up the remains of photographs from the ashes, and pulled out a lavender sweater – whole and unspoiled – from the wreckage. Piling what he rescued into separate, plastic bags, he continued his investigation into the processes of CORD.

In what Ludwig estimated to be the kitchen, he dug up more than a dozen different mugs and arranged them on top of a wooden painting of a magnolia branch. Some of the stained glass had survived as well and Ludwig was smoothing the ashes off of a stained glass Iris with purple petals and green leaves when he heard footsteps in the otherwise silent ashes.

"It's fascinating, isn't it?" A silky, soft voice reached his ears and Ludwig froze. "How many things we can leave behind – how many tales our possessions tell." It was Lucy and he was right behind Ludwig. Sweat broke out on his lips and temples as he gripped the stained glass ornament in his hands, muscles coiling up to strike.

"It seems zhat zhe nature of humanity is to seek immortality zhrough our material possessions."

Ludwig applauded himself for not letting his voice shake. He had defeated Lucy before, when he turned the Grim Reaper into a boy in a costume, but who knew how Lucy had prepared for this? He had somehow managed to penetrate Mara's shields and that didn't bode well for Ludwig. "But zhen I suppose zhat ve of all people know zhat ve cannot take it vizh us." And he swung around, the stained glass upraised in his hands, and brought it crashing down onto Lucy's head, backpedaling in the ashes as he went, trying to put distance between them. His stained glass shield passed straight through Lucy and Ludwig almost fell over in surprise as he pulled it up in front of his body. "Stay avay!"

"Relax – I'm not really here." Lucy looked oddly normal. He had his hands stuffed in his jean's pockets and a slightly open lumberjack shirt over a black t-shirt. "How would I have gotten through Mara's shields?"

Ludwig lowered the stained glass only slightly. "Vell, you certainly are not solid." Stepping forward, he reached a bold hand out and ran it through Lucy's torso. "So, vhat are you doing here? Vhatefer you are."

"I don't know. I think you made me up. Maybe you just needed someone to talk to who wasn't tall, pale, and draconic." Lucy thumbed towards the hotel that had become their base of operations.

"…Ja, but zhat has its own implications." Ludwig replied, setting the stained glass down beside the pile of surviving evidence he had collected. "Vhy vould I conjure you of all people to talk to vhen I need someone, first off, und zhen how did I do it vizhout my knowledge und consent."

"You forget, Doctor, that this place works in your subconscious and your conscious mind." Lucy reminded him. "Just because your conscious mind isn't ready to acknowledge your need for conversation with someone of your caliber, that doesn't mean your subconscious doesn't know. It's instinct, plain and simple. So... What do you want to talk about?"

"I do not know." Ludwig slowly replied, staring over the pit of ashes. "I am missing somezhing. Zhere has to be a vay to understand it."

"Understand what?"

"Vhat I am missing. Vhy is zhere no Shadow of zhe Grandmozher? Vhy did she fanish?" Ludwig bent down and ran another handful of fine, white ash through his fingers. "Vas it because Mara set out to destroy her? To purge herself und her vorld of all traces of her influence?"

"If you're looking for answers, I can't give you them." Lucy spread his hands helplessly. "I can only tell you what you already know."

"Zhen vhat do I know? Vhat hafe I seen, but missed?" Ludwig looked back at Lucy, but the figure out of his subconscious was gone – as quickly and silently as he had appeared. "...Danke, so much for zhat. Fery helpful."

Ludwig began gathering his ragpickings together again and placed the stained glass iris on top of the pile. As he began to lift it, his mind was still locked on what his subconscious was trying to tell him. What did he know? What was he missing? Had the answer been staring him in the face the whole time and all of his fluttering and deduction was for nothing?

Mara was waiting for him outside the hotel, playing with Patches. The dog had become as exuberant as a puppy and eagerly tore into the plush rabbits that Mara threw for him to play with. "What have you found?" Mara questioned when she saw him coming – all of the things he had brought back in bags and piled in his arms like some bizarre Santa Claus.

"Pieces of zhe puzzle, I hope." Ludwig replied, setting the pile down on a luggage cart just inside the hotel door. "But I'm afraid zhat I hafe more questions zhan answers."

"That's how it goes, usually." Mara pushed the cart and Patches bounded alongside them. "Any grand thoughts sprouting in your mind?"

"Nein, I am afraid not." Ludwig decided against telling Mara that he had seen Lucy out among the ashes. That would only worry her about more than her own actions. "I don't vant to zhink about zhis. Vhy don't ve go to dinner? Somevhere peaceful und quiet."

"How about a crab boil on the beach?" Mara suggested. "I know this beautiful part of the gulf coast where you can catch blue crabs right out of the water."

"Zhat sounds perfect right now." Ludwig dumped his evidence unceremoniously on the couch in their hotel room to be dealt with later. "Zhe pick-up?"

"Of course. If we're going to get stuck, we want to get stuck as far from help as possible." Mara flashed a ring of keys with a comedic flair. "And the pick-up has four-wheel drive."

"Zhen vhat are ve vaiting for?" Ludwig fell asleep during the drive and when he woke, they were at the beach. Mara had already changed into her bathing suit and neoprene, of course, bud Ludwig had to pull his shorts up in the shelter the pick-up's open door and a towel made. The sand burned the bottom of his bare feet as he joined Mara on the Lagoona.

"Souzh Padre Island. Not a bad choice."

"Mustang Island." Mara corrected him, pulling a neoprene glove with "The Glove of Death" embroidered onto the back in white onto her left hand. "I brought a second glove for you."

"Only one glofe? Vhy not bozh?" Ludwig questioned as he pulled on his own and picked up a net.

"You'll see. You only need one glove with these little nuts." Mara shot him a side-grin and waded out towards the dark line of red sea grass. "We'll catch as many as we could possibly want, but only about a dozen will be large enough to keep." The blonde woman predicted, tying the lead of a floating bucket around her waist.

"Ja, zhat is likely, but if ve are going crabbing, vhy are ve not using a-!" Ludwig cried out in surprise as Mara struck through the water near his foot and brought up her net full of a struggling crab.

"Because traps are boring." Mara explained with a mischievous glint in her eyes. "And perilously close to fishing."

"Do you not like fishing?" Ludwig poked at the crab in the net and watched as it snapped its claws at him. The joints closest to its body had a blue and purple patch that looked almost lacquered on. The color was so intense that it couldn't be real.

"Dump a piece of food on a hook into the bay, wait for hours and hope that fish bite. No, that doesn't sound like a good time to me." Mara replied, reaching in with the Glove of Death and seizing the crab by its back to untangle it from the netting. "Now, wading through hip-deep water with a gaffe, looking for two beady little eyes sticking up from the bottom? That sounds more like hunting than fishing to me."

"Vell, vhatefer you call it, it isn't my cup of tea." Ludwig walked along with her as they looked for another scurrying movement. "I prefer to sleep on zhe beach vizh a book beside me, or to svim in zhe surf."

"We can do that on the other side of the island." Mara dismissed. "But if you want to get out, I'll just catch the crabs and then we can go over to the other side."

"Zhis vater is a bit hot for me." Ludwig began wading back out of the grass and across the white sand flats towards the generously sandy beach. "Enjoy your crabs, Mara. I vill rest."

"If I'm catching them, you're cleaning!" Mara called up towards him.

"Zhat is fine." Ludwig waved behind himself and settled in on a thick beach towel from the back of the truck to watch Mara as she chased back and forth in the water. All the time, he was thinking to himself about what he could possibly be missing. The shade from the vehicle was just enough for him to lie in as he thought. The sun was sinking down into the sky – mid-afternoon – and the doctor felt lazy and quiet.

Chapter Five

When he woke, Ludwig saw Mara lying on the towel beside him. "Does time pass vhen ve sleep?" He questioned suddenly, pushing the towel that had been rolled over both of them to protect them from the sun down.

"…That's a weird question." Mara grumbled and heaved herself up onto her side. "It feels like it's been at least three hours since you fell asleep and I've felt time pass while you sleep, so I suppose the answer is yes."

"Ja, but zhat is vhen you are avake und zhis is your vorld." Ludwig pointed out. "But I hafe nefer been avake vhile you are asleep, I do not zhink."

"…Yes, you have." Mara replied, thinking. "But it has been a while since then. You woke up before I did and made breakfast. So time must pass when I'm asleep as well."

"…Ah, ja, I did. It has been a long time since zhen, zhough. Our schedules hafe become remarkably synchronized since zhen."

Mara flopped onto her back and sat up. "Yeah, they have. Except it hasn't been our schedules synchronizing to each other – it's been your schedule synchronizing to mine."

"Zhat makes sense. Zhis is your vorld." Ludwig sat up and looked out across the Lagoona Madre. "Is it time to go ofer to zhe ocean side yet?"

Mara looked up at the sun as it sank through the sky. "Looks like it. By the way, I moved the pick-up and everything across to the other side while you were asleep. All we have to do is take a short walk."

"A short valk across zhis burning sand?" Ludwig looked over to his left where the pick-up had been and found that his shade maker had been removed. "Vhat vere you zhinking?"

"I was thinking that we could walk through the tropical jungle that has miraculously grown between the lagoon side and the ocean side and pick some fruit from the trees to go with our dinner." Mara thumbed behind her with that mischievous look she got whenever she was showing him something she had always wanted to do.

Ludwig turned and found himself facing a dense jungle forest with plenty of shade and a soft, bare-earth floor covered in leaves and moss. The rich scent of tropical fruit reached his nose as the calls of macaws rang through the air. The green was such a direct contrast with the white sand that Ludwig instinctively knew that it would be cool and pleasant to walk along the paths cut into the trees. Standing, the doctor barely noticed as Mara gathered up the towels they had lain on and began following him. He felt hypnotized as he stepped over the boundary between two worlds.

"You vould zhink…" He commented to no one in particular. "Zhat after everyzhing ve hafe done – everyzhing ve hafe seen – zhat I vould get used to seeing zhe impossible."

"Never let that happen." Mara smiled up at the canopy, where water was dripping from the waxy leaves. "If you get used to the impossible, then it just becomes possible." Hummingbirds whipped around them, hunting out the bright, red flowers vining around them. "And what's the fun in that?"

"...I zhink zhere is a charm in zhe possible und zhe ordinary." Ludwig reached out and plucked a pink and white hibiscus to weave it into the tail of Mara's braid. "Some kind of comfort in zhe idea zhat zhis is how it has alvays been und vill alvays be."

"It's a charming idea, but it's a charming lie." Mara reached up and pulled the supple branch of a Passionfruit tree down into Ludwig's reach. "There isn't a single thing in the world that's the same as it always was, Bon, and the only thing that always will be is that it won't."

"Ja." Ludwig began gathering the ripe passion fruits, touching their wrinkled hulls gently as he gathered them into his loose, linen beach shirt. "But for now, ve enjoy vhat is zhe same und vhat ve see before us."

"That's as good a philosophy as any." Mara shrugged, letting the branch go. "I think I'll join you in that kind of thinkin'."

"I vould hafe it no ozher vay." Ludwig chuckled and they walked peacefully through the jungle.

By the time they reached the ocean side, the sun was low over the ocean and they only had an hour before sunset. Mara set up a camp stove and boiled the crabs with small cobs of corn and red-skinned potatoes. Ludwig cut into their fruit and scraped it out into bowls, tossing the innards of passion fruits with bright, red Gac fruit and mangoes. The resulting fruit salad was a reddish orange with chunks of sweet mango and creamy Gac dressed in tart passion fruit.

"Here." Mara handed Ludwig a bag of softly toasted coconut. "Want some of this?" She had sprinkled it over her own portion like parmesan cheese over a lasagna.

"Danke." Ludwig took a spoonful and dressed his own as they sat and waited for the crabs to boil – the sun setting in front of them. "Mara, forgife me, but aren't ve facing zhe wrong vay for zhe sun to be setting?"

"Yep." Mara nodded, sinking back into her plastic beach chair. "My world, my rules."

"Ah, of course." Ludwig smiled and turned his eyes back to the conflagration on the horizon. "How could I hafe forgotten?"

Chapter Six

It was only once they were tucked safely into their hotel – clean of all salt and sand and full and lazy on crab and fruit – that Ludwig's thoughts flitted back to the puzzle before him and a thought went through him like a flash.

"Let me up!" He cried, batting at Mara's arm. The woman jumped and her grip about his middle loosened. The doctor tore over to his desk full of notes. "I hafe it! I hafe it!"

Mara followed, bemused by her fiancée's agitation. "What is it?" She questioned as Ludwig began tearing down his carefully arranged notes. "Have you figured out the meaning of life?"

"Nein, do not be so silly!" Ludwig waved her away. "I must start from zhe beginning – I hafe to see it all again in zhe order. Leafe me be to vork! I vill speak to you later."

Mara drifted over to the bed and laid upside-down on it, slightly amused and mostly bemused at the whole thing. She watched as Ludwig wrote notes out on the pad of paper and began laying them out in a new order – some words she couldn't follow, his pen moved so fast, and then on to the next sheet of paper. Mara was certain that some of the words weren't even words – they were symbols or even drawings.

When Ludwig stepped back, his pentacle of notes on each of the five survivors in CORD had been entirely pushed to the side and a flowchart of notes had taken its pride of place in the front of the desk. "Mara, I need pins und yarn – red yarn if you can."

Mara silently handed him a jar full of push pins and a ball of yarn and watched as he began arranging the notes on the wall, affixing each slip of paper with a pin and connecting them with the yarn. "What are you making?"

"Quiet, please, I am still zhinking." Ludwig picked up his pen again and made a few corrections. Then, when he was satisfied, he stepped back from the wall and bowed, gesturing up at it.

"…Bon, that may as well be Greek for all I understand." Mara read a few of the papers.

Ludwig sighed and rolled his eyes. "Look, starting here, zhis is zhe point vhere a mind enters CORD." He tapped the first piece of paper. "Und it vakes here. But zhere is a split. Zhere are zhose who realize zhey are not in zhe real vorld und zhose who don't." He tapped the next two. "Und of zhose who do not realize zhis is not zhe real vorld, most of zhose who do surfife create a vorld of zheir own. It entirely resembles zhe real vorld and zheir minds compensate for zhe changes betveen CORD und zheir own lifes vizh denial."

"You have me so far. That sounds like the difference between the Engineer and me." Mara nodded, criss-crossing her legs beneath her to listen.

"Ja, just like zhat. So zhe people who beliefe zhis is zhe real vorld – vhen zhey are killed here, zhey die. Because zheir brains und zheir bodies beliefe zhat vhat happens here is real." Ludwig tapped the next sheets of paper. "Und zhey die – here in CORD und in zhe real vorld."

"Uh-huh." Mara nodded and continued listening.

"But zhose who don't beliefe zhat zhis is zhe real vorld, zhey do not die!" Ludwig triumphantly stabbed another piece of paper. "Vhen zhey are killed here in CORD, zhey simply vake up! Like vhat happens in dreams!"

Mara straightened up when she finally understood what Ludwig was getting at. "So, you think that when I burned the Grandmother, that I woke her up?"

"She knew zhis vas not zhe real vorld!" Ludwig agreed, pointing to the pieces of paper above the others. "So, her brain knew zhat you could not be zhe end, und it voke her up! It vas enough to startle her avake and zhat is vhy zhere is no Shadow, no remnant of her vorld except for zhe pieces zhat belong to you!"

Flashing back through her experiences with the Grandmother and the Shadows, Mara thought of everything she had heard and seen before. "But that leaves a problem, Ludwig. If the people who believe this place isn't real die and die permanently, then why are there Shadows at all? What's here in CORD that's keeping them?"

"Ah, for zhis my medical career fails me." Ludwig tossed himself down onto the bed beside Mara with the notepad and a pen again. "Fortunately, I did take a course on computers und zheir vorkings in my undergraduate days." He began drawing. "Each one of zhese boxes is a capacitor. A capacitor is one of zhe many vays zhat information is stored. If zhe capacitor is charged vizh positife electrons, zhen zhat is a one, but if it is negatifely charged, zhen zhat is a zero." Ludwig scribbled. "But zhe capacitors can only keep zheir information as long as electricity is running zhrough zhem. Zhey can hold a charge briefly, but zhey vill start to lose zheir charge und pieces of information vill begin to go missing."

"…So the people who don't believe are the ones and the people who do are the zeroes?" Mara questioned.

"Nein, nein, zhat is not vhat I am getting at at all!" Ludwig exclaimed, scribbling again. "Look at zhis – zhe capacitors may hafe lost most of zheir charge und zhey may hafe lost almost all of zhe information, but some remains und zhat, I zhink, is vhat is happening vizh zhe Shadows!" Ludwig tapped the paper again. "Vhen a person dies in CORD, zhe charge zhey leafe behind is recorded in zhe hardvare zhat makes up CORD und it leafes a data ghost – just like zhe capacitors! Zhat is vhy zhe Shadows cannot speak und zhey vander. Zhey are only part of zhe whole person."

Mara opened her mouth, closed it, and shook her head. "I still don't understand."

Ludwig wracked his brains for a few minutes more. "Zhink of it like zhis." He turned to a fresh page in the notebook and picked up a sharpened pencil. Pressing down hard and using clean, simple lines, he drew a smiling stick figure. "Zhis is zhe person in CORD – zhe information stored in zhe brain zhat CORD is able to access und process."

"Got you so far."

"Zhe human attached to CORD is like an external harddrive." Ludwig continued. "Zhe information is accessible by CORD, but zhe computer only keeps an incomplete copy of zhe information being processed." Ludwig flipped over the page and rubbed the pencil across the second page, revealing the outline of his stick-figure drawing. "So vhen zhe hardrife is suddenly ripped out of zhe computer, only zhe outline of zhe information remains."

"But then why don't people who wake up get ripped out like the people who die here?" Mara traced the outline with one finger, thinking.

"Because vaking up is a gradual process." Ludwig replied. "CORD has a chance to close down zhe documents und to finish separating zhe processing information from vhat is safed. Zhe computer doesn't have zhe same data outlines zhat result from zhe sudden termination of deazh."

"Then... what? What would we have to do? Because you and I have done things that should have killed us both and we didn't wake up." Mara pointed out.

"Nein, Mara, you hafe done zhings zhat vould hafe killed you. I hafe alvays been safe." Ludwig leaned up and pressed a kiss to her lips. "Because you hafe alvays been zhere to help me."

"Sweet enough to rot teeth, aren't you?" Mara pressed a kiss to his lips in return. "All right. Say I believe it. That still leaves us with a dilemma – now we can leave any time we want. All we have to do is die here."

"But if ve leafe now, zhe ozhers might be stuck in here forefer." Ludwig agreed. "Und ve should not vake Lucy – I do not zhink zhat vould be vise."

"Who knows what he would do when he was unleashed on the world again." Mara nodded firmly. "I think we should just get it over with. These other guys are just going to drag us down."

Ludwig frowned a the overly callous statement. "You are afraid. You still don't vant to leafe. But zhat is not vhat you're afraid of…" He thought deeply for a moment. "Mara, you vill not lose your nerfe if ve vait und safe zhe ozhers."

The woman beside him blustered a bit in an attempt to cover up her weaknesses. "…You're too perceptive for your own good." She finally bit out. "I don't want to leave and I don't want to hurt your feelings by saying that and I don't know if I can bring myself to leave."

"You can. Zhink of it, Mara. Zhere must be a million new discoveries out zhere for you to see, but you can't find zhem if you're stuck in here. You'll life out your life, imagining zhe same zhings und you vill be bored – I vill be bored." Ludwig reminded her. "Out zhere, ve can learn about a zhousand new zhings a day. Ve can construct our own adfentures. Zhey vill probably be simple adfentures, und nozhing like zhese zhat ve hafe here eferyday, but zhey vill be ours, und zhey vill be amazing in zheir own vay."

Patches jumped up on the bed and barked, pressing his nose in between them.

Ludwig laughed. "Und ve must go und find zhe real Patches." He scratched the dog's ears and hugged him close. "Ve vill hafe to rescue him."

Mara smiled slightly as their sweet dog licked her chin. "Yeah. I guess we do." She pressed her left hand to Patches's back and rubbed, the glint of her engagement ring on her finger. Ludwig wrapped his own left hand around to link with her hand. It was awkward, but worth it when the metal of their rings rubbed against each other.

"…Ve go togezher or not at all." Ludwig told her finally. Mara didn't have an answer or anything to say to that.

Chapter Seven

"As far as I know, the Engineer doesn't believe he's in CORD." Mara told Ludwig as they were planning their next mission. "And he's created some kind of bizarre cityscape to help him maintain that illusion."

"Vhy do you say bizarre?" Ludwig questioned, looking down at the pentacle "map" they had drawn. The Grandmother's space was blacked out.

"You'll see when you get there. The most I can say is that it seems to be designed to create the same week, over and over again. Time passes normally all the same, but nothing changes from week to week. The exact same events repeat themselves." Mara explained. "He hasn't reached out and no one can even contact him. Even Lucy's mystified, and he usually has no problem sniffing out where someone is hiding."

Ludwig nodded slowly. "You call him zhe Engineer... Vhy is zhat?"

"Because he's created a perfectly logical world, with all variables taken into account. There are no accidents in his version of New York and every person's actions leads to a logical conclusion. It's an utter impossibility from any frame of mind, but to an Engineer, it's a perfect world. I should know: My parents were engineers." Mara dourly reminded Ludwig.

The doctor adjusted his glasses and smoothed back his hair. "So you hafe told me. But I vould make zhe argument zhat a perfectly logical vorld has more to do vizh computers zhan engineering. Engineering is zhe process of solfing zhe problems presented by zhe unpredictability of life."

"So sue me: My nicknames aren't entirely accurate." Mara shrugged. "Would you prefer that we called him the IT Guy? 'Cause that has two words and not quite the same ring."

"…I-T. Letters, not it." Ludwig corrected her. "But you're right, zhe Engineer sounds better. So, vhat do ve do now? How do ve find zhis Engineer?"

"We pay a visit to the Big Apple." Mara reached out and grabbed her coat.

Chapter Eight

"Question: Why is it called the Big Apple?" Mara wondered as they walked along a crowded street beneath massive skyscrapers.

"How should I know? I did not name it." Ludwig pointed out, sticking close to her. The Facsimiles around them didn't react to touch or interaction and they parted in front of Mara like the Red Sea.

"It's not logical at all. It doesn't make sense. I don't have a problem with that." Mara reached out and grabbed an apple from a cart on a street corner and offered it to Ludwig. "But it's the weirdest thing ever that it seems to have nothing to do with the actual city. You see, New York used to be New Amsterdam, and that has nothing to do with apples."

"Aren't zhere apples in Europe? Perhaps zhey grow in Amsterdam." Ludwig suggested as they continued to stroll through Times Square. It was unnerving to see all of the cars lining up and stopping as the lights turned red and all of the pedestrians using the crosswalk. "Mein gott... Zhis is nozhing like zhe New York I remember."

"You've visited?" Mara looked down at him. "I never had the chance. Wasn't really interested, to be honest, but I never had the chance either."

"It's a dirty, dangerous, massife city, Mara, und no amount of vindow dressing vill help zhat. But zhis is completely different." He looked around and shuddered. "I do not see any litter or even a badly parked car. Zhere is nozhing, absolutely nozhing, less zhan mazhematically perfect."

"Now do you see why I called it 'bizarre?'" Mara put a hand between his shoulder blades and looked over her shoulder. "I feel like we're being watched."

"Zhat vould not be far off, efen in zhe real New York. Look, zhe traffic cameras." Ludwig pointed up at them.

"They're creepy."

"Zhey help to prefent und solfe crimes, safe lifes… Zhey are not so bad, are zhey?"

"If they were inside your house, it would be terrible, right? And if someone got into those cameras and used them to collect information, organize terrorist attacks, and spy on the citizenry by, say, turning them to face the windows up there or modifying the lenses to take in more than just visual information. What if they find a way to modify the cameras to diagnose potentially infectious diseases and then quarantine the victims?" Mara put the question to Ludwig with the tired air of one who valued their privacy and constantly found it stripped back and tossed away.

"Zhat sounds like a use of public resources to protect zhe public. I don't see vhat is wrong. If zhe person on zhe cameras does not know about a potentially harmful disease zhat zhey carry, zhen zhey most likely vould vish to know, Ja? So zhey can get treatment." Ludwig pointed out.

"All right. What if it was something like Syphilis?" They turned a corner onto Wall Street. "Would you want people to know that you had that? Especially if you were married and your professional life required some form of discretion from you, say, politician or judge."

"If I vere in such a position, I vould not hafe Syphilis." Ludwig disagreed, trailing one hand along a stand of bushes in front of a fancy building.

"In a hypothetical situation where you received Syphilis in some way other than the usual, would you want everyone to know?" Mara gave him a look.

"Nein, I vould not. But Mara, zhere vould be prifacy laws, information security, und efery kind of gauruntee..." Ludwig trailed off when he saw Mara rolling her eyes.

"Our government can't protect its own secrets, much less ours, Bon. You have far too much trust in people in authority."

"Und you hafe far too little." Ludwig looked forwards. "...Vat ist los?" He pointed at a bright patch in the street ahead.

"I have no idea. What do you see?" Mara looked around, scanning with all of her lifeguard skills. "All I see is grey and Facsimilies. Some blue here and there."

"I saw somezhing bright." Ludwig pointed again. "Look!"

"I'm looking. I swear, I don't see anything!" Mara looked again.

"…I must be seeing zhings." Ludwig blinked and the bright patch was gone. A non-descript man in a business suit walked past them and disappeared into one of the buildings nearby. "You said zhat zhe efents repeat zhemselfes at zhe end of zhe veek?"

"I didn't spend a lot of time proving that theory, but I saw the same woman sell the same bunch of flowers to the same young man three weeks in a row when I did visit, and nothing else seems to change. Just look at the newspapers: June, 13, 2005. It never goes past the 17th and it's never before the 10th." Mara pointed at a newspaper stand they were passing by and the dates on the front of the papers.

Ludwig reached out and grabbed a copy, reading through the headlines. "…Fascinating. Zhis is a complete paper. Und zhis lefel of detail in zhe vorld, vizh all of zhe people und zhe buildings in exactly zhe correct order suggests zhat ve are dealing vizh a photographic memory. So vhy is it replaying zhe same veek? Vhat happens on zhis veek zhat is so important to zhe Engineer?"

"…Maybe it was the week that someone close to him died. Maybe he's reliving their last few days of life before some terrible accident or a sudden illness took them away?" Mara suggested, snatching the comics out of Ludwig's paper and reading them as they walked along. "…Oh, that cat…" She muttered, a smile in her voice.

"How long has it been since you had new reading material?" Ludwig smiled at her.

"On the contrary, this isn't new. I read this newspaper the first time I ever came here and I read all seven others on offer." Mara told her fiancée. "I have to amuse myself internally, by remembering old stories for myself to read."

"You seem to be a fan of zhe old classics." Ludwig hummed. "You must hafe been a fery interesting child. I beliefe zhe term in vogue is zhird culture kid."

"Homeschooling tends to do that." Mara shrugged. "But we're not all antisocial idiots, just so you know. Just most of us."

"Mara – You shouldn't say such zhings. I hafe met many homeschooled children und zhey seem quite vell adjusted." Ludwig looked up from the paper and found themselves in Central Park.

"Yes, well, the large majority of us are homeschooled because we're not exactly geniuses." Mara settled on a bench nearby. "In fact, it's usually quite the opposite."

"Zhe actual number of geniuses is fery small." Ludwig reminded her. "Und most genius intellects are associated vizh a number of social und emotional deficiencies."

"Aspergers being the most famous, yes." Mara looked over at him. "Come on. You can't tell me that wasn't what you were thinking."

"Admittedly, I did zhink of zhe tendency tovards mental abnormality, but I understand zhe fact zhat efery group of people has different representatives." Ludwig found himself babbling. "It is obfious zhat zhere are ozher reasons to homeschool, but-"

"No, Ludwig, you're right. Most of the people I know do have something wrong with them. They're ADD, they're Autistic, they're Damaged in some way... But the truth is that what I've come to realize is that everyone is damaged. It's just that some people have parents who see that and most have parents who choose to believe their child is whatever can be called normal." Mara ran a hand through the air, calling up images of children of all colors and shapes. "Do you think the spoiled little brats who make everyone else miserable in high school are anything but damaged? The difference is their damage inflicts itself on everyone else around them. They're poison, and it leaks out. Eventually, they grow-up, internalize their own problems. But the damage they've inflicted is... permanent." Mara listlessly leaned back on the bench.

Ludwig was quiet for a long moment. "Vhen I vas in school, I vas fery unpopular. Zhis accent I hafe... It vas much zhicker zhen. Mein parents, zhey only spoke Deutsch around zhe house, so I did not speak zhe English fery vell until my ninzh year of schooling." The doctor looked down at his hands. "Efen zhen, I knew I vanted to help ozhers, to become a doctor. But zhe children who heard vhen I told zhe teacher und zhe few friends I had, zhey mocked me. 'You cannot be a doctor, Luddy, not if you cannot efen speak.' Und so I studied alone. I decided to become a surgeon und a researcher so zhat I vould not hafe to speak to zhe patients so much."

"And then you considered being a psychologist." Mara looked over with a silent question.

"I got to medical school und I realized zhat zhey vere wrong. Zhat my accent does not prohibit me from communicating vizh ozhers und zhat I could improfe it vizh time. So, I decided to have a moment und explore zhe ozher options." Ludwig shrugged and spread his hands. "But zhen I realized zhat I liked zhe surgery und zhe research better. I liked zhe brain und zhe nerves."

"I can see why." Mara agreed. "I've always loved looking at the pictures in Grey's Anatomy and the systems. The skeletal system was my favorite – I loved the idea that I could take a person apart and put them back together."

"It's not so simple as zhat, but... Zhere is an appeal in zhe idea. Ve hafe come so far vizh Adult STEM Cell research, zhat perhaps someday ve vill be able to take zhe human body apart like a puzzle und put it back togezher. Ve can put togezher new parts for zhe puzzle already – zhe transplants of skin und zhe organs. It is not so far to zhink zhat someday ve vill transplant every piece of zhe human body – perhaps even pieces of zhe brain." Ludwig gestured around them. "Computer Neural Interface is zhe first part of zhat process."

"Yeah, but I wouldn't want to see this place as a mass-market medical treatment any time soon."

Mara pointed out. "Can you imagine all of the Lucy's that would be running around?"

"…It's not a pretty picture." Ludwig agreed. "Zhough, if ve succeed here, ve vill hafe found zhe vay to vake up stable coma patients permanently. Zhat should help vizh some cases at least. Und efery man, voman, or child returned to zheir parents is a fictory."

"But is it worth the terrorization we've all gone through?"

Ludwig stared across the park at the buildings that rose all around them. "I hafe to beliefe zhat it vill be."

Chapter Nine

This pseudo-New York that the Engineer had created made for a remarkably pleasant place to stay. Mara had made their spot inside the Ritz Carlton. "It seems that I can pull a piece of my world into other controller's worlds." The Ritz had gone from a largely grey and uninteresting spot to a thriving, exciting establishment. Mara had let down her hair and was wearing a nearly-skintight mermaid dress with a black velvet bodice and pearl trim.

"You look fery dashing. Vhat is zhe occasion?" Ludwig questioned when he looked over and saw what she had dressed up in. His mouth and face puckered and stretched in surprise and a long, appreciative look at the back of his dress.

"When I turned fourteen, I told my mother that the only place I was wearing a dress was the Ritz-Carlton." Mara was signing the guest register with a fountain pen. She turned around. "Does it look good?"

"I zhink it looks amazing." Ludwig smiled. "...But you should show a little skin perhaps. Zhen, I could read off zhe Song of Solomon from your shoulders und look at zhe illustrations."

"What is it with you and my ink?" Mara questioned, shaking out her braid as they stepped into the elevator. The high, Chinese collar on her neck neatly hid all but the slightest peak of the black-inked words.

"It's interesting!" Ludwig smiled up at her and gestured with his left hand, the ruby winking in the light. "You decided to imprint zhe vords of God on your own skin. Zhat is incredible! Don't you see zhat? It lets me see so much of vhat you hafe in your mind, und zhat is coming from zhe man who is inside your mind, literally!"

"I don't know if I like your fascination with my psyche. If I'm so open to you, then why is it such an object of interest?" Mara gave him a side glance and adjusted her cuffs to cover more of her hands.

"Perhaps because you are so open. It is zhe natural human instinct to hide zhe parts of ourselfes zhat makes us less zhan perfect. But you have alvays been more open vizh zhe pieces of yourself zhat make you human und zhat is fascinating. It makes me vonder vhat you do hide und if I vill efer see zhem." Ludwig looked up at her. "It is zhe openness of your mind zhat fascinates me. Zhe idea zhat you vish to appear as ordinary und lacking in mystery. Most take zhe opposite route."

"Normal may be over-rated, but sometimes it's nice." Mara pointed out.

"Only if you vant to blend in vizh zhe crowd." Ludwig pointed out right back. "…Zhis elevator is amazing. Is zhis real hardvood?"

"Why would I imagine my mental version of the Ritz-Carlton with anything less than the best?" Mara questioned.

"Schtupid question, perhaps. I hafe nefer been to zhe Ritz, at least, not yet. I am not zhat famous a neurologist." Ludwig explained, digging the toes of his boots into the carpeting. "Question: Are you going to vear dresses all zhe time ve are here? Because I could get used to zhat."

"Well, all I'm really doing is projecting the dress over my normal clothes because I hate dresses. So, you can stare away and I'll remain in perfect, pantsed comfort." Mara shot him another of her mischievous smiles. "Want to run down the hall and act like hooligans?"

"On our first day at zhe Ritz? I am not bored enough vizh acting sophisticated yet."

Mara had, of course, chosen to put them up in one of the grand penthouses. It resembled the ones shown in movies rather strongly, being a two-story room with a large, main room and many smaller bedrooms. "Oh, good, we can sleep in a different room every night." Mara joked as she explored the cupboards in their small kitchenette. "Do you want to call Room Service first or shall I?"

"I zhink ve should read some of zhese brochures. Zhey vere all laid out on zhis coffeetable – zhere must be a reason." Ludwig picked up the first one – a map of New York as told by Google Maps. "Did you efer do some research on New York?"

"Only the most famous parts of it. And I spent a lot of time looking at maps." Mara slid down the banister and landed primly on her feet. "Why do you ask?"

"Because I get zhe feeling zhat your subconscious is trying to remind you of vhat you know about New York." Ludwig replied, flipping open the map and laying it out over the kitchenette's counter. "Look at zhis – a map, a guide to zhe skyscrapers, und vhere to find Sushi restaurants, oddly enough."

"Well, what would you want to eat in New York?" Mara questioned, sitting down beside him on the couch and picking up a brochure. "This one is about Central Park – specifically where all the best views are. It's based around a series of Google Images Search."

"Well, zhe internet isn't a bad place to start vhen you're looking for information." Ludwig flipped through a brochure about the new restaurants opening in bad neighborhoods. "Tell me, Mara, is crime logical?"

"In a perfectly logical world or the real one?" Mara questioned.

"Zhis one. Vould ve be mugged for going to say… Zhe Blue Shark near zhe Bronx for dinner?" Ludwig showed her a picture of the front of the restaurant.

"In a perfectly logical world, I find it to be statistically unlikely that anyone would take the risk of a felony conviction just to snatch a purse." Mara replied, leaning back in the couch's cushions. "This is a dangerously comfortable couch, by the way, just sit back and enjoy it."

"But zhere vould still be – in a perfectly logical vorld – desperate people und zhe fery poor." Ludwig pointed out, still reading about the Blue Shark.

"In case you haven't noticed, the people in this world aren't exactly responsive to anything we do." Mara reminded him. "But you have noticed, because you're not stupid and you're a neurosurgeon – you have to notice things. So, I'm going to assume this is a hypothetical situation that would only apply in a real world that runs entirely on logic." She cut him a glance to confirm her deduction. "And therefore, you're asking if, in a real world, we went to the Blue Shark for dinner, we would get mugged. And I have to say, yes. We probably would. It's just logical – do dangerous things and you put yourself in danger. On the other hand, I'm pretty dangerous myself. I'd protect you if you were in danger and you would return the favor if I was. And, in this real situation where we are in one of the largest and most dangerous cities in America or possibly the world, I would not put you in that situation without carrying a beretta strapped to the outside of my thigh and another one under your arm, James Bond style."

"In ozher vords, you vould not explore New York vizhout protection, und stiff protection at zhat." Ludwig put his nose back into a pamphlet about Times Square. "Gut. So vould I."

"I keep forgetting you're from Texas." Mara mused. "They really like their guns down there, don't they?"

"It keeps people safe in dangerous situations und allows us to keep a cultural heritage of lifing off zhe land alife." Ludwig opened up a brochure on birds of New York and flipped through it. "Do you disaprofe?"

"Nope. I have Army relatives and more Texan blood than you think." Mara explained as she put her feet up and began stretching out. "I'm going to sleep. You play around in whatever my subconscious wants you to read."

"... You're tired already? Ve just got to New York." Ludwig concernedly found her pulse in her knee and timed it.

"... Ludwig, I'm barely above a hallucination." Mara reminded him. "What is my non-existent, mental pulse going to tell you?"

"Zhis vorld is already a construct of zhe mind. Zhe brain knows vhen ve hafe somezhing wrong vizh zhe rest of our bodies, und it can interpret zhis information. Zherefore, your mind might attempt to communicate physical symptoms by your neurological self." Ludwig closed his eyes, counting. "But it does not matter. Your pulse is regular for a voman of your height und veight who is resting."

"Thank you. Now, can I sleep? You realize that if you interact with me deliberately, it keeps me up, right? I think we discuss this every time you're curious and I'm tired." Mara reminded him.

"Ja, und I am sorry. I just hafe to make sure you're all right." Ludwig sighed and pulled his hand back out from under her skirt. "It's a doctor zhing."

Mara smiled softly as she covered her eyes with one arm – no sleep mask. "I wouldn't have you any other way."

Ludwig found himself all but alone in the penthouse and free to explore this dream of the Ritz. If he had done his research correctly – and who hadn't looked up the Ritz-Carlton at least once – there was an indoor pool somewhere and he was going to find it. Right after slipping down to the shop to grab a swimsuit and an extra shirt. He was sweating in this one.

Chapter Ten

Mara found him floating in the center of an abandoned pool a few hours later. She was in her usual bodysuit swim suit. "Do you like swimming alone or with people?"

"Vell, until you showed up, I vas completely relaxed und enjoying myself." Ludwig opened his eyes and looked over, smiling. "How do you feel?"

"I seem to have taken a nap and gotten a little bit better." Mara replied, sliding into the water and heading out into the center. "How about you?"

"I have been having an amazing time. I had a massage, went to the shop and found a swimsuit, and ordered dinner to the pool deck for two. It's amazing, but we seem to be the only two guests here at the Ritz, so people are falling over themselves to wait on us hand and foot." Ludwig sat up and turned to dangle his feet off the edge of the floating mat. "Also, this pool is amazing. It seems that it's been made for a race of twelve-foot-tall people to swim in – the shallow end is six feet deep and the deep end is fifteen feet."

"Now, did you do that on purpose, because I didn't." Mara leaned on the mat. "I was thinking it would be a standard, three-foot deep hotel pool."

"You of little imagination." Ludwig dug his squared-off fingers into her hair and cupped her head. "It's the Ritz! Only zhe best, and zhe best has to hafe a dive tank."

"There is no way there's a high dive at the Ritz-Carlton in New York. I'm sure I would have heard of that." Mara turned to look over at the diving board at the other end of the pool.

"You can't trust eferyzhing you read, und you hafe nefer been! How vould you know?" Ludwig turned back onto the floating mat and rolled onto his stomach while Mara pushed the mat towards the ladder in the deep end.

"I guess I don't know." Mara smiled and frog-kicked her way down the pool. "It's a good thing that you've been practicing the few reality-bending skills we've managed to get for you."

"I hafe a lot of skills. I zhink I hafe been able to force ozhers to refeal zhe truzh – like vizh zhe Grandmozher. Vhen you could not go in und face your family, I forced zhe truzh to refeal itself. I showed you zhat she had pushed her own family into your's shoes." Ludwig felt his feet hit the wall behind him. "I zhink I am beginning to find a real vay to control zhe vorld. I can show people zheir own lies."

"…Please don't do that to me." Mara shifted around the mat, dropping under the water to reach the ladder. "Sometimes, my lies are all I really have left. If I had to face them, it would probably shatter whatever slice of reality I've managed to build for myself here."

"I won't. I promise." Ludwig sat up and watched as she climbed the ladder up to the high-dive. "I understand needing to deceive ourselves sometimes."

"I hate lying. And liars." Mara did a flip off of the end of the board and crashed down into the pool, the water catching her with ease. "But I hate lying less than I hate the reality."

"Ve vill get home, Mara. I promise." Ludwig told her, paddling over to hug her and nearly drowning them both in the process. Mara pushed off the bottom and shot upwards to her full height. "I know ve vill."

"You got your glasses wet." Mara reached out and tapped the glasses to clear them. "And your hair is a mess. Let's eat something and go to bed. Tomorrow, we should explore where you saw the bright patch again and see if we can find something."

"Do you zhink it could be important?" Ludwig asked as they made their way out of the pool."

"I think you noticed it. Therefore, it has to be important somehow – or there wouldn't be anything to notice. Get me?"

"Not at all, but I trust zhat ve must start somevhere to find zhe Engineer. If zhis is how he vishes zhe vorld to continue in his logical mind, zhen he must be an ordinary citizen. It is statistically unlikely zhat he vould be famous."

"Maybe not in any circle we would know about, but he might be famous as an Ethical Hacker, say. Or as some sort of expert, perhaps in making the buildings stand in perfectly straight lines as they do here." Mara pointed out as they picked themselves up onto the deck and found dinner laid out on one of the deck tables.

"An Ezhical Hacker vould make as much sense as anyzhing else I could zhink of. Zhey vould most likely be in zhe offices of a financial institution, Ja? Or perhaps in IT for one of zhe banks." Ludwig mused.

"Then I think we should start hanging out in some Wall Street buildings." Mara hummed and steepled her fingers together.

Chapter Eleven

"Are you certain ve can start here?" Ludwig questioned as they returned to the spot where he had seen the bright patch. "According to zhe newspaper, it is Friday. Perhaps zhe person ve are looking for is at home."

"Don't worry." Mara pushed her way into the building the bright patch had stopped in front of. "I think this might be where he works."

"Und how exactly do you figure zhat?" Ludwig questioned as they stepped up into a granite and hardwood lobby. "Zhis is one of zhe biggest investment firms I hafe efer seen."

"We need to find where they keep their IT guys. Either that, or we look out for bright patches. If I'm right, then I think I'm beginning to get an idea of what's happened here." Mara began searching for bright patches with her eyes. "Keep an eye out – remember, I didn't see it last time."

"Vhat do you zhink has happened here?" Ludwig scanned the lobby with care.

"I think that the Engineer is watching himself go about his day-to-day, trying to make sense of something that happened – something illogical." Mara continued to scan the anonymous faces of the businessmen surrounding them. Their suits blurred into smears of neutral colors – dark blues and tan, grey and black. "So, his presence watching himself go about his day is what you see in those bright patches.

That's why he re-plays the same week over and over in his mind. Now, it's just a matter of finding the bright patches and making him show himself so we can see what's going on here and how we're going to break him out. I warn you, though. He's seriously delusional."

"Do you zhink if ve approach him zhat he vill notice us?" Ludwig questioned. "If he is so deep into zhis delusion as you say, zhen ve may go unnoticed as he focuses on himself und his own actions."

"Then we'd just have to make trouble until he notices us." Mara shot a smirk at Ludwig. "Don't worry. We'll get it and he'll be waking up in no time. As soon as we figure out how to kill him or we convince him to kill himself."

"As soon as ve explain zhat he is inside of CORD, he should not resist. I cannot see zhat he vould vant to stay here und not in zhe vorld, learning all about zhe computers." Ludwig looked up and spotted another bright patch – it was a tile on the floor, about one foot by one foot square that afforded a view of the doors and the rest of the room. It was reminiscent of a music video that Ludwig had seen where the singer inside stepped on various squares of road on the street and the squares lit up. "I see a patch, Mara. It is zhat spot zhere – vhere no one is stepping on zhe tile."

"All right. Wish me luck." Mara pushed through the unresponsive crowd and slammed her feet down onto the bright tile. Instantly, the light went out and she turned her head, swiveling and staring. "Did I find it?"

"You are standing vhere it vas, but it is quite gone." Ludwig looked down at the floor under the hundreds of feet. "I do not see anozher one. I don't understand: Vhy can't you see zhem?"

"Maybe it has something to do with the way you've been forcing others to see truth." Mara pointed out. "If there was someone there, where no one should be, then your mind forced something to reveal itself so that you would notice more directly."

"Und zhen I vould speak to you about it und ve vould infestigate. Of course." Ludwig scanned the floor again. "Zhere. By zhe elefator. Hurry!" They shot across the floor and into the open doors of the elevator at the very last moment.

"Where do you see it?" Mara twisted her head.

"It vas zhe camera." Ludwig pointed up into the camera at the corner. "It flashed bright und I saw it. Mara – vhat you vere saying about zhe cameras. If zhis man is a computer expert, zhen perhaps he could be using zhe grid to keep track of himself indirectly."

"Then it might be a lot harder to get his attention – unless he can see us through the cameras and he's not just watching the same, pre-recorded film. But if it's the cameras that he's looking through, why did the floor and the sidewalk light up before?" Mara questioned as they rode the elevator.

"Because zhere vas not a camera zhat showed zhose spots. Zhe cameras in zhe lobby und outside showed zhe doors, zhe desk, und zhe elefator. Zere vas not a general camera zhat showed zhe whole of zhe lobby." Ludwig explained. "So, zhe Engineer's attention must be on himself und using zhe cameras, but also be going out in und of himself to keep vatch ofer himself."

"If that's true, then the brightness of the objects might not be reflecting him as a person, but his attention – where he's focused." Mara mused. The elevator stopped several times as it rose until they were the only two left. "Which suggests that he was on the elevator with us just now – and we didn't even notice."

Mara and Ludwig shot glances at each other and the doctor scrubbed his palm down his face in exasperation.

Chapter Twelve

They rode the elevator up and down the rest of the day, waiting to see if the bright patch would return. "Zhis isn't zhe only elevator in zhis building." Ludwig folded his arms across his body. "He might be in a different elefator."

"Then we should go back downstairs to the lobby and wait for him to come out." Mara replied, studying faces as they stepped into the elevator and took their places around them. "We can't miss him then, right?"

"Of course, ve can. Ve didn't efen zhink to look for more patches vhen ve vere in zhe elefator in zhe first place." The doctor was clearly frustrated and Mara couldn't blame him.

"Hey, it's going to be okay. We know he has to be here – it can't be that bad." Mara rubbed his back with a wool-gloved hand. "Come on – we can have a snack while we people watch."

They found a bench in the lobby and Mara brought Ludwig a salad from who knows where and a couple apples for herself. "It just occurred to me that we could go to London while we're here."

"Ve must not be distracted." Ludwig scolded her, keeping his eyes trained on the floors and the few cameras in the lobby, determined not to let their quarry slip past again.

"We can talk, can't we?" Mara questioned, biting into the pinkish-green fruit in her hand. "You can look and talk – I've seen you do it."

"Ja, but I vas not so focused zhen." Ludwig put a bite of the salad into his mouth and chewed without tasting it.

"Well, you know that if you're too focused, you can actually miss things." Mara pointed out. "It's okay to relax a bit and blink a few times – helps clear your eyes."

"You speak as zhe lifeguard now." Ludwig observed and sighed, sitting himself back upright and rubbing his eyes before adjusting his glasses. "If only you could see zhem as vell."

"Hey – I turn into dragons and merpeople – you see truth. We all have our own talents." Mara stretched an arm around him and bit into the apple again, revealing more and more of the core with each bite. "I bet it's because I lie to myself. I accept reality and twist it in my mind. I'm a grade-A hypocrite, and that's okay."

Ludwig shook his head, smiling. "I zhink you see more of zhe truzh zhan you realize."

"I see the truth – I just choose not to acknowledge it." Mara easily gestured around with the apple. "This lobby is freezing. Is that air conditioning? In New York?"

"It must not be cold to zhe people who life here." Ludwig turned his eyes back to the floor and searched. "I still do not see him."

"It's not quite time for people to go home." Mara looked at the clock. "It should be another hour before we get some serious traffic through here."

Ludwig sighed and sat back in the bench, cupping his bowl of salad. There were matchstick apples on top of baby lettuce and some kind of red lettuce. A light, citrus vinaigrette covered the whole and Ludwig found himself dragging the fork out between his lips – unwilling to let any drop of flavor go unsavored.

If they had been in the real world, perhaps he would have written a post to Facebook. It seemed to be the thing to do these days – to keep up with each other and the world by sharing every experience. But where was the intimacy in that point of view?

What was the quote? The greatest love story is the one that is not and should never be told? There are facets of life that seem to be strengthened in privacy. Ludwig found himself shifting a little closer to Mara – who had given him space – and he felt her body relax slightly as she leaned her arm closer to his shoulders. Something about the moment had that sacred feeling. They were on a mission, there to save others, and sitting in an icy lobby supposedly in one of the Northern States. But there was a closeness as Mara sighed deeply and her clever eyes followed the faces in front of her, noticing details and drawing conclusions. There was a moment of crisp silence where they just sat and watched the passersby and Ludwig knew he would never be able to describe it as he dragged a few matchsticks through the remaining vinaigrette on the bottom of his bowl and offered the bundle to Mara, letting her taste the sour brightness of the oranges and the soft sweetness of the apples.

And then the moment was broken. Ludwig spotted a bright tile, just like he had that morning. "Mara – zhere!" He exclaimed, pointing. "Quickly! Ve must not lose it again!"

Mara stood and chased after him, the salad bowl and apple cores forgotten on the bench, fading away like an ephemeral dream.

Chapter Thirteen

The bright patches turned quickly into traffic cameras following cars down the road. Mara and Ludwig missed the cab that their target stepped into by a millimeter and the woman looked down the road, throwing her hand to her lips to let out a sharp whistle. They threw themselves into a taxi driven by a Rastafarian with foul-smelling breath. "Follow that car!" Mara snapped, pointing, and their driver didn't ask questions.

It became obvious that the Taxi was Mara's mental construct when they began passing through the other cars like nothing was there. Soon, they were riding on their quarry's tail and Ludwig took a moment to catch his breath and to process. There had only been a split-second glance at their target before he had climbed up into the cab. They were chasing a middle-aged, reasonably-fit, mousy little man in a grey suit with a briefcase. Ludwig had been correct when he estimated that the person they were looking for was more likely a computer programmer than an engineer. It was unlikely an engineer would be working in a financial institution.

"Question." Mara suddenly stated as they stood in front of a small house in Staten Island – an idyllic little neighborhood.

"Answer." Ludwig looked up at her, turning his attention briefly from the almost lonely looking little house.

"Cheeky. Seriously, though. If the Engineer is some kind of big-shot computer wizard from New York, then why was he being treated in Albuquerque?" Mara questioned as they stepped up the drive. They had seen their target go inside the house and paused while Mara dismissed the Taxi to take it all in.

"New York doesn't have Doctor Bervick." Ludwig reminded Mara.

"Ah, yes, the sainted Berwick. I almost forgot." Mara put her hands on her hips, studying the green lawn and the sycamore tree. "Kind of a big house for just one man to live in."

"Perhaps it is a family home." Ludwig shrugged and took note of an antique statue of St. Francis of Assisi. "It certainly doesn't seem to be decorated by a young man or a computer programmer."

"Have you met many?" Mara stepped through the front door and looked around. "…I take it back – it's definitely a family home. Look at all these antiques. It's like a museum in here, good grief. Is this a Picasso?" She pointed to a painting and shook her head. "Everything looks… Oddly disjointed, though. As if it was just being arranged and maintained as a matter of habit and not passion. No one would put a Kinkade beside a Picasso like this – look at the way the paintings make your eyes ache."

"Zhe colors certainly do glare slightly, but I zhink zhere is a logic to zhe order. zhis room is predominantly blue und zhe colors of zhe paintings und decorations are also predominantly blue und cool colors." Ludwig pointed out, wincing as he compared the structurally deaf Picasso and the elegantly flowing Kinkade. "But I must look avay. Zhat is awful."

"That seals it: There's no way there's a woman living here." Mara stepped through into a yellow living room and folded her arms, shaking her head. "Look at this mess. There's too much yellow – it's ridiculous."

"I did not know zhere vere zhis many shades of yellow." Ludwig admitted as he took in a painting of a field of tulips across from what seemed to be a yellow and orange swirl. Directly underneath the swirl was a vase with sunflowers, all painted delicately and with a careful, practiced hand. Still, this was clearly a handmade heirloom and not an antique of great value, as the paintings were. Ludwig picked it up, finding it solid, and turned it. There was a name inscribed on the bottom: Ganella Trenchfurt. "Mara, look at zhis."

Mara, though, had taken refuge in the one room not obnoxiously decorated. "No! Come up to the office, it's beautiful in here."

Ludwig set the vase down and followed her up the stairs to the front office where he found Mara easily sprawled on the floor with a book in her hand and a smile on her face. She had found some measure of peace. The enclosed office was full of books and screens and their programmer was sitting at his desk, working away.

He was a small man with a bit of a mousy look behind thick glasses. There was a tilted slant to his eyes and his hair was dark, not even touched with grey yet. In spite of the slightly manic state of his office, he was a bit deliberately put together and everything about him was as logical as the rest of the world. It seemed he had taken care to create a reflection of himself as he observed this one week, over and over. And Ludwig saw that there was a bright patch: The web-camera on top of the shelf above the desk. "Mara, zhe camera over zhe computer is lit up. Zhis must be who ve are looking for – it is certain now."

"I thought we had figured that out." Mara continued reading about old computers through a technical manual.

"You had guessed zhat it vas him und I beliefed it, but ve did not know until now. Now, how do ve get zhe attention ve need?" Ludwig hummed and looked around. "Mara, you take zhe ozher side of zhis shelf. Let's see if ve can tip it over."

"Oh, come on, Ludwig. Imagination, please." Mara pointed out the window. "I think that will get our point across nicely."

Ludwig poked his head out the window to find himself face to face with a unicorn made of cotton candy and lollipops. "You are such a little girl sometimes, Mara." He told her as the unicorn began climbing inside, sprinkling powdered sugar and lemon drops after it.

"I know – great, ain't it?" Mara grinned, grabbing a handful of the sweet and sour candies and pushing them into her mouth. "So, do you think that's enough to get his attention or should I unleash the winged monkeys?"

"I don't know." Ludwig watched as the unicorn whinnied and scattered cotton candy hair all over the desk. "I suppose ve vill find out."

The unicorn had a tongue that looked like it was made of shiny, bright-red gummy candy. It licked the computer programmer all over his face, leaving sparkly trails of sour-flavored slobber. Ludwig watched with a bemused kind of horror. The depths of Mara's depraved imagination had yet to be plumbed.

A sharp, annoyed voice shouted. "End simulation!" And the world collapsed around them until they were standing inside of a white paneled room. "You! What are you doing, making trouble? Can't you see that I'm in the middle of a very important computer experiment?"

"That's the problem." Mara replied, tossing the book over her shoulder to shatter like the rest of the world. "You were so deep in your very important experiment that you haven't noticed that we've been following you, trying to get your attention. You see, we're here for one simple reason: We're going to wake you up. And it's very inconvenient that you've forced us to run all over New York to do it."

"Nonsense!" Their computer expert paced out at them. "I have to insist you leave at once! There is no reason for you to be here!"

"If you haven't noticed, sir." Mara leaned on the computer station in front of her. "You are in a machine called CORD and being quite annoying about it. Ludwig and I have been here for two days searching for you and by the time we find you, it takes a cotton candy unicorn to get your attention. Frankly, I would have taken more subtle hints – like a pair of strangers and a Rastafarian chasing you in a cab." Mara pointed out acidly. "Now we've gone to a lot of trouble to talk to you, so I think you can do us the courtesy of sitting down and eating lunch with us before you brush us off as a pair of troublemakers and go back to your videogame."

"Videogame?!" The man became purple. "This is not a videogame. It is a computer simulator that allows me to observe and create theoretical experiments based on known variables!" Mara held up a hand and began making it "talk" in time with his mouth. "It is a highly scientific pursuit that permits me to observe what we cannot observe with any degree of accuracy and to formulate – WILL YOU STOP THAT!" He cried in outrage.

"I hafe an idea." Ludwig stepped between the two. "Let us go somevhere else. How about a seaside restaurant to hafe a meal und speak?"

"Of course. There's one approximately a mile away in King's Bay that I adore." Mara agreed. "Coming, Mr. Computer Expert?"

"It is a physical impossibility to be a mile away from King's Bay Georgia when in New York! You are quite mad!" The computer programmer followed them out of the room and they stepped suddenly onto a beach of fine, white sand. Ludwig pulled open his coat and tossed it away at once as the heat hit him.

"My mistake. It was less than a tenth of a mile." Mara calmly threw off her own coat. "What a pesky thing: A decimal place."

"This is impossible!" The programmer's face had gone ashen. "How can we be-?" His equilibrium restored itself suddenly. "Of course. You've programmed King's Bay into the computer simulator."

"I wouldn't have the foggiest how." Mara began walking off, passing one arm through Ludwig's. "Come on, Bon. Let's show this New Yorker how the South grills steak."

"We will not be able to interact with anything at the restaurant!" Their computer programmer bustled after them. "Everything inside this simulator is non-corporeal. The moment you sit down in a chair, you will fall through right to the floor."

"Tell zhat to zhe adfenture ve hafe been on." Ludwig told him as they climbed the steps up from the beach to the restaurant's patio entrance. "Ve hafe been staying at zhe Ritz."

"That's… Well, where else would you stay in New York? I mean, the Ritz is the best… Or at least one of the best. And it's certainly world famous." Their follower glanced nervously around. "This can't be real."

"Well, it's not. That's what we're trying to tell you."

Ludwig put a hand on his shoulder as they sat down in the restaurant. "You're inside a machine called CORD."

"CORD?" The Engineer broke into a sweat. "No... No... My name is... I'm... I'm Henry Cho. My grandfather was a Japanese immigrant and he married an Irish New Yorker. I work for Brecker and Sons – I'm their Technology Support Manager. I keep the computer system running. I'm good at my job. I know what it means to be real..."

"Yes, you do." Ludwig assured him. "Und zhis is not efidence zhat you hafe gone insane. You hafe been in an accident or fallen ill, Ja? Somezhing happened und you vere sleeping, perhaps for a fery long time. You vere in a coma, und your mind created zhis vorld to help your subconscious deal vizh zhat fact."

"...But that's ridiculous. If I'm really here, in a coma, why have I been watching myself relive my week for so long? It doesn't make sense." The Engineer looked down at the table in a loss. "...Mom's crab dumpling soup. How did that get here?"

"Your mind knows you're getting upset. It vants you to be comfortable und to calm down." Ludwig explained. "Zhe truzh is, vizh all I hafe seen of zhe ozhers in zhis vorld, replaying zhe efents leading up to your accident is quite normal. After all, Mara here decided to spend her time creating fantastic landscapes und changing into a dragon."

Mara smiled and shrugged. "It was a way to pass the time."

"Wait." The Engineer breathed, setting down his spoonful of the crab-dumpling soup. "If this is a world created by my subconscious, how do I know either of you are real?"

"I guess you don't." Ludwig shrugged. "But for vhat it is vorzh, ve hafe had many adfentures zhat ve could tell you about. Und I don't zhink you vould imagine someone who summons zhe demons of zhe cotton candy unicorns to vake you."

Henry Cho smiled suddenly, laughing. "Yeah… Yeah, that actually makes a lot of sense. I wouldn't imagine something like that – I would imagine myself going home or being called to a conference. So…" He began eating his crab dumpling soup again. "If we're all really in comas… Do you know how to wake up?"

"We think we do." Mara explained. "You see, that's what we were looking for when we started visiting the other people here in CORD – a way to wake up. And we have a theory, but it's going to sound insane and even dangerous."

"Well. I'm willing to try anything once." Henry replied calmly. "And this is just insane enough that my brain is willing to except whatever you say as gospel for the moment. So, what do I have to do to wake up?"

"Simple: You have to die." Mara told him.

"…Is there a way that's less… insane?" Henry almost knocked over his bowl of crab dumplings. "If this is a subconscious world, then, logically, I can't die, but I can't imagine that dying is the proper way to go about waking up."

"I know it sounds terrible." Ludwig held up his hands. "But ve hafe some efidence, if you vould care to listen."

Chapter Fourteen

Henry Cho almost staggered back to his own home when they had filled him in on everything. Though Ludwig had tried to intervene, to give him time to think and to understand, he had insisted on hearing everything at once – shock therapy, as he put it.

"Do you think he's going to be okay?" Mara questioned. "He's a logical man. He's got to be... well, knocked down, kicked around, and off his stride."

"I agree." Ludwig cut into his filet. "I vish he had allowed you to slow down. He vanted to get it ofer vizh, but I zhink he has valked avay more confused zhan anyzhing else."

"That's what I'm afraid of too. If he goes in and conjures up a gun and shoots himself, do you think his mind will wake him up?" Mara questioned.

"I hope so. But I do not zhink zhat he vill try to kill himself immediately. He vould vant to consider zhe options." Ludwig pointed out, leaning slightly closer to her. "Und he may need some furzher proof at zhat. Do you zhink he would agree to take a flight?"

"If our friend Henry wants a flight, I don't see any reason to object. You could come along, Sparrow." Mara sucked the tail out of a crawfish expertly.

"I vould nefer turn down a flight. But I am vorried about our friend Mr. Cho. Vhat if he does decide to do somezhing drastic?"

"Then it makes our job easier, doesn't it?" Mara picked at her own food – a shifting mass that might have been anything and seemed to reflect a lack of focus. "He takes himself out and it doesn't interfere with our plans. Everything would work out just fine."

Ludwig's glasses reflected Mara's face as he looked at her in concern, brows furrowing. "Are you still zhinking about zhe Grandmozher?" When Mara turned her face down towards her plate and pushed her food around the edge, he knew. "You are not to blame for her, Mara. Vhat she did to you vas reprehensible, und you hafe a right to defend yourself und your family vhen you are zhreatened."

"But I wasn't defending my family. I was defending my memories of my family. That's like trying to defend a photo album." Mara pushed away her plate. "I don't even know what I want to eat. So, yes, I am upset and I am thinking about it. I don't want to have to kill Henry. He seems like a nice guy – bad taste in decorating aside."

"It's not his fault. He's probably colorblind." Ludwig pointed out. "Zhe colors zhat ve see might simply be translated as greyscale in his mind."

"How are we seeing the world in color if his world is all greys, though?"

"Zhe vorkings of CORD are as much a mystery to me as to you, Liebling." Ludwig pointed out gently, patting her hand. "Und ve hafe discussed zhem more times zhan I care to zhink of."

"I know. I just can't get used to the idea that I killed someone. Even if she deserved it. Even if she didn't really die." Mara sighed and looked down into her water glass. "All this time, I've been looking out for evil, trying to guard myself against it. I saw Lucy as my enemy because I saw the visceral image of Evil in him. But it's been lurking in me as well. It's there – in my reflection."

"You vere attacked. Vhen you are attacked, you respond." Ludwig put his hands on her shoulder and made her meet his eyes. "It is a basic law of human nature und you are not exempt."

"But I burned it, Ludwig. I didn't just defend myself, I destroyed the enemy and laid waste to everything that once grew there." Mara bared her teeth. "I rendered her and her world ashes and dust. I wiped her from the face of the earth and I will never regret it. I just marvel at what I've done and I can't believe it was me. That I did that. I can't believe that I was the vicious executioner."

"You vere not zhe executioner. You vere zhe fictim. Zhe fictim who struck back. Zhat is all zhat seperates you from zhe Shadows zhat zhe Grandmozher created." Ludwig kissed her forehead. "Und now ve must take some time to rest. Ve vill check on our friend Henry tomorrow und see if he has had time to process all zhat he has learned."

"And learn what he intends to do with what we've told him." Mara darkly replied.

"Do not vorry, Mara. Ve hafe informed him of zhe cure for his condition. Zhat is all ve are ezhically

compelled to do. Ve can take zhe back seat for now."
Ludwig assured her. "Und if Henry attempts to hurt
us, you can block him out, Ja? No need to harm him."

"I suppose you're right." But doubt was written
deep on her face and in her eyes and Ludwig didn't
know if she believed it.

"You really are a meddling little tart." Ludwig
had never dreamed in CORD before. He wasn't sure
that he liked it. Especially since his dream had a
definite flavor of Lucy.

"Get out of here, Lucy." Ludwig snapped into
the whispering wind. He knew he was in Mara's bed –
he could feel her beside him. The sheets had tangled
up around her, isolating her, and her hair was wildly
pooling over the pillows and his neck and ear. "I don't
vant you here. I don't vant to talk to you, see you, or
hear you. Not efer again."

"And yet you're going out of your way to upset
me…" Lucy hissed softly. "You're looking to make me
angry."

"We're not doing any zhing of zhe sort. Ve are
freeing zhem. Zhey are vaking up und you can too."
Ludwig spoke to the would-be demon. "You do not
hafe to life like zhis for zhe rest of time."

"I am happy this way. I am free. And you
threaten that… Who am I to sacrifice if you take them
all away? I will have to stop you…" Lucy's soft voice
was threatening. "And there is so much left to do – it's

a risky task ahead of you both. Why don't you just give up? It would be so much easier... Safer..."

"I am not afraid of you." Ludwig reached out to place a hand on Mara's hip and found he couldn't move. He was helpless in this dream world. Only his voice to use as a weapon or a shield.

"I will make you afraid." Lucy promised. "I can keep you alive for a very long time before I let you die. And I will make the dragon's suffering the worse... before you came, there was a balance to this world. You've upset that balance."

"I saw vhat you zhought zhe balance is: You, free to pillage und torture your neighbors. Not much of a balance at all, is it?" Ludwig barked out. "It seems to me zhat you vere vizhout competition before. You preyed upon zhe creations of zhe Ozher und zhose unfortunate enough to be put vizhin your reach vizhout any challenge. Mara vas content to be Svitzerland in vhatefer is going on betveen all of you, but I vas not. So you are challenged und are finding out exactly how small your piece of zhe vorld is. Vell safor vhat you hafe. Before ve leafe, I intend to see you out of zhis vorld, by one means or anozher."

"Oh, Ludwig... Be glad you have Mara or you would be long, long dead by now. Don't forget, I had you in chambers, and you were snatched away. That makes me interested... what does a lovely, young creature like her see in an old tart like you?" Lucy's sibilant voice whispered through his ears. "Whatever it is, it won't be enough to save you if you cross me. There is still so much you simply don't know." And he thought he felt a cold breath on his face before the message? Vision? Dream? Faded away.

"Vell, zhis is not vhat I expected." Ludwig and Mara stared up at the destroyed shell of a house in front of them. Lucy's message was still ringing in his ears. It was easier to bear in the daylight and with Mara awake and alert.

"Henry?" Mara called as they stepped up into the foyer – covered in the wreckage of antiques and artworks. "We came to visit! Are you... are you all right?"

"Do you zhink zhat Lucy managed to make it in?" Ludwig questioned Mara as they climbed up towards the office.

"I don't think so. Lucy tends to leave a more... sinister mark than a trashed house."

"I zhink zhat destroying a Kinkade is sinister enough!" Ludwig fussed over the torn edges of one of the paintings.

"Ludwig, it's a mindscape. Henry can put it back together." Mara reminded him. "Focus."

The doctor adjusted his glasses as he hurried to catch up with her and they pushed open the doors together to find Henry destroying his own office. There was a hammer sticking out of the monitor, the camera above it was smashed beyond recognition, and his papers were scattered. The desktop tower was on the floor, pushed.

Henry himself was going through his shelves. Most of the books were simply dumped out on the floor, but occasionally, the computer expert would rip out a whole chunk of pages from the book and toss them into the air like confetti.

"Henry, what are you doing?!" Mara grabbed for one of the books. "You're destroying your own home!"

"Don't you realize how long I've wanted to do this?" Henry hissed, ripping one of the volumes in half along the spine. "Out with them! Out with all the things I've kept and stored! Out with all of it! Burn it in Hell's Fires and drown it beneath the River Styx!"

"Henry, you're distraught: Vhat happened?" Ludwig adjusted his glasses in concern and stayed out of the firing range.

"It's all meaningless!" Henry responded, chucking a dozen books at his desk at once and laughing when the live electrics sparked and caught the edges on fire, forcing Mara to grab for a small, home fire extinguisher. "All of these books, all of my work, all of the antiques. 'Henry, if you do your work and live well, then you will not fear death and no one will harm you.' Someone pushed me down the stairs, Grandma!" Henry screeched at the ceiling. "All of your precious computer programming couldn't stop that!"

"Vait – who pushed you down zhe stairs?" Ludwig raised his hands in pacification. "Talk to us, Henry. Ve vant to help you."

"Are you sure it wasn't an accident?" Mara questioned helpfully.

"They meant it! They meant it!" Henry began to chant, throwing books out through the windows – the glass resisted at first, then cracked, then shattered and fell.

"Okay! They meant it, we get it, but you're not making sense." Mara held out her hands like a shield, trying to calm Henry down, trying to protect Ludwig.

Ludwig remembered what Lucy had said before – an old tart. He was lucky to have her, but was she lucky to have him? In this world, he was more of an impediment than a bonus. "Henry, calm down. Zhink logically." Ludwig tried to reach him on the intellectual level where Mara had failed on emotional. "Ve are not your enemies, but you are frightening us a great deal."

"Good!" Henry hissed, throwing a flurry of pages at Mara, who incinerated them before the crisp papers could come near them. "I want to be frightening! I want to rage and scream and do all the things I never could!"

"Henry!" Mara barked, seeing the danger in his eyes before Ludwig did. "Stay back!"

Henry lunged at them with a howl and Mara dropped into a crouch, striking outwards at his chest with two hands. "Run, Bon!"

Ludwig didn't need to be told twice. They raced out of the house as quickly as possible. "It seems zhat our friend is more unstable zhan ve realized." Ludwig panted on the front lawn. "Perhaps ve should retreat."

"He's very strong." Mara's teeth were gritted. "He's fully embraced the unreality of this place."

"It is a logical conclusion." Ludwig helplessly replied. "Und combined vizh zhe suppression zhat Henry has been lifing under, it must be like trying to bottle up a rifer. He is lashing out because he is confused und frightened. Ve hafe ripped avay his vorldfiew und he does not know how to handle zhat."

"In other words, he's completely off his rocker. What should we do?" Mara's antisocial nature could not serve her in these interactions. Ludwig reminded himself that she needed him as much as he needed her.

"I do not know." Ludwig stood up. "I zhink zhe best zhing to do vould be to leafe him alone until he is more himself."

"Well, I can get behind that." Mara looked up at the house as several figurines made of ivory flew through a window and almost took their heads off. "Run!"

They beat a hasty retreat and watched from a distance as more objects flew out of windows and bizarrely, Henry ran out with a spray can of weed killer and began spraying his grass while chanting that dandelions made pretty flowers.

"Zhat is a man who has gone off zhe deep end." Ludwig shook his head in sympathy.

"On the other hand, Dandelions do make pretty flowers." Mara pointed out and they walked away at a more sedate pace. "Should we leave him alone? What if he sets himself on fire?"

"If he dies, zhen he vill vake up in his own body." Ludwig reminded her. "Und ve hafe told him how to exit. Zhe ezhics require no furzher action on our part. If he does not vish to pursue his cure, zhat is his business und ve cannot interfere."

"We should check on him occasionally, though. Just to let him know he's not alone."

"Undoubtedly, but for now, our focus should be on zhe fourzh member of our triangle: Zhis elusive Ozher." Ludwig tapped his chin. "Ve do not know much about zhem."

"Nope." Mara agreed. "Just that they make almost perfect Facsimilies. What does that tell us about them though?"

"Vell, I suppose ve could start vizh zhem hafing a photographic memory." At some point, New York had grown a lot warmer and fresher and he shrugged open his coat to enjoy the Hill Country air. "But zhat does not seem right... Henry had a near-perfect New York, und his Facsimiles are as soulless as any of zhe ozhers. Perhaps I should see zhese Facsimiles for myself."

"I'll be glad to take you looking for one." Mara agreed as they stepped up to a two-story Hill Country cottage and she pushed open the door. "But I'm tired and I want to be home right now."

"Of course." Ludwig agreed at once. It was hard to remember sometimes that the effortless transitions between worlds and domains were actually quite draining on Mara, especially with the controller's mind pressing down on her own psyche. "I could use a break myself. All zhis zhinking can be exhausting."

"…It's the one activity that people try to avoid." Mara muttered under her breath. "Thinking, the bane of the ignorant and the tyrant."

"No vonder zhe Zhinker looks like he has a bad stomachache." Ludwig agreed humorously.

"Or Leonardo has such a twisted scowl." Mara snorted and pushed into the living room – sunk slightly into the foundation and filled with couches and sheepskin rugs.

"Or Einstein has zhe insane hair." Ludwig flopped down on top of her as she sprawled out on the fluffiest rug.

"Or Plato lost all of his." Mara grunted as Ludwig landed on her chest and corrected the angle of her torso to shrug him off onto the rug beside her, leaving only his head leaning on top of her chest.

"Or John Locke looks so lost." The doctor tried to cling stubbornly to his perch, but Mara could be slippery as an eel when she wanted to be.

"Or the Founding Fathers had to wear wigs." Mara's arm came out like an ironband and prevented Ludwig from climbing back up.

Ludwig wiggled against her arm but gave up after a few moments. "Or I put up vizh you."

"Are you calling yourself a great thinker?" Mara tickled his ribs. "I don't think you are." She teased him with a hand in his hair.

"Zhere must be a reason zhat I keep you." Ludwig playfully responded.

"Hmm… You do have excellent taste." Mara mused to the ceiling.

"I vas zhinking more along zhe lines of my mind being gone und zhat is vhy I keep you."

"I should think that keeping me is the greatest argument for sanity that a man can have." Mara's knees pulled up into angles and she crossed one leg over the other.

"Ja, zhat may be so, but it does not explain how I sleep vizh you snoring so badly." Ludwig relaxed perpendicular to Mara's body and forgot entirely Lucy's hurtful words.

"I do not snore."

"Mmm… Ja, you do."

"No, I do not. That's Patches." Mara whistled idly for their pet and the dog rushed down the stairs from where he had doubtless been lounging in the master bedroom.

"Zhen how do you explain zhe 'barking spiders'?" Ludwig good naturedly scratched Patches' ears as the dog licked at his chin and nose. "Stop zhat, you shtupid dog. I do not need my face vashed."

"Good boy, Patches. Good boy." Mara cooed to the dog as she reached up to scratch his ears and gently pull at the folded skin around his neck. "Clean his face."

"Do not encourage zhis!" Ludwig mock-severely ordered her, pushing Patches away.

"Come here, Patches." Mara sat up, displacing the doctor. "Come here!"

The dark brown and white dog rushed to her at once, all wagging tail and enthusiastic tongue.

"Gross, Patches." Mara laughed and kissed his nose, pulling him into a strangulation-strength hug. "I wuv you! I wuv you!"

"I'm going to be sick." Ludwig announced, retreating to a couch to watch Mara and the dog wrestle about with a knotted rope that Patches had chewed into a mass of barely put-together strands.

"Not on the sheepskin!" Mara warned him as she got to her feet with difficulty, pulling back hard on the rope bone. "Come on, Patches! Get it! You can do it!"

Patches let out a playful growl and shook his head from side to side, trying to get the rope away from Mara as his tail waved like a fan. They danced around each other, moving this way and that as each sought an advantage.

"She really is lofely." Ludwig found himself thinking. *"Und so alife in spite of eferyzhing."*

"Why on earth did she choose an old tart like you?" A nasty, creeping little voice that was very like Lucy crept in and poisoned his thoughts. *"How many good years do you have left? Thirty? If you're lucky…"*

"Shut up. It's quality zhat counts." Ludwig set his head a little straighter and adjusted his stance. *"Und I am not so bad. My Vater had a good, long life before he died."*

"But it doesn't always translate and we both know that… what are you going to do when you're a broken down old wreck in a wheelchair and she's still running marathons?"

"I vould-" But Ludwig didn't get to finish the thought because Patches' rope bone snapped in two suddenly, sending both Mara and the dog sprawling. Mara's head made contact with his knee and broke him out of his internal self-flagellation. "Ouch!"

"Woah!" Mara's hand came up to cup the back of her head. "That'll leave a sore patch. You okay, Bon?"

"Just a sore knee." Ludwig assured her, rubbing his own appendage. Patches stared at bot of them, the end of the broken rope bone hanging out of his mouth and his tail slowly wagging apologetically.

"Come 'ere, Patches." Mara sighed, rubbing his ears. "We'll get you another rope bone, don't worry."

Patches rested his muzzle on her breast and stared up at her with soulful eyes, the piece of the rope bone held out like an offering. Ludwig reached down and, with a hand that felt at the same time desperate and sweet, he stroked her hair. If he could have gotten away with it, he might have grabbed her braid and tugged like a schoolboy unable to tell the girl he liked how he felt.

"What do you want to eat?" Mara spoke at some point and after a pause that was long and sleepy, Ludwig answered.

"Vhat do you vant to eat?"

"I asked you first." Mara kicked her feet into the sheepskin and stretched.

"I asked you second." Ludwig retorted to be difficult.

"Ravioli with pesto?" The blonde woman suggested at last.

"Zhat sounds Vunderbar. Vhat kind of Rafioli?"

"Lobster." Mara decided and pushed herself up. "Come on – let's make it from the ground up. It'll be fun."

"Fery vell... Do you hafe a pasta machine?" Ludwig rolled off the couch to follow her – he always would.

"Do you have to ask?"

Ludwig could still smell buttery pasta long after Mara had banished the mess into her mindspace – including the raviolis stuck to the ceiling. She had an arm around him, pulling him close. His weight had to be cutting circulation off in her arm. He would adjust their positions in a moment, but for now he was enjoying the arm around him. In light of the dark turn his thoughts had taken throughout the day, it was nice to be reminded that for all that he loved her like a bird loved its nest, she loved him the way a dragon loved its hoard.

Was that a good thing?

Ludwig had never done his best or most rational thinking when he was trying to fall asleep. In fact, it was rare that his sleep would have been so hard to find. During medical school, he had been famous for falling asleep during the dissection of a cadaver – when other students were leaning forward to make notes and sketches. He had woken to the janitor poking him with his mop and his glasses askew.

Disquiet in the mind had never robbed him of sleep before.

"You vould zhink," Ludwig sat up and thought to himself. *"zhat since I am in CORD, I vould be able to sort out my subconscious problems on mein own, vizhout being kept from slumber."*

Then again, he never would have imagined himself in this situation – inside a machine, speaking to someone through a computer. This had to be unprecedented. Briefly, he thought of the

Grandmother and wondered if she had told anyone about her experiences. He wondered if they believed her or if they thought that she had just had a surreal dream as a result of being kept in a coma for so long. When they woke and corroborated her story, what would the doctors do? It might be better to keep silent, to avoid being branded insane, but this was what CORD was meant to do, after all. It was a computer interface with the human nervous system – a communication system between man and machine. If it could work, it would launch medical science ahead a century at the least. Who knew what kind of damage might be repaired with a simple computer chip one day?

"Ve are in zhe midst of a grand experiment." Ludwig mused to himself. *"Und ve must be brafe, for zhe experiment is to benefit all of mankind."* He had been so willing to donate himself to this machine. When Doctor Berwick leaned over him, when he steadied the pen in his hand, he had been so ready. Perhaps that had been the pain and the medicine he had been pumped full of, but he hadn't been afraid.

He hadn't been prepared either. Fleeing, his thoughts returned to the frozen spectre of his mental train. Mara had full control over her own world, but in Ludwig's, she couldn't even crack the ice that had sprung up over everything. It seemed he had been plunged into an eternal winter. And the lure Lucy had used, the promise of dance and warmth – of human company. The Would-Be Devil had read the doctor's heart, it seemed, and known exactly what to promise him to make him follow a fairy trail to his own destruction.

Speaking of Lucy, that whispering, sticky voice was back again. *"I will take her from you and I will destroy her. I will destroy you again and again… you will never escape."*

"You won't touch a hair on her head." Ludwig scoffed. *"Don't forget what I managed to do to you, Lucy, and Mara is stronger than I am."*

"You think so, do you?" Lucy's voice stroked his ears, sending shivers down his spine and driving him down into that small corner of himself where everything around him was so much more frightening than he was and the distant warmth that optimism offered was a dull flame indeed. *"How can I touch your mind then? How can I whisper directly to your soul? I am growing stronger, Bon. Stronger and stronger. Soon no one will be able to stop me."*

"I need to vake up." Ludwig spoke aloud suddenly.

"Wakefulness can't save you, Bon."

"Mara, vake me up." The doctor forced his mouth and tongue to work.

"You can't escape me."

"MARA!"

"Wake up!" Mara slapped him across the face. "What's going on? Were you dreaming?"

"I don't know." Ludwig put a hand to his temple and rubbed there. "Danke."

"No problem. I'll slap you any time." Mara pushed her loosed hair back out of her face. "What happened?"

"I don't know. I zhink Lucy vas talking to me. He said he vas getting stronger." Ludwig laid back down. "I don't vant to sleep anymore."

"…You need sleep, though." Mara worriedly knit her brows together. "It's the only real necessity we have here."

"Ja… But I do not vant to hafe to face Lucy in mein dreams."

"Ludwig, Lucy can't reach you here. I've Lucy-proofed this place. Whatever you're hearing, it's coming from up here." Mara tapped his forehead. "And your subconscious is messed up over something. I don't know what it is, but I know you can't just stay awake. If your brain is in a constant state of excitement, it'll start leaking out of your ears."

"I know zhat!" Ludwig threw a pillow into her face to shut her up. "Put your mask back on und go to sleep. I'm going downstairs to try to relax."

"No. If you're staying up, I am too." Mara batted the pillow away and slid out. "Come on. We can watch a movie or listen to some music. That might help you sleep better."

"If zhis is all mental, zhen I doubt zhat imagining music vill help." Ludwig followed her down to the den of warm furs and laid on the couch with Mara.

"Maybe if I rub your back too." Mara offered, settling in with him on top of her – Ludwig's favorite position. "Just relax and try not to think of Lucy."

"It's not going to vork." Ludwig closed his eyes as Mara trailed her long-fingered hands up his shoulder bones. "Zhe moment I relax, I vill be zhinking…"

Whether it was the scent of the sea foam perfume Mara wore or her fingers doing their job or the alternately soft and firm body pillow she made, Ludwig managed to get to sleep dreamlessly within moments.

"Zhat vas veird." Ludwig mused into Mara as they slowly woke up in the morning. "I didn't know it vas possible to dream in CORD."

"I dream all the time." Mara yawned. "It's just like sleep anywhere else: Your brain doesn't shut down."

"I hafe nefer dreamed here." Ludwig sighed and closed his eyes. "Did ve leafe my glasses upstairs?"

"Maybe." Mara grumbled and one hand went searching. "No, wait, here they are." She had pulled them from the air again as was her wont and she set them gently on his face where he was pressed against her side. They must have made at once a comical and heartwarming sight there on the couch, in their flannel pajamas. "That is weird, though. That you haven't dreamed, I mean."

"Do you dream often?" Ludwig found that his voice was softer than normal and heavy with sleep.

"Almost every night. Don't ask about what." Mara shifted and arched her back before turning over onto her side, trapping Ludwig against the couch cushions. "Do you want breakfast?"

"Only if it's lobster." Ludwig muttered back.

"That would be quite a breakfast." Mara sighed and sat up. "Will you turn up your nose to pancakes?"

"Nein, I vill not. Vhatefer you vish, serfe it."

They ended up having something that was more like lunch as they lounged and leaned their way up and into wakefulness, enjoying this sleepy flavor of companionship. In the end, it didn't matter what they ate. They ate together. It was good.

The whole day was sleepy and spent mostly horizontal, on couches and in chairs. They ended it with a thunderstorm full of lightning strikes and the alternating soft and roaring claps of thunder. Mara had a crystal glass of Bourbon idly hanging from one hand and Ludwig had a flute of champagne with a never-ending stream of pearly bubbles rising to form a band of white on the top.

"…Mara, vhy do you put up vizh me?" Ludwig questioned suddenly into the thickness of the evening.

"...I thought it was you putting up with me all the time." She had her hair down in braid-crimped waves and it was shining slightly – he remembered a jar of rose-scented oil on the counter in the bathroom.

"You know zhat is only mein little joke, Mara. Now come. Tell me vhy."

"I would think that would be obvious." Mara's tone became slightly grumpy. "I love you."

"...I lofe you too." Ludwig sipped his champagne and tried not to think too much about the insult hanging in his head. "*Old tart.*"

There was a long hour of absolute quiet and Ludwig thought Mara had gone to sleep.

"You're intelligent, resilient, good-looking, grounded, and mature." She finally stated. "You don't need or want to hide behind pretty lies."

Ludwig absorbed that easily and mulled it over. "Neizher do you."

"Ludwig, I imagine myself into a nine-foot-tall giantess with a tattoo of the Holy Bible covering my skin. I think that's enough of a pretty lie." Mara pointed out.

"If you vere lying to yourself, you vould fix zhe vay your nose bulges." Ludwig retorted. "Und do not take zhat as an insult. I like your nose, und zhe rest of your face. My point is zhat you could easily create zhe perfect voman here, but you hafe not. You hafe left your flaws. Your size is a matter of comfort – you do not delude yourself zhat you are a giantess, just like you are not deluded zhat you are in zhe real vorld. You hafe alvays been telling zhe truzh, Mara. It is simply a matter of how you see zhe vorld versus how it sees you. Perhaps you vant to lie to zhem, but you know zhe truzh und zhat is vhat counts."

"…Ya know, it was you looking for reassurance just a bit ago. I'm fine with myself." Mara tipped her glass to watch the dark liquid pouring out to mix with the rain beneath their balcony. "And you should be fine too. I like you just the way you are and nothing will change when we wake up. If anything, you'll take one look at me and run the other way."

"…I hafe seen enough patients in remission to know zhat it is not pretty, Mara." Ludwig assured her. "Ve vill come zhrough togezher."

"Then don't ask me why I love you again. I thought I had made it clear." Mara hauled back with one arm and tossed her glass out. The lightning struck and shattered it into dust. "Had enough of the fireworks, Ludwig?"

"Ja." Ludwig threw his own flute and was gratified when there was a flash of light and the scream of shattering glass. "To bed zhen?"

"Tomorrow we're going to start talking about how we're going to hunt down the Other and pay Henry another visit." Mara decided. "Too much of this resting and I might get used to it."

"Ve all hafe to keep our buns in gear." Ludwig teasingly agreed.

"I've never seen the Other." Mara told Ludwig for the third time the next morning as they spread out a crude map of CORD between them. The Grandmother had been scrawled out in an ashy grey and Henry's territory had question marks all over it surrounded by torn books, paintings, and broken glass.

"You hafe told me zhat. Ve need to see her Facsimiles so I can attempt to determine vhat makes zhem so realistic." Ludwig reminded Mara.

"We were supposed to do that yesterday. Sorry."

"Nein. It vas mein own fault. Mein schtupid dream." Ludwig muttered.

"It was a good day. It's good to take care of yourself." Mara reminded the doctor. "So, we need to visit Henry and hunt down one of the Other's Facsimiles. That's what we're doing after lunch. Get out your notepad, darlin'. It's going to be a long morning."

Ludwig grabbed a stack of sticky notes and began making them. "Vhat do ve know about zhe Ozher?"

"Perfect Facsimiles. Unlike any of the others I've seen. The only way I can tell they're not human is when Lucy kills one of them and they don't become a Shadow. Oh, and they tend to disappear and not come back or come back very different after about a week. Those are the only two differences between them and humans." Mara was pacing around the kitchen table, thinking.

"Perfect Facsimiles." Ludwig repeated back, making a note. "How long has zhe Ozher been here?"

"I don't know. Longer than I have and I've been here eight years." Mara shook her head. "I still can't believe that."

"Beliefe it. Dates don't lie." Ludwig made a note. "Do you know if zhey vere zhe first one here? Zhat might explain some of it."

"I think so. I mean, you get a feel for that kind of thing. I know the Grandmother was pretty recent and Henry was here after her. I was here when Lucy was put in, so I pre-date Lucy, but not by much, but from what I heard from the others and from the people before they became Shadows, no one was here before the Other, so they must be first." Mara extrapolated, letting her thoughts flow out around her like streaming ribbons.

"Zhe Ozher..." Ludwig scratched out notes. "Vas first..." Looking up, he wondered. "Do you zhink zhat zhey hafe some kind of control ofer zhe rest of us? Zhat perhaps zhey are manipulating efents und allowing us to communicate vizh each ozher?"

Mara shrugged her shoulders and spread her hands in confusion. "What? Like they took control of CORD and somehow managed to change the programming to allow the other sleepers to talk to each other? That sounds like crazy conspiracy right there. No, I don't think they're that powerful. At least, I hope not."

"It vould be difficult to deal vizh zhem if zhey had managed to take control." Ludwig agreed, doodling slightly on the map. "Vhat else?"

"…That's pretty much it. The Other keeps to themself and just watches the world go by as far as I know. All of our knowledge is going to be second hand at best. I mean, we can extrapolate, but there's almost nothing to go on."

"Question." Ludwig tapped his chin with the pen. "Do you zhink zhe Ozher's Facsimiles know anyzhing about zhe Ozher?"

"They're very cryptic when they speak, if they speak at all." Mara replied. "Especially on the Other themself."

"Ve are good at riddles." Ludwig leaned on his elbows.

"Only the ones we know already, Bon." Mara retorted and sat down in the chair across from him.

"I zhink ve are good at riddles efen vhen ve do not know zhem." The Doctor sat back in his chair. "I vork ceaselessly, und you vill alvays feel me, but nefer see me. Vhat am I?"

"Heart." Mara held up a tennis ball and began bouncing it on the floor. "That's an easy one. I bite without teeth, mutter without a mouth, and push without hands."

"Vind. Who is gifing easy ones?" Ludwig teased back. "Let us go. Ve are not getting any younger."

They went to check on Henry first. When they reached his house, it was neat and everything had been put back in order almost perfectly. Henry had fertilized the lawn and watered it to get rid of the weed killer and pulled all the dandelions.

"He was destroying all of this the last time we saw this place." Mara stepped through the front door easily and they turned their eyes on the foyer. The sunflower vase had been glued back together, the paintings had been glued… it was almost seamless.

"I can still see zhe cracks." Ludwig ran the tips of his fingers over the tear through the middle of the Kinkade. "Zhey are faint, but I see zhe cracks."

"What do you think? Denial to Anger and straight into Bargaining? If I put my house and mind back in order, I'll wake up and everything will be the same?" Mara questioned as she continued to search for Henry. "He's not in his office!" She called down over the stairs.

"…Nein, he vould not be." Ludwig turned to look out towards the back yard. "Mara, he is outside."

"Bargaining implies a change in his lifestyle." Mara came down the stairs. "What do you think he's going to change?"

"…Vhat does efery busy Vater vant to change more zhan anyzhing else?" Ludwig pulled open the back door. "More time vizh his children."

Henry was playing in the back garden with a young girl – only about three years old. She had his straight black hair and charming, apricot-shaped eyes. They were chasing after insects in the lawn with small, finely-woven butterfly nets.

"Bon, there aren't any pictures inside." Mara stopped on the back porch and they watched the man playing with his little daughter. "Not of a wife or a daughter."

Ludwig folded his arms. "Vhat do you zhink? Zhis is a fantasy?"

"Or he went through a very messy divorce." Mara sighed and shoved her hands into her pockets. "Maybe we should just go."

"Ja… Zhat seems best for now. Ve vill come back und check on him later." Ludwig nodded crisply.

"You all right, Bon?" Mara cut her eyes at him, detecting that subtle note.

"…Zhis is a fantasy vorld, Mara. In a few days, it vill all come crashing down around him und he vill be left alone once more." The Doctor entwined their fingers as they stepped back through the house.

"…He's not you." Mara told Ludwig quietly. "And we're not living in a fantasy. This is real, and it's built on a rock. We're not going to crash down."

"…Ja." Ludwig smiled slightly as they went hunting for a Facsimile.

"Perhaps ve should call?" Ludwig and Mara had walked for what felt like hours through a maze of shapes and colors. The Other's world was abstract and seemed to be made of a crazy quilt patchwork. There was a tree on a verdant hill growing right next to a patch of desert that was sandwiched between a fault and an ocean and it just went on from there. "Zhis vorld hurts mein eyes."

"I know." Mara grimly pressed on. "And calling won't do any good. They come when they want to come."

"Vhy did you not mention how odd zhis vorld vas before? Zhere are so many puzzle pieces zhat are falling into place now." Ludwig shielded his eyes from a child's vision of a rainbow, shining a little too brightly for his taste.

"I didn't think it was important. Everyone has a weird world. Mine is this massive continent made of idyllic surroundings and constantly covered by clouds. Henry's is a mathematically perfect London. I don't need to tell you about Lucy's: You've been there." They both shuddered.

"Ja, Mara, und zhe differences betveen zhe vorlds say a lot about zhe person creating zhem." Ludwig berated her, beating at his head with his knuckles in frustration. "Zhis vorld vas made by a child or someone vizh a child-like mindset. I zhink zhat zhe Ozher – vhen zhey vere introduced to CORD – could hafe been no more zhan fife years old."

"…Is that even possible?" Mara pushed through a stand of bushes that – by some miracle – didn't have thorns or even protruding branches.

"I do not know. Doctor Bervick only informed me of you, Lucy, Henry, und zhe Grandmozher. He mentioned zhat zhere had been deazhs on CORD – but zhat vas expected – und zhat zhere vas one ozher person in zhe system, but he didn't mention anyzhing about zhat person." Ludwig explained.

"If they were the first person on CORD, they have to have been here for, what? Twenty years? …Shoot, Ludwig… No wonder they'd be confused."

"Zhey must have been growing up here, in CORD, alone. Only zhemselfes to explore und understand zhe vorld…" Ludwig stepped carefully onto a complicated stepping stone pattern suspended over the fault. Mara was close behind. "No vonder zheir world is scattered, Mara – look!" The Doctor pointed ahead. "Zhe lodge… und it is snowing. Mara, zhe Ozher has constructed zheir reality entirely from pieces of ozher sleepers'. Zhere is no rhyme or reason because zhe Ozher does not understand vhy zhere should be."

"…Bon…" Mara had a sudden, terrible realization. "If they were that young when they were added to CORD and CORD is all they've ever known… how can they comprehend a world outside this one or even the idea of waking up?"

"...I do not know." Ludwig stepped up to the Lodge and rapped smartly on the door. "Ve may hafe to teach zhem about it before zhey are villing to accept zheir entrapment... If zhey efen can..."

"... Are you sure we have to tell them?" Mara stood on her own stoop and pulled her coat a little closer around her. "Wouldn't it just confuse and frighten them?"

"Ve cannot leafe zhem here." Ludwig rapped on the door again. "Zhat vould not be responsible. Zhey hafe a right to know zhe truzh, efen if nozhing comes of it."

Mara put her hands to her face and pulled her expression taut in stress. "And if we keep waking everyone up, they're going to come to themselves one day completely alone..."

"It is not as if zhat is fery new." Ludwig reminded Mara. "Zhey are not exactly social."

"Only because I keep their Facsimiles away from us. It might be different with Henry and the Grandmother. I know they keep going to see Lucy – Heaven knows why."

"Mara, if ve are to gife zhem a chance to vake up, ve must see zhem und attempt to teach zhem about zhe real vorld." Ludwig reminded her. "Zhey need to be free. Zhey cannot stay here und nefer grow up. Inefitably, zhey vill be taken off of CORD und zhen who knows vhat vill happen. Ve must find a vay to vake zhem up before zhey are gifen up on or vorse."

"…I know." Mara's eyes were dim and her pupils had contracted down to pinpoints. "I can't see how this is possibly going to end well, though – ARRGH!" She jumped about a mile in the air when a Facsimile opened the door, the pleasantly smiling face and glasses a perfect mirror of Ludwig's own.

"Fascinating." Ludwig was nearly as rattled as Mara as he studied his doppelganger. "It seems zhat zhe Ozher creates zheir own copies of zhe ozher Sleepers."

"It's creepy." Mara goggled at the copy. "Oh, it's very creepy… Kill it. Kill it with fire."

"Mara! Nein! Ve must study it first!" Ludwig scolded his fiancée. "Look, it is not a perfect copy." He held up the Facsimile's left hand and showed Mara the empty finger. "It does not hafe a ring."

"That is very, very cold comfort." Mara suspiciously studied the Facsimile. "Well? Say something! I know you and your creepy types can talk."

"Indeed, I can." Ludwig's doppelganger had a higher voice than he did and less of an accent. "And you must be Mara and Ludwig. Come in."

"It knows our names, Bon." Mara hissed to him as they stepped inside. "I swear if there's a me in here too…"

"You just missed Mara." The doppelganger continued speaking as if Mara had not. "But she vill be here later if you vished to vait."

"No, zhat von't be necessary." Ludwig assured the other. "But ve do hafe some questions."

"Ask avay." Ludwig walked into the kitchen and settled at a table. "Shall ve have some tea?"

The tea was flavorless – almost like colored water – and though steam rose off of the surface it smelled like nothing and was lukewarm at best. It seemed that the Other had little concept of abstracts, like flavors and scents. That made sense. After all, Mara and Ludwig had a broad, shared background of tastes and concepts. Even when they were trying "new" dishes with each other, they could logically assume what the dish would taste like based on what other foods had tasted like. The brain could be amazingly deductive.

"How old are you?" Ludwig questioned first, trying to feel out the edges of who he was dealing with before going straight for the heart of the matter.

"I vas here before Mara." The double – it was too confusing to think of him like that. From now on, Ludwig would call him Wolfgang – told them. "Ve have been vatching you. You're interesting and seem nice. But something has kept us away from you."

"That would be me." Mara folded her arms.

"Vhy have you pushed us avay?" Wolfgang blinked his deep blue eyes. "Ve only vanted to talk."

"You're creepy." Mara bluntly answered. "And you scare me. I don't like that you don't show yourself or that you have to speak through Facsimiles."

"...I don't understand. Am I not speaking to you properly? I am not hurting you, am I?"

"Nein. You are not." Ludwig assured Wolfgang before Mara could reply. "Mara has simply been gifen good reason to be suspicious of zhe ozhers in here. Zhey are not all nice."

Wolfgang nodded and blinked owlishly. "No, they aren't. Michael keeps taking my dolls and tearing them up. It's not very nice of him at all."

"...Michael?" Ludwig looked over at Mara with a raised eyebrow and the blonde woman shrugged. "Who is Micheal?"

"He has yellow hair and black clothes." Wolfgang described. "And he likes drinking red punch."

"...Lucy!" Ludwig's eyes opened wide. "You are talking about Lucy!"

"His name is Michael." Wolfgang informed them with the conspiratorially superior air of a child correcting a grown-up. "He told me when he first came here and started taking my dolls."

"I never knew his name was Michael." Mara blinked. "Why did he tell you?"

"I asked." Wolfgang crossed his arms and smiled, smug. "So he told me and then he took my doll and ripped it all up. He isn't very nice."

"Fascinating." Ludwig breathed. "So, you managed to communicate vizh Lucy when he vas just putting togezher his persona."

"Yes. I talk to everyone." Wolfgang stood up and brought over a bowl of fruit to place on the table. "Even the Doctor."

"…The Doctor?" Ludwig raised a brow. "Do you mean me?"

"No! I mean the Doctor. Don't you know anything?" Wolgang dismissively waved a hand in the air. "The Doctor is Michael's friend."

"…As far as I know, Lucy doesn't have friends. Unless you count the Shadows he keeps as trophies." Mara cupped her chin and thought. "I don't remember there being a doctor… but I suppose I didn't exactly talk to all of them before they died."

Wolfgang rolled his eyes. "I'm tired of you. Go avay."

"Can ve come back tomorrow?" Ludwig questioned as they stood up – Mara all too eager to escape from this parody house and Ludwig not wanting to offend the child, at least not yet.

"Maybe, if you promise to play better." Wolfgang told them as they left and he didn't bother to see them out.

"He's quite rude." Mara thumbed back at the lodge.

"Zhey are a child." Ludwig reminded Mara. "Zhey need to be taught good manners und it is clear zhat no one has taught zhe Ozher."

"You would think he could pick it up by watching people." Mara grumbled.

"Vhy hafe you decided zhat zhe Ozher is a he?"

"He chose to talk to us through you." Mara explained. "That seems to suggest that it's a he."

"Ja, but you hafe mentioned zhat zhey hafe many ozher Facsimiles. If anyzhing, I zhink zhe Ozher is a girl. Zhey call zheir Facsimiles dolls und are fery conscious of forms und zhe vay zhings look." Ludwig reminded Mara of the flavorless tea and the fruit bowl. "Zhat is not zhe behafior of a young boy."

"You're very concerned with how things look. You fuss over your spit-curl all the time." Mara pointed out. "Does that make you a girl."

"Nein." Ludwig denied with a sweep of his hand. "But zhat is a learned behafior. I vas trained by my Mozher to keep mein hair neat vhen I vas a young man."

"And there's no one to train the Other, therefore because he has a decorating instinct, he must be a girl." Mara rolled her eyes to the sky slightly. "I have brothers. I know how they act."

There was no point in opening up the can of worms brewing just under the surface of that statement. After her run-ins with the Grandmother, Mara couldn't truly be certain that she did have brothers or what they acted like. That was the nature of manipulated memories.

"Ja, zhat is true. But hafe you efer had a tea party vizh zhem?" Ludwig cocked an eyebrow.

"…Well, not one that wasn't interrupted by the Robotsformers and their cronies in Green Beret Gary." Mara admitted.

"How diabolical." Ludwig chuckled and ribbed her gently. "Zhat is vhy I do not zhink zhe Ozher can be a boy."

"Ya know, he might be a boy who just happens to like tea parties. I'm told that they exist." Mara folded her arms grumpily.

"Does it truly matter, Mara? Zhey are a child und zhey need help. Zhat is enough for me."

"…Yeah, I guess it's enough for me too."

Once home, Ludwig went to sleep easily, but the dreams were not done with him yet. Once again, he found himself paralyzed and listening to sneaky, snaking voices in his ears.

"Well, well, well… look at this. Back again. Are you finally putting it together?"

"Mara und I hafe discussed zhis. Ve know you are part of my subconscious. I just hafe to figure out vhat you vant." Ludwig told the Lucy-voice in his head.

"Vhat makes you think he vants anything?" Suddenly, the high voice of Wolfgang joined them, echoing through his head.

"Eferyone vants somezhing." Ludwig countered this new voice.

"Or maybe… Just maybe… your mind is finally breaking down and your subconscious can't protect you anymore."

"You realize that all of this isn't real? There are wires in your brain connecting you to a computer interface – how much damage does that have to cause?"

"Even the slightest change in voltage could lead to death."

"Or, who knows? Is any of this any more real than a fantasy? Are you actually trapped inside a dying body – frantically clawing to escape from this prison dragging you down?"

"Nein… Nein! I vill not listen to zhis! I know vhat you are doing!"

"Do you? Are you certain? Do you really trust the doctors who pulled you from the wreckage? Don't you remember?"

"Vhat? Vhat should I remember?!"

"They let you fall." Wolfgang's voice whispered.

"They let you fall!" Lucy exulted over Ludwig.

"They LET YOU FALL!"

Ludwig blinked and he was staring up at surgical lights on a slick table. Someone had their fingers inside his chest. Someone else was trying to put his neck back together. A nerve touched wrong and his whole body spasmed, leaping clear of the table as shouts of shock and alarm went off around him. He dropped into the freezing air clear off the side of the operating table. The sound of a heart monitor flatlining followed him down as he fell forever…

"WAKE UP!" And Mara was slapping him awake in a puddle of icy water beside their bed.

"Zhey let me fall!" Ludwig screamed as he gripped Mara's arms, bruising them.

"Not this again!" Mara shook him. "You did not fall off the operating table! What kind of clumsy idiots would the surgeons have to be if they let you fall off the table?"

Ludwig hyperventilated, leaning his head against her shoulder – marveling at how solid it was. "Mara? Zhis is real, isn't it? You're not just someone I made up? Zhis isn't just somezhing I conjured to ease mein own passing, is it?"

"…Of course it isn't." Mara rubbed his neck gently. "I'm real. I know that… What did you see, Ludwig? What is tormenting you like this?"

"…I don't know." Ludwig moaned into her shoulder. "I don't know."

Neither was well rested by the time they dragged themselves out of bed. "Do we really have to go visit the Other again?" Mara asked as she pulled herself together somewhat literally. It seemed that her tattoo was spilling down her skin and she had to put it in order before she could get up.

"Ja. Ve must establish zhat ve can be trusted." Ludwig tried to be a good soldier, putting the mess of his face into order, but it seemed that no matter how many times he smoothed his hair, the moment he turned around, it knotted back into a mess of bedhead.

"You look barely held together." Mara pointed out unnecessarily. "I don't look much better." In reality, she had pulled herself to a point that was almost normal. The only thing that stood out was the ends of her braid, which were undone, and the black words peeking out of her collar – like a pantyhose pulled up too high.

"Ve're bozh tired." Ludwig stated, just as unnecessarily. "I've never felt tired here. At least, not tired vhen I just got up."

"You had a nightmare. It happens." Mara reminded him. "People wake up still tired in the real world all the time."

"Ja, but zhis is not zhe real vorld."

"Wouldn't it be doubly true that people would wake up tired then?" Mara pointed out, kissing the air to call Patches to them. "Because it takes so much more mental exercise to visualize all of this."

"Ja, perhaps zhat is true." Ludwig considered. "But ve hafe been in here for at least a year und ve hafe nefer had zhis trouble before. Or at least, I hafe not."

"Admittedly, I've never been this tired in the morning either." Mara admitted. "But that doesn't mean that something is wrong. We've been doing a lot of mentally strenuous things over the past few days… past week… However long it's been. It's natural to be tired."

"It's also natural to be clinically depressed und zhat is not a good zhing." Ludwig pulled his coat around himself. "Let's go fisit Volfgang."

"You seem more upset this morning than you were when Lucy woke you up last time. What did you see?" Mara questioned as they walked out into the Hill Country. Patches seemed to be tagging along this time, running ahead and sniffing the greenery.

"…Do you remember vhen I vas new to CORD?" Ludwig asked. "How I kept hafing zhe flashbacks to my time on zhe operating table in zhe ER?"

"How can I forget? You were going to pieces all over the place." Mara shrugged. "It didn't happen again, did it?"

"I vas hearing foices-" Ludwig shook his head. "I vas hearing Lucy und Volfgang. Zhey vere tormenting me about zhe fact zhat I vas hearing zhem. Eizher zhey really are able to speak to me in mein sleep or my brain is failing zhe longer ve are on CORD."

"…Then we have to get you off CORD as fast as possible. This isn't something we can just brush aside, Ludwig." Mara stopped dead and Patches rushed back to them, sensing the change in mood.

"You can't stay on CORD with your brain slowly damaging itself."

"I do not efen know if zhat is our only two options!" Ludwig raised his hands in frustration. "I do not know if zhere is damage or if zhere is simply a subconscious part of me tormenting itself vizh zhe idea zhat perhaps I am dying und all of zhis is a hallucination! All I know is zhat I seem to hafe fallen off of zhe operating table. Zhat is zhe only common zheme!"

"That's a very vague and ridiculous theme, though. No ER doctor would let a patient fall off of the table. They would lose their license and that's only to start surely. There are straps and binds and people all around you to hold you in place." Mara reminded him. She took hold of his shoulders and stared into his eyes. "What if the falling is a metaphor? What if you remember falling unconscious or into this coma and that's what your mind is thinking of when you remember falling off the table? What was it you said the first time? They let me fall?"

"I zhink so." Ludwig agreed, listening.

"Then what if your mind is looking for someone or something to blame? What if you fell unconscious and your mind is associating that with a physical fall? You're a great doctor. A neurosurgeon. Maybe you're thinking that if you had been the one behind the knife that day, that you would be awake now. That's reasonable, isn't it?" Mara questioned, searching his eyes with her own.

"Ja, zhat does seem reasonable." Ludwig's subconscious didn't entirely shut up as he considered Mara's proposition, but he was willing to ignore the problem for a little longer. "Und I could hafe done better zhan zhey did. I know zhat."

"Well…" Mara clearly took that as a sign that he felt better because she linked her arm in his. "I think you would have. But you were put into other people's hands and they didn't exactly do a bad job. Here you are after all and here I am."

"But for how much longer?"

"Don't ask questions like that."

Wolfgang wasn't waiting for them alone today. Mara's doppelganger was there as well.

"…Hell, no." Mara muttered under her breath and began back-pedaling. "I can't deal with copies of myself, Ludwig."

"She's not a copy of you." Ludwig laced his hand with hers and refused to let go. "She's a hologram at best. Come on."

"I don't want to talk to a copy of myself, no matter how real or non-real she is, Ludwig." Mara hissed back, trying to tug her hand away from him with sharp, jerky motions.

"Mara, ve hafe to explain to zhe Ozher zheir situation. It is a matter of ezhics, und you are going to grow up und come vizh me because I might hafe need of you. Just imagine zhat she is a cousin who happens to look exactly zhe same." Ludwig dug in the heels of his jackboots and refused to stand down.

"Ugh, fine." Mara glared at her copy. "But I do not imagine my nose that big."

Satisfied, Ludwig patted her hand. "Of course not, liebling. See? A hologram at best."

Wolfgang and Not-Mara waved as they came closer. The two were sitting in their enclosed patio and enjoying the weak, mountain sunlight. "Hallo!" Wolfgang waved enthusiastically. "Velcome! Mara, these are the people I vas telling you about."

"I can see that, Luddy." Not-Mara had an indulgent smile on her face as Wolfgang rushed over to greet them and Patches. "I'll get a tea service, shall I?"

"Of course! Ve must make our guests velcome!" Wolfgang clapped his hands together. "And who is this charming little dog?"

"Zhis is Patches." Ludwig introduced their pet, who seemed very confused as he sniffed Wolfgang and let him scratch his ears. The dog tipped his head to look up at Ludwig with a long-suffering cant to his head and mournful eyes.

Mara burst out laughing at their dog's expression. "Someone's confused. How are you, Wolfgang?"

"Wolfgang?" Wolfgang twisted the word about in his mouth. "Is that my name? Ah, vell, it is not a bad one."

"What did you think your name was?" Mara questioned.

"I thought it vas Mary. Or Margaret. Or something like that." Wolfgang explained.

Mara and Ludwig exchanged glances and the woman sighed and rolled her eyes. "Okay, you were right. The Other is a girl. A girl named Mary."

"Or Margaret. But vhat does it matter?" Wolfgang shrugged. "I am me."

"Ja, but who are you?" Ludwig turned back to the doppelganger and questioned. "Can you tell us something about yourself?"

"I vatch people." Wolfgang shrugged. He was wearing the cream-colored wool coat that Ludwig was so fond of going out for walks in and a hat with a pulled down brim. "I know! Vhy don't ve go for a valk and let Mara talk to my Mara?"

"Uh, no. Please, no." Mara objected with one finger raised. "Bon, I don't want to be left with my evil twin."

"She's not your efil tvin, Mara." Ludwig scolded. "But I am not eager to split up eizher right now."

Wolfgang looked between them and Ludwig could see some confusion in his blue eyes. Then, the doppelganger seemed to come to a realization – his glasses flashed as he nodded sagely. "Oh, of course. You are like me. You cannot be apart from each other?"

"Vell, nein. Ve are two separate people. Ve simply do not vant to be split up right now." Ludwig tried to explain without offending the child. "Sometimes, grown-ups just like staying together."

"...You only split up once before. Are you certain you are not the same person?" Wolfgang tipped his head to the side like a bird.

"Are you and Not-Mara the same person?" Mara questioned.

"Yes. Ve are. Und vhen ve are not in the same room, one of us ceases to exist. Ve can only have one doll out at a time unless ve put the other one away." Wolfgang summed the idea up neatly – childlike.

"...Sweetheart." Ludwig could almost see the moment that Mara changed gears – that she truly decided that this was a child. "How old are you, tweetiebird?"

"...I don't know. I vas here first." Wolfgang's eyes drew more closely on her.

"I bet you could tell me if you thought. Were you... one!?" Mara poked a single digit into the doppelganger's stomach and tickled.

The giggling that spilled out of Wolfgang's mouth was childish and innocent as Mara continued her interrogation – fishing for a number. For a few moments, it was charming. Then, a sick twist in Ludwig's gut explained the reason Mara was so uncomfortable with duplicates. It wasn't about seeing himself in Wolfgang, it was seeing the way that others reacted to him.

Mara treated Wolfgang as a child because she was a child. The Other – Mary, Margaret, or whatever – had made a face to speak out of. Perhaps she had no true concept of what she looked like or what was real. But Wolfgang had Ludwig's face. Ludwig felt his stomach twisting slightly as he watched Mara babying someone who looked and sounded almost exactly like him.

"Mara, do you hafe to sound like zhat? She has been lifing here for Gott knows how long und she has clearly had plenty of contact vizh people who can speak much better zhan she can. Zherefore, she can speak correctly." Ludwig irritatedly asked.

"She's having fun. The only one here being a grumpy guts is you." Mara pointed out.

"You hafe increased your height to zhe point zhat you hafe to squat to be on zhe same lefel as his eyeline." Patches was wagging his tail, tongue lolling out of his mouth as Wolfgang giggled helplessly.

"He is not a he. He is a she, as you keep telling me." Mara calmly kept tickling Wolfgang, who was squealing and protesting at her hands, batting them away. Mara shrank down back to her normal size and stopped the tickling. "And she is a child who never had parents, a real companion, or anyone to teach her about all the subtleties of reality and human relationships. I thought you would be all over this chance to make someone's life better."

"Ve need to vake her up. Now, I don't know if zhat is possible." Ludwig looked across at Wolfgang. "Vhen she might have been able to know zhe difference betveen CORD und zhe outside-"

"I am still in the room." Wolfgang pointed out. "And, much as I hate to admit anything, I can understand you both."

"Oh, good. Then we can cut to the chase. You're in a computer neural interface system called CORD and you've been here since you were at most four years old. Since then, you've been living here in CORD and keeping watch over the other people inside here. You've learned almost all of your primary language skills and what the world at large is like from them. It's highly likely that if you've been in here as long as I estimate you have that everyone close to you before whatever happened that put you in here is dead. Are you capable of understanding what I'm saying?" Mara smiled blandly and blinked both eyes.

"...I want my dolls." Wolfgang was momentarily stunned as he stared at them – she stared at them. "And I want my mommy." The voice that came out of the Facsimile was very young and very female.

"Mara." Ludwig's nurturing instinct finally triggered. "Zhat vas a bit much for her to take in all at once."

"You wanted me to treat her like an adult." Mara reminded him, a slight smirk on her face as Ludwig gently guided the child down to the sofa and pulled the Facsimile close. "Now let's treat her like she is, a child." Mara stroked Wolfgang's hair and leaned over to Ludwig's ear. "If we had kept playing the game the way she expected it, we never would have gotten anywhere near the truth."

"Ve don't need zhe truzh, Mara, ve need to find a vay to get her out of zhis Hell." Ludwig hissed back. "Und I am pissed off at you – you are sleeping on zhe couch tonight."

"What? Where I fall asleep half the time anyway?" Mara threw him a wink and joined the cuddle pile on the couch. "Don't worry, tweetheart. Most people don't actually see the real world. They don't want to see it, so they don't."

"…Zhat's vhat makes eferyzhing so complicated." Ludwig rubbed her back. "Because ve cannot show our real selfes to people. Zhey say zhat zhe truzh vill set you free und zhey're right. Vhy don't you tell me somezhing about yourself, Mary or Margaret?"

"…I like Mary better." The voice was so vulnerable, so small coming from such a large body. Ludwig couldn't ignore that it was his body it was coming from. "I think it's my name. So… I like it."

"Why don't you know your own name?" Mara questioned, pressed against Wolfgang's back.

"I don't know." The child in Ludwig's body grabbed fistfuls of Ludwig's cardigan and buried her face against his chest. "You smell nice."

"I smell like zhe forest ve valked zhrough to get here. Vould you like me to tell you about it?" Ludwig questioned, pressing his palms into her shoulders soothingly.

"…Please." The child whispered.

"Fery vell." Ludwig felt an enthusiastic weight hopping up on the couch behind him. "Patches liked zhe voods as vell. He vas running all about zhe pazh, sniffing at zhe leafes und zhe grass. It vas like being inside of a fairy dream…" The doctor went on to describe the flowers they saw – what few there were – and to embellish with a playfully imaginary chase after a raccoon that Patches supposedly led.

"You tell quite a story." Mara commented after Wolfgang had fallen asleep between them. They were spread out on the couch with their feet up, Wolgang still buried in Ludwig's chest.

"It vas a vay to get him to calm down after zhat stunt you pulled." Ludwig replied, stroking Wolfgang's hair absently. "Vhy did you just zhrow it all out on her like zhat? It vas as if you vanted to rush zhrough it."

"Maybe I did. Maybe I was so tired of being around a child and babying her along." Mara threw out again, like she was guessing at her own motives. "…Maybe I'm just a sorry DOB."

Ludwig rolled his eyes at her. "I zhink zhat you are not as impatient as you say." Ludwig lifted his head to look at her more fully. "Do you vant children?"

"Isn't this a question we've answered before?" Mara questioned. "I'm sure we talked about it at some point."

"Nein, ve didn't. I do not zhink so. Und… I do zhink I know zhe answer." The doctor leaned back against the couch again. "Ve vould not be such bad parents, vould ve?"

"…No. We wouldn't. Provided that every other set of parents on earth had died." Mara quipped. "And by that… I mean that I think I wouldn't be a very good mother. Not that I think you wouldn't be a good dad."

"Vhy?" Ludwig lifted his head again.

"Because I expect too much of children. I expect them to learn how to behave. I expect them to follow rules. I expect them to be rational creatures. In short, I want them to act a little more like me." Mara sighed. "I wasn't an emotional child. I smiled, I laughed, but I don't remember being overjoyed or happy. I don't remember being irrationally despondent over the small things that other children were."

"Some studies show zhat children who are treated as if zhey hafe zhe potential to be mature are more mature." Ludwig pointed out. "Maybe you expect much because you know zhat zhey can gife it."

"Or maybe I'm just unreasonable and I think everyone should be emotionally repressed so that the connections they do form with others only feel genuine when they happen inside a computer neural interface."

"You hafe real connections. I don't zhink you beliefe zhat ours is zhe only real one." Ludwig began to disentangle himself from Wolfgang, but only enough to reach across for Mara's hand. "Vhat about your Mozher?"

"My mother is a saint who would love me if I took a chainsaw and began butchering summer camp teenagers." Mara idly entangled their fingers, lacing them together like the lines of a herringbone pattern.

"Most Mozhers are." Ludwig squeezed the larger hand in his. "…You know, zhis vas strange to me vhen ve vere first becoming vhat ve are today. Your size is… Vell, unusual is a good vord."

Patches muttered and looked up at them from where he had laid his head on Mara's hipbone.

"I think Patches disagrees with you." Mara's other hand played with his ears. "Or he feels replaced. What do you think, Ludwig? Does Patches seem jealous?"

"I zhink he seems tired. I zhink ve all are. How safe are ve if ve fall asleep here, Mara?" Ludwig questioned.

"No. You are not falling asleep here. I don't know about the Other, but I don't want you sleeping in strange places." Mara jumped to her feet, instantly alert.

"Vait! Ve can't leafe her alone!" Ludwig was slower to climb up, not wanting to disturb the sleeping doppelganger. "If ve do, ve destroy zhe trust ve hafe built!"

"Then we'll take her with us, but I'm not going to go to sleep inside of someone else's mind. Especially a child's mind. Children are indelicate und you are in… Well is the word fragile too offensive?" Mara reached down and lifted Wolfgang up into her arms. "Come on, let's go. We'll take her with us to the lodge. Might not even notice we moved her."

"All right. Ve take her vizh us." Ludwig picked up his coat and called Patches. "Come on, schtoopid dog."

They didn't speak again until Wolfgang was settled in on the chaise lounge in their lodge up in the mountains. Snow was falling outside and Mara handed Ludwig a mug of rich, dark hot chocolate.

"Do you want children?" Mara asked Ludwig. "Because I could stand a few of the rugrats, I guess. Especially if I can take a break from them occasionally."

"I saw you vizh Wolfgang, Mara." Ludwig smiled and sipped his hot chocolate. "You do like children."

"I like children – doesn't mean I want to be around them all the time." Mara settled in with her own cup of hot chocolate.

Ludwig smiled slightly and sipped. Mara moved closer to him on the couch. "So, we've adopted a kid. What do we do now?"

"Ve hafe not adopted a kid. Ve hafe found someone who needs our help to vake up so zhey can go on vizh zheir life." Ludwig hummed and leaned slightly against her ribs. "Until ve can find a vay to do zhat, I don't zhink ve should leafe zhem alone because ve might be zhe only adults who deduced zhat she is only fife und vere responsible enough to realize zhat she needs someone."

"We can't stay here to raise her." Mara sighed, staring up at the bare rafters above them. "And it would traumatize her if we suddenly left her behind here in this world."

"Vhat do you suggest, Mara?" Ludwig tiredly questioned. "Ve induce a child to kill herself on zhe off chance zhat she might be able to return to a vorld she barely remembers? Perhaps once ve are out of CORD, ve can make contact vizh her und find a better vay, but for now, she must be protected… und zhat means she vill hafe to stay in CORD."

"And our dear friend Henry? What are we going to do about him?"

"I zhink Henry vill take care of himself as soon as zhe glow of his resolution to change fades. Ve can check on him tomorrow, vhen Wolfgang vakes up." Ludwig sat up and set down his mug. "Ve cannot zhink of zhis as being an impossible situation. Ve still need to vake up und ve cannot leafe her alone vizh Lucy. Vhat should ve do, Mara?"

"I think we need to break the Hippocratic Oath into tiny little pieces and find a way to trap Lucy. Something that he can't just break out of."

"Ve need to find a vay to make his coma a catatonia." Ludwig stood up to pace. "To make him entirely unresponsive und unable to leafe his own realm to cause hafoc for ozhers."

"I would settle for complete brain death. I have no problem making sure that Lucy never hurts anyone else." The dragon rippled in her voice, the warrior waking.

"I cannot condone zhat action. Ve are not law enforcement personnel."

"No." Mara stood up at her full height – all twelve feet – but even from half her height, Ludwig could see that her eyes had darkened and her bangs were shadowing the top half of her face. "We're victims under fire and under United States law, we can strike back against our attackers to preserve our lives. We can't just call the police, but we can make sure he never, ever hurts us again."

"Ve can't just decide to kill him eizher. Und zhis is not a good confersation to hafe at any point vhile ve are sleep-deprived. Ve need rest. Ve need rest vizhout nightmares. I zhink… I zhink I should sleep alone zhis efening, just so I do not disturb you. It is not zhat I am mad – I vas before, but I am not any longer – but zhat vhen I hafe nightmares, you are inefitably disturbed." Ludwig watched the room shrinking back to a more reasonable size as Mara calmed down and shrank.

"Sleeping in different beds isn't going to keep me from knowing when you have a nightmare. This isn't the real world. These walls, these beds, this lodge, are all part of my psyche. It's not a distance issue – if you fall asleep with me, then the world will monitor both of us. I'll know when you wake up screaming regardless of whether I would in the real world or not. We might as well not strain ourselves trying to avoid the nightmares. Perhaps you need to face them. But you can face them with me sleeping beside you." She made a stubbornly effective argument in that unreal way that the logic of CORD worked.

"…How much prifacy do I really hafe, Mara?" Ludwig questioned as they got dressed for bed. "Zhis vorld is in your psyche, but can I keep zhings from you? If you vere asleep und I vas in zhe kitchen, vould you know vhat I vas eating?"

"I would be dreaming vaguely of you. I might have some general idea of what you're doing, but no. I would not know what you were eating. When you're awake and I'm asleep, the world we're in transfers to your control." Mara explained, pulling on her pajamas and setting her sleep mask on top of her head. "That's why – whenever you can't sleep and you get the hankering for conversation – I can't block you out."

"Then – hypozhetically – if all of zhe Sleepers inside of CORD vere asleep at zhe same time, CORD vould cease to exist?"

"As a metaphysical world where we all interact with each other? Yes." Mara hopped onto her bed and covered her eyes with the mask. "As a real computer interface, we're all connected to? No."

"Smartmouzh." Ludwig laid down beside her, curling up.

"…Bon, why do you still sleep in my long underwear shirt? It's getting really old. I would have thought you would have chosen something else by now."

"In zhe real vorld," Ludwig closed his eyes and sighed, "I sleep in zhe nude."

"…Kinky."

"Shut up, schtoopid." Ludwig poked her. "Guten nacht."

"Night, Bon."

"Vhy do you do this to yourself?" Wolfgang questioned Ludwig that night. The doctor was tied down to one of the fleshy, spongy chairs that Lucy conjured out of human flesh and his doppelganger paced in front of him. "You know you are dying."

"Ve are all dying at farious paces. You hafe to do better zhan zhis if you vant to frighten me." Ludwig boredly squeezed the yielding chair arm to feel it squeezing back. It seemed there were advantages and disadvantages to everything being alive in Lucy's hellscape. This chair – now that he was used to the horror of it – was giving him an excellent massage with its echoing heartbeat. "Vhy are ve here instead of lying in a catatonic state in our own bed? Are you resorting to more histrionic means to get your message across?"

"You don't understand. You're a bug in the universe. Vhy do you think you keep on coming here? If I'm in your mind, then you're dying on an operating table, hallucinating in your last moments."

"I hafe been in zhis vorld for more zhan a year now. I doubt zhat efen a dying man's delusions vould last zhat long." Ludwig blinked lazily around at the fuzzy world. His glasses were off. "It's far more interesting if zhis is Lucy's doing, since zhat vould mean zhat he has somehow managed to subfert Mara's shields."

"Far more interesting, yes, but how likely is that? Ve all know that Lucy only manages to enter Mara's mind vhen she invites him. It is how she plays, yes?"

"And you? How do you play?" Ludwig questioned the dark reflection.

"I'm not going to tell you. You'll just have to find out for yourself."

He woke covered in sweat and tangled up in the sheets. A few moments with a towel and sitting up on the edge of the bed left him in a better frame of mind but the sticky thudding of the chair's blood still echoed in his ears.

The only comfort he took from the whole thing was that Mara slept soundly throughout. It seemed he had grown better at hiding his nightmares from her. Either that or this really was all a delusion – in which case there was nothing he could do and no point in worrying about it.

Mary was eating multi-colored cereal when Mara and Ludwig dragged themselves up the next morning and came up from their bedroom. "You brought me here?" The child's voice was still coming from Ludwig's bow-shaped mouth. "It's a nice home. I've only seen it a few times."

"You should have seen it a grand total of no times since I've never seen you." Mara pointed out, grabbing a cup of hot tea out of the microwave.

"You've played with my dolls before." Mary shrugged. "You were much nicer than Michael."

"It's weird to hear you call him that. The name I always call him is Lucy." Mara sat down and sipped her tea while Ludwig grabbed his own mug.

"He doesn't like that." Mary giggled.

"I bet he doesn't." Mara made a funny face at her.

Ludwig smiled at both of them. "Are you sure I am zhe one who adopted her?" He teased Mara.

"Shut up." Mara poked him in the side. "As if you're not enjoying this."

"Ve need to fisit Henry zhis morning." Ludwig deflected neatly. "Mary, I zhink ve should go alone. Henry is in a fragile state."

"Henry is always upset and distracted." Mary commented, stuffing her face with cereal. "But I'll stay here, if that's okay."

"That's perfectly fine." Mara fluffed up Mary's short, dark hair. "Come on, Ludwig. If we're going to see Henry, we should go."

"Ja. Guten Tag, Mary." Ludwig paused beside the chair and looked down at the Facsimile sitting there. His face stared up at him, a touch more youthful than he knew himself to be, a touch more innocent. "Perhaps vhen ve get back, you vill show us vhat Mary looks like, Ja? Not your dolls." He pressed a kiss to the forehead.

"…No promises." Mary replied, pursing her mouth up. "But… Maybe."

Mara ran a hand over Mary's hair. "We'll be back soon."

"Well, this seems… Grey." Mara looked up at Henry's house. The whole area was overcast and the wind was especially chilly.

"I zhink he has reached zhe phase of Depression." Ludwig folded his arms across his chest. "Should ve go inside?"

"We've come this far." Mara pushed the door open and it creaked despondently. If anything, the inside was even colder than the outside. "Henry?" Her voice echoed oddly in the corridor.

Everything seemed elongated and the shadows deepened the longer Ludwig looked at them. It was a hard, lonely place. The child's laughter had long since faded and the Doctor shivered.

"Henry!" Mara grabbed the handrail. "Come on, Ludwig. I think he's in the office."

"…Perhaps ve could check zhe backyard first?" Ludwig suggested, but even he could tell that the Office was where Henry had holed up.

"He's in here, Bon." Mara shot him a look from upstairs. "Maybe you should stay down there, though. I'll handle this."

"Fery vell." Ludwig held himself around his arms. "…Zhis is creepy." He approached a cracked vase covered with sunflowers. Or, they would have been sunflowers if they were yellow. They looked dried out and drained, like something had come and sucked the colors right out of them.

Mara looked grey and her tattoos were invading her neck and face when she came downstairs. "…Bon, let's go."

Ludwig looked up from the vase and didn't protest. "Ja, zhis is a sad place." He fled the house after Mara and found himself – for once – in danger of being left behind as she ran down the street and into the Hill Country sanctum.

"Mara!" Ludwig called after her and took to his heels, practically flying to keep up with her. "Vhat did you see?"

Mara stopped and waited for him to catch up without looking back. "…He asked me to kill him." And she would say no more.

Mary was a small, round dumpling of a girl with a puckered and almost cat-like face and straight, dark hair. Mara's eyes lit up the moment she saw her. "Mary!"

"Hello." Mary waved. She wore a fluffy, pink dress and a string of small, jade beads around her neck. Ludwig studied her cheekbones and facial structure and decided that she was most likely of Filipino descent. "I didn't bring my dolls." She told them.

"I can see that. You're very pretty." Mara crouched beside the child. "You're so big for five years old."

Mary smiled and tipped her head to the side cutely. "I like you."

"And I like you. So, what are we going to do? Want to play a game?"

"I'm really good at hide and seek!" Mary's black eyes lit up. "I bet you'd never find me."

"I bet I would! Let's play a game!" Mara challenged. "I'll count to fifty and you go hide."

Ludwig settled down on a couch to rest and watch them. It seemed Mara needed a bit of light-hearted fun. In the meantime, he needed to think. This whole situation was exponentially more complicated than it had been when they began.

Mary's development captivated the doctor's mind briefly. It seemed that she had remained in her child-like state in spite of the passing years. It was an interesting insight into the effects of society on the child. Perhaps maturity was simply a construct of adults and it was taught rather than inborn. Ludwig had read studies of children who had been indulged remaining in child-like states in spite of their advancing years. After all, who hadn't heard the tales of spoiled brats and the warnings against allowing children to become them?

But Mary's infantilism was not the malicious kind that sprang from overindulgent parent. It was a true innocence born of immaturity. She was a child who had simply never grown up. Perhaps it was a side-effect of life in CORD. Trapped inside their own heads, exposed only to people being effected by the same system.

No wonder Mary had never grown up. She must have never had a grown up who taught her how to grow up. She was a child because she had never been nurtured – like a seed left in a cabinet. And now that seed was in their hands. What were they to do?

Before he had known that the Other was truly a child, he had been so certain that it would be simple to ensure that the sleepers woke and they made it home. But the Other had never known the real world except as a child. She had no concept that the reality created inside CORD was not the true reality. For her, life had always been this way.

It would be unethical to attempt to wake her with no certainty of it working and worse to leave her alone in this bleak system. A child abandoned in an empty world of machinery would surely go mad eventually, especially after spending time in the company of others. It was a terrible thing, to be lonely.

Ludwig couldn't do that to a child. Not for anything. He wondered how Mara would react when he told her they couldn't leave yet. She might be delighted or horrified depending. She was a fascinating web of contradiction: Enjoying the freedom that this mental world allowed her, but longing for her family. The conflict with Henry and the Grandmother seemed to have awoken a need to see them in her.

They would have to talk, long and at length. Perhaps there was a way Mary could be woken from outside of CORD – using stimulants or some other method. Who knew? Perhaps merely being released from CORD might be enough to wake the child.

Mary dove beneath the blanket Ludwig was lying on and buried herself behind him on the couch. "Shh! Don't tell!" She whispered, curling in.

Ludwig smiled and adjusted his position so she was a little better hidden. Mara burst in, eyes wild with a playful fire and scanning. "I'm going to find you!"

"Is she eluding you, Mara?" Ludwig pretended to look up.

"She's a tricky beast, but I'll find her yet!" Mara searched through the room all around Ludwig's couch. "Tallyho!" She rushed back out the other door.

Mary giggled. "Mara's funny." She whispered to Ludwig.

"Ja, und she has ears like a bat, so be quiet if you do not vant her to find you." Ludwig brushed a thumb over her forehead where she was buried in his crocheted throw.

Mary nodded and cuddled in behind Ludwig, hugging him around the middle as he rested back on the pillows and a contented smile spread across his face. This would be home.

Mara pulled back the throw suddenly, waking Ludwig and Mary. "I should have known you looked lumpier than normal."

"Mara, put zhe blanket back…" Ludwig yawned heavily. "I am still tired."

"You're always tired." Mara ran a hand over his cheek and lifted Mary into her arms. "Do you want some dinner, Mary?"

"Mac and cheese…?" The sleepy girl hugged her neck.

"Sure. I'll add chicken and broccoli to it."

"I don't like broccoli…"

"You'll like it when I make it." Mara hugged Mary like a mother holding a child and then slipped her into a chair at the table while she went to the fridge and the stove, the kitchen bowing to her whims. Ludwig drifted after them, watching and holding his own counsel – at least for the moment.

It was only later, when Mary was asleep in a bedroom that Mara built into their lodge for her, and Mara was lying beside him in bed, trying to sleep, that Ludwig brought it up. "Mara?"

"…Is this important, Bon?" Mara rolled over and lifted her sleep mask.

"Kind of." Ludwig sighed, hugging himself. "Do you remember vhen ve first discovered zhat ve could leafe zhis place?"

"How can I forget? What about it?"

"I do not zhink ve can leafe anymore." Ludwig blurted out.

"…What?"

"Ve hafe Mary to zhink about now."

"Mary." Mara flopped back in the bed. "Of course, this is about Mary. I should have expected it. Well, what do you want to do about her? We can't stay here forever. It's inevitable that if no suitable progress is made in your dear Doctor Berwick's experiment, the plug will be pulled."

"But ve cannot abandon Mary eizher. Ve know how to vake up, but Mary has no concept of zhe real vorld. She is still such a child und I do not zhink ve vill be able to teach her about reality." Ludwig explained, reaching out for Mara's arm. "I know zhat I am zhe one who vants to leafe, but… vizhout Mary it vould not be right."

"...I want to go home." Mara quietly told him. "I'd miss my powers. I'd miss the freedom of this world, but I miss my family more."

"I know you do." Ludwig sighed. "I miss mein own. But vhat of Mary? If ve leafe her, she is likely to stay here, alone, for all time."

"...You're right. I know you're right. And at the same time you're wrong." Mara sat up and sighed. "People weren't important to me before she did whatever she did, you know. I could easily stay in my space all day and never really need to see my family, but now..."

"Now you do not know if your family efen exists zhe vay you remember zhem. You vant to experience zhem again, so zhat you can learn vezher your memories are zhe truzh." Ludwig finished for her. "Und zhat is fery human und fery understandable."

Mara was silent for so long, Ludwig thought she had gone to sleep. "We can't stay forever. I won't agree to that. I want to get out someday – I want to see what I've been missing."

"So do I. But ve must stay vizh Mary... for at least a little bit. Zhat cannot hurt anyone." Ludwig smiled softly in the darkness, knowing he had won.

"Fine. I guess we're staying." Mara pushed down her mask again. "Wipe that smirk off your face."

"It vas not a smirk."

"It was too a smirk, you smirking smirker. Now go to sleep."

Mary was cuddled up between them when they woke. Mara tickled their semi-adopted daughter gently to wake her up. "Good morning, Mary."

"Morning." Mary yawned. "I was cold."

"Vell, zhis is a big enough bed for all zhree of us." Ludwig stroked her hair. "Good morning, mein fraulein. Vhat do you vant for breakfast?"

"Mmmm… Nana Waffles."

"Nana waffles?" Mara lifted her head. "Is that like the waffles your grandmother makes?"

"No…" She pouted. "Nana waffles. With Nanas!"

"Bananas, I zhink." Ludwig guessed.

"Yeah!" Mary eagerly nodded. "Nanas!"

"Well, let's see what we can find." Mara pitched herself to her feet with a groan. "Getting too old for everything."

Ludwig drew the letter again. "Zhis is zhe letter A, Mary. A." He was trying to teach Mary to read. It was not going well. Mary didn't seem to understand the concept of letters and symbols were frustratingly vague for her as well. Ludwig was sure that if he could get her to catch onto this, though, that anything else he wanted to teach her would come easily. It was abstract thinking – something that didn't seem to translate as well to someone who hadn't yet mastered it.

"A. It's a letter. A letter is…" Mary furrowed her brow at Ludwig as she looked down at the scribbled drawing.

"A symbol. Zhis is somezhing zhat stands for a sound – for zhe sound a or A." Ludwig enunciated gently. "By reading or writing, you can speak to ozhers vizhout hafing to be vizh zhem in zhe same room."

"…But I can do that by sending one of my dolls."

"But in zhe real vorld, you vill not be able to send a doll to take a message to someone else." Ludwig explained. "Und vhen ve leafe CORD, you vill find zhat many of zhe zhings you can do here vill not be possible zhere."

"Why would I want to go there then?" Mary pouted. "I don't want to leave my dolls."

"I know. But zhink of all zhe zhings you could see und do in zhe real vorld. Zhere are jungles und oceans und forests all vaiting to be explored." Ludwig encouraged her to imagine. "Great, salty lakes of vater filled vizh beating vafes und surrounded by sand."

"Salty water? Yuck!" Mary stuck her tongue out. "No, thanks!"

"You are not supposed to drink it, silly zhing, it is for svimming. Zhe salt in zhe vater bouys you up like a cork und it is easy to float. It is fery fun." Ludwig tried to explain. "Und zhe vafes, zhey bounce you along in zhe vater und it is like bein zhrown up in zhe air und caught und being rocked at zhe same time."

"…That does sound fun…" She frowned. "But why can't I go to Mara's beach and do it there?"

"Because you hafe not experienced zhe sensation in real life." Ludwig explained as carefully as he could. "You see, ve are in a place called CORD und ve are connected by zhis place. Zhat means zhat ve can see und feel each ozher in our own minds. But it is not zhe same as zhe real vorld. Everyzhing zhere is so much better."

"Then why don't we go there?" Mary questioned curiously.

"Because ve are not sure how ve can get zhere as a family. Ve are vorried zhat ve might be separated if ve take you vizh us now." Ludwig explained.

"How will we know I'm ready?" Mary questioned innocently.

Ludwig reached out and ruffled her soft, dark hair. "I vish I knew, Liebling. I vish I knew."

Mary pouted and folded her arms. "What's Lee-Bling?"

"Liebling means zhat I lofe you fery much." Ludwig reached for the child and gently pulled her to him in a hug.

"You call Mara that too." Mary pointed out, hugging his neck.

"Ja. It is vhat I alvays call zhe vomen I lofe."

Mary giggled at being called a woman and Mara pressed a kiss to the top of Ludwig's head from where she had snuck up behind him. "And I call him Bon, 'cause he's sweet."

"I zhought it vas a shortening of mine last name." Ludwig kissed her back and Mary – for her part – looked disgusted and wriggled to get down.

"Haven't you ever heard of bon-bons? Good grief, you're older than I am and I know what those are." Mara teased him gently as he set Mary back down and she rushed away from her reading lesson. "No joy with her letters?"

"Nein. Zhere is somezhing ve simply cannot communicate here zhat she vould need to understand." Ludwig folded his arms. "I do not know how ve vill make her understand zhat zhis place is not real. She vas asking me vhy ve do not go to zhe real vorld just a bit ago und I told her zhat ve vere not sure all of us vould make it zhere. I do not know if ve vill efer make it home."

"I don't know either. Something to think about, I guess." Mara folded her arms around him. "Oh, sinnerman, where you gonna run to? All the walls are closing in…" She sang the lilting and sad melody as Mary ran off to play with her toys – a child, and a shackle – all at once.

"We should check on Henry again." Mara commented into the dark as they were settling down to sleep. Mary was already in her bed and Ludwig had been looking forward to passing out and resting.

The doctor grunted slightly in acknowledgment. "Do you zhink he might be in zhe Acceptance stage yet?"

"Well, depression felt very distinctive." Mara pointed out dryly. "So, I think we'll be able to tell before we actually see him whether or not it's safe to approach."

"Vhat if he asks you to kill him again?"

"Then we'll leave." The woman stated simply, tucking her feet in further into the bed. "Now go to sleep. We'll tell Mary we're going to visit him in the morning. She should be fine on her own, shouldn't she?"

"I beliefe she vill be." Ludwig laid against her back. "She has been efery time ve go to see Henry or leafe her alone."

"She's very independent. Sometimes, I forget that. She can be such a child."

"Zhat is her charm." Ludwig smiled fondly. "As it is yours."

"I am not a child." Mara smacked his backside gently. "And I should think you would know that by now."

"Ja, mein Liebling. I tease, zhat is all." Ludwig kissed her jaw gently. "Now hood your eyes und sleep. I hafe zhe feeling zhat tomorrow vill be fery interesting indeed."

Ludwig and Mara woke to find Mary playing in the snow outside the house – without her coat. Mara sighed when she saw the child and reached for the green, heavy coat hanging on the hook while Ludwig pulled on his own coat and warm Ushanka. "Mary!" She called out, irritated. "You forgot your coat!"

"I'm not cold!" Mary protested as she got up and tried to run from her snow castle – a rather clever take on sandcastles. And really, how was Mary to know that there was any difference whatsoever between sand and snow? Except for the fact that Mara ran after Mary with a coat whenever she was playing in the snow and with sunscreen when it was the sand. They looked similar enough – white sand and snow.

"Listen to Mara, Mary!" Ludwig called, tying down his Ushanka and rushing out to join them. "You could catch cold!"

"I won't catch cold! I won't!" Mary chanted in the snow, turning a few somersalts before running off again, Mara still hot on her tail. And Ludwig, feeling helpless, raced off to join them.

"Come here, you little Mudlark!" Mara bellowed after the child, the green coat raised up like a flag or a cape.

"Mary!" Ludwig laughed and almost tripped over his own feet as he raced after them into the quiet and the clean scent of the evergreen forest. "Bitte, mein Lieblings, vait for me!"

By contrast with their playful dashing through the woods, Henry's world was calm and peaceful. The sun was shining, though weakly, and there was no depressive atmosphere, no suffocation. It seemed... Becalmed. Entirely still.

"Zhis is a change." Ludwig observed.

"It feels slightly more muted than Bargaining, but endlessly better than Depression. I guess this is Acceptance." Mara muttered beneath her breath as she reached up to touch the branches of a tree. "It feels solid."

"Vell, did you expect somezhing else?"

"Did you never notice, when we were here before, that the place felt a bit cottony? That it was wrapped up in something? Now, it feels real."

"Zhat makes no sense." Ludwig reached out and knocked on the door.

For once, Henry answered the door instead of forcing them to come inside. He had looked better, but he had looked worse. He was in a pressed shirt and pants with his hair neat, but without the jacket or the tie. "I wondered when you two would come back."

"Hi, Henry. You look better." Mara studied him with wise eyes. "What have you been up to?"

"Thinking." Henry replied, beckoning them inside. "Can I offer you something to drink?"

"No, danke." Ludwig settled down on a couch with Mara across from Henry. "How are you feeling, Henry?"

"…Better. More like myself. I'm ready to go home. I just wanted to talk to you two one last time before I do."

"Well, that's good." Mara stated more to fill the quiet than anything. "Have you chosen an exit?"

"I have." Henry sighed. "I know you can change your shapes, Mara. I wondered if you would take me flying, on a dragon's back, before I did exit."

"Someone's been doing their homework." Mara airily commented. "And I would be fine with taking you on a flight. If Luwdig is."

Ludwig found himself with both of them staring at him. "Nein, I do not mind. Ve are all friends here, und zhere is no reason to be jealous."

"I should hope not." Henry's smile was wan and thin. "Frankly, I hope I never see either of you again when I wake up."

"Same to you." Mara gave a wry smile. "Well, we're not going to get anywhere by just sitting and staring at each other. Henry, if you're ready, we can go any time."

"Let's get out of the house before you transform." Henry gave a wry and lonely smile around the mis-matched and ordered place. "Somehow, I can't bear to see it disturbed, even here where it's not real."

"Zhat's fery natural." Ludwig stood up and followed them outside to where Mara could have some room to expand.

Mara stepped aside from Henry and Ludwig and took a deep breath. When she began to change, something was different this time. Her whole body elongated and became serpentine. She fell down onto six legs and golden scales erupted from her skin. Ludwig watched with his mouth open as she became an Asiatic dragon.

"Shen Lun." Henry bowed in respect.

The dragon bowed its maned head back and winked at Ludwig, who was still standing gob-smacked. "Climb on. I will take you to the Empire State Building." Mara's voice had taken on a gravely tone and a mischievous smirk was clear in her words. Ludwig found himself smiling as he climbed up behind the maned head, with Henry behind him.

"Hang on." Mara's six legs began to move, faster and faster. Ludwig recalled that Asiatic dragons were not portrayed with wings, as European ones were, but they were still known to rise into the air when necessary. Even as he wondered, Mara pitched herself forward into a momentum-propelled leap that carried them hundreds of feet into the air. Great flaps of skin and scale unfolded like kites on either side of her and they glided, carried on currents of air.

Henry held on to Ludwig's shoulders, hands clenched in the back of his coat as Mara paddled her tail like a flap behind them, guiding them through the air. New York unfolded beneath them in rows of steel and glass. It was an altogether gentle, pleasant ride, nothing like the plunges through the heavens Mara had taken Ludwig on before.

When Mara landed, she wrapped her lower body around the Empire State building, her massive tail almost reaching to the ground below. Henry climbed off over the banister and reached back out to Mara, patting her nose. He said something in Chinese and Mara huffed, flaring her mane.

"Good luck, Henry." Ludwig waved from Mara's back, where he had stayed. "Auf weidhersen."

"Good fortune to you." Henry bowed to the doctor and the dragon and Mara's legs tensed for another leap into the sky.

"Do you zhink he vent zhrough vizh it?" Ludwig questioned Mara as she flew back towards their own home.

"I don't sense Henry or his world anymore." The golden dragon replied, flapping her tail and blowing out puffs of smoke that shaped themselves into Chinese boats and other whimsical shapes. "So I suppose he did."

"Vhy did you change your dragon?" The doctor was holding onto Mara's golden mane. It was much stiffer than her hair, but had the same color.

"Sometimes, we have to take on someone else's dreams for a time." Mara mused to him. "For our own sakes."

"Ja. So, you became his dragon?" Ludwig ran his fingers through the stiff wool.

"I let him change me instead of changing myself." Mara explained. "For a brief moment, I let him shape my reality. It was… enlightening."

"Enlightening?"

"I have never allowed someone else to change me willingly before. It was interesting to be shaped instead of shaping." Mara's scales were darkening as they flew, though she remained in the Asiatic form. "And the dynamics of this dragon's flight – or glide, really – are fascinating. I feel like a boat."

Letting out a surprised laugh, Ludwig questioned. "A boat?"

"Yes, a boat. I'm floating along with a rudder to guide me. It is… amusing. It feels like being tickled all over. I might keep this form."

"Perhaps it vould be pleasant to fly vizh Mary." Ludwig patted the smooth, serpentine scales. "But I hafe a fondness for your ozher form zhat I cannot deny."

"You enjoy the dynamicism of the European dragon instead of the meditative Asiatic." Mara concluded. She lifted her head and the large, pointed ears on either side of it lifted up. "Hang on." Spikes and crests exploded up around Ludwig and he clutched desperately at the distinctly European dragon head with a yelp as the smooth saddle-dip he had been sitting in suddenly narrowed to the bicycle seat of a curved spine.

"Mara! Vhat are you doing?!"

The ride became rough and choppy as Mara exchanged a paddle and sails for two, strong wings, cutting through the wind instead of riding it.

"I smell smoke." Mara explained without any need for detail or elaboration and Ludwig's heart stuttered and froze.

The lodge was on fire.

Ludwig stumbled and fell off of Mara's head as, with a single swing of her powerful tail, Mara sheered off the burning roof and flung it away into a snowbank. "Mary!"

Mara took to the air again, gathering up massive boulders of packed snow and crushing them over the burning house. Ludwig took his scarf and wrapped it over his nose, rushing into the blazing house.

"Mary!" He cried out, coughing on the smoke. The cool sifting of snow wasn't enough to entirely tame the flames and he could feel the acrid smoke burning at his eyes. "Mary, bitte! Come out!"

He stumbled into Mary's bedroom and dropped to his knees beside the dollhouse full of toys. He lifted up the skirt of the pink bed and found nothing. "Mary!"

Mara, human once again, rolled a massive ball of snow into the room and kicked it into the bedframe. It blanketed the room and snuffed out the fires. "Where's Mary?"

"I do not know!" Ludwig snapped at her. "Hafe you been to our room?"

"I'm taking snow down there now." Mara hurried out of the destroyed child's room and back into the main room. She had dropped a payload of snow over their house and then several snow boulders on top of that, rolling them to different rooms of their house to finish the fires off. It was a creative solution, only possible in this odd world.

Ludwig put his hands to the final ball of snow and they rolled it down the stairs to their bedroom, letting it break apart on the steps and coat the furniture – the shell of the scorched bed.

"Mary?!" Ludwig dropped to his knees beside the bed and checked in the last place they could possibly look.

Mara, perhaps sensing what he would find, grabbed him about the waist and dragged him back as he scrabbled for something beneath the bed. "Mary!" The doctor kicked out and grabbed for the baseboard, which crumbled into charcoal beneath his fingers. "Let go of me, Mara! She is zhere... She is zhere!"

"Ludwig, it's too late." Mara put her back into it, dragging him out of the bedroom as he resisted. "She's dead. She's been dead for hours."

"Nein!" Ludwig howled and turned on her, nails out and scratching at her as smoke-smudged glass streaked with angry, irritated tears. His eyes were red and bloodshot from staring into smoke, and his clothes were soaked with melted snow running grey over his cream-colored coat.

Angry red lines opened up and bled down Mara's cheek as she released his body to grab his hands and hold him an angry hostage. "Get a hold of yourself! She's gone!"

"NEIN!" Ludwig strained against her grip, but she truly was a woman of iron. The hands around his wrists might have been manacles for all the good that struggling against them did. Her fingernails bit into the soft flesh of his joints as he threw his shoulders and frame backwards and towards the stairway to Hell. "Mara, let go of me! I hafe to go to her! I hafe to see her!"

"Ludwig, she's gone." Mara pulled him into her arms, keeping his hands trapped beneath her own arms and wrapping him close. "She's gone."

Ludwig laid his head against her breast and closed his streaming eyes.

Mara stroked Ludwig's hair back from his forehead as he lay on his side. "...You have to eat something."

"...I'm not hungry." The doctor dully replied. He hadn't left their seaside cottage's bed in days.

"You know, you can't really starve in CORD." Mara pointed out, sighing as she reached out to adjust his glasses on his face. "You'll just feel hungrier and more miserable the longer you go without."

"Zhen I vill be miserable." Ludwig stated succinctly.

"…She might have made it out. I haven't found a Shadow." Mara told him as she laid off her attempt to groom the despondent doctor.

"…Do ve efen know vhat happened?" Ludwig questioned.

"I assume it was Lucy. He must have broken in somehow while we were with Henry." Mara frowned. "He's never been able to do that before."

"Do you zhink he has grown more powerful zhan he vas?" Ludwig gathered the energy to ask after several moments of silence.

"I don't know how he would have managed that." Mara sighed through her nose. "I've never grown more powerful in all my time here. I've just learned how to use it."

Ludwig sighed and turned over to face her back. "…Do ve hafe an idea?" Ludwig questioned Mara softly.

"Not much of one. CORD is limiting my options, for once." Mara sighed. "But I do think I have an idea."

"Vhat do you need from me?"

"Well, we need to build something to trap Lucy in. Something solid, so that it doesn't break, and we need to cover it with arcane symbols. If we can convince him that we're creating a ritual of entrapment to use on him, then we can convince him that he's trapped. Perhaps for forever." Mara pitched the idea with the quiet certainty of a long-planned thought.

"So, ve need to create a confincing entrapment ritual." Ludwig hummed. "Somezhing zhat vill satisfy Lucy's need for dramatacism."

"Blood. Candles. Chalk." Mara shrugged. "Sounds like we're going to be decorating for Halloween."

"Ve should gife him some adfance varning. So zhat he vill spy on us und see vhat ve are doing. Zhen, he vill build up his anticipation und make zhe ritual more effectife." Ludwig sat up slowly and sighed. "Zhen... Zhen vhen zhis is done, ve go home."

"Yes." Mara agreed, rubbing his back. "We go home."

Mara insisted on physically building Lucy's prison. "It's important to make it as solid as possible." She told Ludwig as she measured stones and planned out the solid floor. "If it looks impervious, Lucy will think it's impervious."

"Ja. Not a stone out of place." Ludwig agreed, mixing together mortar in a large, black tub with a shovel. "More mortar. I zhink it is too vet."

Mara poured in the grey powder. "A little more sand too. Just to give it the extra grit." She had dug out a space for the foundation, thirty feet by thirty feet in both dimensions, and they were going to pour a concrete foundation to build on top of.

Ludwig shoveled in another few scoops of sand and they mixed it up, then poured the concrete into the mold. Mara got a spreader that looked like a giant, metal dust mop and began spreading the grey porridge throughout the mold.

"Does that look like a start?" Mara questioned when they had finished pouring out the sludge and smoothing it over. "Reckon you could roller skate on it, if you wanted."

"I suppose ve could." Ludwig echoed, slightly hollow. "It vill certainly be smoozh enough for zhe Ritual." They were still making up the nonsense ritual. Ludwig was almost ashamed of how much thought and effort was going into their plan to entrap Lucy inside his own mind. In a way, it was clearly a bid for distraction. Distraction from thoughts of poor Mary.

Mara hadn't been lying when she said there wasn't a Shadow of Mary in CORD. She had spent two whole days searching for her and her world was simply gone. So was Henry's. It seemed they had both escaped CORD.

Ludwig, though, couldn't help the rage and the sorrow he felt when he thought about Lucy being in their lodge, setting fire to their house, Mary running to hide in the Master Bedroom, left to die.

They would leave and find Mary. Not her real parents. Not even able to be her parents. But something from a nightmare she had had for years. For longer than she had ever been alive. They would have to see Henry Cho as well, maybe even the Grandmother. Ludwig had to admit that he wasn't looking forward to that. Mara would probably cause a scene. But it was good to see people who had hurt you as human. Sometimes, it made it easier. And Ludwig wasn't convinced she had entirely known the extent of what she had done to Mara. Warping memories could surely be unconscious as well as deliberate.

"Do you zhink he vas vatching us?" Ludwig asked, later on. He was lying against Mara's side in an over-large hot tub. Bubbles and jets ran over his skin. Unwillingly, he began to relax into it. The day's labor had left an aching twinge in his shoulders and back.

Mara's arm twitched where she had wrapped it around his shoulders. The black words were foggy and stark in the steam. "I think Lucy knows an invitation when he sees one. Whether he's clever enough to cotton to our scheme or obsessed enough to fall right into it is another matter."

"Und if he is not?"

"Then we go home, regardless, and round up everyone who was in CORD with us to make sure that he's taken off the system. If he ever tries this in reality, he'll be caught faster than that." She snapped her fingers.

"Vhen ve get out of here, ve must speak to Doctor Bervick about better screening." Ludwig mused slightly.

"…I have a bad feeling about this Berwick guy." Mara reached over, grabbed her water bottle and took a big gulp. "Maybe it's my inherent distrust of people in power, but there's just something I don't like."

"Mara, really." Ludwig scoffed. "Zhat does sound like it is your inherent distrust acting up. Doctor Bervick is an acclaimed researcher. He has made so many contributions to nuerological medicine already und now zhat ve know zhat CORD vorks – albeit in a limited vay – he vill hafe more funding und support for his vork. It is not his fault zhat Lucy vas put into CORD."

"…Have you still been having those nightmares?" Mara changed the subject suddenly.

"Nein. Zhey stopped vhile ve vere taking care of… Und zhey hafe not started up again. Just zhe anxiety, I suppose."

"It still disturbs me that Lucy got into our home while I was away." Mara rolled her shoulders back and laid her head on the lip of the tub. "That has never happened before. Never."

"So you hafe told me. But how vould you know if Lucy vas here?" Ludwig enquired gently. "If zhe vorld conforms to your expectations vhenefer you return here, zhen it vould logically erase zhe efidence of an encounter, vould it not?"

"…Honestly, I don't know. I just feel like I would sense him if he were here. His cologne on the air." She snorted a laugh.

"…Mara, it just occurred to me zhat eferyzhing ve 'know' about zhis dream of ours is unverifiable." Ludwig looked up at her. "How do ve know zhat ve are efen real?"

"I think the option is too frightening to consider." Mara replied and shifted, moving further out of the water, revealing more of the Song of Solomon beneath her defined collarbone.

Ludwig and Mara hefted a flat stone together into place. "We'll alternate the stones' pattern. It should hold together better than just building them up one on top of the other."

"Ve really are lucky zhat your parents vere engineers. Ozhervise zhis vould include a lot more trial und error." Ludwig helped her lever in the next stone and watched as she mortared them into place. "As it stands, how much progress can ve make before ve hafe to call it a day?"

"I think we can put on three layers before the mortar will need time to dry and cure." Mara estimated. "It's a dry day, fortunately, so we should be able to finish these three layers in the morning and maybe put on a fourth in the evening."

"How tall does zhe Necronomicon say to make zhis exactly?" Ludwig questioned, gripping the end of another rock. Mara had chosen to make them about two feet long and a foot wide and deep. They had to weigh almost fifty pounds each.

"It doesn't specify height. It says seven layers of stones. That should be a good seven feet with these stones, then the capstone." Mara explained.

"Are ve going to be able to lift zhat cursed large zhing sefen feet?" Ludwig gestured at a flat slab of dark grey stone, matching the color of the other rocks.

"I think you've forgotten that I can turn into a dragon." Mara reminded him with a quirked eyebrow. "Now, come on, heave." They lifted on the next stone.

"Ah, of course. Zhe dragon can carry more zhan zhe voman." Ludwig smiled as he spread mortar into place according to Mara's instructions. He had never done anything like this before. It carried an odd sort of thrill.

Ludwig's fingers and clothes were liberally caked with grey powder when they stopped. Four rows up, the cell didn't look too impressive, but it came up to Ludwig's waist. "Ve can start zhe inscriptions on zhe inside now, can't ve? Zhey are only on zhe floor."

"No, the book states very strictly that the inscriptions on the floor need to be put down right before the capstone." Mara explained, reaching into her pocket and pulling out a tattered, eelskin book with an ugly inscription on the front.

Ludwig struggled to keep a straight face as she opened it, holding it carefully so no one else would be able to get a look at the pages. Mara had filled them with familiar, old-style comic strips from newspapers and everything about. "You know, Mara, one out-of-place giggle ofer zhis, und zhe whole zhing vill be for not."

"You give Lucy too much credit." Mara hid her smile and shut the book. "But we can read Calvin and Hobbes later."

"I vonder if ve can get a collection of zhem all vhen ve go home." Ludwig sighed and peeled off his shirt, scrubbing his fingers with it. "Verdammt. I'm cofered in mein own sveat. Can ve go inside und shower now?"

"It's well on time for lunch anyway." Mara hummed. "But first, you mentioning the dragon earlier got me thinking. Stand back."

Ludwig made for a safe spot as Mara transformed and unleashed white, glowing plasma on the stones. She only held the beam of fire for a minute at the most, but Ludwig could still feel the heat from the stones from as far off as he was. It made the already warm air decidedly oppressive.

"There. Perfectly dry. As soon as it cools, we can put on the last three layers, lay down the inscriptions, and cap it off. We'll be ready to trap our demon by tomorrow evening." Mara decided, the dragon shrinking down into her own frame again. Sometimes, it seemed like the dragon never fully disappeared. He could still see the lines of the predator in the way she moved.

"And zhen ve put an end to all of zhis nonsense. Once und for all." Ludwig firmly stated.

"Once and for all." Mara echoed.

Lucy wouldn't come without a fight. Mara had prepared Ludwig for the fight as best she could.

"Bulletproof vest… Heat retardant coat…" Mara helped him into the armor. "And I insist you wear this mask." She held up an old-style gas mask with carefully made goggles. "They shouldn't restrict your vision."

"I'm going to sound und look like Darzh Fader." Ludwig complained, pulling it on.

"Mmm. More like one of the Stormtroopers from the history texts." Mara observed, stepping back and folding her arms. The clothing was very heavy, but not too restrictive. It was all rubbery and folded over itself to protect ever inch of his skin against acid, fire, bullets, and anything else. "How does it feel?"

"Not bad. But heafy." Ludwig lifted his arms up and moved them about. "I vould not like to vear zhis more zhan strictly necessary."

"After this, you'll never see these clothes again." Mara promised. "Come on. Dragon's back all the way, then we'll have to go on foot. I know something about Lucy's domain. But once we're there, I expect him to fight with everything he's got."

"Und vhat is it exactly zhat ve zhink he has got?" Ludwig questioned from the saddle-dip between Mara's spines as they flew.

"I know he likes to create nightmares and visions in people's eyes. Naturally, he makes sure to make himself as strong and frightening looking as possible as well, but you can take care of that part. I'll be honest, Bon, I'm going to depend on you to do that grounding thing."

"Of course. You can alvays count on me."

"See, we can drag him physically back and trap him. I know we can do that, if he's in that human form you fought off, but I don't want to risk anything going wrong with his powers intact."

"So, I turn all of zhem into parlor tricks und zhen ve drag him avay physically. How vill ve get him zhere?"

"I'll leave a car outside the cavern. We load him into the boot, drive him to the cell, and bind him in there. Then, it'll be over. It'll all be over." Mara hummed softly. "Have you given any thought to how you want to leave?"

"…I zhink ve should fly up to a fery great height und let ourselfes fall." Ludwig decided. "Free fall. Like a skydife."

"As soon as we're out, I'm going to introduce you to my family." Mara told him, smiling and let out a curling flow of plasma from her mouth to make the clouds sizzle around them.

"As soon as ve are out, I am going to see a jeveler to get zhese rings made in real life." Ludwig tapped his ring on the spine.

"Oh, don't." Ludwig swore the scales on Mara's neck turned reddish. "They're silly-looking things."

"I zhink zhey are beautiful." Ludwig patted her neck. "Und I vould not trade zhem for zhe vorld."

"Yes, but they're stupidly expensive to make in the real world and they would weigh a ton." Mara scoffed. "Let's dispense with rings. Rings are stupid. In the real world, I never wore jewelry unless it was Halloween or Christmas."

"You do not hafe to vear it on your finger. As a surgeon, I vill not be able to vear it normally eizher. Ve can get zhem put on chains." Ludwig suggested as a compromise.

"...I'd like that." Mara admitted, softly.

"I've never done this before." Mara told him outside the gates to what could only be Hell. It was a pit down into the Earth – a great pit – and a river of the foulest concoction Ludwig could imagine was running into it. It was like the blood of a thousand slaughterhouses mixed with the sewage of a thousand cities and caught alight. The river burned sluggishly and in patches. If Ludwig didn't have a mask over his face, he was sure the scent would be searing tracks into his nasal passages.

Mara was covered up in a hazardous materials uniform not unlike the one she had made Ludwig wear. Both uniforms were bright white – for maximum visibility below – but Ludwig couldn't see a way in that didn't take them at least to the hip through the Styx.

"…It's not going to get any better if we stare at it. Ready, Ludwig?" Mara questioned, turning to him. "Remember: Keep us grounded." She reached out and tapped the light on his helmet. "And light up anything you're not sure of."

"Yes, Mara. Are ve going to be able to find him?" Ludwig questioned as they stepped into the slowly-moving sludge. It made a horrible sound around his rubber boots and he could feel the warmth slightly through the protective gear.

"I have an infrared scanner in my HUD." Mara explained. "Your grounding powers aren't going to interfere with it because it's real-life technology."

"Danke Gott." Ludwig closed his eyes and they stepped into a particularly vile sewer.

"A sewer, Bon? Really?" Mara questioned as they waded in. Eventually, they came on a platform beside the flow of filth. "Was this the best you could do?"

"Zhe blood is impossible." Ludwig explained, climbing out beside her. "As is zhe fire. Zherefore, zhat's not real. Sevage on zhe ozher hand, is perfectly possible. Especially in a sever. Und ve are vell protected, are ve not?"

"Very well protected and Thank God for that." Mara looked down at the river of muck and gagged. "…I'm picking up a heat signature through the wall. Someone's in here. Come on."

Ludwig watched as Mara pulled a gun out of her armored coat. He had never seen her with one before, but this was a special occasion all around. Together, they began walking into the dark, Ludwig waving his flashlight occasionally. For a maintained sewer, it was very dark. Shouldn't there be lights in a sewer? And if there were lights… there had to be a lightswitch…

Ludwig's hand found a lever on the wall and he pulled it. Lights flickered on all down the corridor, lighting up the sickly green walls and floor.

"Ugh!" Mara had almost stepped on a dead rat. With ire, she kicked it off into the river. "Good thinking."

Ludwig bowed his head modestly. "Lights in un industrial area. Not too surprising."

"I didn't think of it." Mara cuffed his helmet gently. Ludwig could barely feel it through the thick rubber. "Let's end this."

Book Three: Emotion

Drowning.

It's hard to breathe when you're upset. It's hard to think. It's hard to do anything except to flail out blindly into the shadows. The water gets into your eyes and mouth, you have to spit it out in order to clear your airway. Your head has to come out of water, you gasp in a breath and scream.

But when the water is inside you, it's harder to lift your head. The waves crash over you over and over and over again and drive you down to the depths. Your mind races and freezes. All rational thought stops. All emotional thought kicks into overdrive. Pain clouds everything.

Lashing out at the surface of the water, you don't make any progress towards the shore. Movements become short and jerky and no one makes any progress when they're just short of the air. If you watch television, you might think someone drowning can scream and cry, but when you drown, your mouth is under the water. Your nose is under the water. Everything is under the water. Drowning is silent. Drowning is fast. Drowning is loud. Drowning is slow. It takes three minutes to die from drowning. About halfway in, you fall unconscious, but by then, you've spent a whole minute and thirty seconds in agony – lungs burning and mouth straining, staring up at the surface. At what you need and unable to reach it. Heart bursting and mouth locked as you watch them walk away together – away from you and away from all the promises they made like it was nothing. Moving on. No right. No right. No right. Eyes bugging with rage and pain unexpressed because you've been used. Drowning in it.

Some people get so upset that they have compulsive fits. I'm one of those people. I once became so upset when I was failing all my classes that I had a psychotic break. I ran to the mirror, swiped everything off my dresser and began banging the mirror back into the wall. I nearly lost my hands when it broke and fell in shards and sheets all around me. For months, I couldn't even use my hands to feed myself.

Why did that happen? Why was I so upset?

I don't know… I don't know. I was drowning. I was drowning in my own anger and pain and frustration.

Drowning is silent to the observer, but it's a roar in the victim's ears. Stress makes ears ring. Water fills them and echoes. Waves all around. Waves in your ears. Up your nose. Above your eyes.

Drowning.

They're all drowning. They're drowning and I can't stop them. They're drowning. I'm drowning. It's all come crashing down around our heads.

Drowning… Silence… Sound… Darkness…

Chapter One

They found Lucy in a control room. Mara had to force the door with a crowbar – she had come prepared for anything – and they swooped down on him.

"No!" Lucy roared, drawing himself up. He looked like a boy in a skeleton costume, though, with a black robe over it. The bones Mara kicked aside had a hollow, plastic ring. His weapon of choice was a long knife and Mara had brought a gun.

"Drop it, Lucy! It's over." Mara growled. "You've had your fun and games for far too long here, and now it's come to an end. Drop it, or I'll fire."

"If you kill me, you free me." Lucy growled, handsome face contorting. His blonde hair was matted down and disgusting. "And you don't want that. Too damn ethical for your own good, aren't you, doctor?" He had a manic air. "Do you realize what you've done? In less than a month, you've undone everything. It's all gone up in smoke. All my work, all my time… I'll never get out of here at this rate…"

"What are you talking about?" Mara snorted. "We found the way out. It's absurd how easy it was in the end. It was just counterintuitive, that's all. Now come on. You're going to spend forever locked up inside a nice, grey cell."

Lucy's laughter echoed off of the walls. "Am I?! Am I really?! Your little grey box with those nonsense sigils written on the inside?! Come on, you know as well as I do that all of this is absolute bunk." He roared. "The only real thing you can do is lock me in there. And you know as well as I do that you can't starve in CORD. I'd get out. Eventually. It's made of slate. Fine, then I can use a spoon or a knife – chip at the mortar until I get out and your little scribbles in red paint and chalk can't keep me in there!"

Mara's stance became much more relaxed. "…What? You know all that's nonsense?"

"No, I actually believe that I'm the son of the Devil – OF COURSE IT'S ALL NONSENSE!" He screamed and lunged for Mara suddenly.

The gun went off.

"…Do you feel like all this was too easy?" Mara questioned softly. They had pulled off their helmets and were kneeling over Lucy's collapsed body.

"Ja." Ludwig softly replied. He had pronounced Lucy and they had covered him up in his robe. "…Und he seemed surprisingly sane. Desperate. But sane."

"What I don't understand is, if he knew it was all nonsense, why was he playing the devil? And what was he talking about before? About work and time and effort. What was he doing here?"

Ludwig thought hard as he looked down at Lucy's face. It was a young face – too young. And it was marked by lines – smile and frown. He had lived under great stress and pressure, put apon him by something that had frightened him. "…Mara, I zhink ve need to leafe zhis place as quickly as possible. Ve must go. Now." Ludwig stood. "Come on!"

"What has you in a flutter?" Mara plunged after him. They left the gun behind.

"Zhere is only one person who has been controlling zhis." Ludwig growled. "You vere right, Mara. You vere alvays right."

"Right about what?" Mara questioned, running after him. "Ludwig, Ludwig, you're not making sense. We have to go back – I left the gun."

"Make anozher one!" Ludwig snapped. "If I am right, he vill know soon! He vill see!"

Suddenly, the world erupted into fire and death around them. Mara screamed and tried to push Ludwig out of the way of the blast and the falling debris, but she was too late. He found himself buried and his ears rang with the explosion and the constant beep of a flatlining heart monitor.

"Bon!" Mara's voice seemed to be coming from farther and farther away.

Ludwig couldn't move. Everything hurt. He heard a defibrillator charging. He was so cold. It was so dark. He passed out and it seemed a blessing.

Ludwig woke to the rocks shifting around him. There was a golden light coming from a crevice as Mara lifted the boulders off of his battered body. "…Mara?"

"Hey, Bon." Mara lifted him into her arms.

"...*Es tut mir lied*..." Ludwig wrapped one arm up across her torso. "...Vhere are ve going?"

"Home, Bon. We're going home."

Epilogue

"Is she still asking for him?" A middle-aged woman with curly blonde hair questioned as she was led along the corridors of the hospital.

Doctor Berwick, a smiling man with a ginger beard, nodded. "She seems quite certain that we are keeping her from him. It seems the dreams she had inside of CORD were quite vivid." He opened the door of one of the hospital rooms. "Nevertheless, I do believe Miss Martha is ready to go home."

"Martha." The woman rushed to her bedside. "Martha, did you hear that? You're going home. You're coming home."

"…Bon." Martha turned towards her mother – a skinny, fragile young woman with hair that had been clipped unevenly. "Is he coming to? I said I wouldn't leave him. I said we would go together…"

"Martha, there is no Bon. It was just a dream."

"I want Bon. I'm not leaving without him." Martha laid her head back down. "I'll wait for him to wake up. He knows the way out." Her eyes tracked to the corners of the room, always searching. "…He knows the way out."